Impostor

Impostor

F M M MacLeod

Wardgate Press

To Rachel, Eimer, David and Rob

Copyright c2007 by F M M MacLeod

First Published in paperback in 2007 by Wardgate Press

The right of F M M MacLeod to be identified as the Author of the Work
has been asserted by her in accordance with the Copyright, Designs and
Patents Act 1988

Published by Wardgate Press
A division of Wardgate Associates Limited
PO Box 6234, Ashbourne, Derbyshire DE6 3ZL

ISBN: 978-1-901957-01-3

All papers used by Wardgate Press are from fully sustainable forest areas
Printed by Ripley Printers Ltd, Derbyshire
www.wardgatepress.co.uk

Impostor

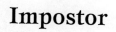

Prologue

Sweep down over the fields and the tiled roofs. See the wedges of garden, carefully bounded by thick smudges of green hedge. See the power lines, the telephone poles, delicate connections to light and power and the world.

Come closer and note the cars set beside each home. Biarritz blue, gunmetal grey, opalescent white. We can just make out the colours, half washed by light, for it is dawn. In the distance the glow of a city fades as the sun raises a wild majestic red across the eastern sky.

Rip up the tarmac road beneath us. Roll it back, push it aside. Pile it up against the bungalows, let the walls sag and burst with its weight. Let poles snap and lines of power tangle and snag. Be decisive. Go deeper, pull aside the neat sewers, see the rats arrow away on either side in fear.

Look around you. The world has changed. You have changed it. You are standing on the hard packed soil of an old track. Feel it beneath your naked feet. The smooth surface, dimpled by the stone which lies underneath the clay and dust, is glinting white as the sun lifts up above the hills. Now we will travel forward along the line of the turnpike and enter a wood.

A small wood, made of scrubby deciduous trees. Field oak, maple and straggly elder. It is dawn. But it is still dark in this wood, the sun has not yet penetrated beyond its boundary. Over to the left, at the foot of the largest tree, lies a bundle of brown cloth. The cloth merges into the brackeny soil around it. It would easily be missed. Just a sodden mass of fabric. But there is something lying beside it. Light in colour and curved. Perhaps a stick, a sliver of rock. You come closer and see that it is a human hand. Half open as if begging, with the thumb turned up. Now the bundle of cloth begins to take shape. Here is the bend of an arm. There the ball of a head. The rounded curve of a hip. There is no movement. You move forward. You are curious. Is this a dead body? With a thrill of excitement edged with fear at what you might touch, you flick the hood of the cloak, for that is what it is, away from the head.

And you see the white face of a young woman. Her mouth is open and edged with blood, her eyes are shut. Her face is turned away and you hold your hand to her cheek. It is cold and damp. You touch her shoulder. It too is cold and damp. There is no feeling of life. The body inside the cloth is still. After the slightest hesitation you slide your hand across her ribcage to feel for a heart beat. A last check. An act of care. Sanctioned. But you are well aware that it is a violation. As you touch her torso you are startled by the unexpected softness of a living body. There is some life in her, stored in the central core. She moves, twists round and moans. For a moment you hold the warm weight of her left breast in your cupped hand and then you stumble back, making your apologies. She sits up, gasping for air as if she had been drowning. Now she is on her knees, now standing. But she is unsteady. She stumbles and lunges forwards at you and you put out your arms to catch her.

And she goes right through you.

For a split second you feel the ageless beat of another human heart pass dangerously close to your own, like two great liners passing unseen on a dark ocean. You feel another body's struggle for breath harsh in your own throat. Panic rises in you as your body senses its rhythms being disrupted at their very core and you begin to suffocate.

And then she's through you and you stagger a little with surprise at what has happened. You were expecting the weight of a body against you. You turn around clumsily, gulping for air and clutching your chest. There she is, on all fours on the ground behind you. In one swift movement she turns, still crouching, and looks back. She has heard something. She is afraid. But not of you. She is not looking at you. You do not exist, not yet. For this is the past and you have no place here.

8

Chapter 1

February 26th 1755 Bradley Wood, outside Ashbourne

The woman crouched on the wet ground, muscles strained and tense. Something had woken her. She shook her head and opened her eyes wide to clear them. She darted her head from side to side like a wild animal. A mist was rising off the ground and enveloping everything. She could see nothing. By her reckoning she was over ten miles out of the town – but was it enough? She held her breath and listened into the whiteness of the mist. Nothing.

Nothing yet. But they will follow her. That was for sure.

She became aware of the weight of the damp cloak across her back and the ache in her arms. She sat back on her haunches and shook her arms to release the stiff muscles. She crawled forward and positioned herself against the base of a tree, curling her body up and holding herself tightly, her arms wrapped around her knees. She pulled the damp hood up over her head and then forward and down around her face. She made herself as small as possible. It began to rain steadily. The sound of the water on the leaves above her had a soporific effect. Against her will, her head began to fall forward. She began to sink back into sleep.

And then suddenly her head jerked up. There it is again. The sharp chinking sound of metal on metal. They have come.

Then a softer sound. Bells. Intermittent, faint. She recognised them instantly. Her heart slowed and relief flooded through her. She knows what this is. And it is not a danger to her. She stands up, leans against the tree for a moment to gather her strength, and then begins to walk towards the sound.

The packman stood up slowly, rubbing the side of his face. He had a bad pain in his head and neck, probably from sleeping on the wet ground. There had been no choice for him but to stay out in the open last night. He had to wait here for a while, he could not risk going into the town too early. The pain in his head intensified and located itself at one side. He couldn't shake it. It was beginning to affect his thinking and he had to keep alert. He bent down and wet his hands with dew from the grass then wiped them across his face. As he straightened up he saw a woman coming slowly out of the wood towards him.

As she drew nearer he could see that the left side of her mouth was streaked with what looked like blood and the bottom edges of her brown cloak were heavy with caked mud. She kept her eyes on him as she walked towards him. The pain in his head receded, overtaken by this new problem. She stumbled slightly but ignored it and kept on walking. Her eyes on him. He scanned the woods behind her for any movement. There seemed to be no one else. The wood was quiet. He looked back to the woman. He had no contingency plan to deal with anything like this.

She stopped some way from him.

They stood in silence looking at each other. He pushed back his leather jerkin and freed his sword. His hand closed over the hilt as his eyes scanned the wood behind her. Checking again.

He's looking for the rest of the gang, she thought. He is standing like a soldier, not a packhorse man. A soldier. She was confused, unable to decide whether to go forward or not. This was not what she had expected. The relief she had felt when she heard the bells of the packhorses disappeared. 'Sir,' her voice faltered and died away. She found she was too tired to make up a convincing lie, and the truth would mean he would turn her away. She had wanted a simple packhorse man. She needed to sit by the fire he had built, to eat some of the food he was cooking there.

'Sir, I...' She must think of something. But nothing would come. She was unable to think. It was hopeless. Overwhelmed by cold and exhaustion, she turned slowly and started to retrace her steps.

He watched her. What did she think she was doing? Did she think she could simply disappear back into the wood? She must be far gone. He caught up with her and took hold of her arm.

'What are you doing here?'

She attempted to release his hand. Fear at last made her brain quicken. She had to find something convincing. 'Walking to my home. I am in service at the Hall up there. I have leave.'

'You have blood on your mouth.'

She raised her hand up to her face, finding the roughness of dried blood, genuinely surprised. Looking down, rubbing the flakes between her fingers.

'It must be a small scratch... the bushes.'

'The bushes. People don't usually walk home through bushes.' He brought his head down close to her, tipped his face up slightly and sniffed. Startled by his action, she pulled away.

'Prison. I can smell prison on you. Even under the mud.'

He heard her quick intake of breath as she leaned forward, closing the gap she had just tried to make between them. 'You must know prison if you can smell it so well... sir.' The last word was a challenge.

He was not what he seemed and she knew it. Her voice had been low, sharing a secret. Anyone standing more than two feet away would not have heard what she said. Her face was less than six inches from him. Her hair was dark where it was wet and clinging to the sides of her face but dry wisps curled up fair. There was a faint blue bruise on her forehead, tiny veins smudged and broken under the skin. Her eyes were fixed on him, wide and bright blue but red rimmed with exhaustion and shining, not with defiance as she hoped, but fear.

He relaxed his grip on her arm. She would be no danger to him. Unless she was being followed. He looked back down the road, in the direction from which she had come.

'What is your name?'

'Ann' she replied. 'Ann Dance.'

'When did you escape?'

Ann thought. The dark, the fear, the cold, had all confused into one desire to get away. Keep moving. How long had it been?

'Last night. No, the night before.' It seemed days.

'Will they follow you?'

She nodded.

'You need to get through the next town, then.'

She nodded again.

'Where have you come from? Derby?'

'Yes.'

'Where are you going?'

She shrugged. She had no idea. 'Away. North, I think.'

'The next town is Ashbourne. You must get through it and onto the Leek road.' Shared information. Help. She felt weak with the relief of it. Her legs buckled. She must sit down and eat. She looked across at the fire. He saw her glance, understood her need but was not prepared to give her anything until he had secured what he wanted. She realised he was bargaining. But did not understand what she had to offer.

'You can get through it as my wife. It would serve me well too.'

'Your wife?' Now she understood. They both needed cover. She looked at him. His eyes were constantly flicking up and down the road as he spoke. She saw that there was a greyness to his skin. He had his own exhaustion to contend with. His own dangers to face. He turned his attention back to her.

'Well?' There was an urgency in his voice.

She dipped her head once in agreement.

He took her hand in his and shook it in a parody of formality, and then looked up and gave out a great laugh of relief. One sharp bark, like the sound of a dog on the morning air. Surprised, she laughed back at him. The noise exploded into the trees, startling the crows, black flags which spiralled upwards, flapping and crackling above them in response. He smiled at the woman as they both turned towards the fire and the pot which was steaming there.

He stepped forward and turned slightly to catch a clearer sight of her face. He smiled again. 'Clean your face of that blood. I don't wish to be known as a wife beater.'

She did not reply. Her eyes were already on the pot.

He slipped the hilt of his sword back behind the jerkin. This would make the next few hours easier.

His mind turned to Cluny, who should be riding towards him from the north. Where was he? How did it go with him? His mind swooped up over the countryside and he could spy the small figure of a man on horseback, moving slowly across the road ways of England. Inching further and further south into this dangerous terrain. Dark forces gathering around him. Around them both.

He rubbed his thumb over the familiar emblem on the hilt of his sword. He did not look down at it. He knew it held the profile of a man. A king. Around this face were inscribed the words. 'Look, love and follow.'

The call to the heart which had killed thousands.

'You are Ann Rudge. My wife.'

He ducked down to tighten the girth. She was to ride on the second horse in the line.

'We are going back to Nantwich.'

'Nantwich,' she repeated.

He had given her food and water and as she settled down

into the space between the two bales of soft cotton she allowed herself to enjoy the comfort of a full stomach and the certain increase in safety of her new role. The packhorse train moved forward, steadily covering the mile of road before Ashbourne, the warning bells on the lead horses tinkling as they moved. Rudge, if that was his name, swayed ahead of her.   Saying nothing. Resting before the next danger had to be faced and overcome.

Ahead of them Ann could see the houses of the town beginning to line either side of the road. And the red sign of the Plough Inn, their destination. She   closed her eyes. 'Mrs Rudge. Ann Rudge.' She sounded the words out.

The horse beneath her faltered in its step then stopped. They must have arrived. Ann opened her eyes and looked ahead to the pack man.

Something was not right. She saw that he was flopping sideways in his saddle.   There was something slow and graceful in his movement, but it was frightening in its incongruity. Something was wrong. He had fallen asleep. She yelled at him to wake him up but his body carried on sliding to one side. He fell to the ground. And lay there. Not moving. The horse stepped delicately to one side to avoid standing on him. Ann scrambled off her horse and ran to crouch beside him on the road. She pulled him over onto his back and slapped his face. From his throat came strange grunting sounds and froth was appearing on his lips. She wiped it away with her sleeve and looked around desperately for help. They were outside the Plough, first inn of the town. She heard her voice saying, 'My husband. You must help my husband.' Her desperation was real. What would happen to her now? People were crowding around. She was exposed. Her face seen. In the most memorable way possible – as part of a tragedy.

A crowd herded around the body on the ground, lowing their sympathy for the woman looking so wildly up at them. Her husband was going to die. Looking at the inert body on the ground with the strange noises rising up from it, it was easy to see that.

Some of them lifted the man up and in through the door of the inn. All the time he made the same strange inhuman sounds. And Ann followed behind them. 'Here you are, my dear.' Hands. A white apron. Dark wood, a glint of pewter. She was aware of people standing up to come to the side of her, behind her.

Someone took her by the arm and she was taken upstairs to a small bedroom. Then she was sitting alongside the nearly dead body of her husband.

She had to escape. Get away. A doctor had been sent for. She had to get away before he came and questions were asked of her to which she had no reply. But it was difficult. How could she get out? She left the room and climbed down the stairs into the tap room. As she entered all eyes turned to her. She was a curiousity. An excitement. The longer she stood there the more clearly they would remember what she looked like. She explained that she had to check the horses and the load and was taken outside to the yard. The horses were tethered at one corner, the bales stacked against a wall. There were less people here. The yard was almost empty. Just the boys tending the animals. Ann walked over to the stack of bales. Beyond them was the open gate. She began to walk slowly towards the gate. And then her eye was caught by a wooden box beside the bales. She stopped. It was a small strong box of some sort. It must belong to Rudge. She hesitated. She should run. But if she opened it she might find some identification. Some papers which would give her story credence. Every minute she stood there doing nothing made her capture more certain. Go or open it.

She bent down and tried to prise open the lid. She tried to pick the box up. It was surprisingly heavy, and then, as she shifted it around, she heard the dull chink of heavy coins sliding against each other. She stood up and looked up at the window of the room where Rudge lay. The packhorse man had money. She pushed the box with her foot. It was so heavy it hardly moved. A lot of money. She looked out of the gate. What was he doing carrying this much money on the open road. What did it mean? One thing was for sure, left here it would be stolen. She picked up the box, balancing its weight on her hip, and carried it back to her room.

Minutes later, Ann sat in the hot little room and watched the breath continue to force itself in and out of the body of the man in front of her.

In her hand she held a key; under her feet stood the box. She had found the key when she had returned to the room. It had been thrust down a deep pocket on the inside of his leather jerkin. It was well concealed, tightly wrapped in a linen cloth; but as soon as Ann's fingers closed around the neat little package she recognised it for what it was. The key to the money box.

She thought about it. Money; a lot of money. A lot of money in an inappropriate place. More money than a packhorse man should have. Much more. Gold. French Louis D'or. Ann recognised them. She had seen a fair few in 1745, when the Jacobite army had come into Derby. Business had been brisk. But what would a packhorse man be doing with French gold, and so much of it? Under the gold Ann made another discovery. Cut to lie flush with the edges of the box was a letter. Ann had pulled it out and shut the box.

The letter was not written in English. Ann could not read it. What was its purpose? Ann tried to make out the address. Janvier 2nd 1755, Chantilly, and the name signed across the bottom with a flourish. Choiseul.

Choiseul... Janvier... Dutch? French? It didn't matter. A letter. Or a bill of sale – or a receipt? The important thing was to destroy all trace of it. She took the letter to the fire and threw it in. It fluttered over the coals and then flared up and was gone. She should leave this well alone. Take a few coins and slide away as quickly as possible. However tempted, however hungry, desperate or greedy, all of her acquaintances would put the money back and melt away from the situation, leaving no trace of their involvement. They knew that if they did not do this sometime, somewhere, there would be retribution. Not prison, but a sharp knife quietly given. By those much more powerful than them.

Ann knew this as clearly as any other thief living off the streets of Derby. She had climbed the stairs with the box lodged on her hip, the gold solidly shifting with each movement of her body, intending to take a few coins and wait for a chance to escape. The coins lay in the small pocket of her over skirt. She would leave the box by the bedside. The remains of the letter were nothing but grey ash in the grate.

The door slowly opened. Ann's body tensed and she put her hand to the pocket where the coins lay. But it was only a young girl. Her face round with curiosity as she paused in the doorway. She brought over a jug of milk and some bread to the bedside. She looked at Ann, taking in every detail of her clothing, of her face, of her mood – it would be described again and again downstairs and beyond. 'What is your name?' she whispered. 'No one knows.' No one had thought to ask. But the girl needed it for her story. No one at home would believe her without a name.

Ann did not reply.

'What is your name? Please?'

The packhorse man lay in front of Ann. She stretched out her hand and touched the coverlet. He should be dead before morning. And his name could be dead with him. Ann Dance could be gone too. And the trail cold. It was her chance.

'I am Mrs Challinor, Ann Challinor, and this is my poor husband, James. James Challinor, of Nantwich.'

It seemed to Ann that the name hung uncertain in the air

between herself and the girl. Then the moment passed, the girl left the room quietly and Ann was alone again with the box of money and the dying man.

Mrs Challinor. Mrs Challinor. She had created another territory and passed into it. At this very minute, the child would be speaking that name out loud.

If Rudge had never been here, then those who asked for him would be turned away.

Unless they asked to see the man lying on the bed. In which case they would recognise him.

If he lived long enough. If they came before he died and was buried. She let that thought find its own place. She circled around it and then faced it again. If they came before he died.

The money sitting beneath her feet would have trapped her here. She should get away. She half rose, then sank back onto her chair again.

How long would he take to die? It could be days. And every day that he lay in this room brought danger closer to her. But he could die quickly.

Another thought asked to be considered. It waited. Then became impatient.

It broke down the flimsy barriers she had created against it and flooded in. She should kill him.

She thought it through.

Holding the pillow over his face.

Being caught. The door opening. Disbelief, then outrage, disgust. The child's face.

Back to prison, this time for murder. She could feel her hand closing again over the stone balustrade at the top of the prison steps as it had done six months ago. She could smell the stench rising from the dormitories as she descended. Prison. Walking to the gallows. The crowd jeering.

And she rushed back from it, trying to take her mind elsewhere. Insidiously, it would begin again.

Holding the pillow over his face. The door opening.

But – if the door did not open. The gold coins, used with care, would last for a long, long time. For an hour she sat teetering on the edge of action and then retreating from it. It was not murder, although it would be seen as murder. The man was dying. To all intents and purposes he was dead already. But he could lie here for days, and each day trapped here as his wife would make the chance of her being found out more likely.

She looked at the man on the bed. A thin trail of spittle was being sucked in and out of his mouth with every breath. Under his head lay a feather pillow, the only one in the place. Donated for his comfort by the landlady. It was dirty but thick and soft. Ann gently raised Rudge's head and slipped the pillow out. She laid it on her knee and continued to stare at him. Her hands were sweating and she wiped them on the pillow. Her mouth was dry and she swallowed uncomfortably.

The breath continued to hiss moistly in and out of his mouth. The thin trail of spittle continued to appear and disappear. Ann leaned forward.

Then she jolted out of the chair as she heard footsteps on the stairs. She fumbled to lift up his head, heavy and lolling, and put the pillow back. As Ann sat back down steps passed by her door and entered the next room. She sat perfectly still. Someone was making up a bed. Walking round, tucking in. Closing the curtains. The bed would be for her. So that she could be near her husband. The steps passed by her door again on their way downstairs.

For twenty minutes, Ann continued to sit perfectly still, staring at the wall opposite as every part of her attention strained to hear any more movement on the stairs. Then she began slowly, methodically, to eat the bread and drink the milk. This was the first action. When it was all finished she would take the second action. She put the plate on the floor beside her chair. She pulled the pillow out from under the head of the pack man, leaned forward and pressed it over his face. At first she pressed too lightly and the pillow seemed to make no difference to his breathing.

Sitting in the chair meant that she could stop quickly if anyone entered the room but the angle was wrong, she couldn't get any leverage. She stood up and put her weight on her outspread hands. She could feel the contours of his face underneath them. Then his body started to buckle and twist. She could not hold the pillow on to his face. It slipped and his body fell back on to the bed and then lay still. His breathing steadied. She saw that the spittle had gone from around his mouth. She felt some wetness on the pillow and dropped it quickly. Her legs gave way and she sat down suddenly on the chair. She heard the rapid tap of one of the chair legs against the uneven floor and realised that it was caused by her body shaking violently as she sat there.

She took a deep breath and stood up again. She touched his face. 'Wake up. Can you?' There was no response. She tried to shake the body, first gently and then she was on her feet shoving him from side to side with more and more force. 'Come on. Come on.' She was shouting. Her voice was loud in the quietness of the room. She must be quiet. She must stop this. Those movements, which had so shocked her, did not mean that he had real life in him. It was just a reaction, an involuntary survival mechanism which caused him to move so powerfully. The physical cage of him fighting for itself. With no direction, for the mind had gone already. She had to carry on. He must be got rid of before someone came who could name him as Rudge and then ask for the money. For that was what would happen. She was certain.

Quick and hard. She had to be quick and hard. She parted her legs and braced herself against the side of the bed. She closed her eyes and put the pillow over his face again. Then pushed down. And held on as the body beneath her hands convulsed and writhed. The arms and legs flailed and the torso arced upwards. He was going to roll off the bed. Ann got on to the bed and knelt on his chest, all the time keeping all her weight on the pillow. It was a fight now. She had forgotten how uneven the odds were. She was fighting a strong man, and she had to win. His arms came up. The fingers of his hands were stretched apart. One hand found her skirt, gripped it, and she couldn't shake him off. She lurched forward and almost straddled his face. She stretched her neck back, arched her spine, and pushed with all her strength down through her rigid arms, down to the face beneath the pillow between her thighs. Her arms and legs shook with the tension and she could feel herself weakening. His other hand scrabbled on her back.

He would win and she was finished. She brought her left knee up to his throat and gave one final, terrible push. Suddenly she realised that the inhuman grunting sounds had ceased, the body had gone limp. The room was still. Ann kept the pillow on his face and crouched over him, her head resting on the bed head. She could hear the low murmur of voices coming from the tap room below. She listened for any change, anything to indicate that this struggle had been heard. But the voices continued to rise and fall gently. Doors opened and shut, men laughed and from outside she could hear the faint sound of the warning bells on the pack horses as they dipped their heads into the feed buckets. Then she started, for she heard a low moaning. It was coming from within the room, and she thought with horror that it was him, coming back to life, but it was not. It was her own voice.

She looked down at the shape on the bed and then she slowly brought her hands up and lifted the pillow from the man's face. The skin was discoloured, mottled blue and purple, and the mouth hung open. The tongue was beginning to protrude between the teeth. She wriggled her body backwards, still straddling his body, and looked further down. The body was contorted, twisted to one side, and the hand which had gripped her skirt was still held stiff and tightly closed. The other hand had fallen open, the fingers slightly curled as if expecting to be taken and held. She shuddered and felt the milk and bread rise in her throat. She slid off the bed and turned away, holding one hand over her mouth. She took a deep breath and put her other hand on the chair for a moment. She was not finished with this business yet. She had to continue. He had to look as if he had died in his sleep.

It was easy enough to straighten his legs and arms. But his fingers were stiff and she had to massage them, bending them back until they lay flat and limp. She worked quickly, aware that someone could come up the stairs at any minute. She avoided looking at his face. Then came the part that she had left to last. She put her finger against his pink tongue and tried to push it back into his mouth. But it would not go. She put fingers from both hands in to his mouth and gently pulled his jaws apart. His mouth was still warm. The tongue strong and springy. She had to hook her fingers around it and push it sideways. At last she was satisfied. Now to tell them. She smoothed her dress, rubbed her hands on the coverlet and went to the door.

Before she could reach it, the door swung open and the girl stood there again.

'Mrs Challinor,' the girl's eyes widened as she took in Ann's stricken face. She looked beyond Ann to the bed. 'What has happened? ' The girl took a few steps into the room. 'Oh! he has died!'

The simple, incontrovertible statement of a child. Innocence. It had to be believed.

Great sobs of relief began to rack Ann's body.

Noise. Voices raised. Steps on the stairs. The room became crowded. Every kind face, every comforting hand on her shoulder, leading her further towards safety. People murmuring to her about arrangements. At last she was taken to a smaller room on the same floor. The door was shut quietly. She was alone.

She lay fully dressed on the bed, her eyes staring into the darkness while she listened to the distant sound of her story being repeated and passed around the room below. She waited, expecting an excited rise in the voices, incredulity, and feet returning on the stairs. Wanting to get up and leave but preventing herself from doing it. She had to hold on. Pushing down the panic which rolled in waves across her. She waited. The sounds grew less, and then fell away altogether.

Only a formless noise filled her ears and beneath it the steady whoosh, whoosh of her own blood. After a long time it seemed to Ann that she was apart from everyone, a sentinel on the furthermost edge of darkness, listening.

She got out of bed, wrapped a shawl around her shoulders and quietly entered the room next to hers. The dead man lay on the bed, covered by a sheet of linen. The doctor had come. Taken a cursory glance at the body, pronounced the man dead, and gone back to his dinner. There was no coffin yet, but the undertaker had washed and laid out the body, ready for burial.

Ann sat down in the chair by the bed. The chair she had sat in earlier in the night. She took the sheet away from his face and upper body. The room was dark. She stood up and opened the curtains. She wanted to see him. Now she could make out the shape of his face. The skin with the curious matt density of death. The eyes closed. The tongue beginning to protrude again between his lips. She sat down again and after a moment she laid her hand lightly on his chest. It felt cold and she realised that she was surprised by that. She was still locked into an intimacy with him. Could still feel his body moving under hers and feel the wetness of the spittle on her hand as she stood clutching the pillow. She looked around the room and saw his sword lying on the

23

floor. She got up from the chair and picked it up. On the hilt was an emblem of some sort. She took the sword to the window and turned it curiously in her hands. She could make out the image of a man and the words encircling it. 'Look, love and follow.' She looked back at the body on the bed.

Now she understood.

She laid the sword back down gently, crossed the room and stood looking at the dead man for a moment longer, then she bent down, pulled the linen sheet over his face, and went back to her own room.

She lay back down on her bed, her mind too agitated for sleep. Look, love and follow – the motto of the Jacobites. The money. The dead man. No wonder she had thought he was a soldier. He was, but not in the pay of the government. What did this mean for her? Did it make her safer or did it increase the danger of her recapture? At least she was unlikely to hang for killing a rebel. On and on she went, turning each piece over in her mind.

And then the early morning wind came, bending trees with its rushing weight and bringing with it the light of the next day. She heard a boy shout and a gate being swung open. The daily rhythm of the town began.

What did she now know and what did it mean? No matter. What was important was what she had done. What she had changed.

Mr Challinor had first existed and then had died in his sleep. There was no Rudge, there was no murder and there was no Ann Dance. She closed her eyes and slept.

As Ann Dance had stretched her hand out to place it on the dead body of Mr Rudge, another man was riding into Ashbourne on the last part of his long journey from the north. Half an hour before, as Ann had stepped from her bed, he had stopped at the foot of Swinscoe Hill and swung heavily out of the saddle. He was tired, near the end of his strength. He looked down at the lights of the town ahead of him and laid his hand on the trembling flank of his horse. The animal was finished, he knew. And he was sorry. He had ridden it too hard. But there was so little time. Every moment he was here, this far down into England, the danger to him, to them all, increased.

Echan. The Green Man. In the town of Ashbourne. He was almost there. His heart filled with a sudden rush of exultant hope. He grasped the top ridge of the saddle, put a foot in the stirrup and heaved himself back up on his horse. He needed to get to the Green Man before too many people were about. He had to stay out of sight until the next night and the time came for his rendevous with Echan Dhu.

Twenty four hours later Cluny left the safety of his room and climbed down the narrow back stairs to the ground floor of the inn. He waited by the door to the tap room for a few moments and then slipped in amongst the crowd of drinkers, walking along by the wall until he could slide into a bench in the fire recess. Here, with his back resting against the bench, he could see both the door from the street and the door to the narrow staircase. For many hours, he sat, a darker shadow in the darkest corner of the tap room at the Green Man. A silent man whose face was drawn with the fatigue of travelling. But as time passed and Echan Dhu did not come, Cluny's body crept with the need for action - and with fear. He imagined Echan fighting to get to him - or trapped. Perhaps being followed. Perhaps wounded.

He took a deep breath, half closed his eyes, forcing himself to sit still and wait out the long hours of the night.

Hours later, Cluny watched as a long strip of light gradually fattened and spread across the tap room floor. He was sick at heart. Like Ann, he heard the early morning wind rise. And as she fell into a deep sleep, Cluny stood up, stiff from his night-long vigil and asked the sleepy bottle boy to prepare him a room. The boy could not understand his northern accent at first. Cluny had to repeat his request. A man, one of the few left in the room, raised his head from his drink and looked across curiously. Their eyes met. For a moment Cluny held the man's gaze and struggled to prevent his hand moving upwards towards the dagger. Was he being watched? The man turned back to his drink; Cluny's hand relaxed back down by his side.

He sat down again, leaned back against the seat and briefly closed his eyes. There was no danger to him in this room. But something was wrong, and if Echan Dhu was lost they would all fail.

Late that morning, when Echan Dhu had still not made contact, Cluny knew he could wait no longer. He left the Green Man by the side door. He visited the stables and made sure that a new horse was got ready for him. He had to be able to leave this place quickly. He wrapped his plaid cloak tightly around his body as if to protect himself from discovery and under it he kept his right hand near his short sword. As he walked through the streets, he could feel his skin prickling with a strange mixture of excitement and dread, as it did before battle. He did not expect to survive this day. Somewhere in this town they would be waiting for him to show himself. What he was about to do would lead his enemies to him even more quickly but it had to be done. It was the course of action he had decided upon as he had lain awake in the half light of his room at the Green Man. He could not simply turn and go back north. He had to trace Echan. He had to find out as much as he could. And if he survived, take that information home. He must visit every inn, every stables, asking for a packman named Rudge. There was a small chance that Echan had gone to the wrong place. But Cluny thought of the careful, meticulous Echan repeating his instructions, folding his map, edge to edge, and knew that this was not likely.

Echan standing by the boat at Arisaig. 'I'll see you, my friend, on the 26th day of February, in Ashbourne, at the Green Man inn. Tha Dochas an.' The Gaelic soft from his throat. His firm hand grasping Cluny's shoulder in farewell. Ashbourne. The furthest any known Jacobite could go into English territory with any chance of returning.

As the day progressed, and people shook their heads at him again and again, briefly wondering who this strange man was and what was his business, Cluny felt despair overtaking him. He almost hoped for a flash of recognition, a hesitation before answering – anything which might tell him that one of the people he spoke to was lying. At least then he would have found a lead, however dangerous, that might take him to Echan. Fear for himself was lost in this despair. Somewhere in this inhospitable place Echan lay dead, or worse, was captured and faced torture. And he could do nothing. Nothing.

In the late afternoon, as the sun was casting its long shadow before him, Cluny reached the Plough Inn.

The inn was dark and cool and almost empty. Cluny felt safer than he had all day. He wanted to eat. He did not want to ask his questions again. He wanted to be just an ordinary traveller for a few moments.

'A pint of ale and bread, if you would, mistress.' Cluny eased his cloak off and laid it on the bench beside him.

The landlady of the Plough Inn brought the food and drink to his table. Cluny ate without tasting, his mind going back and forth over the day. Echan. He had repeated the name so often in his mind that day he was sure he must have said it aloud. He caught movement out of the corner of his eye and he looked up in time to see the back of a young woman as she went slowly up the stairs. He had an impression of a narrow waist, a downward turn of the head and a delicate hand as she bent to gather her skirt away from the stairboards. In her other hand she carried a tray of food. She paused to regain her balance and as she did so the landlady called to Cluny, 'More ale, sir?'

'No, thanking you, mistress. I still have plenty.' Cluny raised his pot. As he spoke he had the impression that the young woman had turned to stare hard at him, but when he looked back, she had gone.

Ann pressed herself close into the curve of the stairwell. From here she could hear what was said in the tap room but she could not be seen. She tried to still her harsh breathing. She would be heard. The voice of that man. The accent - the same as the packman. She listened as Cluny asked his questions. The landlady couldn't help him. No one named Rudge and, no, certainly no big man with fair hair and who spoke Scots under any name. Only packman they had seen was flat on his back, couldn't tell his height, name of Challinor and had died last night. Her customer was immediately curious – had there been a fight? No, the man had died natural, poor chap. Couldn't be the man he was looking for – had a wife, poor creature, said they came from Nantwich, not Scotland. The landlady dropped her voice. Ann could feel that they were both looking at the stairwell, thinking about the young widow who had stood there a moment ago. She swiftly carried on up the stairs, entered her room and softly closed the door. She listened to the muffled voices from below. There was no rising excitement in their tones. No discovery. She went to the window and watched until she saw the man leave and walk back down the lane to the middle of the town. He looked dejected, tired. He did not look like a man who has a lead. Who knows that behind him in the inn is a woman who could tell him about the last few hours of his friend, Rudge. She wished he would turn around so that she could see his face, she might need to recognise him in the future. But he did not. And try as she might that evening, she could not bring his features to her mind. She had had too little time when she had felt the shock of hearing his voice and she had turned. The sun was behind him in the window. All she got was an impression of straight shoulders, a certain holding of the body... a soldier, like the packman. What was this? That now she was a part of. What did it mean?

That night, as the wind got up and the rain splattered on the glistening cobbles, the solitary figure of a horseman could be seen riding down St John's Street. Cluny was travelling north by the Leek road. He had only bad news to carry with him. All the evidence told him that Echan was dead and his precious cargo had been lost. The Scottish clans gathering below Letternich would have to be stopped. Sent back to their glens. Their leaders would have to understand that without the French money and information there could be no glorious third rebellion. The prince would have to wait in France a little longer. Cluny pulled his reluctant horse into the wind as he rode up Swinscoe hill. The horse slowed to a steady walk. Cluny did not urge him on. There was a long journey before him and, at the end of it, only disappointment for the men who waited.

Ann twisted both of her arms around to the back of the black dress. It was too big for her. She pinched the fabric together at the waist. Then let it go and swung from side to side looking at herself in the mirror. The stiff wool dress swayed around her body like a bell. It was not made for her. But it would do. The landlady had rushed up the stairs twenty minutes ago, carrying it proudly like a prize.
'It was made for Hettie Ffoulkes when her man died – but she's out of mourning now – doesn't need it any more.' She leaned forward. 'Between you and me, she's on to a new man, any road.' The landlady's happy smile faltered. She wasn't sure if that had been the right thing to say to a new widow. She helped Ann into the dress, pronounced it a perfect fit and left. Now, alone in her room, Ann took the matching black bonnet from the bed and placed it on her

head. She had never worn a bonnet before. Her hands were trembling slightly as she carefully tied the ribbon under her chin. She pulled on the black silk gloves and picked up the bible the church warden had pressed into her hand at the funeral. She stood up and examined herself in the mirror. Ann Challinor, widow. She took a deep breath and stepped out of her room.

'Two pence please, mistress.'

Ann opened the beaded purse and took out two coins. Her fingers were stiff and clumsy. She put the coins down on the glass counter top and the shop woman scooped them up. 'Wait here would you , Mistress…?'

'Challinor,' replied Ann. The woman hesitated. Ann cleared her throat. 'Challinor,' she said more loudly.

The woman disappeared behind a curtain of lank fabric which concealed the back shop. Mistress Challinor's purchase, a set of tortoiseshell combs, her first purchase in this town, lay on the other side of the counter. She could stretch out and take them – but there was no point – she reminded herself that she had already paid two pence. She looked around, it would be easy to steal from this shop. Ann tried to quieten her breathing. Challinor. Challinor. She sounded the name out in her head.

The shop bell rang. She started, as guilty as if she had actually been caught in the act of stealing. Three women entered the shop, talking to each other. Ann felt her mouth become suddenly dry. She would be found out for sure. She turned away to hide her face but, with horror, she felt one of them touch her arm.

'Mistress Challinor, is it not?'

Ann turned.

'Yes,' Ann's dry lips fumbled over the word.

'Let me introduce myself. Mistress Martin.' Ann caught a drift of sweetish perfume as the woman leaned forward, taking Ann's hands in her own. She was offering her condolences. Talking. Shaking her head from side to side in sadness.

Behind her, Ann heard the shopkeeper clatter back into the room and the rustle of tissue as the tortoiseshell combs were wrapped. Good. She would be able to get out soon. She forced herself to give her full attention to the woman in front of her.

'St Oswald's – our church.' Mistress Martin included the women behind her with a wave of her hand, 'The funeral. The sexton tells me that you had no family there. It was so sudden, of course. But Mistress Wibberley at The Plough was saying that no one has come to you since?' Curiosity swam in the woman's eyes. 'We,' she glanced back over her shoulders at the other women, 'we wondered why you had not left Ashbourne – have you no-one to go to. No family?' The other two women moved back as if to distance themselves from Mistress Martin, their skirts rustling in disapproval. This was a little too much – Mistress Martin could be accused of being impolite. For an uncomfortable moment the question hung in the air. Then Ann began to cry. It was all she could think to do. The women rushed to her, glad to make redress for being part of this. Someone brought her a chair, a glass of water.

'My dear,' said Mistress Martin, full of guilty sympathy and searching wildly for something to make amends, 'you must come to our church meetings. Come tomorrow, please.'

Through her tears, Ann nodded agreement. 'I would be glad to,' she said, although the prospect terrified her.

'...and for this we are truly thankful'. The prayer came to a close and for a brief moment the last syllable echoed faintly in the silent hall. Ann kept her eyes closed and continued to listen intently. She heard a multitude of small sounds around her as people shifted in their seats. She opened her eyes and raised her head slowly. Mistress Martin, who sat beside her, was handing her prayer book to a child who was eagerly collecting them. Ann leaned across and added her book to the pile the child was carrying.

'Now, come and take some tea.'

Mistress Martin stood up, brushed down her skirts and set off across the floor. As Ann followed her she was conscious of many eyes taking in every detail of her appearance. She was handed a cup of tea and, as Mistress Martin bobbed between one person and another, Ann was able to slip away from the throng to a chair by one of the huge stained glass windows. For a moment she felt as if she was completely alone in the room. She closed her eyes again and let out a sigh of relief. How to speak, how to move. She had to learn all of it. And once more she doubted her ability to do it. Every day, for the rest of her life. That thought surprised her. The rest of her life. Here. A curious idea. She tried to imagine her future in this town. She felt a kind of longing for it. For the ordinariness of it.

She opened her eyes and saw Mistress Martin coming towards her with her hand firmly under the elbow of a tall, fair woman in a pale blue dress.

'Mrs Challinor, Mrs Challinor,' Mistress Martin, unable to hold back her good news, called out before she reached Ann, 'Here I have some one who says she might know you. Isn't that delightful?'

Ann lurched to her feet; her tea cup fell forgotten from her hand. As she stared at the woman being propelled towards her, she heard, as if from a long way away, two loud separate cracks as the cup and then the saucer hit the floor. She had the impression of all the faces in the room turning towards her. In a flurry of skirts the two women bent to pick up the shattered pieces of cup and saucer while Ann simply stood there, her mind racing. As they stood up she stared dumbly at a dark streak across the front of the woman's blue dress. Tea from her cup must have splashed it. Ann raised her eyes to find the woman staring back at her.

Mistress Martin, now a little breathless, continued her

introduction. 'This is Jane Horsfield, who also comes from Northwich. Is that not fine?' She beamed at Ann, confidently expecting her pleasure.

Jane Horsfield put her hand out to Ann, 'I am indeed from Northwich,' she frowned, 'but I do not think that we have met, have we?'

Ann took the woman's hand, it was cool and slightly damp from the tea. Northwich. Where had the packman said? What had she said to the landlady at the Plough? For a moment she had lost track of it. She thought back frantically. Remembered the packhorse man saying the name to her. Nantwich. It definitely was Nantwich. Not Northwich. Ann felt a great flood of relief. This was a simple mistake on the part of Mistress Martin. The two women were looking at her expectantly.

She took her hand away and shook her head sadly. 'Oh, I am afraid that there is some mistake. I have come here from Nantwich, not Northwich.' She tried to look suitably upset.

Mistress Martin was immediately contrite. 'My dear, I am so sorry. To raise your hopes like that... my silliness, I misheard you...'

After drinking a new cup of tea, and making small talk with the woman from Northwich, Ann explained that she was tired and left the hall.

At the bottom of the graveyard, she found a seat secluded by yew trees. She sat there for a long time until she felt calm enough to walk slowly back to her room in the Plough Inn. She thought about her story, the story she didn't yet have. In a town like Ashbourne, where everyone knew everyone else, it was not good enough for her to simply look like the poor widow – she had to have a credible past, to be able to deal with a situation like the one today. She shuddered when she thought of what might have happened in the church hall... the confusion and then suspicion spreading on the face of Mistress Martin – and all her friends. She had to be prepared for meetings like this. If she wasn't careful, it wouldn't be a bounty hunter, but a woman from Nantwich who would expose her for the imposter that she was. If she had come from the right place, that woman in the blue dress could have sent her back to prison.

At the next meeting, surrounded by a circle of townswomen whose faces were strained with curiousity, Ann told her story. It was sad. As sad as Ann could make it in the week that she had had to invent it. A romantic story of a young woman marrying beneath her and then being disowned by her family. A young woman whose family had moved around the country, and who would now be difficult to find. The reconciliation she had hoped for would, by now, be impossible. She indicated all of this without being so crude as to actually say it and, in this way, allowed her listeners to discover her story for themselves. As she walked back again to the Plough Inn, she knew that the women she left behind were comparing their impressions, creating Ann Challinor for themselves and looking forward to offering their new creation to the rest of Ashbourne. Ann considered the women who had listened to her so intently. The story of the untimely death of her husband, the story of someone else's life being shattered, had both fascinated and comforted them. But they had also looked at her with genuine sympathy. If she wanted it, she could create a place for herself in this town. It would be her protection.

She considered the practicalities of her position. How to have enough money to settle here but not so much as to arouse suspicion? To start buying with the French gold was too dangerous but she could sell the pack horses and their cargo. She looked up. She had walked quite far down the street and now above her, she saw the sign for the Green Man. Underneath it was the great arch where the daily London coaches rolled in. Without any hesitation, she turned and walked into the yard. The ostler, Mr Shoesmith, came out of his tack room to see the small, black clad figure of a woman picking her way towards him across the cobbles. It was that poor young widow. He went forward and reached out his hand.

'Mind yersel, lady. It's slippery here.'

Ann took his hand and smiled at him, 'I am hoping that you can help me sir,' she said. Her voice was hardly above a whisper so that Mr Shoesmith had to lean closer to hear her. As he helped her across the yard towards the only chair in the tackroom, Ann knew that she was going to get a good price for the pack horses and the loads.

With the money from the sale of the horses Ann was able to buy more clothes and pay for her room at The Plough. The French coins she kept secret. She would only use them sparingly. One at a time. Exchanging them for English coinage at the jeweller's shop on the market place in town. Every day she walked down Church Street, wearing her black dress, to visit her husband's grave in St Oswald's churchyard. A slender symbol of piety and a constant reminder to everyone in the town of who she was and of why she was here. And every day she fought the desire to run, to get as far away from the Gaol in Derby as was possible. Sometimes, when she walked out on the streets, a kind of blind panic threatened to overwhelm her. But reason kept her hand steady and her walk slow and measured. She made herself meander when she wanted to slide quickly from doorway to doorway. She stepped forward to pick up fruit or cloth on a market stall, quelling the desire to merge back into the anonymous crowd of shoppers. She spoke in shops, asking for soap, thread, a cake, mimicking the tones of the women around her and dreading all the time to hear someone behind her say. 'Why, I recognize that woman, that voice…'. She scanned the bills pasted up on the walls of town buildings, expecting to see an announcement of the escape of Ann Dance. Offering a bounty for her recapture.

And one day it appeared. Ann had been walking towards the main street of the town when her name sprung at her from the wall of the town hall.

A good Reward offered for the capture of Ann Dance, pickpocket and thief, who escaped from Derby gaol on this day February 25th 1755. A handsome faced woman of young age, being five foot five inches high, pale complexion, fair hair and blue eyes, looks very sharp, commonly known as The Sparrow and belongs to a notorious gang of Gamblers. Her father is well known as a pickpocket and lately is imprisoned in Leicester Gaol to take his tryal at the next assizes for the stealing of Great Coats from Melton Fair. Whoever will apprehend and secure the said Ann Dance, in any of his Majesty's gaols in England, and give notice to John Greatorex, Gaoler at Derby, shall receive 10 guineas Reward.

She pulled her bonnet further down on her face, afraid to even glance up and down the street. She took a step closer. The poster was old and dog-eared but she was sure it had not been there the day before. It must have been lying in the town hall for weeks. Someone had finally noticed it and felt duty bound to put it up on the notice board. She plucked up courage and looked around quickly – no one was watching. She put her hand up to take it, then she stopped. She glanced up at the windows on either side of the street. They looked blank and empty but she could not take the chance of being seen tearing the poster down. She must leave it there.

Every day after, no matter where she intended to go, she found herself taking a route which brought her past the town hall. She had no need to go up to the notice board for she could easily tell from a distance that the white rectangle with her name on it was still there.

Now her reactions to every inflection in a voice, every look towards her became heightened. Where were the bounty hunters? Had they been and gone? Would they come back? She changed her back room at The Plough for one which had a window overlooking the Derby road. She began to sit at the window of this room for hours, anxiously trying to make out the demeanour and face of every man who came riding in to Ashbourne – it would be a lone man – bounty hunters never wanted to share their prize money. For days she hardly left her room and the landlady began to talk to her customers in a hushed voice about the way grief can lead to madness.

On the sixth morning in her new room, Ann woke late. In one rapid movement, she swung herself out of the bed, intent in getting to the chair by the window.

She had only taken a few paces, when she stopped and stood still in the centre of the room. She could hear the shouts of the stable boys in the yard below as they led new horses into the stalls. How many had she missed already that day? How many horses had ridden into Ashbourne that morning – with riders whose faces she had not seen?

She wiped her bleary eyes, walked forward, picked up the chair and moved it back to its original place by the fire. She either ran or she stayed. Either way only luck and wit would save her. She sat back down on the edge of the bed. Waiting to be caught was pointless; she needed work and a place to live. So far, she had managed to convince people of her story. She was accepted as Ann Challinor, but living in The Plough like this was dangerous; it kept her connected to the death of Mr Rudge. And only a rich woman would have no need of work.

She got up from the bed, went to the writing bureau by the window and sat down. She took a piece of paper, folded and ripped it until she had a small piece about the size of the palm of her hand. She took the quill pen from its wooden slot in the table top and unscrewed the ink jar. She sat for a few moments, staring out of the window with the pen raised in her hand, and then she wrote with large, curling letters on the scrap of paper:

Ann Challinor
Embroidery
Fine work for ladies

She held it up to the light and looked at it. Her calling card. She imagined offering it to prospective customers. Taking it from her purse, smiling.

Sewing. Mistress Greatorex, the gaoler's wife, had said Ann was her best pupil, even though she was a prisoner. Ann had not forgotten any of it. Cross stitch, fern stitch, overlock, then a bowl of thin soup before she went back down to the prison dormitory. For the first time since she had come to Ashbourne, she thought of Mr Meynell, the prison doctor. She shivered, suddenly aware of the cold air through her thin nightgown. She had thought herself lucky then, when Mr Meynell had chosen her for his great experiment.

Later that day Ann stood in front of a house in the business part of town. She carefully read the brass plaque on the door:

Mr Waldron
Solicitor and Notary
Magistrate and Attorney at Law

She looked down at her sombre grey gown, shook some of the dust from the street off its hem and smoothed the black gloves she wore. She reached up and knocked on the door.

As she was led up the curving staircase by Mister Waldron's clerk, she had an impression of cool, dark quiet; of time being measured more carefully than on the street outside. She was ushered from the dark upper hallway to a room at the front of the house. She sat down on one side of a large desk, blinking in the sudden brightness. On the other side of the desk, framed by the light from the huge windows, she could just make out a figure rising from its chair to greet her. Before the figure could speak, she blurted out, 'Sir. I wish to rent a property. A shop, here in Ashbourne.'

The figure stood up and leaned over the desk. Her eyes rapidly adjusted and she saw a small neat man, holding his hand out to her in greeting. He looked a little annoyed. She knew immediately that she had been too abrupt. There was a formality to everything, to every occasion she entered now. She must learn that, or it would be her undoing.

'Mr Waldron, madam. How pleasant to meet you, Mrs...' He looked down at the sheet of paper in front of him, ' Mrs Challinor.'

He sat down again and leaned back in his chair.

'Madam, pray continue. You say you wish to rent a ... shop?' There was the faintest hesitation and then a slight incredulous rise in his voice as he spoke the word 'shop'. Perhaps shops were beneath him or perhaps she did not look as if she could run a shop.

'I am a seamstress. I have need of employment – my circumstances have changed...' she proceeded to explain about the death of her husband. As she spoke, he nodded. He looked at her sympathetically. He held his hand up to stop her.

'Madam, I fully understand your position. Please accept my condolences for your loss...but...I have to ask...so you,' he stumbled over his words in embarrassment, '...I mean ...can you afford to take on this venture?'

Ann nodded. She explained to him about the pack horses. The sale.

He listened to her intently and then tapped the table decisively. It would be possible. He would find her the kind of property she needed. In fact, there could be one. Then words came which she could not understand. Leasehold. Flying freehold. Indenture. What was he saying?

The door opened.

'Yes, Mrs Jessop – what is it? I have a client with me.' Mr Waldron was impatient.

'It is Mr Jamieson – from the court. He says it is an urgent matter.' Mrs Jessop hesitated in the doorway, looking at Ann with concern; she did not like to disturb Mr Waldron when he was with a client.

Mr Waldron got up. 'Very well. Tell him I will come down.' He turned to Ann, 'My apologies, Mrs Challinor. I will be back directly.'

Alone in the room, Ann fought a rising panic. The court. Her hands slid with sweat on her purse, her legs felt weak, but she gripped the arm of her chair and forced herself to rise. They had found her. She had to get out of the room. She was, even after everything she had done, just a street thief. Her plan was presposterous. It would not work. Her attempts to dress, to move, to sound like the women at the church meetings were doomed to failure. And her secrets were about to be discovered by this man of law. She reached the door just as it opened.

Mr Waldron stared at her, his eyebrows raised and eyes wide open with shock. Without taking his eyes off her, he went to the desk and picked up the brass bell which sat there. He shook it vigorously and a sharp tinkling sound rang out. Ann imagined it travelling down the stairs to where the clerk sat at his desk. Now, now he is going to send for the constabulary. She returned to her seat. There was no point in trying to run. It was hopeless. She could not get down those stairs quickly enough.

Mr Waldron got up and came round the desk to her, still without taking his eyes from her face.

I won't admit to murder, I will only admit to my escape, there is no proof... what have I done... sold goods which don't belong to me...nothing else. Ann heard the door open behind her.

Mr Waldron took his eyes away from Ann for the first time.

He spoke softly. 'Mr Jamieson, would you be so kind as to ask Mrs Jessop if she would make us some tea. Mrs Challinor is feeling faint.' He went to the door with the clerk and Ann heard the words – widow... recent... very sad.

Gradually, her panic subsided. She realised her hand was aching and she relaxed her grip on the arm of the chair. Her fingers shook as she tucked some stray wisps of hair under her bonnet. Mr Waldron was not about to discover the truth about Ann Dance. He could not smell the prison on her. Now he was coming back in, not even looking at her as he spoke. And then she understood – he had simply been horrified at the thought of having to deal with a fainting woman in his office. He stole a look at her and seeming satisfied that the crisis was over, he took a key from his waistcoat pocket and opened a large cupboard set into the wall. Soon, papers, plans and ledgers were strewn across the table.

'Mrs Challinor, good book-keeping is the basis of any successful business, I cannot stress this enough. Now, I do know of someone...' He looked up and smiled at her kindly. In this world she had decided to enter each person had a role, and taking care of her was his. She had become one of his clients. He opened a leather-bound folder and reached for a quill from a wooden pot on his desk. She saw with pleasure that her name, Ann Challinor, was being written down and filed away.

The house she wanted was on Church Street. She had seen it on the first day she had walked out on the route of the Manchester coach. She had walked past it three times before she knew that she had to stop and look at it more closely. She had cupped her hands to peer in at the window. By squinting against the glass she found she could make out a wooden counter, three long shelves and just a glimpse of a staircase turning up and away to the next floor. Ann imagined a sitting room up there, a fire with coals burning in the grate and a table with supper laid. Her hands resting on the table, picking up a knife, cutting bread. She could live here.

'Yes. I know the house.' Mr Waldron was pleased. He could see a transaction ahead. 'Church Street – Frost's Yard to be precise – as luck would have it, it has been empty all winter and the lease is for sale.' He slapped the file in front of him in satisfaction.

But Ann did not feel that it was luck, she felt certain that the house was meant to be hers. She liked its position, poised on the far edge of town on the Leek road.

'How long a lease do you wish to take?' he had asked, 'six months?'

Ann had shaken her head. 'No,' she said firmly, 'a year – at least.'

It was true that when she had first looked in through the window she had dreamed of it as simply a place to hide before her journey north and away. But even a few weeks later her plans had changed. She would stay in this town. She reasoned that a lone woman travelling on the coach north was more likely to be an object of suspicion than a widowed shopkeeper living here in Ashbourne.

But there was something else. Taking the keys in her hand had given her that first thrill of possession. Mr Waldron had handed them to her, an ordinary everyday moment for him, and had stood back with a flourish to let her open the shop door. 'This could suit you very well,' he murmured. Part of her was aware that he would say these words to any client but oh – the act of opening the door and stepping into the empty shop. Running her hand along the wide wooden counter. Opening each of the wall cupboards.

She walked through the house in a sort of daze. Her life ahead unfolding in front of her. Here the kitchen, where she would stand at the sink. Here the sitting room where she would bend to stoke the fire and here the bedroom where she would slip in between taut sheets and turn her face into soft, cool pillows. Moving, standing, working, she already inhabited this house. Back on the street outside Ann hardly listened to the solicitor's words as he shouted to her above the noise. Around them the street was filled with the sound of stone cutting, of carpentry and the yelled instructions of men hanging on scaffolding high above her head. Church Street was filling with the great square houses of the new rich of this area, the merchants of Ashbourne. Soon her house would no longer be the last one on the town road. Mr Waldron was apologising for the dust, the confusion, the heaps of yellow sand lying on the pavements. But Ann liked it. She felt anonymous amongst all this activity. No one was paying much attention to the small, fair-haired woman in her widow's dress as she stood there looking up at the windows of what was going to be her parlour.

Chapter 2

July 1755 Frost's Yard, Ashbourne

Ann plunged up into consciousness, her heart thudding as if she had been running desperately through the night, not sleeping in this soft bed. It is six months since the packman died, three months since she came to live in Frost's Yard and every night it is the same.

She rolls off the mattress onto her knees in one practised movement, born of obsessive repetition. Yes. Good. It is still there. She feels the rough calico of the money bags and the cold weight of the coins within. She will place it back in the box and under the floorboards tonight. This is her pattern. Sometimes she puts the money above the floor, hidden somewhere out of the box, and at other times, she places it back in the box and puts it under the floor boards. In her mind, at all times, she knows where the money is, and where it will be next in her sequence of hiding places.

She climbs back into bed. This night, of all nights, she tells herself, she should be able to sleep. She dragged the covers up and tucked them around her body.

Today as she had passed the town hall on her way to the market, she had half glanced, as usual, in the direction of the notice board. Something had changed. What was it? And then she knew. The bill with her name on it had gone. Her eyes searched the ground around the noticeboard desperately. Had someone taken it? Had a bounty hunter come? Was he watching her now? Forgetting that she should show no interest, she ran towards the noticeboard and there to her relief, in the dusty summer street, lay the poster, crumpled and torn. She longed to pick it up and destroy it completely, but, as she stood there, uncertain of what to do, she felt the first heavy drops of summer rain. She watched in fascination as the rain flattened the torn edges and blurred the black letters proclaiming her escape, gradually merging them into one greying, indistinguishable pool of water on the surface of the paper. Eventually even the letters of the name Ann Dance, in thicker ink than all the others, had gone. She had realised that rain was soaking into the collar of her jacket and she had turned for home.

She moved her legs restlessly. The blankets felt heavy, a damp weight pressing down on her. It was hot and thundery, there would be more rain tomorrow. Through her open window, she heard the sound of a child crying in a room across the street. Then the sound stopped. Ann rolled over on her back. She imagined the mother putting her arms around the child to comfort it. Hush, it was only a dream.
Ann rolled over on to her back. Her dreams are all nightmares. Nightmares of Mr Meynell and his machine. Suddenly there was a sharp noise, as if something had been dropped. It sounded close, directly beneath her window. She sits up, straining to hear. Now there are voices, a man and then a woman, whispering. Then a laugh, quickly suppressed. Two lovers stealing a good night kiss. Ann lay back on the pillows and closed her eyes.
She cannot believe that her nights are safe. All of her life, except for that brief time in the molly house, she has slept ready to defend herself from some kind of stealthy attack in the darkness. A hand sliding over a breast or curving around her thigh, seeking entertainment and relief. Fingers slipping between the folds of her skirt to extract the few coins she had secreted there or fists pulling at her sack of provisions, gathered for safety under her head. Now she awakes alone, to silence, but even more in fear. Ready to react to danger, she hears nothing but her own breath in the empty room. Each night she fills the silence with the great threat of recapture. Lies awake in the half light and sees prison. As time passes these fantasies become more

exquisitely painful. She knows she could not come through a return to Markeaton Gaol. It was not the stench, the disease, the need to be always alert, ready to avoid someone's quick rage. Ann could deal with all of that. It was simply an extension of the life she led outside. But the shining machine belonging to Mr Meynell, the prison doctor, it was this which filled her with such fear.

At first, she had been pleased - to be chosen by Mr Meynell. Word in the prison had been that you got extra food if you helped Mr Meynell. The women prisoners had jostled at the door of the dormitory, clamouring to be chosen, joking about why he had only asked for women. He had tried at least ten women before she had her chance.

She had passed all his tests. She had enjoyed the puzzles. Smooth wooden blocks, all different shapes, to be put into their own slot on a board. Metal links to be separated. Everything to be matched. To be put in order as quickly as possible. And always food afterwards, which she was allowed to eat in the room or in the prison kitchen - otherwise it would have been snatched from her as soon as she entered the dormitory.

Then, one day, she had entered the room and seen that a cloth screen had been rigged up in a corner of the room. Mr Meynell was seated at his desk. He waited until the guard had left and then he pointed to the screen, 'You will find soap and a clean garment there.' He gave a small, nervous cough. 'Please wash and put on the shift.'

Ah, so this was what he wanted after all.

Obediently, she went behind the screen. There was a bucket of water, a bar of soap and a piece of sacking with a cotton shift folded neatly on top of it. She started to take off her clothes. After a few moments she heard Mr Meynell leave the room and the sound of his steps receding as he went down the stairs.

Ann was alone. It was the first time she had been alone

since she had been brought to the prison over a year ago. Almost automatically, she looked up at the high window. Too high, there was no chance of escape. And part of her didn't want the terrible effort of escape – if Mr Meynell wanted her just for himself then she could do well out of it. She was surprised – she hadn't thought that this would be it. He'd gone to a lot of trouble – all those tests. And to offer her the privacy of a screen while she washed... he was a queer one – still – it could be to her advantage. He'd taken a great deal of care to get someone who could pass those tests. That must mean that she couldn't be replaced that easily. She looked around for a cot or a mattress, then she tested the floorboards with the heel of her shoe. Surely he wasn't going to have them lie on the floor? Perhaps that was why he had left the room, to find something to lie on.

It had felt strange to be standing naked in that room, with no eyes watching her. She had straightened up and slid her hands over her naked body, stretched out her arms and examined her narrow wrists. She felt for her ribs one by one under their thin layer of flesh, and cupped her small breasts. She looked down and watched the soapy water trickle across her stomach, between her thighs. She had not touched or been touched by a man since she had entered the prison. She knew how to keep her eyes down or feign illness if any guard looked like taking an interest in her. There were plenty of other women who hoped to get some favour, some kind of trade with the guards, but she knew better. There was no trade to be made if you were a prisoner, anything you had could be taken. She dried herself on the piece of sacking lying by the bucket and slipped the shift over her head. She came out from behind the screen and sat down on the chair to wait. After a few minutes she heard his slow steps coming back up the staircase.

And Mr Meynell had come in, carrying, not a mattress, but a china bowl slopping with soapy water. Over his arm lay a towel. He put the bowl and the towel on the table, picked up a measuring tape and metal rule which had been lying there and asked her to stand and hold out her arms.

He measured her height, the length and circumference of her fingers, the span of her outstretched arms. His fingers had hardly touched her, just a single, firm moment of pressure as he held the tape against her wrist, her hip or the tips of her fingers. Once he had fumbled, trying to find the correct positioning of the tape, feeling for her shoulder blade through the loose shift. He was standing behind her, close enough for her to hear the shake in his breath as he tried to place the tape. For a moment she felt the warmth of his hand held flat against her back. Curious, she shifted her weight slightly to press against it. He sprang away quickly. She didn't dare turn around, knowing that if she did she would find him staring at her. After a moment, he carried on with his task. Eventually, she heard him give a deep involuntary sigh of relief as he moved back to the table to copy his findings in his dossier. She watched him wash his hands meticulously in the china bowl and wipe them on the towel before he sat down to write. She had been far wrong to think that he wanted to bed her. He could hardly bear to touch her body. When he had finished transcribing his notes, he had asked her to sit with him at the table.

'You have done very well. Very well indeed. Yes, a great deal has been covered.' He shuffled the papers in front of him. 'I have some further tests. They are measurements I must take of your head, and, for them to be accurate, we must shave off your hair. Mrs Greatorex will do it.'

She had tried to refuse but her reaction had only made Meynell impatient.

'I cannot proceed without it. You,' he pointed one finger at her, 'cannot continue to take part without it.' It was a threat. Ann knew that she had no real choice. She nodded her agreement.

Ann remembered the shame of it. First the silence when she had been taken back to the dormitory and then the jeers of the other prisoners, delighted that she had got her come uppance. 'Not so good being the doctor's pet now, eh?' She had fashioned herself a scarf from a strip of her petticoat and tied it tightly over her head.

It was after that that she had met the Reverend Parker for the first time. It was the Reverend Parker who wrote down the measurements while for two days Mr Meynell endlessly turned her head this way and that, feeling, probing – with none of that nervousness she had sensed when he had touched her body.

Ann was exhausted by it. After the first morning, she had swayed, dizzy with fatigue and if the Reverend Parker had not caught her arm she would have fallen.

'Meynell. Must we use a woman? They are not as physically strong.'

The doctor had held up his hand, 'Parker, it is essential that we use a female. They are not so steeped in crime as the male of their class. They have more natural morality. And they are malleable.'

Reverend Parker had suggested that she be given a chair but even so the endless turning and twisting and the need to hold completely still tired her. She listened as they discussed the bumps and ridges under her skin. She thought over what Meynell had said. What did it mean – more natural morality? They leaned over a table covered with diagrams of the human skull. They consulted a china head, covered with sections, each one filled with writing. They stood in front of her, asking her to turn this way and that, comparing her head to drawings which showed other heads with lines and sections covering them. From what she could see, each of these sections was named and numbered. At last, late into the night of the second day, they completed their calculations and they both seemed satisfied by what they had discovered about her.

She had watched them, their heads close together at the table, peering at their results in the candle light. 'She is a suitable candidate, Parker. I think we can be sure of it.' She remembered how Meynell had rubbed his eyes – just for a moment, he had seemed to her like an excited child. 'We should start the programme.' He looked intently at the other man, there was an urgency in his voice, 'Are you still willing?'

And Parker had nodded his head.

Meynell turned to Ann. 'This is a great opportunity for you, Ann Dance.' It was the first time he had used her name. 'You are to be taught to read and to sew. I have designed a full series of lessons. Tomorrow we will start.'

Ann had stared at him. Neither of those two things seemed appealing. But they would mean better treatment. She remembered saying. 'Thank you.' They seemed to expect it. But she was tired. She wanted to go to sleep.

Every day after that she had been taken to what the guards now nicknamed the school room. She had two teachers. Mistress Greatorex who taught her to sew and Mr Parker who had elected to teach her to read.

The sewing was tedious but Ann was entranced by the books - by that winter of learning to read. Reverend Parker was a good teacher. The big picture books at first, with their coloured illustrations and then the stories and the ballads. Ones written down that she had heard sung. Reverend Parker brought her stories. Stories of terrible misfortune. Shipwrecks and unjust killings. Love and desperation.

Oh Mary left her house to go on the wild moor.
Oh Mary left her house, and was never seen no more,
her love he lies adying on the near sea shore,
but Mary has left her house and can hear of him no more
The soldiers they came calling in the light of day

but Mary they never found for she had gone away
the sand on the sea shore stains red as any rose
and the cries of Mary's lover are lost where the sea wind blows.

Once she could read without a finger guiding her through the words on the   page, the minister brought Ann simple histories and books of religion.

'Once you can read, Miss Dance, any learning, from any age, can be yours.'

Back in the dormitory, she whispered this name over to herself. Miss Dance. It was her name, but it was as if it belonged to someone else. She sounded like someone of importance. 'Would Miss Dance come for tea?' 'Good afternoon, Miss Dance.'

Mr Parker sometimes brought her sweets and once a dog-eared pamphlet with London fashions and court gossip for her to read. She learnt quickly. One afternoon, when she had finished reading a particularly difficult passage, he brought a small book out from his pocket and asked her to read the cover.

'A journal thro' the world…an Explanation into the Beginning of Our Existence.' She sounded out the unfamiliar words. The author's name was inscribed below. The Reverend Benjamin Parker. She looked up with an exclamation of surprise.

'Yes, I have had some small fame,' he had said, pleased by her reaction. 'There was a man in Cambridge,' he continued, 'Isaac Newton, who believed that we can turn lead into gold.'

He made her repeat the name. Isaac Newton.

'Why is that important, Miss Dance? Hmm?'

She was confused, 'His name?' she offered.

'No. No.' The Reverend Parker shook his head. 'No – turning lead into gold. Do y'see.'

She nodded, although she did not.

'It means – that we should always seek for what seems the impossible. This is science. Perhaps you think it is impossible that you can change – but Meynell and I do not.' Change from what to what, thought Ann. If she knew what it was that they wanted then she would certainly do it – if it meant less time in the cell and more food. Who wouldn't?

The next day he brought a tall young woman with him to the school room. Her tiny waist was tightly encased in a green velvet bodice with a row of pearl buttons down the front. She was like a doll. A pretty toy. Ann found herself greedy for the sight of something so rich, so colourful in the dismal room. She drew in every detail of this woman's clothing. The grosgrain skirt with its dull sheen, flouncing out from the tiny waist and then the scalloped edges of layers of creamy lace petticoats just visible beneath its bottom edge. The dark woollen shawl around her shoulders, the way her hands clasped its soft folds close to her body as if she were cold. The rings on two of her fingers. She shone. All of her shone. The pamphlet, with its fashions, it would have been hers.

'This young lady is my niece, Miss Dance.'

Ann stood up and held out her hand, unsure if it was the right thing to do. The young woman looked around the room with interest, but did not acknowledge Ann. Ann clasped her hands awkwardly in front of her for a moment and then sat down.

'Catherine, here it all is,' Parker was already at the table, opening up the folders, one by one.

Catherine walked over to the table. Ann could hear the precise click of her wooden heels against the floorboards. 'Ah – are these the measurements that you told me of, uncle?' she spoke quietly, her voice held a mixture of fascination and revulsion.

'Yes,' Parker was proud to show her what he was doing, 'some of them. There are others, more detailed – of the skull... here.' He reached up and took a folder down from the topmost shelf. His niece looked at them, giving her full attention to each page before she turned them. 'How strange,' she said, finally, 'and you can tell from these measurements that she's a felon?' She glanced down at Ann – she had no hesitation in saying the word.

They have discussed this before, thought Ann. Around a dinner table, in a library, in a carriage on the way to the theatre.

'Are you sure?'

'Oh yes. Meynell has been very thorough.' Parker turned to the next page, 'Look here – the detail.'

'And can you change her?'

Parker nodded.

'Yes. It is very curious, and it is very good work.' Now she has had enough of him. 'But, uncle, I must go to meet Mama...'

'Yes, yes, of course.' And Parker had called the guard. As Catherine left he had called after her and she had half turned, indulging him for another few moments.

'Mr Meynell is going to write to the Royal Society in London about this,' his hand waved to include the whole room, 'this – experiment.' It was a last try to gain her approbation.

She smiled again and was gone.

The Reverend Parker had carried on with Ann's daily lesson but he was unsettled. In his mind he was still talking to Catherine, but words, nuances, glances were being altered as he thought. Catherine's eyes were opening wide in amazement, her lips were parting in surprise. She was catching her breath in wonder. Finally, he was satisfied with the meeting. Ann was aware of all this as she sat beside him, her voice unheeded as she dully recited the verse he had chosen.

At last she was taken down the stairs by the guard, into the kitchen where, as usual, she was given food.

'Good food,' as the cook pointed out, 'better than the other prisoners.' Ann took the bowl of watery soup in both hands and lifted it up to her lips. No one else in the busy kitchen spoke to her as she stood by the door chewing on threads of cabbage.

I am an object then, a thing, something to be changed. An experiment. Nothing more.

She put the empty bowl down on the table.

'Are you finished, Miss Dance?' the guard's voice dropped with sarcasm on the last words. She nodded. She was ready to go back to the dormitory, and for the first time she preferred it to the school room.

The lessons continued. Benjamin Parker was at his most serious when he talked to Ann of the heavenly father. She was obedient. She listened. She gloried in God for him. She told him that her heart was uplifted. She read on and on, through the books with brightly coloured pictures, travelling in a hot country with rounded hills of sand and yellow sun in a blue sky. She skimmed over the simple poems and then the pages of large black print which told stories. Stories of tests and of goodness and of reward. Of women with huge brown eyes and oval faces and men with tangled beards. Each of their faces showed the twisted anguish of loss in the first drawings, and this look was always replaced by an expression of grateful relief in the last picture. The message was clear. Faith would save you. If only you could believe.

She could not. There was no proof. She could not believe in an almighty and caring God. Although, curiously, she could still fear him.

She considered sharing this difficulty with the Reverend Parker, but decided against it. She had understood something about him now. She was only of benefit to the minister as an example of salvation. An unbeliever would be of no use at all to him.

Eventually, her lack of faith ceased to trouble her. After all, she reasoned, if there was no God then there could be no Retribution; a release from faith would mean, finally, a release from fear.

And she had carried on along this docile path, allowing herself to be comforted by the pattern of each day. Until the terrifying moment when she at last fully understood her role in the scheme of Mr Meynell's ambition.

She had been taken from the lower prison up a long flight of steps to the school room as usual. In this room which had not changed in the year that she had been coming to it she was surprised to see a strange machine. She had seen nothing like it before. A long glass cylinder, held in position by two brass cradles, some kind of paddle and, most curiously, a metal spoon hanging from the end of a chain. Mr Meynell was standing to the right of this machine. Mr Parker was also there. Mr Meynell had been turning the cylinder rapidly with the wooden paddle as Ann was led in. He looked up and over his shoulder, registering her presence. 'Mr Parker,' he said, nodding his head to indicate that she was to be seated in a chair directly beside the machine.Then, before she could be seated, there was a loud crack, a flash of light and she saw what appeared to be a blue, jagged line leaping through the glass tube.

Ann sat down. She was startled, curious, but, at this point, she was not afraid. On Mr Meynell's command, she obediently stretched her arm out. He pushed back her sleeve and attached a metal cuff to her upper arm. He held her arm with one hand and took up the metal spoon in the other. The chain attached to the spoon clinked against the table and the brass fittings. He laid the spoon carefully on her lower arm. Suddenly, she felt as if a great force had entered her. Her body curled up in spasms as, just behind the force, came enormous flooding pain. She drew her breath in over her teeth in a high pitched whistling sound. She had never felt such pain. What was this horror? Then it stopped.

Mr Meynell observed her for a moment and then turned back to his machine. 'Too much,' she heard him say to Reverend Parker. She recovered her breath, although her teeth chattered and her body shook.

She attempted to stand up, but her legs gave way and she reached for the table to support herself. The metal cuff clanked against the table edge.

Mr Meynell turned round, glanced down at the cuff and then up at her. There was a mixture of irritation and surprise on his face.

'Sir, what punishment is this? Why are you doing this?' Ann heard her own voice, weak and gasping.

Mr Meynell gestured to the chair. 'Sit down. This is not a punishment. This is a cure. I am offering you a cure.'

Ann took a deep, shuddering breath, 'Sir. This is a punishment. Are we not in a prison?' She sat back down slowly.

Mr Meynell held up his hand impatiently. 'Madam,' there was a deliberate irony in his use of such a formal term, ' you showed willing to come here. You wished to take part in my work.'

'Mr Meynell...,' began Reverend Parker, uneasily, 'this does seem a very different reaction to...'

Mr Meynell turned to give the younger man his full attention. 'It is my theory, Parker, that if the appropriate part of the body is supplied with these electric shocks, then the bodily harmony will be restored and the person will be freed from their affliction. I believe that this is true for mental or social ailments, just as it is true for the physical.' His words were emphatic. 'This is not a punishment.'

The words jumbled in her head. If he was talking then at least the next shock could be delayed. 'No, sir. I did not agree to this... this pain.'

He picked up a folder from the desk and handed it to her. The cuff made the folder difficult to hold but she managed to open it. She realised that it was about her. Small, neat writing covered each page. The results of a year of more measurements and tests, which he had completed each week, charting her progress in reading and writing. Between two pieces of tissue paper were samples of her sewing. Each one dated. The last one was a fiery cross which she had sewn for Mr Parker. She turned the last page to find a diagram of her skull, named and dated. The skull had carefully drawn lines crisscrossed over it, each section containing a word or two, written small and neat in ink. She looked more closely and could make out the tiny words. 'Philanthropy, Honesty, Anger, Love'...

Mr Meynell took the folder from her. 'You are here because you are a pick pocket and a card sharp are you not?'

He means in the prison. She nods. They both know this.

'Young woman, I have read your history. It is my contention that you and your kind could be made into something useful for society. I have chosen to help you.'

She said nothing. He walked over to the window. His voice softened and dipped.

'You are young. You could have a different life. There has been some work done already in Germany which shows that the desire to steal can be taken away from a person such as yourself.'

He turned his attention again to Reverend Parker. 'Benjamin, this is great work,' his voice trembled. He longs for this. Now he is saying that English prisons could be transformed by his work. He will publish soon. He walked quickly back across the room and sat down on a low chair beside her. He hesitated and then placed his hand lightly on her arm in a deliberate attempt to feign kindness. She sensed it was a great effort for him. He gently slid his fingers over the metal armband. His voice reached a higher note and was suddenly tremulous with an excited sentimentality. 'I am offering you freedom. Freedom from the life of crime and degradation which you now lead.'

He sat in silence for a few moments. He needed no response

from her. Or from Mr Parker. Now he was walking out across a platform to wild applause from the men of science. Then he spoke again. This time his voice was a whisper.

'Of course, Adams, down in Southhampton, has some great part in the original design. But the application. This is all mine.' He pauses. Adams soars in his mind, a great dark cloud gathering in the south of England. London, the fineness of the men of letters. Their eyes alighting on Meynell of Derby with curiousity and then disdain, whilst they smile in welcome at Adams.

He tapped the machine gently and leant forward to make some adjustments to what he called the electrometer, below the cylinder.

Then he gripped her wrist and made her touch the metal spoon. She screamed in anticipation. Mr Parker gave a small cry and took a few steps towards them. He stood, undecided, and Ann knew her only hope was that a guard might appear in the doorway to prevent this inhuman treatment. But, as Mr Meynell forced her fingers over the metal, she realised to her amazement that there was no pain. He spoke rapidly to her, explaining what "electricity" is. That it can be controlled. That he can control it. But she looked into his eyes as he spoke and saw the mad determination there. She had thought that assisting Mr Meynell might be a useful way to survive the next few years, but to be a subject of his experiments was the stuff of nightmares.

'Sit upright, I wish to measure your skull again. Maybe there has been some change. Something I have missed.'
Mr Parker shook his head impatiently. 'Meynell. We have missed nothing.' Mr Meynell had taken a metal instrument out of a drawer and was approaching her again. He looked at Parker and laid the instrument down on the table.
He spread his fingers out lightly on either side of her head.
'The phrenologists tell us that the shape of the skull could indicate pathological tendencies.' He gently twisted her head

from side to side.

'I have been able to examine the heads of hanged felons …but the flesh swells after death and so my results will always remain inconclusive. Of course I can take away the flesh from the skull – that is best – but the prison governors are reluctant to allow this after every execution … and so I am hampered in my explorations. I must measure the living.' He took his hands from her head and straddled the low examination chair placed close in front of her. His silky knees almost brushed against hers as he settled himself but he seemed completely unaware of it. He paused, head down, arms akimbo, troubled by thoughts of the prison governors and their obtuseness. Then he looked directly at her. He leant forward and she smelt the sourness of his breath. He examined her face, but she knew it was not like the examination of other men. Mr Meynell was seeing her skull, the bones under the flesh. She felt his eyes track across her forehead, around each eye pit, lingering on the ridge of bone on the outer edge of each socket, then on across the bridge of her nose and up under the jaw bone.

'You will have your head shaved again, and, in a few days when I have completed this last set of notes,' he indicates her dossier on the table. 'I will begin to properly map the contours of your skull.' She thought of the fleshless skulls of the hanged felons.

He was smiling at her. 'And perhaps find some way of aiding you. You have been a good subject so far. But now,' he nodded in the direction of the machine, 'now, we must take things further.'

'Meynell.' Mr Parker's voice was more forceful this time. 'I beg you to reconsider – in God's name, to cause pain is not …'

Meynell lept up, his body quivering with sudden rage. 'Parker,' he screamed, his voice unnaturally loud in the small room, 'if you cannot bring yourself to support,' he paused, sucking breath in through his nostrils and then his voice curled around the next words, fluffing them out, making them bolder, 'this scientific experiment, then leave.' He pointed dramatically at the door.

'Meynell, I insist, this cannot be right.'

'We have worked together on this for fourteen months, and now you question what we are doing, Parker. I had thought better of you.'

The Reverend Parker put his hand up to his clergyman's collar and touched it as if for comfort, 'We can carry on as we are, Meynell. With the teaching. This is the way ... There is no need for this.' He indicated the machine with a kind of horrified distaste on his face. 'There is no proof that it will be of any use and...'

Meynell held up his hand. 'Precisely, Parker, precisely. You have given the answer. We have no proof – and that is what we are about here – to gain proof.' He emphasised the last words by walking over to the table and bringing one fist down on to it.

The Reverend Parker shook his head. 'Science does not justify ...'

'Of course it does. Of course it does, man. What else is there? Religion.' He spat the last word at Parker.

'Meynell. I appeal to you as a friend.'

'Friend? Friend? This is more important than that, Parker. There are other men working on this. Do you want them to steal a march on me, eh?'

Meynell brushed past him and walked back to sit once more in front of Ann. He brought his hands up to her head again. His voice was quieter but still full of anger. 'Get out, Parker. If you cannot help me, then get out.' Ann felt some spittle land on her cheek.

Parker looked across at them. His eyes met hers briefly and then he had looked down, ashamed.

Without saying anything else, he turned and left the room.

And quietly, carefully Mr Meynell continued to measure her skull. She had known then that she had to get out.

Ann forced these thoughts of the prison to the back of her mind. She dressed and went downstairs to unlock the shop door. As she turned the sign to 'open' she nodded to the post boy who was walking down the street. He smiled at her. She closed the door, sat down in her chair by the shop window and picked up the work she had put down the night before. She enjoyed this part of the morning, the quiet order of stitch after stitch; the ladies did not come out to shop until after eleven as a rule.

The blunt end of the needle slipped between the weave of the fabric pulling a bright red line of silk with it. Push through, pull and knot. She was embroidering a row of strawberries around the edge of a handkerchief. Between each strawberry were three bars of gray silk. They reminded her of the bars on the prison windows.

Each night after she had been taken to see Mr Meynell's machine, Ann had made sure that she slept nearest the door in the crowded dormitory. Late into the fourth night, her efforts were rewarded. There was a big card game on and a prisoner was needed to serve ale in the guard house. A woman, of course, they were too timid to run. Ann was first to stand up when the door to the dormitory was unlocked.

As she moved around the table filling the men's pitchers with ale she saw that they were playing with 'Frenchies'. She did not recognise the design on the cards. She had been surprised, she thought she knew most of the cards in use in town. Four times Ann filled the pitchers and sat down. The night wore on. The playing became erratic, one by one the men threw in their cards and stumbled to collapse heavily on the long benches around the room. Eventually only the chief gaoler sat at the table, staring glassily at his winnings. At last his head had fallen forward and the only sound in the room had been the slow steady breathing of the deeply drunk. Ann knew she did not have much time. It had taken longer than she had thought it would. She stood up, watching them all the time. She stretched her hand out slowly to the keys hanging on the board by the door. As her fingers closed around them, tight, to deaden any noise, the thought flashed into her mind that now there was no going back. To be found with the keys in her hand would mean that she would be sent back down for a longer sentence and put to stone-breaking in the yard. She wouldn't last long at that, none of the women did. She got out of the room and down the short corridor to the outer door as quickly and as quietly as she could. Behind her she heard the sound of the prison waking up. From the kitchens directly below came the scraping sound of the ovens being raked out. In twenty minutes one of the prison children would bring a tray of hot oatcakes up to the guards.

The biggest key, that was the one. Her fingers fumbled agonisingly, then the key caught and turned smoothly in the lock. Ann pushed the door open and stepped out into a silent alley way. She made herself wait long enough to turn around to lock the door from the ouside and then she started to run. As she crossed the Markeaton bridge she threw the key in a high arc over the parapet. She was already off the bridge when she heard it splash into the water below.

An hour out on the Ashbourne road she had heard the distant sound of hounds coming after her. The dogs were useless, everyone knew that, but the unearthly sound of their baying had made her feel that there was an unseen thread of her scent leading them to her. But the sound gradually faded. They had gone off in all directions on other scents. No one had trained them. Thank God.

She had walked in the fields parallel to the road for the whole of that day. The going was harder but she could duck down out of sight whenever anyone appeared on the road. By that first night she had got as far as a little clump of trees known as Bradley Woods just outside of Ashbourne, twelve miles away from Derby and the prison. She had had to stop there, exhausted, only having enough strength and sense to walk far into the wood and conceal herself with bracken before falling asleep. The next morning she had met the packman.

She looked up and out at the street. And now the packman was dead. The packman was dead, but no one had found Ann Dance – yet.

This was where she felt most safe. Sitting in the shop she had bought with the money from the sale of the horses, stitching fine stuff for the ladies of the town.

The morning sun shone through the piece of muslin Ann held in her hands. Beneath it, she could see the wool of her skirt, stretched across her knees, black for a widow.

The money. The French money. She located it in her mind. Upstairs under the floor by the door of her bedroom. That restless fear rises to the surface again. She puts down the muslin, rises, locks the door of her shop, and begins to walk through her house, on a route she travels many times a day. She picks up the jug, the ewer. She slides the palm of her hand across the smooth surface of the table in the kitchen, then pulls open a drawer and takes out the spoons laid there. She climbs the stairs, crosses her bedroom and opens her wardrobe. There are a coat and two dresses, limp, empty, but retaining the shape of her body. She stands in the centre of the room and listens for the small recognisable sounds of her house. The sounds that she has learnt perfectly so that she can discount them in the middle of the night when she awakes from another nightmare of chase and murder. She can hear the rolling of carts and the shouts of men on the street outside. She feels the familiar longing wash over her. To leave. To join those on the street outside. To slip away. Why not? Just go. But again she goes through her reasons for staying. To go would not be safer. This life is her safety. Her escape. Although it feels every day like an imprisonment.

She is not used to this. These things, this house. They require tending. The clothes must be kept fresh; the jug, the ewer, cleaned. Each time she leaves her house the door must be locked. She must not lose the key.

And when she is not there, like her clothes, the house retains an impression of her. To be gathered by anyone who entered. Clues.

She turns and runs downstairs. In the kitchen she takes a chisel from the back of the drawer of cutlery. The bell for the shop rings. She ignores it. She runs back upstairs and kneels down and begins to open up the floor boards.

There it is. The calico bag. Heavy with gold. She drags it out and crouches over it. She closes her eyes. Through her fingers she can feel the round coins.

The packman. She hears his hoarse breath filling the dark room. She sees his face as he turns his head up to see the crows flying in the wood. Ann brings her head slowly down until her face rests on the bag of money and she weeps. After some time, she carefully puts the money back in its hiding place.

The bell for the shop rings again, and again she ignores it. There is a small pile of books and newspaper cuttings lying on the windowsill. Ann gets up from the floor and takes a piece of paper from the top of the pile. She sits back down on the floor and starts to read. She has read it before, many times. It is a cutting from a London newspaper about the great earthquake at Lisbon in 1755. She knows most of the opening paragraph by heart.

It is certain that those who now tell us that it is Nature, Nature without the guiding hand of a Supreme Being, that directs our pitiful lives, will come to realise only at the moment when they meet their maker the error of their thinking. The Portuguese nation, who flocked to their churches after the earthquake, to

pray for forgiveness from the almighty, even in their dim
understanding of the world, have more knowledge of the truth
than our so called men of science, who debate such matters as if
their own lives were not forfeit. We must all prepare to meet our
maker. Events such as this terrible earthquake are a part of a
scheme of things directed by a hand far greater than our own.
We would do well to remember that we do not know the will of
God, or his purpose, which directs all things.

'Which directs all things,' she breathed, looking down at the
paper. She closed her eyes. 'Murderer.' She spoke the word
into the empty room. 'Murderer,' she said again. She got up
and stood for a moment, as if waiting for a reply. The shop
bell rang for the third time. Ann turned and went back
down the stairs. In a few moments she had unlocked the
shop and was greeting her first customer of the day.

Ann's shop was the front part of a narrow red-brick cottage.
She had been told that it was built as part of a row by the
Hemsworth family only a few years before she rented it. It
had three storeys and a small cellar with a rounded roof.
Vaulted, she had been told was the name for it. The ground
floor was a shop front, which was really only the usual
cottage parlour with a large four-paned window and a
wooden counter running to the side of the fire place.
Behind this room was a small washroom and store. Steep
wooden stairs led off and up to the two floors of living
quarters above; the first floor room having a large cast iron
cooking grate and her table and chairs, the second floor
being a bedroom with only space for an iron bed, a night
slop bucket and a mirrored wardrobe, which she had bought
from Black's Emporium on Dig Street.
Her back door opened into Frost's yard, which was made of
four terraced cottages with one dirty wash-house between
them. Each evening in the late summer of 1755, as she shut
up shop, she could hear the talk of the families sitting out on

doorsteps or upturned boxes to catch the last warmth of the sun. The children of these families were dirty and many of them were sick. Ann could pick out the children who would not survive the winter, they sat listlessly against walls and in doorways while the others ran around. She knew that they would steal from her if they got the opportunity. She ignored them when she went out to draw water from the well or to empty her soil bucket into the open drain.

It was tiring, always waiting for the first warnings that she should leave. Rumours. A sudden surprised recognition on the face of a customer. A mistake made in the telling of a story. But as the months went past and no one challenged her, she began to allow herself to take some pleasure in the place in which she had chosen to live.

From her bedroom window she could look up Church Street and see the gates and stone frontage of St Oswald's Church, with its church spire rising into the sky behind the great yew trees. In the evenings she walked down Church Lane to the bridge over the Compton Brook and looked back at the town houses with their long gardens reaching down to the water. Some evenings the whole area was drenched with the nauseous smell of Morleys skinyard, and she could see through the dusk the flames licking the huge vats as they boiled the cow hides over fires in the back yard of the Church Street house. In the mornings, as she opened her shop, she watched the schoolboys arriving at the house opposite, and she could see Mr Harrison standing in the doorway in his black jacket, upright in his role as headmaster. She has observed Mr Harrison closely. He came across the street to her shop one day, after all his boys had gone in. He entered with a flourish, one arm behind his back and the other firmly pushing open the door of her little shop. Doors were nothing to Mr Harrison.

'Good morning, Mistress Challinor.'

Ann observed him carefully. At the end of almost every

short utterance, his lips sought to rise up in the beginning of a smile. A smile which was intended to indicate that he was a successful, settled man, satisfied with his position. That his place in this society was his by right. That he had time to greet a widow in her shop. To show kindness, which would be reported. The exaggeration of every part of his manner made Ann uncomfortable, and she recognised him quickly for what he was. A practised dissembler. She had met too many in the gaming houses of Derby not to recognise him as one of this type. She was suspicious. What had been his life and how had he come to be here in Ashbourne? The Head Master of Harrison's Academy for boys. Day and Boarding.

He picked up the week's edition of the Derby Mercury which was lying on the counter. Ann had it open at the notices. Her customers liked to read of great parties and balls, and failing that, the funerals of the wealthy. Mr Harrison turned the pages till he reached an article informing on the corn prices and the plight of local farmers. 'This is a dreadful business, Mrs Challinor, is it not?' His mouth turned down.
'If these prices are not improved we shall suffer in this town.' He shook his head and looked down at the page.
'But notice, sir,' she was unable to resist contradicting him, 'the other article at the foot of the page. It tells us that the poor benefit from these low prices. Could this not be true?'
And then she made a most astounding discovery. The Headmaster of the Boys' Academy could hardly read. She almost laughed aloud with the pleasure of it. She had watched as he struggled to quickly digest what was on the foot of the page so as to make a reply. And could not. Ann had immediately understood it. He must choose certain articles each morning and read them carefully so as to be able to discuss them with ease, but ask him to stray away from his prepared material and he is lost. Lost. As he

glanced up at her from the paper, he fully saw the expression in her eyes. She had that look of discovery which he dreaded to find on the face of any in the town. She could see him thinking out the danger. She was only a seamstress. What could it matter? Not much. The rest of their discussion was short and guarded. But this was a dangerous moment. Ann shifted the conversation back to the plight of the local farmers. She wished to appear guileless and he wished to leave.

She watched him cross the street. He did not look back. He walked at his customary pace with his customary style and stopped to converse with what must have been a parent of one of the children in the school. She could see how well he played his role. His manner did not betray that he was preoccupied with what had just occurred between them. As he entered the school, he made one sweeping glance of the street. To any one interested he would be looking, quite rightly, for any late pupils, but his eyes paused on Ann, as she stood watching him behind the glass of her shop window.

He will be my enemy from now on and I must be careful of him, she thought.

She needed to gather as much information about Mr Harrison as possible. After that day she stood at her bedroom window each night and watched the school buildings for hours. She was rewarded by seeing his tall, thin frame slipping out of the side door of his school one evening and heading off down to the alehouses of Dig St. She suspected he would not be an easy target for any woman hoping to use one hand to take away his purse while the other one stroked his stockinged leg. He was, however, in one respect, at least, a foolish man. Foolish to think that his visits to the drinking houses would not be noticed in this small town. He was a city man, Ann thought, unused to small town life and not clever enough to adjust to it. It might be his downfall. So keen to get to the delights of the soft flesh of the girls on Dig Street that he might overstep the mark.

He reminded her of the men who used to come to the molly house on Pickard Street in Derby. Taking chances because they were driven by their need.

The Sunday after Mr Harrison had come into her shop Ann watched him march his boys down the street to the early service at St Oswald's Church. He carried a bible in one hand and raised his hat graciously to everyone he passed. He looked every part the headmaster. But if his head was shaved – what then? Would Mr Meynell be able to use his careful fingers to trace the evidence that this man was a liar, a debaucher? Or was the Reverend Parker right and only God knows all?

In Markeaton Gaol, as she had nursed her arm after the searing pain of his electric machine, she listened to Mr Meynell talk to the Reverend Parker of his theories. Was he right? Although he frightened her, his ideas had appealed to Ann in that like her, he had no time for an all powerful, magical God.

Was he right – did Mr Parker's God not exist? And was there no free choice, simply the mischance of the shape of your skull, which indicates the set predilection of your mind? Is Mr Meynell's machine the only hope to improve mankind? And without his treatment was she now condemned to be a liar, a thief and – she hesitated on the last thought – a murderer.

She felt a kind of empty hopelessness wash over her. She had stolen a new life for herself, but what hope was there that she could make it any better than the last one. And the life of another human being, the packman, had been forfeit for it.

Surely she would have to make some kind of payment for that.

Chapter 3

The Walker Family of Ashbourne

'Lord, Mrs Challinor, if I am not a virgin then I am nothing. But Mrs Challinor, nobody will tell me what a virgin is!' The woman jumped up, hand on heart, fingers splayed, in a parody of innocent surprise. ' If a man were to touch my ankle, Mrs Challinor, as I stumble upon a walk – then have I been compromised? Am I to marry him? Would you marry a man who had touched your ankle? Did your packman touch your ankle and then that was it – love or condemnation for ever to the ranks of the soiled spinsters?' Ann moved back, uncertain how to reply.

The young woman leaned over the counter, staring into Ann's face. Miss Walker, richest young woman in this town, was fascinated by Ann Challinor. She sensed something hidden, something secret in her. And she was determined to find out what it was. Ann looked back at her. There was a curiousity, a determination in the girl's face, but no malice.

Amanda Walker enjoyed visiting Ann Challinor's shop. There was no item in it, or available to it by post chase from London, which Amanda could not afford. Anything desired by any of the other young women of Ashbourne could be hers if she requested it. It was a fairly empty power but it gave her a mild thrill to see the look of gaunt despair on the face of some rival in the marriage market as from Amanda's bonnet dangled the latest gold satin bow or Dutch lace floret.
However, she enjoyed visiting Ann's shop for another reason. She sensed that there was much more to Ann Challinor than met the eye and she enjoyed seeking it out.

Ann was clever and it was difficult for Miss Walker to get anything out of her. Still, it certainly relieved the boredom of frocks and polite dinners. Gradually, Miss Walker began to visit Ann's shop every day and rather than continue to attempt the hopeless search for information about Ann's past life she described to her the horrors of society life in Ashbourne. She would enter Ann's shop and begin to trill and coo over some cheap piece of hessian before collapsing into laughter; and then she would tell Ann of Miss Dale's terrifying brush with a spider.

'Do you know, Mistress Challinor, Miss Dale was near to fainting with the horror of it. A spider. Imagine – Only ten feet away from her. How awful.' She placed her hands on her chest and raised her eyes to the ceiling. 'Luckily James, my brother, don't y'know? He was nearby, heard her screams and came to her rescue.' She ducked her chin and looked up at Ann through seductively fluttering eyelashes, 'Miss Dale told me that she thinks my brother is so - oo brave...'

Then there was the important news that little Sarah Boothby had learnt to ride her new pony with hardly any help.

'Sarah Boothby is obviously a natural horsewoman. Why, she was able to ride her pony with hardly any help from the groom. He was just holding the reins. Oh, and the stirrup on one side. Oh, and the leading rein. But the rest she did herself, and she is only eight. She is obviously a natural horsewoman, just as she is a gifted pianist and an accomplished water colourist.' She paused, 'Or so her mamma says.'

She would describe the way the older women policed the behaviour of the unmarried girls. Lolling across Ann's counter sighing. 'Honestly Mistress Challinor. It is not possible to dance with a man once without the two Misses Pidcock asking about his family. Being two of them – if one leaves the room then the other is still there, watching. Caroline Cardwell offered them a piece of paper so that they

71

could take notes at the Thornton's at home last Saturday. And, d'y'know? They took it. And asked for a pencil! I'm sure that you have never had to suffer such indignities.'

At this point Amanda would come to a halt and stare closely at Ann's face, looking for her reaction. Looking for the knowledge of another kind of life which she sensed Ann understood. Amanda knew it was not the life of the wife of a packman. She knew Ann had escaped from something which had been clawing her down; she knew that the escape had taken a great toll on this secretive woman. Confident and strong but kind in the rich, sensuous health of her youth she never questioned Ann beyond a certain point. She respected that what was secret from the past had to remain so for Ann to continue to function in the present. Ann was thankful for this tacit kindness on the part of this rich young woman. She sometimes had to struggle not to tell Amanda, tell anyone the truth about her arrival in Ashbourne and the fears which surrounded her at night, but she did not give in to the need. It was too dangerous, a friend could become an indifferent acquaintance, a confidante could become an enemy.

Amanda was tall, dark haired and full of a quick energy and physical confidence which made her attractive to all. Men and women alike enjoyed Amanda's presence. Her surefootedness spilled over onto the most timid of souls and gave them strength. Her father was a tanner from Compton, who had made his money by work which meant he came home every night stinking. A man who very much wanted his daughter to be able to enter society and leave that stink behind.

Amanda was enrolled at, and became a survivor of, the Young Ladies' School on St John's Street, where the Misses Pidcock sold the codes of behaviour which they implied would offer the daughters of tanners and the like certain entry, at an appropriately humble level, into the gentry.

Amanda at first learnt and then discarded these manners and politenesses. The physically restrictive movements, the picking up of skirts, the holding of cups and the weak little handshakes irked her.

She was also a survivor of the winter balls held in the Town Hall, where her perceived betters nervously, eagerly examined her clothing for anything they could call vulgar. Amanda already knew what her father did not – that there was no door which could not be pushed open, however reluctantly, with his money. There were no signals and rituals that she need to learn in this rapidly changing country to become one of the elite. Her father's money had already secured her place.

Ann began to receive invitations to the Walker's home, Hulland House. At first, she refused them, but Amanda was insistent and eventually Ann agreed to attend a card party, where she hid her nervousness by concentrating on the cards. She was careful to lose, but she enjoyed holding the cards again, playing out the familiar sequences of each game. She accepted the next few invitations. And soon Mrs Challinor was invited to other houses to take tea or to play cards. There was a danger in going out in public like this but she reasoned that the more accepted she was by Ashbourne society, the better. What she did not realise was that part of her sought the danger. She had created a tranquil life for herself and it was tedious. She was seeking out the slight frisson of fear as she entered an Ashbourne drawing room. The feeling of success when she carried it off once again.

At Hulland House, on the occasion of the Christmas gathering on the 14th of December 1755, Amanda's elder brother, James, met Ann.

Later, James would say that the very first time she entered the drawing room of his home he fell in love with this woman. It happened in a way which was so out of his control that, as it happened, James felt a fearful rush of embarrassment and confusion. This could not be. One moment, one event, one person could not have such an effect. Later on, when he thought of this moment, he sought to protect himself from its impact with humour. He described himself as becoming like a peasant who has misinterpreted the eclipse of the moon to mean the end of the world. Wondrous. He could not place her entrance into any ordinary sort of context. He could not explain or justify what happened. A woman entered the room he was in and his existence changed. Instantly, his heart seemed to dissolve and reform around her.

James was twenty-six years old; he had benefited from his father's money by the sort of education which Mr Walker thought the gentry gave their male children. He could ride to hounds, had read Plato and Socrates, studied Milton and he had shivered in a cold bed while at the other end of his dormitory a master quietly, gratefully buggered one of the less sturdy boys.

He had come home to stand knee deep in slimy bones in the main rendering house so that his father could teach him about the business he was to inherit. And then he had met Ann. After that first meeting his life had appeared to go on as normal. He had attended business meetings with his father. He had sat at glossy mahogany dinner tables while young women around him shook out ringlets which were adorned with slivers of silk which had been teased into shape by Ann Challinor's fingers. He had picked up a delicate handkerchief dropped coquettishly for that very purpose by Amelia Dale and he had hesitated before giving it back. The heart of Miss Amelia Dale had trembled with delight but he only hesitated because he touched the tiny stitches which made up the strawberries on this handkerchief and he saw the figure of Ann Challinor as she bent over the water magnifier; he felt the regular exhalation of her breath as she concentrated on her task.   He had wanted to leave the table, leave the house, cross Church Street and find her in the room with the light he could see every night. The light which surrounded and enclosed her.

But he did not do this. Ann Challinor would never let him in. She was enclosed in her own interior even as she walked out. She was separate from James, from all the others with whom she appeared to mix. And therefore he hesitated. She would not let him in, he knew it, and he would rather not face that moment when she would lower her eyes and turn away from him and he could not ask again. He would wait.

And what had James fallen in love with? What did he see when Ann Challinor came into his presence for the first time?

That night the door of the drawing room of Hulland House had opened to admit a slender twenty seven year old woman of middling height. He saw a sharp oval face with the nose just a slender, delicate line of bone and beneath it a small but plumply curved mouth. Lips, he thought, and one part of him knew how ridiculous he would sound if he said it aloud, lips to part with cherries or sweets. Blue eyes set deep and round, with faint shadows underneath, tired lines around their edge and a wary look concealed behind a polite blankness. Thick fair hair, caught in two plaits wound tightly around the head but with a myriad of separate curling hairs escaping to give Ann a moving, fuzzy kind of halo against the bright lamplight of the room. Tension was expressed in her whole body; betrayed by an awkwardness, an angularity about the way she stood.   There was a stiff squareness about her shoulders which caused the delicate outline of her collarbone to be thrown into relief as she twice made a slight downward sweep of her head to enable her to look around the room. Ann remained close to the door and as James drew near to talk to her he could detect the speedy, rising movement of her breath against the fine white silk of her dress front.

As Ann stood by the door of the crowded room she had concerns other than the young man approaching her. She had given him a cursory glance and she knew that she had never met him. First, as at any public occasion, she looked for danger from her past, thrown up, however improbably, into her present. A magistrate who had last seen her standing in the dock accused as a thief. A woman of property, who had lost her purse after helping Ann with directions and remembered the connection just as she entered Babington's Emporium on Duke Street in Derby. A card player who had lost his stake to this creature. Danger was anyone who could look into Ann's face and suddenly realise that, however incongruous it was – Yes. This was the same woman who... who... now in this drawing room... astounding!

Ann had to wait; not all of her victims were known to her. Some had merely been a faceless being, attached to a greatcoat with a bulging pocket or a velvet purse on a thin chain.

Sudden, shocking recognition was what she waited for when she entered the room in Hulland House. After a few moments, when she could sense there was no untoward commotion directed towards her, she could feel relatively safe. As she stood there, assessing the situation, she became properly aware of the man walking towards her. A tall, strong, fleshy young man, who had an air of purpose and who was smiling at her.

Although neither of them ever knew it, his first words to Ann were probably the ones which eventually led to her acceptance of his proposal of marriage six months later.

James, having found out her name from his sister, determined to speak to this woman. Longing to impress and with no real practice in flirtation he searched for some amusing way to introduce himself.

'May I be your guardian angel?' As soon as he spoke, he knew that the words were absurd. But, much worse, his voice sounded too high. Thin and inconsequential against the noise of the room. He brought his chin down, took a breath, leaned a little closer to Ann and tried again.

'I could start by escorting you through this throng,' He offered his arm to her amid the hubbub of the drawing-room of Hulland House. Guardian angel. Drawing-room talk. Ann took his arm.

The milk rose in a froth to the rim of the pan. Ann moved it to the side of the stove. She poured the milk into a large cup, grated some nutmeg over it and added a lump of sugar. She stirred the milk slowly, watching the specks of nutmeg disappear under the milky froth.

James Walker. Amanda's brother. He had stayed beside her the whole evening. Once he had touched her hand as it rested on the table. Then he had looked quickly at her to guage her reaction. She had done nothing. She had looked away. But she had left her hand there, between them, as if asking to be touched again. Why had she done that?

The noise of the carriages drawing away from Hulland House filtered through from the front of the shop. She had left a little early. James had wanted to take her home but she had pointed out that her shop was only across the street. In the hallway he had folded her shawl around her shoulders and told her to wait. He had rushed back into the dining room and had reappeared carrying a bag of confits. 'Take them. Have them for breakfast. You said you liked them.'

'No one has confits for breakfast,' she had replied.

'And look!' he said,' look! A golden ribbon!' He teased out a twist of gold silk which encircled the neck of the bag. 'Golden. Like your hair. So you must take this home.'

She had laughed aloud at him, he had seemed so earnest. Then, taking the confits from him, she had turned to leave. At the door, Amanda was suddenly standing beside her. 'My brother seems to like you a lot. Do the Misses Pidcock know?'

She put her arm around Ann and lightly kissed her cheek. Then she was gone, before Ann could think of any reply.

Ann took the cup of warm milk to the chair, sat down and stretched out her legs. Under the lacy edge of her dress she could see the round toes of her pink satin shoes. She touched the coral necklace around her throat. There was a small mirror above the kitchen sink. She put the cup down on the table, got up and held the oil lamp up to the mirror. What had James Walker seen? The soft light of the oil lamp left most of her face in shadows. Disappointed, she put it back on the table and sat down.

What did it matter what he thought he had seen – he had most surely not seen the truth. She looked down. The truth about this woman in her silk dress and satin shoes.

What kind of men had she known? None who would put a shawl around her shoulders and bring her confits. She thought of the molly house, Mistress Arbour, and then, before she could protect herself from it, that familiar, aching sense of loss returned and she clutched the warm cup of milk for comfort as she became once again a cold, frightened child.

The molly house was at 18 Pickard Street in Derby. Ann would sit on the steps and beg, but the men going up the steps ignored her. Intent on their pursuit and afraid of lingering too long outside. When she had got into the molly house, wearing Billy Chad's trousers and with her hair hacked off, she had seen that at first these men had a kind of pleading in them. So eager to be liked by the boys but then, once they had gone into the kitchen and talked business with Mistress Arbour, they lost their fear. They no longer looked the boys in the face. Their eyes would become calculating, their sole aim to satisfy their needs. But still when Ann thought of the molly house it was with an aching, a pleading of her own heart. The warmth of the molly house had saved her life that winter. She had walked in one day, wearing boy's clothes taken from poor Billy Chad, the half wit, who couldn't even steal to save himself. With winter coming it was an action born of desperation. Her heart hammering in her chest. If she could pass herself off as a boy then she would eat, she would sleep inside not in the corner of an alley way. If Mistress Arbour had not taken her into the molly house that winter then she would be dead. Her plan had been preposterous – a girl in a molly house, when boys were what was wanted. But she had nowhere else to go. Ann had been ten years old when she entered the molly house at Pickard Street. She remembered that day so clearly.

'Come on, lad. Come in. Eat some bread. There's plenty.' The man smiled and his brilliant red mouth turned up at each corner. Like a clown. He pushed the loaf of bread across the table towards where Ann stood. With one hand she gripped the door. This was the second day that she had dared to stand in this door. The first time she had refused an offer of food. But now she was faint with hunger. She put the other hand to the jagged edges of her hair where she had sawed it off with a knife taken from the same boy whose ragged trousers she now wore. Would it work? Girls never got in the molly house. All the children knew that.

She walked in and took the loaf of bread in both hands. For a moment she took her eyes off his face and concentrated on eating. Cramming as much as she could into her mouth in case he took it away.

Finding food was the obsession of the children who lived on the street. Their days lifted and fell to the rhythm of it. Children over seven years old could be imprisoned for thieving. They were therefore more trouble than they were worth to the gangs who controlled the streets. They would be pushed out, told to go, and would be beaten if they tried to work on their own. They lived on the streets, sleeping shoaled up in dark corners during the day and, when night fell, waking to slide near the walls, ghost-like, unseen, as they moved constantly, looking for food.

Houses had dogs and coachmen who woke up as their horses whinnied at the smell of intruders. But in the centre of the city it was different. A meeting at the Assembly Rooms would draw to a glittering close and through the streets at the backs of houses and halls the children would come. To gather in doorways until the last carriage wheeled away and every light was doused. And then they would move silently forward, crossing the street and slipping round to the back of the building, their eyes seeking for the food spilling out of the make shift bins.

'Come here.' The man stretched out his hand and indicated the chair beside him. Ann sat down.

'Do you want to know my name?'

Ann nodded.

'My name is Mistress Arbour.' He ducked his head to one side and the brown curls of his wig shook. Ann could see the fine veil of stubble on his chest where it bulged out of the tight corset of his gown.

'This is my house.'

Ann continued to eat the bread.

'Do you like it?'

'Yes.'

'Would you like to stay?' Again the red mouth widened into curve.

'Yes.'

'And what is your name?'

'William.' Ann replied.

'Where do you live, William?'

Ann hesitated. A vivid picture of her father came into her mind. Her father telling her to get out and earn herself a living.

'My family live at St Mary Street, by the river.'

Mistress Arbour nodded. ' When did you see them last.'

Ann was not ready for it. She could think of no reply.

Mistress Arbour watched her. He was saving this child from the streets. Tears welled in his eyes at the thought of his own goodness. He pulled a tiny lace handkerchief from between his breasts and dabbed at his cheeks. But the child would have to work for a living. He wasn't a charity.

'Come with me.' His silk gown rustled as he stood up.

They walked down a hallway, patterns of blue and yellow on the floor. Ann looked up and saw a stained glass window, brilliant in the sunlight.

'This is the blue parlour.' Mistress Arbour opened the door. 'And over there is Mr Smith. I would like you to go and talk to him.'

Ann looked across the large room. A thin, dark haired man sat quietly by the window. In front of him paraded a constantly shifting group of young boys, men in shirttails and men in rich dresses, brocade and lace. Ribbons and embroidered panniers. They walked and talked from behind fine fans. Their heads were supporting great wigs with elaborate feathers and flowers sprouting from them.

Mistress Arbour gave Ann a push. 'Go on. Go and speak to him.'

The seat beneath her was soft and she sank into it. Her legs pressed against the hard wooden edge. She put her hand down and ran her fingers along the row of brass nails which held the velvet onto the wooden frame. One, two, three nails. Then a gap and three more. Mr Smith did not speak to her. They both sat watching the room for some time and then he stood up, took her hand in his. She felt the sweat on his palm. He led her out of the blue parlour, across the hall and into another room. He shut the door. Ann looked around. A chair, a cabinet with a jug and ewer, and a day bed. He began to unbutton his pantaloons. He did not want to touch Ann; he wanted her to touch him. She followed his instructions. Guided by his hand she took his cock into her mouth. At first it was soft and pliable between her teeth but it grew bigger and harder. It filled her mouth. She shifted her face sideways so that she could breath. He moved her mouth up and down on himself. She felt his grip on her head become almost unbearable as he forced it to move faster and faster. She was near to choking when she felt him pulse against the back of her throat. Then he slid away from her and lay back on the bed. Ann's mouth was full of salty sticky liquid. She spat it out onto her sleeve quietly.

She looked at the man. His eyes were closed and he had brought both of his hands up to his face. She waited for a moment. Then she opened the door and looked up and down the hall. There was no one there. She crossed the floor with its blue and the yellow circles of light and walked back into the blue parlour. Unsure of what to do next, she sat down once more on the seat. She curled her fingers under the chair frame. She counted the first three nails again. One, two, three.

She was not surprised by what had happened. Every one of the children knew what happened in the molly house.

But the taste and smell of the man was something new to her. A strong overwhelming scent. A secret, private pungency. She put her fingers up to her face. Some of it still clung there. She rubbed her neck. It hurt. She noticed that there was food on the table by the window.

Ann got up, went over to the table, took a lump of currant bread and some cheese, and went and curled up behind one of the sofas to enjoy her meal. As the winter came nearer those children without shelter on the streets would die of hunger, cold and fatigue. She would not. Not here.

And for four months she escaped detection. Many of the men who used the molly house did not want full sex with the boys there. Mouths and hands gave enough satisfaction. Ann was never asked to undress. She was never touched except by a man to guide her this way and that on his body. She was rarely looked at. Hardly spoken to. Except by Mistress Arbour who checked how many men she had been with.

There was always food in the kitchen and during the day, when the house lulled into a restful wait, she would lie with the other boys, rolled up in exhausted sleep under the plush sofa beds or in a corner of a room. Like a puppy, she rested, fed and grew.

There was a hierarchy amongst the boys. The favourites were allowed to braid the hair of the wigs. Four weeks after she had arrived one of the older boys called Seb allowed Ann to braid a wig.

Mister Davidson had become Margaret for the few hours he had to spend at number eighteen. Margaret sat on the edge of a wooden chair, stiffly upright in a crimson gown with a delicate Italian fan held in his large hands. Ann was devising a huge coiffure at his direction. She had a tray of ribbons and combs at her side. All of her attention was on her task, and at first she did not see Mistress Arbour enter the room. But gradually she became aware that she was being watched. She turned her head and caught the intense gaze that rested on her. Her fingers became clumsy, her breath was caught in her throat and a sense of foreboding came over her. Finally Mister Davidson was satisfied with his appearance and left the room to join the other visitors for tea in the blue parlour.

Ann began to fold away the remaining ribbons, keeping her head down but all the time aware that Mistress Arbour was still staring at her.

'Take off your clothes.' The voice held no menace but Ann's heart began to race.

She pretended not to hear, as much to herself as to her questioner.

'Take off your clothes.' This time the voice was louder.

Ann did not look up but slowly began to unbutton her waistcoat. Then her shirt and pantaloons. The sounds of the house seemed to recede. There was only herself, breathing in this room and her fingers on the rough fabric of her clothes. Finally her clothes lay on the floor around her feet in a pitiful heap. Ann still kept her head down. Blood rushed in her head and the red and black tiles of the floor, which was all she would allow herself to see, became blurred into splodges of contrasting colour.

Ann stood what seemed a long time and the tiles became sharp and distinct once more to her eyes. She dared not look up until, with a shock that made her jump, she heard the silence broken by a frightening, gasping sound, growing to a screeching, tearing crescendo. It sounded like terrible pain and Ann looked across the room, startled out of her fear for her own safety. Mistress Arbour was crying. The black painted eyes were squeezed shut into pencil lines and the painted pout of a mouth was distorted and stretched out of its pretty bow into a red gash.

Mistress Arbour was crying.

She had stared at what stood in front of her. A child, naked. A little girl, of maybe nine years old. Thin and white and trembling like an animal caught in a trap. Strange little buds where her breasts would be and between her legs, a secret fold of flesh.

Mistress Arbour took the lacy shawl from her shoulders,

crossed the room and laid it gently around Ann's body.
'My dear, my little girl,' said Mistress Arbour, with all the gentleness of a mother.

Ann was given dresses. She was placed at the table beside Mistress Arbour. 'My daughter,' Mistress Arbour would sigh and all those at the table would look at Ann, some with curiosity, some with loathing. She helped to serve tea at the molly house tea parties, where men sat, comfortable in their petticoats. Ann turned her head away when boys she had curled up with in the corners of the rooms were placed on knees and fondled, then led out to the private rooms off the hall. Ann would sit on, expected to stay primly upright as Mistress Arbour talked and laughed with her clients. Every now and then Mistress Arbour would stroke Ann's smooth hair or fondly adjust the bodice of Ann's dress. The men would smile and utter soft noises of approval. They would hold hands and talk of their own imaginary children. For this was the strange, dark world of the molly house. Where other lives were reached for, with a tentative fear that it would not be possible to grasp them. That nothing so out of the ordinary could survive.

Sometimes two of the men would ask Ann to be bridesmaid at their wedding in the large parlour. The visitors would gather, there would be a vicar, a bible, some loudly spoken words and then a celebration with ale and songs and dancing. Mistress Arbour had ordered a bridesmaid's dress to be made for these occasions and Ann would stand, dressed in a pink velvet gown, smiling at everyone, holding a posy of flowers, while the couple were pronounced man and wife.

On some nights, there would be a birth. Always in the dead of night. Ann would recognise when the time was coming for this scene to be enacted. For days before the house felt active and unsettled. Fights broke out on stairs. Voices were raised. Couples split off to talk alone in low whispers. And then in the middle of the night, Ann would be shaken awake by one of the visitors and rushed to the birthing room. There she would be asked to bathe the brow of the straining, groaning man who would be lying, swathed in a nightgown, on the low birthing bed. Often Ann was given the honour of being the first to hold the baby. A wooden doll, wrapped up in white muslin as it was lifted from between the legs of the new mother. For days after this event the house would be tranquil, men consulted each other on names for the new baby and everyone took small presents in to the mother and child.

And then, it would be over. The baby discarded, the new mother bored with the role and a party would start in the afternoon of one day and continue on until the sunset of the next.

Ann would pick up the wooden doll, wash each part of it, dry it all over carefully for fear of the wood splitting, and then put it back in a box which was stowed in the back cellar. Sometimes she would stay in the cellar and play with the doll. In the cellar, beside the box, were packages, presents which had been given to the baby at each birthing over the years. Ann had unfolded all of these packages and had found treasure. Two silver rattles and four feeding spoons made of creamy translucent bone, with each handle fashioned into the head of an animal. If she held the spoons up, one by one, to the light which came from the coalhole, she could make out the details of each separate head. There was a cat, a cow, a duck and what she thought might be a pig or a horse. She would pretend to feed the baby with the spoons and try to tuck the rattles in alongside its shiny, varnished arms.

But it was the clothes she loved best of all. Tiny knitted woollen jackets and cotton nightgowns. Although some of them were mouldy with age she would pull them over the stiff wooden limbs of the baby.

Over and over again she would start this part of the game knowing that it would end with disappointment. She would dress the doll in two nightgowns and one of the night caps, then she would lay out all the jackets and choose what she thought to be the one which was thickest; she would put this on the doll and finally wrap it up tightly in a woollen shawl. Then she would take the doll in her arms and put her face against its round head. But always, even through the softest satin cap, she could feel the coldness of the hard wood underneath.

For another year, until she was twelve years of age, this life continued. Until her father asked for her to come back.

By chance, she watched his arrival from the landing in the hall. She had been sitting in the middle of the landing playing with some old chess pieces when she had seen a man come in and stand uncertainly in the hall. Then she had heard him speak, asking for Mistress Arbour, and she had realised immediately who he was. Her father. He had looked around but she had moved back against the wall and he had not seen her.

Slowly she had crept forward to peer down at him from between the banisters. She had not seen him for three years. She could hardly believe it, but there was no doubt. It was her father.

When she had first come to the molly house, she had sometimes slipped away and walked to the place where she had lived. She would see her brothers and sisters on the streets, but for some reason she found that she could not bring herself to speak to them and would do little more than give them a curt little nod. Once her mother had come crying and drunk to the back door of the molly house. Sobbing that these queers had taken her daughter. Mistress Arbour had given her a small sum of money and, strangely, she had never come back for more.

Ann heard with a hopeless dread the tone of brave

forbearance in her father's voice as he told of the illness of Ann's mother and the need for Ann to be with the family at this time. She knew that he was lying. There was too much quivering exaggeration put into his speech. Her father had to look up at Mistress Arbour. She towered above him.

She won't let me go. She won't let him take me. She will know he is lying. Ann crouched quietly on the stairs listening, secure in the love and the cleverness of Mistress Arbour.

Her shock as she heard an agreement being made for her to leave was enormous. Mistress Arbour hardly argued. It seemed from where Ann sat that very little had been said at all. Her father had mentioned the constabulary and that was enough. Ann was to leave 18 Pickard Street by the end of the week.

On her last night there, she had crawled into bed beside Mistress Arbour. Stripped of his wig, the heavy makeup wiped from his face and his body released from its enclosing stays and petticoats, Mistress Arbour became James Arbour again. A man of middle age, snoring on his back. Ann crept up onto the bed, slithered between the sheets and pushed herself up against his warmth. She laid her head in the crook of his arm. She could smell on him the sweat of the day that had just passed. She pushed her nose in under his arm, where the smell was strongest. She closed her eyes and reached her arm over him. She drew her hand lightly back across his chest, Her fingers catching briefly on the prickly stubble which steadily grew back there throughout each night. Tomorrow, he would rise and shave his upper body, ready for the day as Mistress Arbour. And, as always, Ann would hold his shaving cup up to him as he stood in front of the bedroom mirror. But the day after that, she would not be there. Ann began to cry, quietly, so as not to wake him.

Four days after she had left the molly house, she saw

Mistress Arbour, dressed soberly in pale grey worsted and a black cloak so as not to draw too much attention to herself, walking in Derby market. Ann's breath caught in her throat with joy. The four days had seemed so long. With a rush of love, she was certain that Mistress Arbour could not have wanted to give her up so easily. She must speak with her. But just as she started to move forward, she saw a young girl of about eight return from a stall and slip her hand confidently into the hand of Mistress Arbour.

For a moment Ann became completely still. She stood, with her right foot partly raised, still ready to run forward, and watched as the two made their way through the market. As Ann watched, Mistress Arbour half turned, bent down from her great height, and stroked the child's head. Even from where Ann stood, it was possible to see the adoration in Mistress Arbour's face. A stall holder shouted out 'Bless you, mother.' Mistress Arbour looked up and smiled graciously. She looked around her to see if there had been any other audience to this touching scene. As she gazed around the market her eyes seemed to slide over Ann without seeing her, even though the girl whom she had called her daughter stood only feet away, waiting, hoping with all of her being, for recognition. Mistress Arbour turned away and walked on with her new child.

Ann became aware that the stallholder was signalling to her. She looked back at him. He waved and smiled in a conspiratorial way. Ann realised that it was Mr Davidson, or Margaret, to give him his molly house name. He called her over.

'Haven't seen you down there,' he bent his head in the direction of Pickard Street, 'for a while.'

'No,' said Ann.

'Pity.' He leaned forward and lowered his voice. 'I liked the way you did my hair.' He smiled at her again and handed her something from his stall.

It was a doll, small enough to fit into her hand, with a tiny, painted face and a red and white checked dress. The arms and legs were made of china and the elbows and knees moved on smooth round pivots. It was beautiful. She threw it into the gutter and walked away.

Her mother had not been ill but had left with a trader from Leicester and twelve-years-old Ann, just tall enough to be taken for someone much older in the candlelit rooms, was to take her place at the gaming tables. After two years at the side of her father her play was the best in the family. From when she was very young, Ann could compute the outcome of the cards, and now she was big enough to sit at a table in one of her mother's frocks and play them out. And this part of her life gave her great pleasure. She returned to what she was resigned to as her real life. An avoidance of turning too many tricks and becoming infested with the clap before she reached twenty years of age was the best she could hope for. Better to be a gamester and work the tables.

By the age of seventeen, when the Scottish army entered the town, Ann had become the centre of the family business. In 1741, her father had shrewdly taken a long let on a small set of upstairs rooms in an inn just back from the waterfront on Duke Street, and, as long as there was no trouble, the innkeeper was happy to let gaming go on above his taproom. Ann could play the cards. She enjoyed it more than the random nature of dice throwing. Some of the men who came to her tables were skilled and she had to use all her knowledge and experience to win. These were the clients whose brief company she enjoyed the most. The gamesters, the men who made a living from working the tables. They seemed only to live at night, appearing after darkness had fallen, the candlelight giving their threadbare velvet jackets as great an air of elegance as that of their richest victims. Men who were by their nature alone. Who did not settle in one place but had to move from table to table, town to town for fear of being caught by the outraged shouts of a player who suddenly realises that the gentleman across the table from him is surely a trickster. Her father would have had them warned off. Tipped the wink to his gang of thugs. A bloody beating in a dark side street and that would be the end of it.

But Ann liked to deal with them differently. She liked to beat them at the cards. To show them that any business to be had that night was to be hers. To show them that there was no point in coming back. The look of surprise on their faces as they realised that they were going to lose always gave her a small thrill of delight.

Occasionally Ann would allow one of these men to take her back to his room somewhere in Derby. And she would succumb to the languorous pleasure of allowing this unknown man to take control of her body, letting him exert a kind of physical power over her just as she had exerted her power at the tables. But she would always leave before daylight came and she couldn't avoid seeing the dirty floor where she put her bare feet, or the stains on the jacket flung over the back of a chair.

For the most part, Ann slept alone in a cot in her father's house. Although she was hardly alone, for the room also contained the large bed still used by her three sisters. In the next room slept her father and her two brothers. Ann's father had not taken another wife. And seemed to do almost completely without female company. If he were lonely at all it was only shown in the early hours of the morning, when after a night's work, he would sit by the range in the kitchen and steadily drink himself into oblivion. In the winter of 1750, Ann's father fell after one of these drinking sessions and hit his head badly on the grate. Ann's youngest sister found him cold and half dead in the morning. He lay silent on his bed for weeks until one day he sat up, called for his clothes and drank a glass of porter.

Ann continued to try to run the gaming rooms but her

father had become a serious liability. He found it difficult to concentrate on the cards. It was easier to take stolen goods and sell them on, or set up Ann's younger brothers in thieving.   In September of 1753 Ann's father was imprisoned in Leicester gaol for thieving. Ann knew that he was not likely to return. That winter she and her sisters had to turn to pick pocketing and then sometimes prostitution to survive. There was always the terrible danger of getting the clap. Ann instructed her sisters to wherever possible only use their hands and their mouth. Like the children at the molly house. This way they could avoid disease. The gentlemen they serviced were often happy with this arrangement. They also wanted to avoid disease.

But as the months wore on, Ann knew that her sisters were no longer following her advice. On the streets where her sisters now chose to work the men were too dull-headed and the women too desperate to attempt to protect themselves from disease. Ann looked at her two sisters and knew that they would not survive. She said nothing; she had the strength now only to look out for herself.

In September 1754 Ann was imprisoned for the first time in Derby Gaol. Pickpocket. A branded felon. She was thin and filthy and was unable to raise her head to show interest when her sentence was passed.

It was a relief to be given one meal every day. She kept her body completely covered, her hair scraped flat and her head down whenever spoken to, and she easily avoided the attentions of the guards or the male prisoners. After all, they had their pick. As long as she could get to the food, when it was distributed each day, she would survive here.

She was horrified to be released along with three other first offenders at Christmas time as part of an amnesty brought about by the Christian Women's Prison Visitors. Ann just happened to be one of the lucky ones. Her name picked out at random from the list of new inmates. 'I hope,' said the chairwoman of the Christian Women's Prison Visitors, 'that this will be an opportunity for renewal.' She laid a gloved hand on Ann's arm. 'God will always welcome a sinner reformed.'

But in 1755 Ann had found herself back in prison. This time with no prospect of release, since it was not likely that a chance intervention by the Christian Women Visitors would happen for a second time. Mr Meynell's experiment had seemed like her only chance of surviving her long second sentence.

Ann stood up. And now she was here, in Ashbourne. Her body was stiff; she must have been sitting in the kitchen for a long time. She had decided. She must not let James Walker fall in love with her. It could only spell disaster.

Before she left the kitchen, she held the oil lamp up to the mirror again. She peered at her reflection and, with one hand, she pulled the pins out of her topknot. She slowly wound a curl of her hair around her finger. Golden. He had said it was golden.

Chapter 4

Spring 1756, Ashbourne

'But you would, James, for you are just a child.'

Ann lifted the corner of her muslin skirt and stepped across the muddy track. March was too early for muslin. Already the weight of the damp air was dragging the fabric down and there was a delicate rim of dark mud on the very edge of the hem. She had to swirl the fabric up against her body to avoid more damage but as she did so she slightly exaggerated the movement of her hips and glanced back at James with a smile. The movement was fluid and quick and if James had not been watching her carefully he would have missed it. But James was watching and he recognised that Ann was flirting with him. For three months they had gone for walks, they had danced, they had talked, but Ann Challinor had remained a quiet, sometimes silent, part of any group. She had never let herself betray even the slightest acknowledgement of his obvious interest in her, far less respond – and now, now, she was flirting. James followed her over the pathway.

'And on what do you base that last observation, Mrs Challinor?' Flirting lightly back while his heart seemed to expand painfully with love within him.

'On your foolishness, Mr Walker,' cried Ann, but her voice held no rebuke.

On the bridle path below, Amanda paused in her supervision of the servants and the picnic basket and watched her friend and her brother. As James reached Ann he turned and Amanda could see his delight. She heard Ann laugh in reply and saw her toss her head back so that her bonnet fell behind her into the mud. James leapt to retrieve it. Ann stopped and turned to watch him and even from this distance Amanda could see that her face was suddenly suffused with a tired sadness, so unlike her voice and actions of a moment before that it made Amanda catch her breath. Then James turned back to Ann, holding her bonnet out with a flourish, and Amanda watched as Ann's expression returned instantly to that of a happy, teasing young woman. As she watched the pair, Amanda felt unease spread inside her.

There was a shriek from behind her, and she turned back to see the wine basket roll off the cart and spill its contents. Glasses and bottles smashed against the stones of the path and claret wine splashed across the apron of one of the two shrieking serving girls, spattering the starched white fabric with a rich blood red. For a few confused moments everyone but the girl involved thought that she had been badly cut by the flying glass and Amanda, in dealing with the hysteria caused by the accident, forgot her disquiet about Ann Challinor.

The world was dark and quiet. Ann slipped into a doorway and looked up and down the street from her hiding place. She leaned back against the stone and sighed in frustration. 'I do not love James Walker.'

Her words echoed back, amplified by the hollow of the doorway. Startled by the loudness of her voice, she gathered her cloak about her and moved out of the shelter of the doorway. She walked down the street quickly, keeping as near to the buildings as possible. She hadn't meant to speak aloud. She looked up at the windows of the houses as she passed. Dark. No sign of life. She slowed her pace. It wasn't likely that those few words would wake a household. The town clock struck three. She found a narrow gitty and turned in to it, sitting down on the low wall which ran its length.

This was the time of night she liked best. The time when she could move freely through the streets, as she had done as a

95

child. She knew it was a dangerous thing to do. No respectable woman would walk through the streets at night. There was a night watch of sorts and if she was recognised it would be difficult to explain. But she could not resist it. The silence and the emptiness of the night streets. The fragments of sound coming from behind doors and windows; tiny cries of babies, the short sharp shout of a man. The eyes of the town closed. The minds of the town wandering in dreams behind shuttered windows and locked doors.

The dead of night. The time to steal. What was it her father had said? 'When the eyes of people who own things are closed and the eyes of those who have nothing are open.'

She had shared nights like this in the past. There had been comradeship, silent signals passed across empty spaces, the feeling of someone's warm breath on the back of your neck as you hid together. Watching. Holding your breath as the guard went by. Pressing your face hard into someone's shoulder to stifle your laughter while your heart hammered with fear. But now she was alone.

She leaned back against the wall behind her, feeling the coldness of the damp stone slowly begin to penetrate the thick wool of her cloak.

James. She looked down at the ring on her finger.

The Saint Valentine's Ball at Lichfield Hall. Their engagement had just been announced in the Lichfield Gazette and they were the centre of attention. As Ann and James had entered the great ballroom, she had the impression that everyone had looked up. There had seemed to be a momentary pause when all conversation ceased, when all eyes turned to look at this little widow who had been so fortunate. Then people began to rush forward to murmur their congratulations. Ann felt a rising panic as the young women in the room pressed around her, leaning forward one by one to pick up her hand and exclaim over the ring. With great difficulty she held her hand out for their use, resisting the desire to snatch it away. Beyond the circle of women she could see James, deep in a throng of men, shaking hands with everyone. He looked back and smiled at her, rolling his eyes up in mock despair.

Someone was touching her shoulder.

'He is the happiest man in the world.'

Ann turned and got an impression of old, powdery skin and meticulously painted eyebrows. The woman handed her a glass of champagne. 'French. But what else should we drink at an event like this?' She shrugged her shoulders, dismissing the idea of enemies when there was good wine to be drunk. 'I have known James since he was a baby. Congratulations. He is such a fine young man.' Little bird eyes took in as much as possible of Ann's face and then the woman squeezed her arm and moved back into the crowd. Ann put the glass to her lips but the champagne tasted sour in her mouth. She felt sick.

How could she carry on with this? How could she have thought it? It was one thing to take on a new identity, to live incognito in the town, but to marry this man, James Walker! She stood on her tiptoes trying to keep him in sight; he seemed to dip and rise up again on wave after wave of congratulations. These are his friends, Ann thought, looking at the crowd around him. They have known him for years, they love him. What she was doing was preposterous. But behind that thought came another one. If she became Mrs Ann Walker she would be safe, for who would connect Ann Dance, escaped prisoner, with Mrs Ann Walker of Hulland House? Who would imagine that they would find Ann Dance in a room like this?

And now James was beside her, laughing and holding her arm. Then they were through the crowd and out, pushing open the french doors and on to the terrace, standing together in the cool darkness of the night. Behind them, the company closed the gap they had left and turned to organising itself into the first dance.

She placed the glass down on the flat top of the stone balustrade and put her hands on either side of it, raising her face up to the cool night air. After a moment, James leaned forward and touched her fingertips with his hand. Still with that little hesitancy, she noted, still unsure that she would accept his touch.

He deserved better.

She took a deep breath. She must explain. 'James...I do not feel as you do.. I have to say this to you... I am afraid that.' She gestured back to the glowing ballroom, trying to encompass all her misgivings. She stopped.

He looks at me and does not know who I am, what I have done. I must tell him. And then the raw fear of being hunted down and taken back to prison made her mouth dry and no more words would come. Only one word seemed to form itself on the very edge of her lips. Murderer. She imagined it being spoken aloud, first whispered by a few and then screamed by a crowd.

And there it was. She knew then that she was not going to tell him. She looked away from him into the dark night. There was a full moon and she could see the trees on the ridge above the lawns. She thought of Bradley Wood. Of everything that had happened after it.

Now James was smiling at her, his face glowing gold from the hundreds of candles in the room behind them.

'Ann. I understand. Your life has been different from mine.' He pulled her close to him, 'But it will be like mine from now on.' He tightened his arms around her. 'It will be the same life.'

She could not reply. She leaned against him, her face turned towards the ballroom. She could see the serried ranks of dancers taking their place. Women turning and twisting, the better to show off their brilliant silks and satins. Three officers in their bright red coats were taking the first row of the dance, smiling at their partners and all of them aware of the effect they made, grouped in front of the great fireplace.

Near to the door sat two mammas taking tea, their feathery caps nodding as they greedily spooned sugar into their cups. Mr Meynell came to her mind – the spoon held so delicately between his fingers and the chain looping to the strange cylinder, and then the sad, apologetic face of the Reverend Parker as he stood in the doorway of the prison room. She gave an involuntary shiver as the cool night air riffled through the thin fabric of her ballgown.

'Ann,' said James, 'you are cold. We should go back in.'

They walked back together through the great glass doors and down the wide stone steps. She smelt the warmth of the crowd rise up to meet them, a mixture of powder and sweat, and felt the music from the ballroom flow over and around them as they stepped out onto the dance floor.

'You see, you see – I think love is something you can make...' James broke off embarrassed. He leaned forward and poured more brandy into his glass. Edward was his brother, but still, it was difficult. They had not been close when they were very young but then they had endured school together, huddled late at night in their dorm, talking of everything, trusting each other against everyone else, but even so what he was about to say was not a usual subject for discussion between them.

 Edward smiled at him. 'Oh, James.' He raised an eyebrow superciliously and James remembered what it was about Edward that had so attracted everyone at school. That casual acceptance that the world was ordered around him. That he was right.

'James you are in love. What else is there to say? You know you are going to talk drivel now for years until it all wears off, and then I will have to listen to how cruel she is.' He sighed exaggeratedly, 'It will be so tiresome.' He looked directly at James, and there was a brief hesitation before he spoke. 'I'm so glad I will never have to suffer this.'

James opened his mouth to make a loud reply, to protest that there was no way that his brother could be so sure... then he sensed rather than understood that Edward was trying to tell him something else. Something important and too painful to broach directly.

Edward held up his hand, 'Ah James, don't look so confused,' he said softly.

'I am trying to say that I will never put a ring on a woman's finger. Or if I do, it will be a sorry day for her, for my...my...' He struggled with the word. 'Interests, shall we say, will always be somewhere else.'

He smiled wryly but his eyes were serious, questioning and uncertain. James felt his heart lurch with the pleasure that Edward should share this with him. He wanted to say something, everything, that tumbled into his mind, but he did not. Instead, he smiled at his brother and slowly raised his glass. 'To you, Edward, you who will never have to suffer this.'

Edward returned the salute. For a moment they seemed to sit there, suspended in time. Two men on either side of a fireplace with their glasses raised and a friendship confirmed. Then Edward leaned forward and poked the fire. 'Come on then James, tell me your great theory of love.'

James began. 'Well, I think that it is possible to make someone love you.' He tried to make it a little less personal, 'I mean make one person love another. By means of the rituals of courtship.'

Edward raised an eyebrow again. James put down his glass and ran his hands through his hair.

Edward watched him. He has always done that, when he is excited by something. This must be important to him.

James hurried on, 'Like love potions or amulets or spells. After all, through out time man has sought to control, to evoke, love. And who is to say that it can't be done?'

He was aware that he was slurring his words. He paused to take a breath, then continued. 'Who is to say that that is not how love works? One person loves another and then proceeds to make that person love them back.'

'So you are saying two people do not fall in love. One person falls in love and then has the job of persuading the other?'

'Yes.' James nodded vigorously. He leaned forward and picked up his glass. A little brandy slopped on to the knee of his britches. He stared as a dark circle spread across the pale fabric. He frowned and dabbed at it with one extended finger.

'And this is always the case?'

James gave his full attention back to his brother. 'Yes,' James nodded emphatically again, this time with a hand placed carefully over his glass.

'You are saying that this is the nature of love?'

'Yes.'

'And the means to do this might be through potions or spells?' Edward stopped. He was looking incredulous.

' Yes, but only if the other person knows about them. You see, I am not saying that spells actually work. I am not saying that magic works but that people can be made to believe, that everything we do is a matter of belief, of faith. When you shake hands on a business agreement, when an army goes to war, all of these work on a moment of change when one person, or a number of people, believe, believes.' He stumbled slightly, the numbers were confusing him. 'Believes that what the other says is true, so why not love?'

'So you are saying that love is like a business transaction - or war?' Edward was laughing now. 'It's not very romantic, James.'

"No, not when you interpret it that way, but that is what I mean.' James frowned again. It was difficult to explain. It sounded like madness.

At first he had waited for Ann Challinor to fall in love with him. He had felt helpless, sometimes full of hope when she had smiled at him and then in despair when she walked past him on the street without an acknowledgement. It had been almost unbearable. He had come to the point of giving up,

101

and had decided to take himself off to London and forget about her by immersing himself in work.

But then, at four o clock on the morning of what was meant to be his last day in Ashbourne, he had woken up and thought: What if you don't wait for someone to fall in love with you? What if you make them love you? What if that is what you are meant to do?

There was no area of his life where he waited for others to make the changes happen that he wanted. Why should love be any different?

It took form. It was a hypothesis. Over the next few weeks he worked on it, with the same energy with which he worked on contracts and transactions. He looked into historical precedent. This was how love had been done, it was how it was done, if you read ancient legends and tales. He sat through a production of Shakespeare's Othello on Dig Street and cried as a wooden Desdemona stated why she had fallen in love with her Moor, 'such wondrous stories, who would not be beguiled.'

He had left the auditorium quickly and climbed over the fence at the back of the theatre then strode off down the empty bridle path by the Henmore Brook, his face wet and cold with tears in the night air. Love was manufactured and maintained. At last, he had a way forward. He realised with a great burst of joy that this was a process which he understood. He could, he would, manufacture and maintain love in the heart of the woman he wanted so much. He could not explain that night to Edward. It did sound like madness. Or like a cold and calculating plan. But it was neither of those things. It was a profound and precious truth.

He became aware that Edward was speaking again. 'But you would agree that here in Ashbourne, very few people will be using spells, not amongst the families you know at any rate?' he smiled. James could see that he had not convinced him. Edward was still minded to make fun of this idea.

'No, of course not. People do not use spells now, but we have rituals, ways of doing things. I think it's something similar. Has the same effect.' James stopped.

'Very well. James. What constitutes the 'spells' of our lovers nowadays?'

'Poetry,' said James, thinking of Shakespeare. 'Poetry.' He picked up a pamphlet from the side table, 'Words. And rituals.'

'Words?' said Edward.

'Yes, words. What else, Edward? What do you use when you want to convince someone to take out a contract with you?'

'Yes, but surely that is different. I want to convince someone of my honesty or that I have enough money to pay. I am not trying to make them fall in love with me.' He shook his head.

"Aren't you? Think about it Edward – isn't love just a very extreme, very exclusive contract?'

'You sound cold, James. I cannot accept this calculated picture of love that you describe.'

'No - No! Edward it is not calculated – it is magical – but this is how it is expressed. I am not explaining this well to you.'

'Explain the rituals to me, then. Leave the words aside.' Edward brushed the words away with his hand. He was still smiling with an air of indulgence.

James sat quietly for a moment, gathering his thoughts. 'All the rituals of courtship, playing at being in love. There are rules. And the rules define the love They exist because love exists. They confirm its existence. Without them it would not continue to exist.'

'Is it so weak then? So flimsy?'

James hesitated. 'Yes. Yes, it is. Everything is, Edward – you know that.' He looked at his brother and suddenly remembered standing beside him at their father's graveside. 'Every agreement we make. Every day we assume that we will not be dead by nightfall. There are no certainties. There is no permanence. Everything is flimsy, if you want to call it that?' He leaned forward in his chair, 'We make things appear important. Love is made important. The small, wrapped presents, the careful passing of a teacup from one to another, then the presentation of a ring, dancing, the walks on the streets, the nodding of heads, the, the … all of this. This is what takes the place of the spells and potions of the past. And it works, Edward. It works.' He used his hands to make a rounded form in the air. 'It weaves love around two people. But one of them has to convince the other one first.' He emphasised his point by bringing the fingers of one hand down upon the palm of the other, 'And everyone else of course. Everyone has to be convinced.'

'Everybody? Like a great army going to war? All marching in perfect unison?' Edward asked.

James tipped his head to show that he recognised the joke in this but carried on. 'Perhaps. Yes, perhaps, like an army. You have to have conviction.'

'Passing teacups?' Edward raised both eyebrows.

'I know. I know it sounds ridiculous.' James shook his head. 'But it is true. Look, Edward, you want to see someone but you cannot; the rules forbid you to break someone's door down, and so you have to wait. And that moment in someone's house when that hand touches yours as you take a cup from it, that moment you may have waited days for, is charged with the stuff of spells and potions.' James turned away from his brother and stared into the fire, lost in a recollection of that touch.

Edward watched his profile. 'James – there is a flaw in your argument.' He spoke gently. 'This person who has to convince the other that he is in love and that his love is real. No one had to convince him. So isn't that real love? Isn't that different in quality from the love that is 'manufactured'?'

James took a long time to answer. He picked up a log and placed it carefully on the fire. 'Perhaps. You may be right, Edward. I have thought there may be another love.'

The excitement had gone from his voice. He turned and smiled ruefully at his brother. 'A love where both parties are equal and there is no effort.' He turned back to the fire. They both watched as small flames began to climb on either side of the log.

'I wish you well,' said Edward, after a pause. It sounded clumsy but it was the best he could say. James left the room to get another bottle and Edward half dozed in the flickering light of the fire. Love. How could it be necessary to persuade someone to love you? If you did then surely it could not be love? He was suddenly overtaken by a great sense of sadness.

'Ann, look!' Amanda pointed across the Walkers' drawing room at a pale young man who was curled like a cat by the side of the harpsichord. Every now and then he leaned forward to turn the pages of music for Miss Sarah Newland, and her dark ringlets dipped prettily in thanks.

'Look at Mr Sanderson, see how he watches Sarah. He believes that she can be his.' She turned back to Ann. 'Yet I saw her let Robert Hamblyn kiss her hand yesterday. And Mr Sanderson saw it too.' She raised her fan and tapped it on her chin. 'What is it on Mr Sanderson's part, do you think, Ann? Blind stupidity or is it,' there was a hesitation, ' hope? What do you think, Ann?'

There was something oddly brittle about her voice, Ann thought. What had happened to her?

'Amanda...'

But Amanda cut in with a rush of words. 'You don't love him, do you? My brother. You do not love him.'

Ann was too surprised to be careful with her reply. 'No, I do not believe I do. I do not know what you mean by love,' she said, as a kind of excuse.

Amanda understood, as Ann knew she would, that Ann meant everyone in that room, everyone that Amanda knew, to be included in the 'you'.

'I mean,' Ann carried on, laying her cards carefully down upon the table in front of her, 'that you all have expectations of being 'in love' of being 'loved' – but,' she shrugged, 'what do you mean by it?' She genuinely wanted an answer.

Amanda stared at her.

'Was there no love where you have come from, Ann?' Ann sensed some anger under the teasing tone, some frustration at Ann's months of silence. 'Did your parents not love you. Did you not promise to love your packman?' Their eyes met. Then Amanda smiled and said softly, 'but I have asked you that before, haven't I?'

Ann nodded.

'And you will not talk of it, will you?'

Ann shook her head. She was aware that her heart was beating faster, her hands felt clammy. Then, vividly, the writhing body of the packman lay between them. Ann blinked to get rid of the horror of it.

Amanda leaned forward. Ann heard her voice coming from a long way away. It sounded concerned. 'Ann, are you unwell?'

With a great effort, Ann pulled herself back.

'No. no, it is warm, that is all.'

'Yes, it is.' Amanda beckoned a maid and asked for some water. Ann drank the water and for a few moments they sat in silence.

'Are you well now, Ann?' Amanda was sorry for her actions earlier.

Ann nodded.

'We will speak no more of it.' Amanda picked up the queen of hearts, fanned her face with it and her voice became louder, the voice of every young woman who attended country balls and drank tea. 'I will be going to Lichfield tomorrow,' she said. 'I am looking forward to it. The Markham's have built a new ballroom. Would you believe it! Above the kitchen.' She gave a mock frown. 'How odd!' Miss Newland lifted her head from the harpsichord to smile across the top of Mr Sanderson's head. Amanda lifted her hand in languid recognition. She slipped the queen of hearts back in the pack and got up to walk around the room.

So she did not want to pursue her accusation. But Ann did. She took hold of Amanda's sleeve to detain her.

'I have talked of this to him,' she said quietly. 'He knows everything I have just said to you.'

Amanda looked down at her. 'I am glad. I think he hopes you will love him.'

'I hope so too,' said Ann.

Amanda took a breath as if she was about to say something else and then thought better of it. Ann let go of her arm and she walked away.

Ann stayed at the table, wanting to say more but glad that she had not.

Amanda left for Lichfield the next day, without saying anything more to Ann. Over the next few weeks, Ann sat at tedious tea parties and quietly lost endless card games in plush drawing rooms. Why had Amanda chosen to speak to her? How much more did she know? Why had she mentioned the packman? And Ann had lied to her. She had not spoken to James. Not even tried since that night at Lichfield. And since that night she knew for certain that she was not prepared to tell him the one thing which would change his view of her forever.

She was careful not to let any of these thoughts disturb the smile of sweet, slightly foolish, expectation on her face. She was pronounced charming wherever she went.

Six months after their first meeting, Ann and James were married in St Oswald's Church. All of Ashbourne was there; the Walker money provided a superb feast, the sun shone and the bride, a widow and a seamstress of no family, looked more delightful and ever more acceptable as the day progressed. Amanda had been her bridesmaid and, as they had sat together in the carriage listening to the bells ringing, she had placed her hand over Ann's.

'Ann, I know you will make him happy.'

Ann nodded, her heart filled with relief but, before she could speak, the carriage door was flung open and then she was entering St Oswald's Church to the sound of the choir echoing around the high vaulted ceiling.

And so, on July 10th 1756, Ann lifted her skirts of white silk over the stone steps of Hulland House as the new Mrs Walker. She heard her tiny heels click on the marble floor as she walked forward to greet the servants as their mistress. As she walked down the line, each one bowed or curtsied and she felt the power and protection of money draw itself around her. The thick walls of the house, the solid depth of them, made even the very sounds of the outside world fade. In the first weeks after their marriage she would lie in their bed and listen for the voices of people walking home to Mayfield after drinking in the town. She was here in this bed while they were outside, in the street below her, with only a few coins left in their pockets until they worked to earn some more.

Some nights she would go downstairs and tiptoe across the hall. She would go up to the great double entrance doors, press her ear hard to the thin gap where they met and listen to these voices, a few feet away from her. She, by some quirk of fate or by her own endeavour, name it as you like, was here, with every satisfaction around her. Mrs Walker of Hulland House.

One night, as she stood by the door it came to her that there could be another interpretation. She was not here because of fate or because of her own endeavour.

She was here because of love.

The sheets slithered to the floor. Ann raised her body upwards and then let it sink onto the body of the man beneath her. She felt him enter her again and just before she pushed forward she caught sight of his eyes, wide open in surprise. Then he turned his face to one side and she heard a moan of pleasure, low and deep in his throat.

Later, when James was asleep, Ann lay on her side with her knees tucked up to her stomach and watched him. After a while she wriggled across the bed to lie against him. She ran her hands lightly across his chest and, as she did, memories of that last night with Mistress Arbour came flooding back. She thought of the child that she had been, lying sunk in hopeless misery as the hours of darkness slowly passed. Crying as if it might make him wake up, take pity on her and allow her to stay. Bewildered, because nothing should matter as much to him as the enormity of her being sent away.

She understood now. The fear on his face which closed her out. The calculations he had had to make as he listened to her father's threats.

She could understand those calculations now. She rolled on her back, turning her head at right angles on the pillow to look at James again. His face was untroubled, his breathing soft and even.

He was like that child. The child that she had been. He would not understand. She turned her face towards the window and watched the strips of pale light that were slowly appearing between the shutters.

No, that was not true. He would understand but then, when he did, he would be horrified. And then, would he give her time to run, to get away? She lay and imagined his face when he heard the truth. The love turning to incredulity, then disgust, then fear.

She placed her hand on her stomach, her fingers tracing the concave dip between her hip bones. She thought about Alice, the kitchen maid, scrubbing at the sink with her belly round and hard under her apron. Even though she was near full term, still trying to carry the buckets of coal and having to bend sideways to pick up the tea tray. If the new Mrs Walker was with child she would be treated like a precious object, waited on and pampered.

If she had a child by James it would change everything. Even that terrible moment when he finally knew the truth about her. She would be the mother of his child. It would be a protection.

'Well?' Edward put down the shipping schedules from Bermondsey docks and looked at James questioningly.

'Well, what?' replied James.

'Well, were you right?'

'About what,' said James, although he knew the direction in which the conversation was going.

'About love.' Edward watched him closely. It was a year since James had married Ann.

Unable to take that stare, James turned away. He did not reply. Edward turned back to the shipping schedules, acting as if nothing had been said. Later, as Edward stood in the stable yard with his heavy satchel of orders and bills of sale, he clumsily put his arms around James and hugged him.

'Goodbye James. Keep well.'

James stood and watched as his brother rode out of the stable yard. He thought of his wedding night. He remembered her wedding dress lying discarded across the high back of the chair by the fireplace. The tiny sequined flowers which covered it had seemed to gather every scrap of light from the dying fire until the dress shone gently in the darkness of the bedroom. There had been no maid allowed in the room to put it carefully away. Newly weds. James had lain quietly beside his wife.

Wife. He was saddened. It was as if when his body had penetrated hers, she had moved further away from him. He had entered her and immediately she had retreated somewhere else.

This was the first time, he had said to himself. It would be different. He had bunched the pillow up under his head and watched the shifting light on the wedding dress until he had fallen asleep.

But, as the days and then the weeks passed, he began to understand that it would not be different. He was shut out of her. The love that he had tried to describe to Edward remained out of his reach. Ann was keeping herself closed to him but he did not want to taste the bitterness of it. He tried to ignore it.

And then there was something else. Something unexpected. She had brought a tension, a kind of watchfulness which ran under their life together. He did not understand it but his sense of it in her leant a sharpness, an excitement to being near her. He could not get enough of her. He sought her out during the day just to touch her hand or slip his arm around her waist. He walked a little behind her on the street so that he could see the sway of her hips under the stiff taffetta and imagine holding the weight of her soft warm flesh in his hands. He would stand close to her to feel the energy that came from her. As if her body was attending to everything around her, all the time. Like something wild. A fox. My little fox, he called her. She smiled.

Love-making with this sliver of a woman was something deep and dark. She led him and teased him until he was confused with desire and his body felt clumsy and his head felt thick with wanting her. She goaded him until he found himself sliding dangerously on the edges of cruelty. Often James came out from the other side of it all, exhausted, fascinated and a little ashamed. He would look away from her until she took his face in her hands and forced him to look at her, her eyes open and bold. She would throw her head back and laugh, then hug him fiercely and rock him back and forth on the bed like a child.

111

He was so amazed by the pleasure she brought him that he almost forgot what else it was that he wanted from her. But his desire to know her resurfaced again and again, no matter how far it sank in the daily pleasure she offered him. It became a struggle between them. He had waited too long to know her, he was determined to succeed. He thought it would be sweet, for her as well as him, when they reached each other.

'What kind of child were you, Ann?' He would ask, his breath on her cheek. 'I think you were a beautiful child. A clever child. Am I right?'

And Ann would lie beside him in the darkness and think of the molly house, of the streets, of her sisters. She tried to shut the thoughts out. She did not want them. She knew where they led.

To a murder.

Two months after they were married James had brought Ann a present.

They lay sprawled across the coverlets. A few moments ago they had made love and he could feel a slippery film of sweat forming where Ann's thigh pressed against his back. There was a fire in the grate and they could hear the rain being blown intermittently against their window by a summer squall, the thought of the cold wind-driven rain outside only increasing their sense of comfort. Although the weather was stormy, it was still only September and the fire had made the room luxuriously hot. Ann lazily wiped her thigh with the edge of the coverlet.

'Are you awake?' he asked.

He could feel her nod in reply. 'Hmm.'

He leaned over, opened the drawer beside the bed and handed her a card and a pretty paper package.

'This is for our anniversary,' he said.

'What anniversary?'

'Our two month anniversary.' He stroked her damp hair,

smoothing it across the pillow.

Ann turned the package over in her hands. 'It's very small,' she said. 'What is it? Can't be much!' She rolled away, laughing as James tried to slap her .

Then she lay back on the pillows and balanced the flimsy package between her breasts. She opened the card – 'To my dear wife,' she read aloud, ' to whom I have been married so long that I have forgotten what it was like to sleep peacefully alone.'

'James' she cried, pulling the pillow from underneath her head and throwing it at him. The package had tumbled onto the mattress.

'Open it!' he shouted back, pointing at the package and cowering in mock fear at the side of the bed. 'Open it before you judge me.'

Ann knelt on the bed, undid the ribbon and unfolded the outer paper. There was a thick wad of tissue paper around something small and solid. She ripped at it, impatient now to see her present. Something tumbled out on to the bed.

She stared at what lay there in disbelief. It was the key to the packman's box.

He knew. James knew everything.

She flung the key away from her and leapt off the bed, to stand, half crouched on the other side of the bed from him, the muscles of her thighs tight and bunched as if she were ready to run. James slowly stood up. His eyes went to her face, it was stretched and contorted with fear. He hardly recognised her.

'Ann…' he began, stretching his hand out to her.

'How did you get it?' She tried to keep her voice low and calm. No need to bring people running to their door. She might still be able to get away.

He could see that even speaking was a huge effort for her. She was trembling from head to foot.

He stood up and started to move around the side of the bed.

She moved a step nearer the door.

'Tell me, James. Tell me everything. How did you get it?'

'Ann.' James was at a loss. 'It is a present. It is the key to your own strong box. You must have one as a lady of the house, you know.'

The key lay on the edge of the carpet. James went over and picked it up.

At least she did not move any further away.

'Here. I'll show you.' He pulled a blanket off a chair and there lay a new strongbox. Unmarked and unfamiliar.

Ann stared at it then she sat down suddenly on the bed as her legs gave way underneath her. James brought the box over and laid it on her bare knees.

It felt cold against her skin. She touched the lid. The box was made of fine wood with an inlay of flowers made of something lighter, shinier... mother of pearl. She traced the pattern slowly with her fingers. She opened the box and it was empty. She had half expected to see the money. The packman's money. She looked past the box at her two feet gleaming pale on the dark floorboards. The money must still be where she had hidden it two nights ago, under the floorboards, under their great bed. Almost directly under her bare feet now.

She realised that James was speaking. He was asking her a question.

'Ann, what did you think it was? Ann?'

She turned her head to look at him.

'Ann.' He leaned over and stroked her arm, but his voice was more insistent, 'what did you think I had bought you?'

She shook her head. Mute. Her eyes were unnaturally wide, her gaze flicking back and forward across his face. For a while they sat there quite still in complete silence; the only sounds in the room were from the battering drops of rain on the window and the hissing of wet wood on the fire.

'Ann. Tell me. What did you think it was. What do you

think I have found out.' He smoothed her hair. 'You must tell me. You must let me know everything.' His voice whispered on, insisting, 'Why were you so frightened?'

At first she sat still, but then she could bear it no longer. His innocence made her angry.

'Stop!' she cried and stood up, her hands clenched by her sides.

'Stop, James!'

She sat back down on the bed. And then she told him how the packman had been a cruel man. How he had accused her of stealing money from him. How he had become strange with drink. How he had hit her and how she had dreaded the times when he pulled out the key to the strong box and the beatings would begin.

'And now James, you know…' she kept her head down and looked at her hands, 'I am ashamed. Ashamed to have told you all this.'

He tried to remonstrate but she held up her hand.

'Please stop, James. I cannot bear it, I will be ill. I do not want to have to talk about this ever again.' She looked at him, pleadingly, 'Do you understand? Can you see why it is better for me not to… think of this?'

James nodded. She slid into the bed and pulled the coverlet over her naked body.

James sat silently beside her until the fire died in the grate, then he also slid under the covers and held her close. She had fallen asleep, her breath even and deep. He lay awake until morning. He made a decision. If that was what she wanted, they would never speak of this again.

Ten months after they were married, the child Ann had imagined that night as she had lain by her husband was born. Here he was in reality. And it was different to what she had thought it would be. She was surprised by him. She kissed his cat mouth and stroked his fat limbs, curled his tiny fingers around hers. And marvelled at him. At herself.

A mother.

His grandfather, Mr Walker, had taken ill with some bleeding disease of the gut and had died six months after James and Ann had married and so did not live to see his first grandchild, named Adam Walker, for him. But every other member of the family was there to welcome him.

Adam lay in Ann's arms and as they leaned over to look and to murmur a welcome to him so she felt that they were murmuring a welcome to her.

Amanda swept Adam into her arms whenever she saw him. 'Only practising for my future motherhood,' she muttered in mock resignation.

'Ann, to produce such a boy tells me you have come from good stock,' cried Kitty as she reluctantly passed the baby back to his mother. 'Amadeus would have been so pleased.' Her eyes filled with tears and Ann wanted to comfort her. Tentatively, she reached out and put one arm around Kitty, and for a moment the weight of the baby was shared between them.

There was a rebuke only half hidden there, she thought, as she touched Kitty's wet cheek with her lips. I have never said enough about myself to her. All they know is I have no family left and that I had come from the south. That is what I said.

When Kitty left the nursery, Ann sat in the nursing chair and looked down at the sleeping baby in her arms. Now they will want to know if that dark hair or these flat little earlobes come from my blood. What did his grandparents look like? Does he have any aunts? Ordinary questions. She felt a sudden restlessness. She stood up and walked to the window with the baby against her shoulder. Her sisters dead by now, her father rotted away. She held the child close to her and felt his faint moth-breath on her neck. They must all wonder, and believe that James knows more than they do. None of them, not even James, must ever know.

116

James stepped out across the marble hall, his coat flapping and his spurs striking on the stone. On his way to make money. He and Edward had begun to scent real success as their business expanded to the London docks and the import of coffee and cloth from exotic countries far away. The tannery had seemed to slowly close itself down after his father died. Workers left and orders dried up. The Walker brothers had turned eagerly to the south and to trade, to the great city docks where ships groaned and creaked against each other and exotic cargoes of coffee and silk were stacked high on the wharves.

They were excited by it as they had never been excited by the tannery. They had seen that as a terrible, stinking place, dragging on their hearts since early childhood visits where they had stood hand in hand by the heaped bodies of dead animals, white and ghostly without their skins. The fear had never left them but as long as their father had lived the tannery was the centre of all the family business and they had to share in it. Now James felt at last free of it. And in this house he had a wife and a child. A son who would follow him.

He opened the door onto the busy street. As he walked down the steps, he felt foolish with happiness. Ann loved their son and it was her way of loving him, he was sure of it. This child, the birth of this child, had brought him contentment. Ann gave him what she could, in the ways that it was possible for her to do it, he understood that now. He looked up at the house and caught sight of his wife watching him from the window. She held up Adam to him and smiled. He raised his hand in salute and smiled back.

As the first few weeks after Adam's birth passed, something changed for Ann. His dark little presence in the nursery began to disturb her. She could not find a boundary between herself and this child. She told herself that he came from her body, but he was a separate soul. If there were such things as souls.

Then the baby became ill. For two days he screamed and his hot little body kicked and struggled against whatever it was that had invaded him. The house became a thoroughfare. First their doctor, followed by neighbours, and friends of Kitty with advice about cold cloths and clove oil. Then it passed, Adam's screams stopped and for hours he slept in Ann's arms, only waking to feed desperately at her breast. Then, his belly round with milk, his mouth would slacken, his fingers would uncurl their grip on her dress and he would drift back into a deep, healing sleep. Ann would close her eyes and try to sleep with him.

But as soon as her eyes closed she saw the packman. Her head was filled with the fear that her baby's life could be the retribution Mr Parker's God might extract. The God she had had the temerity not to believe in.

On the fifth day after his illness, Adam was pronounced fully recovered and the mood of the whole house lightened. But Ann's mood did not change. Her fear did not abate. She would not allow anyone else to care for the baby. She must keep him safe. She lived in a half world of exhaustion and constant readiness. Alert at his first cry in the night and sleeping fitfully beside him on the bed during the day. Sometimes she imagined that she was the child and sometimes she knew she was separate but also knew that she lived inside him as he had lived inside her. She also knew that he might have to survive without her. Her time with him could be short.

For this baby's mother had murdered a man. She could hang.

Alone with him in the nursery, she began to tell him what had happened to her. What she had done. Why she had done it. How each step led to the next one. She was driven to talk on and on, leaving nothing out. Going back night after night, over and over each explanation of each event, trying to fully explain, fully understand. In this inarticulate, vulnerable child, sleeping securely against her, she recognised herself. For the first time she wept for her own weakness and fear. In the half dark of the nursery of Hulland House, with its pretty friezes and nursery book pictures, she wildly conjured up all those who had mistreated her, who had discounted her, allowed no voice to break out of her as she knew it should from every human soul. She had so much to cover. All had to be exposed, examined, understood. She was calling back in time to comfort her young self, to redress the wrongs, to change things.

The household noticed that Ann was becoming increasingly pale and silent.

Ann rarely sat down to eat in the evenings with the family and when Kitty or Amanda tried to talk to her the conversation died away. Ann was always eager to get back upstairs.

Her excuse was the child, but everyone knew that the care of Adam could be shared with Kitty, or his nurse, or any other member of the household whom Ann chose to call upon for help. They watched, concerned. Although Ann said very little she appeared to be sure of her actions and her air of self absorption meant that the family hesitated to question her. James was troubled but he did not know what to do.

One night, as he came to the nursery door to say good night to his child, he was surprised to hear Ann talking to someone. He had stopped for a moment with his hand on the door knob. Then the urgency in her tone made him uneasy. He pushed the door open, dreading what he might find.

'Ann. Is he well? I heard you speaking to someone. I thought perhaps you had called Hargreaves again?'

He looked around the room. There was no one there but

Ann and the baby.

She looked steadily back at him. There was a silence, as if it took a long time for her to recognise him.

'He is very well.'

'Thank God!' He crossed the room and kissed them both. Had Adam fed well? Was he sleeping? She nodded her head but she seemed to be waiting for him to leave.

As he shut the door behind him he heard her voice resume in the same low, urgent tones. He tried to comfort himself with the thought that women did behave strangely after a confinement. He would speak to Kitty.

After that visit by James, Ann told herself that the words she spoke to Adam night after night had to be whispered. They could not be spoken aloud even in this place which had become her home. Sometimes during the day, when she left the nursery to get linen or to eat some food she had to bite hard upon her lips. The words wished to come out. She had to hold them in. But not with the baby. Not with him.

By the nursery window, persuaded to sit there on the plush nursing chair in the bright early sunshine, Ann presented an ideal picture of motherhood, smiling at morning visitors and directing the maid to hand out tea. If the visitors commented to each other afterwards that she seemed a little distant then it was only to be expected. The Walker money would make anyone arrogant. And now she had a son. Well, there would be no stopping her.

But at night Ann clung to the sleeping baby as if it could give her comfort, as if it were her parent. Sometimes, in the quiet hours of the morning, she would stand by the window looking down the long street to the lights of the taverns and hostelries on St John's Street at the other end of town. She would long to walk outside. Dark streets held no fear for her, often they had afforded her protection. She knew how to slide from point to point, using the shadows thrown by the moonlight to her advantage. As she unravelled her

120

understanding of her past, she began to feel less and less safe in the house on Church Street. It represented something got by trickery. A trickery so enormous that it defied belief. Here she was, a little city slattern, whose only true skill lay in extricating a purse from a pocket, now the wife of a man of property and the mother of his child. Loved by his whole family, respected by the whole town.

One night Ann laid the sleeping baby in his cot, put on her heavy cloak and went outside to stand on the other side of the street and watch the house. She could see the faint light from the nursery lamps behind the thick curtaining. She could see the solidity of the shape of the house as it stood in the dark, making an edge, a line of its possession in its space on the street front. She waited. Poised on the edge of the pavement she watched for some signal from the house that she had been missed. That this would not be allowed. But James had grown used to his wife leaving their bed for hours to tend their child. He slept on. She crossed back over the street and stood in the portal of the side door and looked out on to the town. She could hear far into the distance the faint noises of a busy coach town. Horses neighing and stamping in stables. The occasional shout, proving that even at the dead of night someone was awake. Closer to her, in the leafy garden the long cries of a hunting owl and the horrified shriek of its prey. If she stood still long enough she would see rats moving quickly round the walls, scavenging. The rats brought thoughts of the prison back to her mind. What was she doing here? Ann drew back into the shelter of the portal. She gripped the door handle. She drew a deep breath. Money was why she chose to stay here.

Money was everything. Ann was part of the Walker family. She could remain unquestioned in her present role almost without danger. It was in nobody's interests to question her background. Only the greatest misfortune could harm her. She would be Mrs Walker of Hulland House for the rest of her life – if she chose. She began to turn the door handle and as the door began to open she breathed in the warm musty scent of the housed. The thick spicy smell of wax polish and the acrid sourness of ashes from the doused fires of the downstairs rooms. She looked down at her hand, white on the door handle, and as she looked it seemed to change shape with that property of the dark which changes things as we stare at them. Her hand seemed to become smaller until it was the unformed hand of a tiny child. She pushed but the heavy door would not open further. For a moment Ann was perplexed. And then her heart jumped as she realised that she had no strength. This was no illusion of the weak light: she was transformed to a child. The door swung back on its oiled hinges and clicked shut. Ann was overwhelmed with panic. It seemed that she could not enter the house. She stepped back and looked up at the house. It seemed enormous, its high roof revolving against the clear sky. Ann closed her eyes. She tried to shout but no sound would come from her body. She tried to hit the door but her fists made no impression on the panels, no matter how she tried to pound. She felt weak and near to fainting. She stood completely still for a few moments. Only the sound of her breath existed. And suddenly the night seemed a safer place than the perimeter of the house. She tried to move her weak body as quickly as possible down the arched side entrance of the house and out on to Church Street. As she came out on to the street she stumbled and fell against the wall of Hulland House. She took hold of the sill of the dining room window and dragged herself upright and continued to walk down the pavement towards the church of St Oswald's. She felt as she had on that first night of escape, only now she seemed to be a child escaping. The dark pointed shape of the church seemed to move in front of her. The moon seemed to move in the sky. Ann's vision blurred and the street in front of her fell away into darkness. As Ann fell for the second time a tall, thin figure moved out from the doorway of the Grey House on the other side of the street. The figure moved quickly across the road and bent down to look at the crumpled body on the ground. Ann moaned and the figure straightened and turned down the street back towards town, leaving the woman lying there.

Ann came back to consciousness and rolled on to her back. Above her was the round moon surrounded by a white glow and star studs. She rolled her head to one side and recognised the stone front of the Elizabethan school house. She felt the cold, hard cobbles beneath her and realised that she was lying in the middle of the road. What was she doing here?

She struggled to sit up. As she came upright she realised with a shock that someone was moving quickly away from her down the road back into Ashbourne. She shook her head to clear it. A man. Tall, thin. Even in the moonlight she could make out that he was wearing dark clothes. A tail coat. Not a thief then. But who was he? Where was he going?

To get help. To get the night watch. To take her back. Back to prison.

Panic gripped her. She had to get away. She pushed herself on to her feet, steadied herself and began to walk. She had to get off the street before they came for her. Ahead of her she could see the dark mass of St Oswald's church, silent and watchful, its wide open gates seeming to offer a sanctuary. Of course, this was the Leek road, the road she was to take out of Ashbourne. But that had been before... before she was Ann Challinor... before she was Ann Walker. The effort of walking was almost too much for her, her legs felt impossibly heavy and her head span. She stopped for a moment until the dizziness passed and then she forced herself to walk on. She had to get to the church. She had to hide.

Ann passed between the gates and stumbled down the church path. To her right she could see a small side door cut into the stone of the church. It was lying ajar in the moonlight. She walked the last few yards across the damp grass between the gravestones, feeling its coldness beneath her feet, and pushed the door open. She entered the church and at once she was aware of a vast still emptiness spreading around her. She could make out rows of wooden pews receding into the darkness and above her, etched against the night sky, were the familiar, intricate shapes of the stained glass windows. She moved forwards and her heavy, dragging footsteps echoed across the stone floor. Her cloak was damp. The wool had soaked up the dew from the grass. She wrenched at its ties, letting it fall to the floor behind her. She reached the first stone pillar, put her arms around it and laid her head against its smooth surface. She began to cry. She cried for the innocent packman, riding ahead of her in the sunlight. She was a child walking the streets of Derby, crying for her family. She cried because she felt weak and could not run away. And they were going to come. They were going to come. She sank to the floor and began to crawl over to the pews. The floor seemed an endless space. Her knees kept getting caught in her dress and jerking her head downwards. Twice she hit her head on the flagstones and she whimpered at the pain. She reached the first pew, pushed herself as far under it as she could, and put her arms over her head. Her eyes closed and she slipped into unconsciousness again.

A few moments later the side door was pushed further open and a figure entered and stood by the door, listening. There was no sign of the woman although he knew she had come in here. There was her cloak, lying on the floor. Then he heard it. A tiny whimpering, mewling sound like a wounded dog or a child. He located the sound. Carefully and quietly he walked over to the first pew and knelt down. There she was. Wedged under the seat. The strange sounds she was making muffled by her arms over her head. He took hold of Ann's body and began to pull her out. At first her body was limp and she seemed unaware of him. Then she started to fight. She turned and struck out at him with her clenched fists, screaming a high pitched litany of 'No! No!', the noise echoing around them. Someone would surely hear this. He put his hand over her mouth and she twisted her face from side to side, her hands finding a brass rail on the pew and gripping it. Then suddenly her body went limp again and her hands fell away from the rail. He quickly took his hand from her mouth, leaning down to peer at her face. Thank God. She was still breathing. He pulled her out into the aisle and sat beside her. He propped himself up on the side of the pew, wiped his mouth and tried to catch his breath.

It was Mr Harrison. He had been coming out of Mr Hodgson's house, comfortably full of wine and good food and he had seen Mrs James Walker standing across the street staring up at her house. At first he had thought that there was something had happened at Hulland House. Perhaps a chimney fire. He had started forward, ready to help. A good neighbour. But then he had realised that she was alone. No servants, no husband. Something about the way she stood there told him that this was something stranger than a chimney fire. He had slipped back into the porch of the Grey House and watched her. She was swaying. Her hair was dishevelled and she was wearing her night clothes under that cloak. There was something far wrong with her. He smiled. This could be useful to him. It was what he wanted. For a long time he had had the uneasy feeling that Mrs Walker could destroy his position here in Ashbourne. She had looked at him in such a penetrating way on that day when he had entered her shop, catching him out, knowing the game he was playing. He had watched her rise in Ashbourne society with horror.

As he watched, Ann seemed to fold in on herself and then

there she was, lying flat on the street almost directly in front of him. He looked up and down the street. It was deserted. He left the cover of the porch and crossed over to where she lay. He put both hands on his knees, crouched down and examined her face intently. She did not seem to have a fever, or any discolouration. Her breathing was not laboured. Not a disease then. Something of the mind, perhaps. He looked down at her with satisfaction. Here was Ann Walker lying on the street in the dead of night. No reputation could withstand that. He looked up at the house and then up and down the street again. Servants would find her – or early morning farm boys on their way to the market place. And soon Ashbourne would know that Mrs Walker had gone mad. She moaned. She was coming round. He started to walk away quickly. He didn't want to be the one that found her.

He went straight to his study. Poured himself a celebratory brandy and settled down to enjoy it. But he kept picturing her lying on the pavement in front of him and he could hear the slight moan she gave as she struggled back to consciousness. He suspected that Ann was like him, someone who had always had to live by her wits. That day in her shop, when their eyes had met, they had recognised something in each other. Part of him admired her. Whatever her past was, she had done well in Ashbourne. There were things here that she would pay dearly to keep. It occurred to him that it might be better for him if Ann Walker kept her position in Ashbourne – with his help.

He had sprung out of his chair, put his coat back on and hurried out onto the street to help Ann and seal his bargain. He was shocked to find that she had gone and was about to turn back to his house when a sudden thought made him walk towards the church.

And now he sat patiently waiting for her to wake up. His only concern was that her mind had completely gone and he wouldn't be able to make it clear to her how grateful she should be to him. Then it occurred to him that if she had truly lost her mind then that would also mean that he was safe. He looked down at her, another smile spreading across his face.

Ann opened her eyes and stared up at him. She put a hand up to take hold of his sleeve. She was looking directly at him although her eyes seemed to be focused elsewhere. 'I did not kill him.' She took a difficult breath and paused to recover. 'I did not kill him. He was dying.' She swallowed. 'I escaped from prison.'

'Prison?' He leaned forward and shook her. 'Prison. What do you mean? Mrs Walker, listen to me. What do you mean?' She closed her eyes again but he realised that she was still speaking. He got up on his knees and leaned down to catch her words. 'Dance,' then something incomprehensible, then 'dance' again. Then, more clearly, 'Ann Dance.' He realised that it was a name. 'Ann Dance. Ann Dance.' She was saying that name over and over again.

He did not answer. His first thought was that she was talking nonsense. But the name seemed familiar. Something from the past. Ashbourne. The town hall notice board. His mind was racing. Ann Dance? Could he remember that name? Wanted for theft; called 'the sparrow'. Yes! He knew of her. He remembered it - the name 'the sparrow' had stuck in his mind. He took a professional interest in these things.

She pulled him closer. 'I did not kill him...' her voice cracked. 'I did not, d'you hear?' She tried to sit up. Her voice getting louder and stronger. 'D'you hear?' And then she fell back, sliding out of reality again.

He knew the history of Ann Challinor, the tragic young widow, and now he reformed it in his mind. The packman, who died that night in the Plough Inn. The woman lying beside him was a murderess. She could hang.

Mr Harrison sat for another hour on the floor of St Oswald's

Church, listening to fragments of Ann Dance's life. As her fever rose and she moved in and out of consciousness she talked to him as she had to her child. He hardly listened to her. There was nothing else he needed to hear. But his plan required that he waited until dawn.

When light began to stream through the eastern windows of the church Mr Harrison stood up. He was stiff from sitting on the stone floor and he hoped that he had not caught a chill. He was eager to get home and have some warm milk-perhaps with the rest of the brandy he had left on his desk. He picked Ann up and carried her out of the church, down the street to the door of Hulland House. He was surprised by how easy it was. He remarked to himself that Mrs Walker was all bones. It took a while to raise the house but eventually he had an audience of the bootboy, the cook and Mr Walker himself listening to his story in the morning room. Ann had already been taken upstairs to bed where Kitty was sitting with her.

Mr Harrison explained how he had been taking an early stroll to pray in the fine old church when he had seen Mrs Walker enter the church ahead of him. No doubt on the same business as himself. Imagine his consternation when he had seen the poor lady sink down in a faint in front of the altar, as she made her obeisance. Of course he had brought her straight to Hulland House and no, he would not stay– all care and attention must be given to the poor lady.

Mr Harrison walked the few yards to his school in good spirits. A thief, and, from what she said, a murderer, and not to be found out? For how many years? And married into the Walker family. It was astounding. He smiled. A clever woman. A clever woman, but, unlike him, weak. And now she was paying the price of having a conscience. He climbed the front steps of his academy and paused to look up and down the street. He raised his hand to a carriage that was passing, turned and went inside.

Ann lay in bed for many days. She hardly spoke and barely touched the food that was sent up for her from the kitchen. She seemed to have lost interest in her child and would stare listlessly at him when he was brought to her bedside. Two weeks after Mr Harrison had brought Ann to the door of Hulland House, Mrs Walker took James aside and suggested that he should take Ann away for a rest, a change of surroundings.

'It often is of help in such cases, James. Ann is just tired after the birth. Perhaps somewhere by water will suit her? Take her to Matlock Bath. She can spend a few days taking the waters at the new hotel there.'

James and Kitty were in her room. Their anxiety pressed around her. She realised that there was something they very much wanted her to do. She tried to concentrate on what James was saying. Eventually Ann nodded her head. She would prefer to stay in her room but she understood that James and Kitty wanted her to go to Matlock Bath and she did not have the strength to argue with them.

Matlock Bath

James and Ann left Ashbourne by the Brassington turnpike on the morning of August 17th 1757. As the carriage jolted through the market place, out onto King's Street, Ann watched the people of Ashbourne. Traders doffed their caps to James as they rode by on their sturdy horses; strolling ladies stared into the carriage with curiosity. Most of the town knew that Mrs Walker had been unwell and was going to Matlock Bath to take the waters.

Amanda was coming with them as far as Kniveton, where she was to visit a friend.

'Ann, I must instruct you.' Ann turned to Amanda and smiled. She understood what Amanda was trying to do and she loved her for it, although it seemed a pointless task. Ann felt quite satisfied to be quiet.

'Ann. Are you listening?'

Ann nodded.

'To all those who strain to be fashionable in Ashbourne, families like ours, Ann,' Amanda gave a little flourish of her gloved fingers, 'the Walkers, are expected to offer direction and novelty. If Mrs Walker is going to take the waters then, before her carriage has passed, there are those who can already feel that they too had the need of a visit to Matlock Bath for rejuvenation after the long exhausting summer.' Amanda adjusted her bonnet and raised her eyebrows, 'Anything which gives taking off half one's clothes and getting wet a thoroughly medical – and therefore irreproachable – purpose is bound to catch on.'

To her surprise, Ann found herself laughing out loud. James leaned across and touched her hand.

After they had left Amanda in Kniveton, the carriage continued up across the rough gritstone road to Wirksworth. This was Ann's first journey out of Ashbourne since she had entered the town on a packhorse over two years ago. She rolled the carriage window down and took a deep breath, drinking in the rich, sweet smell of the hay which lay drying in great heaps across the fields. Morning mist still lay in the low dales and on either side above the hills stretched a bright blue sky.

She was conscious of a heightened sense of everything around her. She stroked the soft fleece of the white angora wrap which lay across her knees. She took in the fine trellised detail of the lace cuff which circled her wrist and the deep yellow glint of the wedding band against her pale skin. She looked up and smiled briefly at James as he turned to look at her and then she closed her eyes and put her head back against the cushioned seat. She told herself that it was stuffed with eider down, riveted with brass, encased in velvet made from the best Egyptian cotton.

Then, catching her unawares, fear rushed back in. She had forgotten what it felt like. That familiar feeling of dread which had receded to the edges of her mind as she had lain in her bed. The same questions. What was she doing here? How long could it last? She sat up and stared out of the window again. She put her hand on the soft plush of the seat and reminded herself that she knew people who could value this carriage in a glance. And find a buyer for it. No questions asked.

But it was a ridiculous thought.

She closed her eyes briefly and longed for the return of that state of numbness which she had inhabited for the last two weeks. She was not sure that she had the strength to carry on this life, this constant need to be on her guard, and then she thought bleakly that she had no other choice. She could not return to being Ann Dance. She thought of her child, Adam. He was only safe with Mrs Walker as his mother. Ann Dance was a thief – and worse.

And then, in the way of catching something from the edge of vision that can never be seen by looking directly, she understood that she would not stay as Ann Walker only for Adam's protection. There was something else.

Mrs James Walker. It was an identity recognised by others. It preceded her, it explained her. And it had begun to alter her. She could not leave it. Not yet. But that frightened her. She felt weakened by the changes happening in her. It was as if she did not fully know herself anymore. She felt her spirits drop as anxiety formed itself into a queasy knot in the pit of her stomach. The coach passed two young girls carrying farm stuff into market. Ann caught sight of their upturned faces, wide eyed and greedy for a glimpse of the fine lady who rode inside. She wished for a moment to be Ann Dance, out on that road, and then she mocked herself for that thought. Who would choose to live a life by begging and theft? Where was the freedom in that? Ann closed her eyes and drifted in and out of uneasy sleep until she was thrown forward by a great jolt as the coach turned into a courtyard.

The carriage had stopped at The Miners' Arms in Hopton. It was a hot day and the horses would be thirsty. James was taking no chances. He wanted this journey to be as easy as possible for Ann and fresh horses were less likely to stumble. While James dealt with the ostler, Ann was taken to a seat by the fireplace at the far end of the empty taproom and a tall glass of claret was put in front of her. She sat listening to the distant activity of the inn kitchens as they prepared for the London coach which was due in one hour. She sipped from the glass of claret, trying to find comfort in the half darkness and quiet of this normally bustling space.

Two men, grimy from their journeying, entered the taproom. They called for ale and drank deeply. Ann found herself unable to avoid listening to their conversation. They were packhorse men. Jaggers. Who led their animals across the country side whenever the weather made passage possible. Much of their conversation was concerned with the state of the roads. Ann had heard many of these conversations in the past, as she had waited for a traveller to get so drunk that she could safely slip her fingers into his pockets. Then she heard something unusual. One of the men was explaining how he had been questioned by a Frenchman at the Michaelmas Compton market. Looking for a man called Rudge. There was a reward... but it had seemed a bit funny to him. What's a Frenchman want with a packhorse man? The man obviously was still regretting that he had not had the sense to spin the Frenchman some tale and take the money... Unfortunately, the Frenchman had looked like the type who might come back and slit your throat if he suspected you lied.

Ann listened on. Now with her full, terrified attention. The

132

Frenchman had gone. Apparently giving up on his search. The second packhorse man agreed that it seemed very strange. Maybe this Rudge owed the Frenchie some money. Well, no sense in helping a Frenchman, even if you had heard of a Rudge on the roads...

The money. Now lying under the floorboards directly beneath the mahogany cot of her baby in the nursery of Hulland House. Still in its original wooden box. Three thousand Louis D'or. A good sum of money. Enough to fund a small army let alone a gang of cut-throats. The questions Ann had asked the night she had found the money came flooding back, still unanswered. How would a packhorse man get that sort of money? Must have been a thief and a big one. Travelling incognito then. Why? And why French money? Why Louis D'or? Ann had recognised them immediately that night in the Plough inn; there had been a few around Derby ever since the Scottish army had passed through ten years before. And the letter. The letter. She had not forgotten the words she had tried to decipher in the inn yard on the morning of the packhorse man's death. Janvier. Chantilly. Choiseul. Not Dutch but French. French business.

Ann suddenly sat upright, spilling wine over the table in front of her. Could he have been a spy? An agent? But for whom? The French? The Hanoverians? Ann knew as well as any one in the country that the war presently being waged with France had begun to rumble into life in 1755 and was inevitably connected to the hopes of the Young Pretender.

She had been seventeen when the Jacobite army had billeted themselves across Derby. The whole of Derby wore white cockades. For a few days in 1745 it felt as if there was to be a Stuart king.

She thought rapidly over the possibilities. A man travelling alone in the spring of 1755 with a huge amount of French money. Travelling from Derby on the northern route. Maybe carrying funds for an uprising, funds which she had taken. And a letter. Information. Instructions maybe. Of course such a sum, destined for political purposes, would have brought seekers. Only the change of name she had made had saved her from discovery. But how long could it offer protection?

If it was French money then, of course, the French would have come seeking it. But why now, so long after the event? If it had been destined for the Scottish Jacobites then they would have come looking two years ago. If the packhorse man had been a Hanoverian agent who had already intercepted the money then Government men would search for their agent and his treasure. Perhaps they had also already been there in Ashbourne and found no trail. Questions had been asked, but no satisfactory answers given. So why return now? Almost two years later?

Could they connect her? Mrs Ann Walker of Hulland House. Not likely but there was danger. The right questions into her original story could quickly reveal the extent of her lies. For not only was Mr Challinor a fiction but it would now appear that Mr Rudge of Nantwich was certainly a fiction, too. He could easily have been a Highland Jacobite.

The headmaster – Mr Harrison. He was a real threat to Ann's safety. He had picked her up that night and had not revealed the truth about how he had found her. Why? Out of a sense of honour? Or for some future negotiating card? What had she said to him that night? How long had she been with him?

Ann stood up and began to pace back and forwards. She could not focus her attention on finding some plan of action because she did not know the direction or form of the threat.

134

But what she was certain of was that she should go back and get her child. The baby would have been safe from thieves deep in the Walker stronghold but no one could be safe once they had entered the world of espionage and assassins. She had made a dreadful mistake by keeping the money. She had known that even as she had hidden it in her knapsack at the Plough Inn but she had not foreseen the extent of her mistake until now. How could she? And yet that was no excuse, as Ann knew. There is always a commensurate price to pay for a theft. Usually thieves weigh up the price and adjust their actions accordingly. Ann had taken a great, unnatural step and she had faced the possible consequences honestly – but she had not thought of this. That there were government spies after this money. She should have thought it through. She had seen the Jacobite emblem on the sword of Rudge. She had heard the soft accents of the north in the voice of the man who had come looking for him. How could she have been so stupid to think that money like this would be allowed to disappear? Of course there would be English agents after it.

Ann walked towards the door. She must get James to turn back. As she reached the entrance, James came in.

'James, James,' Ann's first words to him were almost no more than a whisper as panic made her struggle to breath. Her heart was beating unnaturally fast. She pulled at his jacket to bring his face closer. Her face as she brought it up to his was white and strained. Her eyes wide.

'We must return for Adam.' She swallowed and caught her breath. 'We cannot leave him alone. James, he is in danger.' For a moment, the directness and certainty of Ann's appeal almost convinced James. He hesitated, but the moment passed, the chance went, and James saw in front of him an example of the very reason his mother had insisted that Ann be taken to the waters. She was over-excited, fevered and imagining horror in every place.

He spoke quietly and slowly. 'Ann, Adam is very safe. He is not alone. My mother and his nurse are there with him all the time. He is strong and healthy and they can take care of him.' He put his arm around her shoulders and led her back to her seat.

Ann realised that, in her outburst, she sounded like the woman they thought she had become. The indisposed Mrs James Walker. Nervous about her child. Hysterical. She would not persuade him unless she told him the truth. The truth. She looked at James, standing with the landlady, talking with concern about his wife.

His wife. Escaped from prison and a murderer. She would have nothing. Worse. She would lose the protective cover of her false identity just as her need for it increased tenfold.

She sat back down by the fire and accepted a further glass of claret and let the sympathy of James and the landlady provide her with time to think. She had to make a decision. Get up now and leave, on foot, as she had once been used to doing. Go back to Ashbourne, get her child and disappear back to Derby or even Nottingham. The only other decision – to take all of the money or some of the money or none of the money. This became uppermost in her mind. How much could she take and not have bartered away the safety of herself and her child? How much? Voices around her brought her back to the present.

'Why, Mrs Walker. How nice to meet you here.' Ann looked up to see the Misses Brockham. Two young women who were part of the Ashbourne circuit. Friends of Amanda Walker.

'My husband is taking me to Matlock Bath, to take the waters.'

They were trillingly sympathetic, and curious. They surrounded Ann, hemming her in with their abundant skirts and round, smiling faces. With their knowledge of her.

136

Ann realised that she could not get up, walk to Ashbourne and take her child and leave. She would not be allowed to do it. The Walkers would be in pursuit of her. James would want his son. She would be caught. She would be returned to prison. She could not just disappear into the back streets of Derby.

James was coming across the room with one of the kitchen girls. 'Alice here will help you upstairs. You should rest, Ann.' Ann didn't protest. She went quietly upstairs with Alice, and allowed herself to be put to bed.

Ann lay in the front upstairs room of the Miner's Arms. Everything was quiet and she was alone. Through the bedroom window she could see that the weather had changed and the sky was dull and cloudy. She stared at the clouds forming and reforming as her mind churned relentlessly over the danger she faced.

There was one possible way of escaping her pursuers and avoiding the added pursuit of the Walker family.

She could leave both Adam and the money. She could get up and walk out of the inn, leaving her child to a good life, hopefully taking most of the danger of discovery with her. She could take the money out of the Walker house, leave it hidden somewhere and then let these French spies know where it was. She knew people who would carry messages like that.

She thought of her old life, the people she remembered there who would still help her. If they were paid. She saw the face of a man who could be trusted to take a message to the French. His business had always been with strangers, foreigners, but nobody asked him too much about it. She wondered how much of the money could she keep without causing a chase. She thought of James and his shock at learning even part of the truth about her. She thought of Adam.

Big drops of summer rain began to hit the window panes. Slowly at first and then with a sudden, ferocious intensity. She got up from the bed and took her woollen jacket from the wardrobe where Alice had carefully hung it. She slipped her feet back into her travelling shoes and sat down on the bed to lace them up. She stood up, took a brush from the dressing table and smoothed down her hair. Then she turned to look at herself in the mirror by the window. And she knew that she was not going to leave.

She wondered how long it would be before someone tracked down Ann Dance. When they did Mrs Walker must be ready to defend herself.

Chapter 5

'Monsieur Macpherson, you can see that to give you thirty thousand Louis D'or when you never accounted for the first three thousand is somewhat beyond my command, even if I were to think it a good idea, my king would not. Not without some guarantees...' The speaker sat back with a graceful movement and looked enquiringly at the dark, stocky man seated opposite him.

Cluny Macpherson frowned. He had not expected to be successful on his first real attempt to gain some financial support from the French for this new Jacobite adventure. However, he knew that Frederick of Prussia had signed a treaty with France and that England now stood alone. What better time to attack from the north as they had during the Glorious 45? What better time to ask their French brothers for aid?

He leaned forward. 'My dear sir, I hope you do not think that the money was misappropriated by one of our clansmen. These are all men who would die for their rightful king. The money simply disappeared.'

The Frenchman raised his shoulders in a deprecating way. 'Ça va. Are you certain that the Hanoverians did not get it?'

'As certain as we can be. Our spies at the court of St James would have eventually heard about it. The Hanoverians could not but boast if they captured a sum of money such as that.'

There was a short silence. Outside the sea shushushed

gently against the brown shore and the seagulls cried.

'Quite so,' replied the Frenchman. 'I hope you know your men.' He turned out to look through the door at the beach and the bleak sky. 'And there is the letter. From Choiseul, our spymaster. It tells you of another seven thousand Louis D'or waiting for you in Glasgow – and the name of its keeper. This was bad for us, Cluny McPherson. That keeper was never apprehended by the Government but what if they are waiting? Waiting for our next move. It could be very bad, very bad indeed.'

'If we could find or at least trace the events surrounding the theft of that money would you reconsider our request for help?'

The Frenchman nodded slowly. He smiled. 'It is two years ago. I doubt you can discover this thing, but... Mais oui. Try.' The Frenchman stood up and brushed his muddy cloak with his gauntlet. He had a long and dangerous journey in front of him and wanted to be on his way. He doubted Macpherson would have any success in finding the whereabouts of the money. This year his agents had already repeated their search, once again painstakingly retracing the journey undertaken by the money on its way across Europe. The trail stopped at a little town in Derbyshire Ashbourgh... Ashburton... some such name. If Macpherson was to be believed, some extraordinary mischance had befallen the agent carrying the money. In the Frenchman's experience, this sort of unexpected thing did happen. Often. And, unlike the intricate plots and counterplots of espionage, these were unplanned, uncrafted things impossible to unravel. In his idle moments he liked to speculate that all across Europe there were letters of the most urgent secrecy and sums of money which would save a kingdom concealed in secret cachets, but lying, lost. Concealed under the seats of carriages, behind cabinets or clutched in the dead, rotting hands of some petty thief, apprehended by others of his kind before he could make his escape. Information, dearly bought, could lie in the hands of people who had no idea of its significance or even perhaps of its existence. Perhaps to be discovered many years later when the cause which they could affect so much no longer existed.

When some unquantifiable factor entered the equation of his world of spy and counter-spy then he recognised his inability to overcome it. The Scots wanted money but Choiseul was loath to give that drunkard Charles too much help. This could be seen as an honourable delay while Macpherson struggled to dispel the cloud of guilt hanging over his men.

After he had seen the Frenchman off in the longboat of the privateer L'Heureux, Cluny MacPherson stood staring out across Loch nan uagh.

L'Heureux. Fifteen guns lined up on each sleek flank and well able to defend itself if it should come across any of the Government frigates which continually cruised like marauding sharks through the cold, wild waters of the Inner Hebrides. Cluny Macpherson had last seen that boat on the 19th September 1746, when his Prince and his uncle, Lochiel, had boarded her, headed for safety. Macpherson had stayed behind to protect the Arisaig treasure. The precious money collected by English and Scottish Jacobites and supplemented, of course, by the French. After the failure of the uprising it had been buried near Loch Arkaig. Over the years, most of the money had been taken to France at the request of the Prince. Cluny sighed. The news of the Prince was not good. His enforced exile and the failure of his plans had brought the prince to the edge of absolute degeneration. The Arkaig treasure, so dearly paid for in men's lives, had been squandered on one man's life of indulgence and dissolution. He stood a moment longer. Soon the Prince would not be fit to lead an uprising. They had to act now, the chance may never come again.

The French had to be persuaded to help them once more.

Ashbourne. The packman. It had to start there.

o o O o o

The water felt shockingly cold. Although it was said to be a constant two degrees warmer than surface water. The spring that supplied the spa never froze, even in the coldest weather, because it came from underground, carrying the warmth of the earth with it.

The baths which provided the Hotel's revenue were in a small vaulted cavern down some steps by the Hotel's main entrance. The baths were no bigger than a reasonable wine cellar and were lit by small windows set into the half submerged walls. These walls were tiled with thousands of mosaic chips, blues and turquoises, which reflected off the surface of the pool creating a glittering, shifting appearance. If Ann half closed her eyes, the division between water and air became deliciously unclear. Only defined by the extreme, advancing cold when the margin of water crept up her legs as she felt her way down the stone steps.

Her bathing dress billowed out around her, and for a moment she could feel her feet being lifted from the floor of the pool. Then the penetrating water began to weigh the fabric of her costume down and she found it difficult to wade forwards against the cumbersome folds of cloth. She looked over her shoulder. The pool attendant had gone, leaving a thick stack of towels by the pool edge. There were no other women staying in the hotel who would be likely to rise so early for the first ladies' session so Ann was certain she would be alone. The pool attendant had locked the entrance door on her way out and Ann had the only visitors' key in her box of toiletries which lay on the stone seat in the alcove by the door.

She slipped the straps of her bathing dress off and stood up. The sodden material fell away from her body. She stepped out of it and sank back into the water, feeling the water flow unimpeded across her naked skin as she swam forwards. She rolled over onto her back and let the water shunt back and forwards across her stomach as she rose and fell in the water. Pushing her head back and pulling at pins and ribbons she let the water swirl into her hair, separating each strand of what had been quite an elaborate coiffure, carefully concocted by the insistent pool attendant for a small additional fee. Ann swam up and down the tiny pool until she was breathless.

She turned over and lay face down in the water. The sounds around her became distorted as the water entered her ears. She could hear the beating of her heart and the increasing roar of the trapped oxygen in her system. If she lay completely still they were the only sounds she could hear.

Then ... she was sure she could hear a voice calling her name... ...

Dance.

Ann Dance.

Her real name... how could that be? Her heart jolted.

She turned back over in the water and crouched down. For a moment she could see nothing but as the water cleared from her eyes she could make out a figure standing in the shadow of the alcove. She shook her head and rubbed her eyes. The figure became a recognisable shape.

It was Mr Meynell.

For a moment they both were completely still, staring at each other. Mr Meynell walked forward from the shadow cast by the alcove. From his right hand dangled the key to the baths. Her first thought was that he was alone. He had got hold of a key from somewhere and let himself in. This was the ladies' session so, by rights, he should not be here.

He saw her eyes upon the key. 'I told the clerk at the desk that I wished to see you and he gave me this key. I think it is not uncommon.' He looked a little embarrassed. It was not what he had come for.

Of course, thought Ann. Liaisons. What a perfect place.

'I saw you arrive and I enquired about you.' He held up his hand, 'Discreetly, you understand. I find that you have become Mrs Ann Walker. I am curious to say the least. How has this happened?'

Ann remained in the water and said nothing. If he spoke to James everything she had would be taken from her, including her child. Why had he come here alone? If he intended to have her arrested then he would have brought the proprietor with him at least.

Finally, she spoke. 'What do you want?'

Mr Meynell hesitated. 'I do not know. First, I think, to hear your story.' He took a step closer to the edge of the pool. 'You have risen in society. By what means? I last met you in a prison.'

By killing a man, stealing his money and living under a false name, thought Ann.

'Mr Meynell, do you intend to tell anyone what you know about me?'

He hesitated again. 'Not until I hear what you have to say.'

'Then, sir, would you leave here and allow me to dress. I will meet with you outside by the sun terrace. Do you know where that is?' Ann calculated that his curiousity would prevent him from talking to any one else until he had listened to her. At least she would have a little time to think.

'How can I be sure you will not run?'

'Mr Meynell.' Ann rose to her feet in the water.

Mr Meynell looked away from her exposed body in horrified embarrassment.

'Madam. Cover yourself, for modesty's sake.'

Ann made no move to cover herself. She smiled at his discomfort and remembered the way he had so assiduously washed his hands after touching her in the prison.

'I cannot run, Mr Meynell. I do not have a carriage ready and to attempt to escape on foot would surely not be possible. I intend to follow you out of this place in no more than six minutes. I will meet you by the plunge pool. If I am not there in six minutes you are free to set up a hue and cry for me.'

He nodded, turned and left.

March 1757 Benalder, Scotland

Cluny returned to his hiding place up on the rocky slopes of Letternilichk. This was a rough bothy, part made out of the trees and rocks which made a natural shelter and partly built up by succeeding bands of men who hid there as the troops of the Duke of Cumberland scoured the countryside hunting for Jacobites. The Prince had spent some time there in the autumn of 1746, waiting for a rescue from the French. Cluny knew he was as safe here as he could hope to be in his homeland. Until the day when it became Jacobite again.

He thought long and hard before returning to Ashbourne. He was about to undertake a well nigh impossible task. A trail dead these two years and a sojourn in what had become a very unfriendly land for the Scottish Jacobites. He thought of the last war he had fought on English soil. If they had pushed on that year, all of England would have drunk to the health of the Jacobites by December, and Charles, with his easy manner, would have been a much loved King. But that hadn't happened and Cluny Macpherson would now struggle to find friends among the English. Friends who weren't too afraid of reprisal to welcome him into their homes and offer him help.

Before he had last visited Ashbourne on that night in 1755 he had considered using a name given to him by his father-in-law Lord Lovat, just before Lovat's capture at Morar. Lovat had been most insistent that he take down this name and be always reminded of it as the name of a staunch Jacobite supporter. The name of a gentleman who had helped the cause when the Prince had stayed in Ashbourne before his hopeless but glorious procession to Derby.

Mr Amadeus Walker.

It was to the home of Mr Amadeus Walker that Cluny Macpherson wrote, asking for help in his search. He could not give too much information but he hoped that Amadeus would realise the importance of his request and see fit to help him.

MacPherson's letter arrived on the 17th May and was opened by Mrs Kitty Walker. After reading it, she sat in the study from the morning until the evening, chasing away anxious maids and heeding nothing around her. She was harking back to events which were ten years distant but still painfully fresh in her heart. The letter was addressed to her dead husband, but, as she read it, she could almost imagine that he was alive still, just as the writer thought.

Borrodale , Moidart
20th March 1757
My dear friend
I write to you as a common sympathiser in a great cause, your name being given to me by Lord Lovat, some ten years ago. I enclose a trinket which will show to you the truth of what I speak. A matter of great urgency requires that I visit England and your very town. I beg that you see fit to offer me discreet hospitality on the occasion of my travels this summer. No more can be written at this moment.
Yours
Cluny Macpherson

When Kitty Walker opened the letter a small silver medallion fell out and rolled across the floor. After she had read the letter, Kitty retrieved the medallion from where it had rolled under the window seat and examined it. It was about the size of a penny with the unmistakable profile of Bonnie Prince Charlie stamped upon it. Around the edge of the medallion were the words 'Look, love and follow'.

Kitty opened the hinged lid of the bureau at which she sat and pressed the back panel. On the top of the bureau a small catch silently sprung open. From the sliver of a secret drawer she carefully withdrew some discoloured, mottled silk which, although obviously old, yet still showed a rich blue colour in parts. She unfolded this silk and withdrew a small object from its folds.

It was a silver medallion which exactly matched the one sent to her dead husband by Cluny Macpherson.

It was these two medallions which Kitty held as she sat in her study thinking back to the past.

○ ○ O ○ ○

August 1757 New Bath Hotel

At the side of the plunge pool, admiring its views of the wild limestone gorge, sat Mr Meynell, waiting for the appearance of Mrs Ann Walker. He found himself a little excited. This was a strange business but it could be useful for him. He had taken the trouble to go to the stables and find the coach belonging to the Walkers; it was fine piece of carriage work. They were obviously a wealthy family.

Ann appeared from the hotel and approached him. She looked around. There was nobody about. It was too early in the day.

'Mr Meynell, I would rather we were not seen talking here. Perhaps you would be so kind as to walk a little way into the woods?' She indicated a rather overgrown path leading behind the hotel. 'I will go first, and then if you would be so good as to follow me after a reasonable interval?'

Ann walked off and, after few moments, Mr Meynell got up and followed her.

They met some way along the path, under the green shade of the elms which covered the slopes of the tor. It had rained earlier that morning and the air felt clean and fresh. As they walked forward together Mr Meynell found his mood changing. His certainty that Ann would be in his power began to recede. She hadn't spoken yet and seemed almost unaware of his presence.

The path narrowed and they were forced to walk in single file. Ann took the lead, and then she spoke. 'Do you remember the prison, Mr Meynell?'

'Of course I do.'

'Were you able to carry on your experiments after I left?'

'Of course. It took some time to find another subject, and the direction of my experiment was somewhat changed. But, yes.'

'A woman?'

'Yes. Mary Dilkes. A serving girl who murdered her own baby. She came into the prison two days after you …went. Perhaps you have heard of her? She was something of a notoriety by the time she hanged. Her story was told in the Derby Mercury.'

Ann shook her head.

Mr Meynell looked surprised.

The public had been fascinated and horrified by a woman who could murder her own child almost as it drew its first breath. His anatomy classes had been well attended when the body on the slab belonged to the infamous child murderer. Mr Meynell recalled with satisfaction a very profitable few days dissecting her body for the young men of the academy. 'I had hoped that the brain would be of especial interest. I have been thinking of publishing an article on the peculiarities of the brains of the criminals I have dissected.' He paused, looking a little disgruntled. 'But unfortunately so far I have not been able to discover any discernible anomalies yet. All brains look remarkably similar.'

'How much time did you have to work with Mary Dilkes before she hanged?' Ann thought of the condemned woman. Perhaps the experiment had given her another year of life.

'Very little, I'm afraid... it was difficult to get support from the prison governers immediately after your escape.' He looked at her reproachfully. 'Although in the last few years my work has been accepted to be of the greatest importance.' Mr Meynell was warming to the task of explaining it to her. 'Yes. The electrical stimulation of the nervous system. She had become mute you see. On entering prison. But,' he raised his right hand up and lightly tapped his chest triumphantly, 'I was able to make her talk again.' He sighed. 'Unfortunately there was some severe damage to the tongue. Burns, you know. And then some kind of paralysis of the facial muscles, and so what she said was unintelligible. But, nevertheless, she did try to speak. So – a success, I think. Most certainly.' He smiled with satisfaction.

He picked his way carefully around a puddle, still engrossed in his subject. 'Of course, my machinery was crudely developed then. My latest work has been more rewarding. The current is now much more extensive in range and I can almost always guarantee a response, even if only an involuntary one from the spinal area.' They had reached a viewing point. From here, walkers who wished to stop and take a rest could stand together on a small semi-circle of trodden earth and look down the steep scree towards the village of Matlock Bath. As Mr Meynell drew alongside

Ann, she briefly touched his arm to steady herself. His eyes travelled down to the fine curve of her waist, encased in close fitting silk brocade. She moved towards him and stood very close to him. He found her proximity disturbing and attempted to move away but he was pressed up against the safety rail and could retreat no further.

Ann put her hands up to take off her hat. Then she turned to Mr Meynell and smiled directly at him. To his horror she reached her left hand up to stroke his face affectionately and brought her other arm up to clasp his neck. Mr Meynell thought he caught a glimpse of something metallic as the sun burst out from behind the clouds. But he could not be certain.

Ann pushed the six-inch hat pin she held in her right hand into the indentation just below Mr Meynell's skull, exactly at the centre of the back of his neck. Her hand was shaking but she pushed hard and firm. The hat pin entered at an angle of ninety degrees, fatally perforating what Mr Meynell would have identified as the cerebellum, the centre of all human movement. She then gave his sinking body a shove which sent it out over the lip of the viewing point and plunging down the steep slope towards the village. Mr Meynell's life had ceased long before his body came to rest precariously against a young sycamore tree in the copse above the nearest house on the Matlock road.

His body would lie there for a few hours before it was noticed by a boy using the path as a shortcut. The body didn't seem to have been badly damaged in the fall. The local doctor who examined it could only find evidence of the right leg being broken in two places and the neck being twisted. There would probably be some serious damage to the brain, the head did seem somewhat swollen. Of course an autopsy was out of the question so far from Derby and anyway, cause of death was obvious. A fall.

Late that afternoon, two workmen from the hotel put up a sturdy fence at the viewing point.

Ann spent all of the evening in bed. As she had told the concerned under-manager, she had taken a walk down to the village and had returned exhausted, having walked up the long drive in the heat of the afternoon. James was concerned on his return to find her so low. He was only glad that she hadn't taken a walk along the top path and found the body of unfortunate Mr Meynell. She would have scarcely been able to withstand the shock.

In the early hours of the next morning, Ann got out of the bed she shared with her husband and sat on the window seat of their room. She wrapped herself in the softness of her shawl and hugged her feet up in her dressing gown. She found herself crying, and knew that she cried from relief. There had been only one thing of which Ann had been uncertain. Could she be quick enough, decisive enough, sure enough to look Mr Meynell in the eyes, pull him close, and kill him? And she had.

If she had failed, if she had just wounded him, then what? She thought about the possibilities. Mr Meynell could accuse her of a vicious attack. He could attempt to expose her as an imposter. He might succeed. She could imagine the scenes at the hotel.   But that far out of Derby, with no-one to verify his story, he might just as well fail to be convincing. Yet she had to remove his threat. If he lived he would make sure that Ann Walker ceased to exist.
The packhorse man had been on his way to death. But the killing of Meynell had been a deliberate taking of life. She had murdered him. Again, she saw his startled eyes as she had moved closer. Felt the sudden slump of his body as she thrust the pin in deep under his skull. She knew that it

could be done, a clever way of killing that couldn't be detected, but had not trusted her ability to do it. She felt no remorse, but a strange, dull dreariness spread its way through her.

She had to sleep, but she could not get back into bed beside James. She was afraid that somehow the thoughts that swirled through her head would transfer themselves to him, and he would know what she had done. She squeezed herself into a corner between the folds of curtain and the wooden shutter on the window seat. She closed her eyes and felt sleep drift over her, only to struggle to wake up, a few moments later, from a sudden, vivid dream of hanging. A rope around her neck and then the drop.

Gasping for breath, she laid her hot face against the window. Gradually her heart slowed. She glanced over to James but he seemed to still be sleeping soundly. Below lay the empty hotel garden, a silent, private place closed off from the outside world by a high stone wall. Everything was bathed in bright, cold moonlight. Her eye was drawn to a wooden door set into the wall. That would lead out to the walk. The walk she had taken with Mr Meynell. She had an overpowering sense that the door was going to open and he would walk in to the garden and stare up at this window, knowing where she sat. Something swooped silently across the lawns and she shrank back against the window seat, but it was only an owl. She shook her head. Ridiculous. The dead did not come back.

She thought of Mary Dilkes.

It was Mary Dilkes who had been murdered. Who, by rights, should come back to haunt those who had killed her. She had been murdered by men and women like Mr Meynell, who could crowd round her in a dark, filthy cell and observe her reactions to the exciting electric-shock machine, careful to keep their fine cloth away from the ordure around them. Mary had walked to the gallows unable to speak, an object of hate and derision, with no one to raise a voice for her.

Anger welled up inside Ann. But there wasn't time to indulge in anger. She took a deep breath. The realities of her situation had to be addressed.

She considered what her meeting with Mr Meynell meant. He had recognised her, that was true. But he was a man trained to be observant. Few other people would share his perceptive eye and few would have his confidence in their own perception. As the years went by, she would look less and less like the woman from the streets of Derby. Danger would decrease, not increase. The same was true of the danger from the money. As the years went by, the likelihood of any search being made receded. She would become increasingly safe.

Her legs were getting stiff. She stretched them out in front of her and yawned. She was tired. It was time to go to sleep. She crossed the moonlit room and slid into the bed beside James.

Ann let herself sink gently down into the routine of their days at the hotel.

When her mind turned to Mr Meynell she deliberately brought it back to the present. She allowed herself to be cared for, to be an object of concern. At meal times she smiled at the waiters, accepting small gifts of food, possets and warming soups. Out of the trunks of clothes chosen by Kitty came light cotton jackets and skirts for the morning, heavier plaid or woollen dresses for the afternoon and dresses of slipper satin and velvet for the dining room in the evenings. Three times a day Ann was dressed by her maid. First the layers of under skirts, then stays, then a bodice which the girl laced tightly down the back and then the final outer layer, a swirl of colour and rich fabric. Buttoned and laced and tied, Ann's appearance said what she was. Maids curtsied as they passed her in the corridor and she inclined her head a little in return. If she stepped outside and the air was cool she waited patiently while a girl was sent to fetch her warm cloak. If the sun shone, a parasol was put into her hand. Ann took exercise, as advised, by walking around the hotel grounds and as she was deemed stronger, she went out on trips by carriage to see the sights of the area.

She continued to turn her mind away from the moment when she had pushed the hat pin into the brain of Mr Meynell.

His death had been necessary. He would have destroyed her as quickly and with less conscience. The only difference being that he would have had someone else to do it for him. Someone paid by the law of this land to deal out justice to people like her. Like Mary Dilkes.

Hulland House Ashbourne August 1757

Kitty had sent word to Mr Macpherson telling him that, although Amadeus Walker had died over a year ago, Mr Macpherson would be welcomed in her home as he would have been welcomed by Amadeus and, on the 21st of August, Cluny Macpherson presented himself at the door of Hulland House. He had come to Ashbourne, as before, on horseback and alone. On the morning of the second day after his arrival, Kitty received him in the drawing room, hardly knowing what to expect. The Jacobites who had visited her house so briefly in 1745, had been well mannered men. Soft of speech and able to enjoy good wine and good company. But she did not remember this man and the urgency and the secretiveness of his letter could imply something else. And what could he tell her of the prince? Charlie. She had waited years to hear that name spoken aloud again.

'Madam, first may I thank you for your generosity. I know this could cost you dear and I promise efforts to reduce the danger to you and your family will be uppermost in my mind.' Cluny spoke with sincerity and with that respectful formality which Kitty remembered so well.

'Thank you, Mr Macpherson, I appreciate your concern, but England is no longer at war with Jacobite rebels and so I think I am quite within the law to have you as a guest in my house.'

Cluny smiled wearily. 'Unfortunately matters are not as simple as that. Would that they were.'

'Mr Macpherson, there is a matter on which I would like some information and it strikes me that you may be able to help.' Kitty gathered the scrap of faded blue silk which she held in her hand. ' The Prince.' Her voice faltered. 'He is safe, in Italy? Not captured ...' her breath failed on the word, 'as we read ... sometimes. Tell me Mr Macpherson, were you with him when he escaped.' She looked at him with such piercing intensity that Cluny replied immediately. Matching her passion with his own.

'Ay, madam, I was there and no man was braver than the Prince.'

'Tell me some of it... if you will. I beg you. It is better to know something of these things. I have come to think that over the years.' She spoke very quietly now and it seemed to Cluny that he was witnessing the result of many hours of struggle with great sadness. He would tell her all that he could.

For a moment, Cluny became lost in memories of those terrible days in London. Hiding from Hanoverian agents, hoping that the impossible would happen and the nightmare of failure would end in a wild surge of London Jacobite fervour. But the people watched as Scottish lords were put to death and cheered as the executioner's axe fell. Among these people stood Cluny Macpherson, determined to be near as his kinsmen and brothers in arms faced their fate. Near enough to mutter a prayer in the Gaelic... *Agus tha duil agam ri Aiseirigh nam marbh, Agus ri beatha an t-*

saoghail a tha ri teachd Amen... as each man died. But amongst all that, the Prince had made him smile.

Kitty saw the smile pass over his face. 'Pray continue, sir.' She wanted to know everything that he could tell her.

Cluny cleared his throat and began to speak again, his voice deep with emotion. 'He made light of his predicament, madam. Treating all with courtesy but refusing to give the courts that would catch and try him any credence. He conducted himself with no fear, madam and kept up all our spirits. He took great amusement in the fact that he was in London, under their noses, while his double was busy escaping off the coast of Scotland.' Cluny smiled at the thought. Then his mood changed. 'Only once I found him in tears.' Cluny remembered the Prince with his head in his hands. 'It was after he heard of Lord Lovat's death on the scaffold.' He said to me, 'Cluny, Lovat has died a hero. God willing, I can do the same.'

Kitty did not speak. She stood up and crossed the room to the fireplace, reaching up to take down the highland Skean Dhu which lay on the mantelpiece. The heavy dagger lay across her hands. As Cluny watched, she brought it up to her lips and kissed the ornate hilt then she carefully placed the dagger back on the mantel. She stood for a moment with the fingers of both hands spread on the edge of the mantelpiece and her head bowed. She seemed to be reciting something under her breath. There was a weariness in her body which told Cluny that this ritual had been repeated many times over the years.

Eventually she turned to him. 'Your Prince handed the Skean Dhu to me on the day he left Derbyshire.' She crossed the room, stopping at the door to look back at him. 'I would like you to meet my youngest son, Mr Macpherson.'

Macpherson sat waiting. His mind was still back in London at the foot of the scaffold. Then the word 'son' came to the front of his mind. Kitty had said 'son'. There had been a particular emphasis on the word. Why would she wish for him to meet her youngest son? In a few moments Kitty re-entered the room with a boy of about ten years of age.

Macpherson looked a long time at the boy who stood patiently where his mother told him. Kitty then ushered her son to the door, sent him on his way and turned to face Cluny.

He said nothing, too overcome with emotion to speak. Then he crossed the floor and knelt at Kitty's feet, taking her hand in his and kissing it. 'Madam,' he said, rising.

'Madam, I will guard that boy's life with mine.' He bent his head and kissed Kitty's hand again.

'I thought you would see the likeness. I see it in the blue of his eyes. The Stuart blue,' said Kitty. 'My husband saw it, but said nothing. He preferred to leave it all uncovered. He was a wise man. I loved him dearly.' She came closer to Macpherson. 'But, for your Prince, I would have given my life,' she whispered.

'Madam,' replied Cluny Macpherson, 'I am glad that that sacrifice was never needed. But I must explain to you the nature of my business here in Ashbourne. After listening to me you may feel that, for the safety of your family, you had better ask me to leave.'

How would she take what he had to say? She would be afraid, and she might refuse to help him.

'Madam. Another uprising is planned in the north.'

Kitty's eyes widened.

'The French will support us.'

Kitty nodded and began to speak but Cluny raised his hand. 'There are conditions. Two years ago, the French sent us 3,000 Louis D'or but it was lost. I came to Ashbourne to take it from its carrier but he did not meet me. I could find no trace of him.' Cluny thought again of that night and the hopelessness which had overwhelmed him as time had passed and Echan had not appeared. 'I have come back to try once more to find out what happened to the money. That is why I am here. If I cannot trace this money then the French will refuse to give us any further help and the third rebellion will not take place.'

He looked around the room. 'Madam, it is dangerous for you to help me. It is dangerous for you to have me staying under your roof.' He paused. 'Yet I need your help.' He wanted to persuade her and yet he wished to be completely honest. 'It is possible that Government agents are also looking for this money. They will certainly be looking for any known Jacobites who suddenly appear in an English town.'

It was Kitty's turn to put up her hand. 'Mr Macpherson. Firstly, you are not a known Jacobite. In the last few moments you have become Mr Anderson, who is in trade. I seem to remember you, Mr Anderson. You were a friend of my husband's.' She smiled. 'Not every Scotsman is a danger to the crown.' Her face became more serious. 'Secondly, I thank you for your warning but I do understand the danger to myself and my family. I know that Hanoverian agents are often to be found in places like this.' She glanced out of the window. 'Where else? A town with many roads, one of them leading to London. This is a market town, Mr Macpherson, used to strangers, where a man might hide undetected – for a time.'

She leaned forward. 'Mr Macpherson – two French muskets were found in a cart of cloth two weeks ago.' She sat back. 'Who had smuggled them in? Who had told the government men where to look? It has to be someone in this town.'

She shook her head. 'This is how it is now. My sons take their trade to Holland, to Amsterdam, and they tell me that every English port, every market place is guarded and every trader who ventures into Europe with his goods is watched. However innocent.' She paused thinking back.

'We were under a little particular suspicion after the '45. The friendliness of my husband to the invading Jacobite army ensured that, but since Amadeus' death, we have been considered safe enough to leave alone. So you see –' She smiled again, 'I doubt one strange Scotsman will make any difference.'

'Brave words, Madam, but surely your known connections to the Jacobites in the past mean that you should be all the more careful to show me your door?' It had to be said. She had to understand.

Kitty shook her head. 'Oh no, Mr Macpherson. Amadeus is dead, and as I said, as a poor widow woman I would not be suspected of furthering his dealings with rebels. I will not show you the door. You can rest assured.'

She looked away from him then and her face saddened as she thought of the man they called the Young Pretender. He was not part of this, she thought. He had not hidden in doorways or kept watch on his enemies, waiting his time. He had followed his cause and led his men because it was his clear duty to do it.

'Do not fear, Mr Macpherson. This is not recklessness. I am not a foolish woman. I know the possible consequences of my actions.' She hesitated. How to say it? 'But I also know the consequences to myself if I stand aside and do nothing. And they are certain.' She folded her hands in front of her. 'Quite simply, Mr Macpherson, I could not live with myself.'

'The Prince is a passionate man' – that was what Lady Dungeld had said to her on the second night Kitty had stayed in the royal rooms and Kitty had understood that she was being given a warning.

'And, my dear Kitty, Charles Stuart has a desire to generate the same degree of passion in others. He will do this with man or woman, with politics or love. His delight is the chase of another person's allegiance. Of course, when he has won you,' Lady Dungeld had paused for effect, 'his interest quickly cools.'

Kitty had seen the jealousy in the other woman's eyes and had dismissed her words. But now she could see that Lady

Dungeld had been telling her the truth. Charles Stuart had left Derbyshire within three days of his arrival, leaving her pregnant with his child. She had never heard from him again. She placed her hand protectively across her stomach as she thought of those months.

Amadeus. He had come to take her home from the house on Friargate, a house whose owners wanted back now that the rebels had gone. Amadeus, finding her sitting alone on the great bed. Gathering all her things into two great holdalls and placing her in the carriage. He had wrapped a blanket around her legs as if she had been ill.

She had wanted to die. Time seemed out of shape. Each day stretching and stretching unbearably. She felt that she had sunk under the surface of life into some slow-moving under-pool of the dead. And then she had found that she was with child, and her head seemed to come bursting through the surface again. For a few days she had thought of sending a message to the Prince, but then she realised that it was too late. The rebel leaders were in London. They would die. The father of her unborn child had fled for his life. He could be of no help to her.

Amadeus had watched her for years as she tended her grief. Accepting Charles as his own son. Never questioning her about her time in Friargate. And she had continued to cling to the small, unspoken hope that somehow the prince would remember her. He might escape his watchers in Italy. He might come back for her. Now, Cluny Macpherson sat in front of her, the lilt of his voice redolent for her with memories of this man. A man she now knew for certain had never spoken of her even to his closest companion. She closed her eyes for a moment and drank in the sound, the idea of him. The Bonnie Prince. It was a heady pleasure. Made more powerful because of Cluny's presence, and more painful.

Kitty looked at Cluny. He wore no wig, his dark hair was matted and tied behind with a makeshift leather strip. He did not look like those elegant men who had entered her house in 1745. He smelt of the sweat of his long journey and his eyes betrayed his terrible anxiety. Only that softness of speech reminded her of the Jacobite lords who had sat at her table all those years ago.

Then, with a shock she realised that if Charles had been caught he would have looked like this man. Worse. His fine clothes would have been fouled, they would have broken his body with torture and his eyes would have been dark with fear as he stood in front of the executioner.

'Tell me again, Mr Macpherson, what did the Prince say?' she said softly.

Cluny tried to find the words he thought she would want. 'He said to us that the English were chasing a pretend Pretender up in the Highlands, when if they came to London they would find the real Pretender very near their throne!'

Bravado. But more than that, a signal, an arrow of courage flying out to the men who stood there, listening to him. Men who had drifted inexorably to Tower Hill to see their leaders executed one by one. Who needed to dredge up enough hope to keep themselves alive.

She sat quietly for a moment. *She had not known the Prince. This man had known him.* Had fought beside him. She was struggling to understand. If she had not known the man then what had she loved? It was something in him, something she had recognised because it was also in her. And she had not known what it was until today.

Courage. The courage to take action.

Cluny saw her smile. 'Perhaps I am a foolish woman, Mr Macpherson, when all is said and done. If it is foolish to offer you help then I am a fool. But I am glad to be one.'

She held out her hand to him and he grasped it in both of his own.

Chapter 6

September 1757 Ashbourne

Ann and James returned to Ashbourne on the first day of September. She seemed stronger to James and had showed no signs of a relapse into her former state, not after that first day of over exertion, at any rate. The visit to Matlock Bath had been a success.

That first night of their return there was an air of celebration as the the whole family sat down together to dine for the first time in many weeks. Kitty was pleased to have all the members of her family together again.

'This is Mr Anderson,' she said, looking to the other end of the table where Cluny Mcpherson was seated. 'He is an old friend of your father's. A very good friend, and he has come to Derbyshire on business.'

She raised her glass, 'Mr Anderson, I am delighted to welcome you to our house once again. As would be Amadeus if he were here.'

Cluny raised his glass in a silent return of her salute.

'What business brings you to Derbyshire, Mr Anderson,' asked Edward. It was more than a polite enquiry. There could be trading to be done.

'I deal in oats and wheat from the port of Glasgow.' Cluny leaned forward and toyed with his glass. He shrugged, 'I had some farmers to see in Derbyshire with a view to taking their surplus crops. Your mother kindly invited me to stay with you here. I am very grateful.' Cluny looked around at them all, this part of his story was true. 'And only sorry to hear of your loss. I did not know.'

Edward nodded. He had no interest in wheat and oats. Kitty had suggested this area of commerce to Cluny as it was one in which neither of her two sons dealt and therefore would be less likely to uncover any untruths. As it so happened Edward was eager to discuss with James the possibility of trading in fine glass with the Netherlands through a mercer in London, who would act as agent. This discussion took up most of the evening and Mr Anderson was free to retire early.

Ann left the dining room and made her way back to the nursery where she had mostly been since her arrival back. Mr Anderson appeared to be relaxed and unconcerned with matters other than common politenesses. But she could not quieten her fears. Was it just coincidence which brought Mr Anderson here from Scotland, so soon after a French agent, for she was sure that was what he had been, into Ashbourne? And a close friend of Amadeus, who had been dead for over a year, and yet this Mr Anderson did not know of his death?

She straightened the coverlet on Adam's cot and lightly brushed her fingers across the baby's forehead. How could she find out more about Mr Anderson? She could hardly question him, and in any case, she felt it was better that she stayed away from him. A glance or the wrong word – anything might betray her. If he had been sent by the government he may already have some information, only be waiting for the final pieces of his jigsaw. A thin wail of hunger rose from the cot. She picked Adam up, cradling him against her shoulder. He turned his face towards her, his mouth seeking food, but she had no milk since her illness. Mary had set a dish of cow's milk and honey to warm by the fire. Ann picked it up and settled in the nursing chair. She began to spoon the sweet mixture into Adam's mouth. Soon his eyes began to close again. She put him back on her shoulder and rocked him back and forth.

She would keep away from Mr Anderson.

Cluny Macpherson spent his first weeks in Derbyshire

retracing the route by which the money must have come from Derby. He rode out from Ashbourne down the sixteen miles to Derby and spent a night in each of the hostelries on his way back along the route, asking if anyone had knowledge of a packhorse man named Rudge. It was not likely that anyone would know the names of any packhorse men, since they quite often would sleep out with their beasts and their loads, not leaving them for fear of theft. However, Rudge had been travelling in the early spring and therefore may have sought shelter. But no-one could remember a Rudge, at any time during the last two years.

Before he had left Ashbourne, Cluny had visited the Plough Inn, where he remembered the landlady telling him of a packhorse man who had died. But she had moved on and no-one seemed to remember the incident.

On the fifth night of his journey, Cluny entered the Black Horse Inn at Hulland Ward and asked his questions again. Mr Cooper, the landlord of the Black Horse Inn recognised the Highland accent and was curious about Cluny's reasons for asking questions.

The marching Jacobite army had passed through Hulland Ward on their way to Derby. It had been a memorable occasion for the landlord. He could still taste the fear in his mouth as he listened to the rumble of the gun carriages and the sound of the marching footsteps of the approaching army. And then, to his horror, in a flurry of tartan plaid and jostling horses, the Prince himself had appeared outside.

He had leaned down from his horse and looked straight through the doorway at Mr Cooper, eyes as blue as his bonnet. 'Come on, landlord, serve your new king!' There was laughter from the men behind him, but Mr Cooper thought he saw the flash of a sword.

He had rushed to serve them, putting his very best on the table, playing the game of mine host but with his mouth dry as parchment, not expecting any payment and only hoping to avoid pain. The Prince had drunk his claret, thanked the landlord for it and had thrown two Louis d'or on to the table and got up to leave.

'Sir! This is too much.' Mr Cooper had remonstrated, picking up the money and offering it back to the prince. 'Two Louis d'or is a ridiculously large sum for some pots of ale!'

A tall, hitherto silent man of the party, laughed heartily at this and clapped Cooper sympathetically on the shoulder as the entourage left. The innkeeper had not understood why until he had gone out to his stable to find that all of his horses, even those for the London coach, had been taken and, with them, every bale of hay and piece of tackle which had lain there.

Since then, a Scots accent brought an involuntary shudder to the landlord and he had been delighted to read of the executions in London. But he still listened out in case he heard that dreadful rumbling, jingling sound again. Who could tell? The world was not yet securely set upon one path, as the innkeeper told his customers. The Prince had seemed so sure of himself that morning.

He now took an interest in any strangers, but particularly ones with northern accents. Best to appear helpful to all. There were two packhorsemen in the stables, eating their supper. Did Cluny wish to speak with them? They travelled the Derbyshire roads at all times and must know everyone in the business of moving goods.

Cluny met with the two men. In the peaceful, musty stables, with the horses tethered nearby, he watched the men companionably share their supper of pie and ale. They weren't in a hurry to answer his questions.

Eventually one of them stopped chewing and wiped his face. He shrugged dismissively. 'There might be something for you.' Cluny's heart leapt.

At last, and against all probability, by the greatest good fortune, had he found the last traces of the missing money?

The Jacobite cause looked possible again.

But he was to be disappointed.

'Last Michaelmas a Frenchie came asking the same question as you. Now there's some as would ask,' the man looked meaningfully at his companion, '– what are a Frenchie and a Scotchman doing asking the same questions? But I don't.' He shook his head to emphasise his indifference.

'Did he also ask for a man named Rudge?'

The man nodded. 'But couldn't oblige then and can't oblige now. Sorry.' The two men carried on eating their supper, without rancour and without further interest in Cluny's business. They knew their information wasn't worth payment. As Cluny left the stables he was overcome with weariness. He remembered eating on the road like those two men, sharing food and drink with friends. Many of those friends were dead now and others waited for the call to arms that would absolve them of the guilt of those deaths.

Cluny returned to the barroom and thought about the implications of the recent French search. Obviously, they were anxious to find out the truth of the matter. And if they had not found anything then Cluny knew that his chances were reduced. He also knew now that the French expected him to fail. Had made sure of this probability by searching themselves. He knew that if he could find nothing then the French would not expect to be called upon to honour their "auld alliance" with the Highlanders and fund the Jacobite cause.

A figure stopped at his shoulder. Cluny thought it was the potboy and shook his head. He never drank overmuch ale. He must always keep a clear head. The figure did not move away. Cluny looked up.

'Sir,' the boy said. 'Mistress Wibberley asks would you be so kind as to join her in a drink?'

Cluny shook his head at the woman sitting over by the

window. He had no need of her kind of business tonight.

'No, boy. Thank her, but I would not.'

Cluny finished his ale, took his leave of the landlord and climbed the steep stairs to the back bedroom of the inn. He had no wish now but to lose himself in sleep. The bed, which he had checked earlier, was a lumpy straw pallet, but clean and sufficient. The inn was quiet and, since there was only him and the two packhorse men, who preferred to sleep in the stables, he could be sure of having the room to himself.

The next day Cluny arose and attempted to put himself in a better frame of mind. As a soldier he was accustomed to setbacks and just as accustomed to facing them and designing ways of surmounting them. He would continue his search. He must be methodical. However unlikely the possibility of his success he had to carry on. There was simply no other course open to him at the moment.

In the stables, the boy who had spoken to him last night was brushing down the horses. Cluny gave him a coin and talked to him about the horses for a while as he saddled up his horse. For the want of something else to say, he teased the lad about his errand for Mistress Wibberley the night before. The boy looked confused.

'Oh no, sir,' he finally said, at last understanding Cluny's drift. 'Mistress Wibberley was not doing that kind of business. She's a respectable woman. Used to be a landlady in Ashbourne until she took bad with gout. She used to keep a fine house. My brother worked there. The Plough Inn on Sturston Street.'

Cluny leapt towards the boy and gripped him by the collar of his jerkin. 'The Plough Inn, you say? Where,' he said, 'where does Mistress Wibberley live now, boy?'

The boy saw how eager Cluny was for information and became sly.

He turned his face away. 'I don't rightly know sir,' he said

167

slowly.

Cluny let the boy go and straightened up. He attempted to control his eagerness. It would only bring suspicion. He reached into his pocket and brought out some coins. Quite a few coins. The boy looked at the coins and then at him, speculatively.

Cluny jingled the coins in his hand. 'There's some money in it if you take me to Mistress Wibberley's house.' He darted forward and gripped the boy once more by his jerkin collar. 'On the other hand I'll break every bone in your body if you don't,' he hissed.

The boy recoiled as Cluny's warm spittle landed on his left cheek.

'All right, sir.' He realised that there was no more room for argument.

Mrs Wibberley lived not far from the Black Horse. As they got near to her cottage, Cluny gave the boy his money and let him go. The fewer people who saw him visit Mrs Wibberley the better. She must have something to tell him. But what? The landlady of The Plough. She must have recognised him in the taproom. He had asked her questions, the same questions he was asking now, two years ago. But why had he stuck in her mind. A brief discussion in the yard of her inn on a chilly February morning? Two years ago? What else had happened to make the name of Rudge stay in her mind?

Mrs Wibberley was pleased that he had come. She had no need of money but since leaving The Plough her life had lacked interest and here was an opportunity to be, however briefly, at the centre of something. She told Cluny Macpherson that the day after he had come to The Plough asking questions about a Mr Rudge two men had appeared at The Green Man. She took a breath. They enquired if anyone had been looking for a Mr Rudge. She had only known because she often shared deliveries of hay from Cockayne's fields and had been told about this by the stableman from the Green Man. The gentlemen had asked if there had been any visitors from northern parts. The stableman had been able to tell these gentlemen that they had had a Northener staying overnight but that he had gone. She hesitated and looked at Cluny. 'That would have been yourself, sir?' Cluny nodded. The men had then asked to see the room where he...Mr... her voice tailed off until he helped her.

'Mr Anderson.'

She nodded. 'Well, Mr Anderson.' A slight disbelieving emphasis on the name. 'Well. Those men ransacked your room.' She shook her head at the memory of that story. The stableman had told her that the men had shut themselves in the room and proceeded to rip it to bits. Nothing like it had ever happened at The Green Man before. When the landlord and his men broke into the room to protest, the two men said that they were Government agents and could do as they pleased... and that the landlord of The Green Man and his henchmen would all be hung for traitors if they didn't shut up. Mrs Wibberley looked steadfastly into Cluny's face as she recounted this story. She was eager for a reaction but Cluny simply nodded solemnly.

Cluny asked if anybody had been given the name of these men or could describe them to him but Mrs Wibberley couldn't help him further. They had not visited The Plough so she had no more information on them. Perhaps The Green Man? She believed the same man was in charge of the stables there as was on the night of the disturbance two years ago. Mr Shoesmith, William Shoesmith.

Cluny rode back into Ashbourne later that morning. Down the road Ann had walked along after her escape from prison. He passed Bradley Wood where Ann had lain sleeping on that February night two years ago and had no idea how near he was to the beginning of his story. At The Green Man he asked for Mr William Shoesmith and the stableman presented himself to Cluny in the yard of the inn. 'Well sir, ye've asked for me and you've got me. Now, what do you want with me?' He looked over his shoulder at the men cleaning the yard as if impatient to be off and join them.

Cluny swung down from his horse. 'I have spoken to Mrs Wibberley, who was once landlady of The Plough.'

Mr Shoesmith's eyes brightened. Obviously the landlady of The Plough was a fond memory.

'She tells me you were here on the night two years ago when two ruffians calling themselves Government agents caused some trouble here.'

Mr Shoesmith considered him carefully and thought for a while. 'I was, sir.' He flicked some dirt off the prongs of the fork he was carrying as if he had lost interest in the story, then he stared hard at Cluny. 'What would you be wanting to ask me about that night?'

'Do you know the names of the men who were here asking for Mr Rudge?'

'No sir. They didn't exactly give their names.' There was a touch of irony in the man's voice which did not go unmissed by Cluny.

'I suppose they didn't tell you why they were looking for Mr Rudge either, did they?' he said.

Mr Shoesmith smiled. 'Now that you say, sir, I don't rightly think that they did.'

Cluny sighed. Even if these men had been Hanoverian agents it merely confirmed what the Jacobite spies at court had said. The money had not been taken by the Hanoverians. But it looked like it soon would have been. The English Jacobite band must have been penetrated by government agents or exposed by their own carelessness, which was often the case. Few men were disciplined enough to live daily in the country of their enemy without giving themselves away by a word or a look. Mr Rudge, alias Echan MacLean, would have been dead by Government hands and so might he, had they been a day earlier. But, if Government agents had not found Echan MacLean and the French were still looking for him, then who had killed him and taken the money? Cluny Macpherson would not accept the other possibility. That Echan MacLean had taken the money and left no trace of himself.

Mr Shoesmith had been watching his inquisitor. Obviously the man had some kind of trouble. But he was keeping most of it close to his chest. Mr Shoesmith liked that.

Which was why he told Cluny what he knew. He had mistrusted Mistress Challinor from the start. She was a fake, he was sure of it. He had bought her packhorses off her after her husband had died so sudden. He remembered it clear. He hadn't believed her story. She had surely been a trollop, picked up by the packhorse man on his travels. It often happened. Bit of company for the man, protection of a sort for the woman. Now he wasn't saying she knew nothing about packhorses. She did. But she didn't know those particular packhorses any better than some she'd caught sight of in a field. And that's what alerted his suspicions. She should have known 'em. If she'd been on the road with her husband, she couldn't avoid knowing the darn things. Their hooves, their habits, their names, even. She knew none of this and yet she sold those horses to him, bold as brass. Only that wasn't the right description for Ann Challinor. Not brass. She was quiet. A quiet woman. But bold. Yes, she was bold. Mr Shoesmith's storytelling came to a climax and he stopped to draw a big breath, keeping watch on Cluny's face, to see if he still had his attention. Cluny Macpherson's face showed nothing. 'So, you see, sir. If you want to find out about what happened that night, what happened to that Mr Rudge, you'd better ask Mrs Challinor.' He emphasised the name with clumsy sarcasm. 'I've thought about this long since. There were no other pack trains in

Ashbourne that night. So if you're looking for one, then that has to be it. I fancy something strange has gone on.'

'Where can I find this Mrs Challinor?' he asked, not convinced that Mr Shoesmith's reasoning was sound but aware that it was the only lead he had.

'Where else but at Hulland House. Down Church Street.' Mr Shoesmith pointed in that direction. 'Mrs Challinor's become Mrs Walker. But I don't forget who I deal with. She'll always be Mrs Challinor to me.'

Cluny was dumbfounded. For a moment he thought that the stableman meant Kitty but then he realised. Ann Challinor. Ann Walker. 'You do mean Mrs Ann Walker, wife of James Walker of Church Street?'

'Aye. That's the one. That's the one.' Mr Shoesmith moved off. A backward glance over his shoulder told him that he could be confident that his story had been a good one, told to the right person. Cluny Macpherson stood as if paralysed, heeding nothing as the din of the busy yard continued around him.

This news was of the utmost significance. Mrs Ann Walker was not, apparently, what she seemed. And if she wasn't what she seemed then what was she? How did she fit into this puzzle? Had it been a Mr Challinor who died that night or had it been Echan MacLean? Had Echan somehow picked her up before Ashbourne and... then... had she killed him? For the money? Had she seen the money? Was it simple theft? Or was she working for some other agency? But what? And did Kitty Walker know? Cluny swung his horse out along Church Street towards Hulland House, determined to find out.

As Cluny led his horse into the stables behind Hulland House he caught sight of Ann Walker in the garden, sitting by the bassinet which contained her infant son. She made a pretty picture but it did not affect Cluny Macpherson's heart. He had seen too many other pictures. He looked away for a moment and thought of his clansmen in hopeless battle, of their children starving.

Cluny had not immediately rallied to the standard of King James. He had not been among the Jacobites to greet Prince Charles when he landed at Lochanna in July, 1745. Like Donald, Young Lochiel, the chief of the Camerons, he was wary of embroiling his clansmen in another exhausting struggle with the superior fighting machine of the Hanoverians. He held a commission in Lord Loudon's English army. He could have stayed on the side of King George.

When the Government forces were gathering in the highlands in response to the landing in Scotland of Prince Charles Stuart, Cluny Macpherson had reported for duty at Dalwhinnie. When he made his decision to turn himself and therefore his clan to the banner of the Jacobites he had known that the chances of success were slight. He had made the decision knowing the bloodshed that might ensue and knowing that the responsibility for that bloodshed would lie with him. He had made the decision because of his great love for his country. When he had waited with his clansmen in the streets of Dalwhinnie to be seen by General Cope he had realised that in this place he was no longer a leader but a useful vassal. Cope's officers had no interest in the people and the land of the highlands. The traditions and the honour of fealty from each man to his clan was useful in swelling the numbers of those fighting but not of any other value. As Cluny sat upon his horse, watching the

Lowlanders and the English at their business, seeing the extent of their armoury, the extent of their combined investment in this exercise, he knew he was witnessing the successors to his culture. He sat there, a dark, swarthy man, wrapped in rough plaid, who had lived in France and who spoke Latin. Cluny was a product of a way of life which was a man's only possible response to the inhospitable nature of the mountain land. One man was leader, the cost of learning was invested in one man who would then use it for the benefit of all. The land would support no other way. Above all, a clan chief was of one blood with his people. His leadership was a tacit agreement which brought with it a terrible responsibility, the honouring of which could exact death.

To the merchant entrepreneurs of Glasgow, he was a remnant of out-dated feudalism and to these men of Cope's army, the dark figure hunched against the rain on the back of his horse was a barbarian and his men were scarcely human. After one hour, Cluny had turned his horse and ridden out of Dalwhinnie with three hundred of his clansmen walking behind him. He had decided to fight for his land, his culture, his traditions. He suspected the hopelessness of his cause but he also knew the impossibility of turning aside from the duty invested in him.

Now, some years later, each move forward, each action taken made it less possible for men like Cluny to find a compromise. The Jacobite Highlanders were on a collision course with the new order of trading Europe, where allegience to kinsman would eventually be weakened by allegiance to commercial partnerships. James and Robert Walker represented this new order, while Kitty, with her passionate loyalty to a half-imagined nobleman, represented the old. Between them stood the enigmatic figure of Ann Walker. Cluny did not know what she represented. How she might be expected to behave. Could he explain to her the real reason for his visit? Would she pledge to assist him? Could he find out anything at all from her without first telling her his story?

He was undecided on this as he walked towards the house. But the events of the next few moments decided things for him. As he approached Ann, she looked up. She saw in his eyes the knowledge which she had been dreading. They stared at each other briefly and then Cluny greeted her formally and passed her by on his way into the house. Ann sat staring unseeingly into the distance. She had to decide what to do next. She found herself getting up and entering the house, intent on finding Cluny Macpherson. No plan, just the blind need to find out what he knew. She saw Charlotte, the second under maid, polishing the hall table, and sent her out into the garden to sit with Adam. Apart from the servants, Ann and Cluny were the only ones in the house.

The door of the library was ajar, and Ann could see Cluny sitting in one of the large chairs by the empty fireplace. There were no books in the library as of yet although Edward had ordered a cart full from London which should arrive soon. The windows had no hangings to soften their angular edges and, as she entered, Ann walked through dust motes dancing in the sunlight above the bare floorboards. She took her place opposite Cluny where she could see his face clearly.

He had ordered tea, although it was still morning. They both sat without speaking while a small tea table was carried in and set up and then tea was brought and served. Ann noted that there were two cups. He had known that she would follow him. She watched as Cluny carefully mixed the tea with sugar and bent his head to sip from his two handled cup. She took her own cup from Mary and looked down at the garland of flowers which circled the interior rim of the delicate porcelain. Green leaves, blue and yellow flowers, repeated over and over again in a circle, just visible above the brown liquid. Ann shifted on her chair, ruffling her skirts prettily and put her cup down. She gave her full attention to the man sitting opposite her.

'My name is not Mr Anderson. It is Cluny Macpherson, Clan Chief of the Macphersons of Ben Alder,' stated Cluny. He paused to sip again at his tea. He had decided that the only way he was going to get some truth out of this woman was to be honest himself. As far as possible.

'And my name is Ann Walker. It was Ann Challinor. I was the widow of John Challinor, a packman out of Stafford.' Ann had not decided to do the same.

'I am a Jacobite, Mrs Walker and I am here on Jacobite business.' If she was a government agent she would already know this, if she was not then she had to know his background, if she was to be persuaded to help him. But the name – Challinor, a packhorseman, out of Stafford. Something tugged at the edges of Cluny's brain, some thread of recognition, but he could not grasp it and pull. It eluded him. Yet something made him certain that this woman could help him. She knew more than she would say, or perhaps, more than she really understood.

'Mr Macpherson,' Ann said slowly, 'what would that business be, may I enquire?' Her brain seemed to pound against the bones of her skull. She could scarcely remember what could be told and what could never be told. She frantically tried to put things in order. Murder. She must not say she murdered Mr Rudge. She must not speak it. That could be hanging. But could she tell this man that Mr Challinor probably, almost certainly was Mr Rudge? Would he know that already, and therefore she could appear to give information which he already had, gaining his trust while losing nothing?

She stood up and went to the window, to play for time. She did not need to worry, for Cluny had as much need of time to think as she did. They were like chess players who could not see the board. They had to keep up the momentum of the game by making moves but they did not know what significance each move would have.

'My business is to find a Mr Rudge, or at least find out what happened to him. He was a compatriot of mine. He was travelling as a packhorseman on important business and seems to have disappeared at this place about two years ago.' Ann considered quickly. Mr Rudge was therefore a Jacobite. The French had been sending money to the Jacobites. He had been carrying it but the money never got to its destination. Ann turned to face Cluny.

'Mr Macpherson, I am now going to tell you something that no one else on this earth knows.' She clasped and unclasped her hands nervously. 'I long suspected something of this sort would be the case... I believe that my deceased first husband, so called, and your Mr Rudge, are one and the same man.' It came out in a rush and Ann closed her eyes briefly as if with relief at this unburdening of herself. Cluny watched her closely. 'I met with this man...'

'Describe him,' said Cluny sharply.

'Tall.. fair... with a Scots accent,' said Ann, still with her eyes closed, as if remembering, using her hand to describe the height of the man. 'I met with this man and his companion...'

'What companion?'

Good. Ann opened her eyes wide in surprise at his reaction. 'Why the southerner who was riding alongside of him. A well spoken gentleman. Dressed quite fine and carrying a... a pistol. I saw it under his frock coat.' Her voice dropped to a frightened whisper. She looked at Cluny for understanding.

'A southerner,' repeated Cluny.

'Yes. They had done some business together from what they said and they parted at Bradley Wood, just before Ashbourne, where I met them that morning.'

'They parted at this wood?'

'Yes, I don't know how long they had been travelling together... but not long, I think. They seemed very nervous of being seen together.'

'Then what happened?'

'The tall man and I came into Ashbourne together. He said I was to say I was his wife and told me his name.'

'And what was that?' asked Cluny Macpherson.

'Why, Challinor, of course, but now I fear that he may have been Mr Rudge,' replied Ann.

Cluny thought for a moment. Mary came in to take the tea things. As Mary moved about the room between them, placing cups and lifting away the table, Ann watched Cluny Macpherson. He doesn't know whether to ask me about the box of money, she thought. He doesn't know whether to bring it up or not. He must see that his man has betrayed him and has done a deal with the Hanoverians. Or maybe he thinks the two men have done a deal together and cut out both their organisations. Must be one of the hazards of this trade, just as in all thieving. She mulled over her master trick of giving the invention of the name 'Challinor' to Mr Rudge. Rudge being a name, by implication, she had never heard until spoken by Cluny Macpherson himself. It proved her case. She thought she had been travelling with a Mr Challinor. Rudge was attempting to conceal his identity, with a new name and a new wife to escape pursuit by the Jacobites.

'What happened to Mr Rudge?' Cluny could hardly bear to ask.

Ann hesitated. It would seem preposterous, but it was true. "He died, Mr Macpherson, as we entered the town. He fell from his horse...there were witnesses... a natural death.' For a long time Ann had allowed herself to believe this. She sounded convincing.

Cluny took it in, and examined it. Echan, not in battle, not even a knife in your back in a crowded room but alone in this town of strangers, with only this woman for company. 'What was it?' he asked. Ann raised her hand to the side of her head. Cluny raised his hand to stop her explanation. He believed her now. Sometimes Echan had been thrown to the ground by terrible pains in his head

Cluny looked at Ann again. She stared steadily back at him. She knew what his next question would be and she waited for it. She was fully in control of the situation.

'And why were you in these Bradley Woods?' asked Cluny. It was the question she had expected.

Ann had a choice of answer. She could tell him the truth. She was an escaped prisoner. He would not be concerned by the jurisdiction of an English gaol and might even be more sympathetic and less critical of the rest of her story. Always tell as close to the truth as possible, that was the rule. Or she could avoid any future connection with Derby gaol, Mr Meynell and all of that episode by giving him a simpler story. 'I was on the run from my employers in Derby,' she said. 'The mistress had taken a dislike to me and accused me of stealing silver. No one would believe my version of the story so I thought it best to leave. I had no idea where to go.' She stopped and sighed. 'Of course, because I ran, now there will be a price on my head. Or there was. I suspect it has all died down by now. I was glad to become Ann Challinor, widow of Mr Challinor.' It was the story of many a servant. No redress in court, false accusations left standing. No option but to run. But in Ann's case a chance meeting which had transformed her life.

Ann turned to look fully at Mr Macpherson. 'I was lucky, Mr Macpherson. I sold the packhorses, rented a little shop, started a new life. If I had not met and married James, I would still be in that shop, across the road and you would pass me by on the street without so much as a glance. But I have all this and I am grateful, I can assure you. Whatever reason makes this family welcome you into Hulland House is a good enough reason for me to count myself as your friend, too. I would be honoured if you would accept me as such, sir.' Saying this Ann got up, curtseyed low in front of Cluny and left the room. She climbed up the stairs to her bedroom, confident that she had convinced him.

But Cluny did not believe Ann's story.

Ann was an ordinary street thief. She had always done what was expedient. She did not understand the passion and loyalty of men who fought together for a common cause. A cause that was shared in every prayer before battle half sung in the Gaelic, in every lament at the graveside of a friend. Or in the simple act of breaking bread after a day's hard work together.

Cluny Macpherson had known as soon as Ann described Mr Rudge, the turncoat, that she lied. It was cleverly done. But it was a lie. Once again, he felt weariness sweep over him. He longed to be home in the clean air above Loch Ericht.

He thought of Echan MacLean. A man who would not betray his friends as long as his heart was still beating. Dead. By the hand of God, as the witnesses would seem to prove? Or helped by that poor, perfumed creature who had swept up the stairs after delivering her pretty speech?

Well, he would play her game. Let her think that she had succeeded in laying a false trail and let her believe that he now considered her a friend and confidante. He would wait his opportunity to find out more of the truth. Now he knew in what direction to turn his gaze, it shouldn't be too long before he should pick up more information.

The day after she had left Cluny in the library Ann received a request from Kitty to go to her bed chamber. Kitty sat very upright by the window. She had a shawl wrapped around her shoulders. In one hand she held a letter and in the other she held what looked like two silver medallions.

Without taking her eyes from the medallions, which she

turned constantly over and over in one hand, Kitty began to speak.

'Ann, since May, when I received this,' her head tipped slightly towards the letter, but she did not take her eyes from the medallions, 'I have been heavy of heart. I have known that this morning would come, when I would have to speak to you and I,' her voice faltered, "I have dreaded it. I cannot prevent you from judging me, and judging me badly, but you must be told.' She paused. 'The safety of my son depends on it.'

Ann was alarmed. What other dangers could there be for James? Other than her, that was? How could danger come to James from Kitty? She wanted to ask questions but Kitty was still speaking.

'Over ten years have passed since I spoke of this aloud, although the consequences of what I am about to tell you have been with me every day. In one way they have been with me as a delight and in another as a great source of fear.' She dropped her head. 'I know that I have not felt the shame that the church teaches me I should over this matter.'

She turned and looked directly at Ann. 'I did feel guilt. And sorrow for the pain I caused my husband.' She opened her hand and looked at the medallions. 'I cannot say that I regret what happened. I long to see him again. But I cannot.' Kitty turned her face away and Ann had to strain to hear her next words. 'For he will not come back to me. There is not the smallest doubt left.'

Kitty stopped and for a moment she seemed to be lost in thought. When she spoke again, it was as if to herself alone. She looked up at the window. 'I did not truly believe it until Cluny told me.'

Ann was struggling to understand what Kitty was talking about. It involved Amadeus, and some wrong Kitty had done him. And did it involve danger for James? She leaned forward and laid her hand on Kitty's arm.

'Kitty, Kitty,' she said gently, 'you must tell me more. What

181

is the danger for James?'

Kitty turned to face her. 'Not James, Ann, but Charles. Charles is in danger.'

This young woman had to know. She was the only one in the household who would have the guile, the vision to protect Charles. Kitty hoped she had judged well and that Ann would be worthy of this trust. She must tell her everything.

'Ann, with the Jacobites in 1745 came one Lord Lovat. He was a close companion of the Prince. He billeted here, in this very house, and the Prince would come here each day to speak with him. The Prince, Ann, the Prince. He ate at our table. Sometimes he would get us all to leave the dining room and eat at the kitchen table. 'We are all equal in a war' he said, 'the kitchen is fit for a king – and a lot better than the roadside.'' Kitty smiled, her eyes wide, reliving it, the nervous diners, in awe of their guest, being suddenly whirled up into action. The Prince striding ahead, holding the candlesticks aloft.

She paused and for a moment her face became secretive, then she took a deep breath and looked straight at Ann. 'When the army left for Derby I...' there was nothing but to say it, ' I followed him. We lay together for some nights whilst the Jacobite army stayed their hand in Derby, waiting for information from their spies. Ann, Charles is the child of that union. '

Ann sat back, trying to take in what Kitty had just said. Kitty raised the hand holding the letter, as if to stall Ann's questions. She must finish what she had to say.

'Amadeus knew. When the Scottish army left, I was bereft. I would gladly have died. I should have been an outcast. What I had done was unforgivable. Amadeus came to our lodgings and brought me home. He never remonstrated with me and when the baby was born he accepted him and loved him as his own son. It was Amadeus who named him.'

Kitty stood up. 'Ann, Charles is a son of the Stuart line. His father could be drawn and quartered for a traitor. And now I fear that rebellion is stirring again. Cluny has told me as much. There will be a bloody war before many years. And the son of Charles Stuart would be a great prize. I must trust you to care for him. Keep this knowledge safe, even from your husband. Charles' life may depend on your secrecy and watchful care. If I die, when I die, as we all must, I charge you to keep Charles safe, and tell him the truth when you think it time.'

Ann nodded her head. 'I will. I will do this.'

She felt an almost unbearable need to tell Kitty the truth of her own story. Here in this warm, tranquil room, sitting with a woman who had lived in subterfuge for so many years, Ann longed to share her fears of pursuit, her guilt at her actions, her shame at the uneasy compromises she had made of other peoples' lives. Here, in the place where Ann felt most ill at ease had all along been someone who would understand the choices Ann had faced. But she did not speak. The effort to keep the words from leaving her lips and changing everything about her life in this house was almost unbearable. She felt disturbed. Agitated. There were uncertainties, secrets, of which she had known nothing. And at the centre of it there was this quiet woman, offering her such a trust. Such a duty.

Ann hugged Kitty and kissed her on the forehead.

'Ann. You must swear.' Kitty laid the letter down and grasped Ann's arm.

'I swear,' said Ann. She suddenly needed to move, to take action.

She left Kitty by the window and rushed upstairs to her dressing room. She pulled out her riding clothes and got herself into them, cursing buttons which required a maid to do them up. Then she went to the stables and shouted loudly for the stable boy. She waited impatiently while her horse was saddled and then, at last, she was out on the road, riding her horse fast until she was clear of the town on the north road. She reached the top of Mayfield rise and allowed her tired horse to slow to a walk.

She was breathing hard. She pulled off her riding hat and wiped her face with its veil. She tried to think about Kitty's information. But for the moment thinking was no use. There was only an incomprehensible pleasure welling up inside of her. She had been given a gift. Kitty had freely chosen to trust her with some precious and dangerous knowledge.

Everyone worked alone. You kept a lookout for information and what you found out, you put to work for your own good. Sometimes you were the quarry and sometimes you were the other. That was what she had understood, at any rate. But now she realised that for the first time in her life, she was in possession of information about another person which she had no intention of ever using for her own gain. She thought of Kitty's quiet voice, explaining the unforgiveable. Kitty had broken rules and survived. She had stepped out of this world which surrounded her, and then, in a most extraordinary fashion, and by the grace of the man who loved her, had stepped back in again. Kitty had taken a chance, she had relinquished control, maybe foolishly. She could be ridiculed. But, although what she did had led to pain, also, more importantly, it had led to change. Something in the world had been altered by Kitty's action.

Ann saw Kitty's trusting face and felt a sudden, bitter anger. They were fools, Macpherson and Kitty Walker, and their thoughts were the thoughts of fools. Look, love and follow. The motto of the Jacobites. The words inscribed on the medallions cradled in Kitty's hand. As if those three actions were all that was needed to win battles and hold nations. And now they were twisting her up in their stupidity. Making her a part of it.

She told herself that she knew so much more than Kitty, and what she knew was that this loyalty she saw in Cluny, in

Kitty, was a false, flimsy construction. There was no proper reasoning to it. And yet they thought it illuminated their lives with purpose. Kitty was a foolish little woman. A poor, stupid woman, impressed by a soldier on a great horse, riding into her life and out, with hardly a thought for her.

And Cluny Macpherson? Cluny was a rat in a trap. Did he even know that French spies were also tracking down the Louis D'or? Did he realise the danger he had brought to the Walker household. Where Kitty had protected the blood-line of the Stuarts for over ten years? And Kitty...? Did she realise to whom, to what, she had entrusted her son's life? A thief, an escaped prisoner, a murderer? Someone who could now bargain for her freedom with the son of the Stuart Pretender.

Ann had an escape route now. She could go. She manoeuvred her horse out on to the top of Mayfield hill and turned him to face the valley where Ashbourne stood. She stretched upright in the saddle and drew the cool clean air into her lungs. She was free. She could take her son and leave. Other people could pay the consequences of their own actions. She turned in the saddle and looked up the road snaking north behind her. She could continue her journey, but this time without fear of pursuit. She raised the reins in her hands ready to move her horse forward.

But she knew she could not go.

She could not betray Kitty's trust, she could not see James and his brother destroyed by law suits and actions for treason. And as she turned her horse back to the road, riding up to the right, through the village of Calton and down the bridle path to the Manifold river she knew she could not leave the Jacobite Cluny Macpherson to take a knife in the gut from a French spy, before he had even time to fight for his life. He would have to be given the money. Only that would make him leave, and only that might prevent the threat to the Walker household overtaking them all. Ann rode on, devising a plan, looking for a hiding place.

And, again and again, returning with wonder to the moment when Kitty put such trust in her. As she approached the river, she saw the green mass of Beeston Tor woods lying to her left. This would offer her a good hiding place for the money box.

When Ann made the decision to give Cluny the money, she stood on the very edge of his world of causes and loyalties. In twenty four hours, she would bring Cluny to the woods at Beeston Tor. Her nervousness when she speaks to him here will be engendered by a kind of excited, heady fear at being part of a world for which she did not have the language. A world where her old standards did not apply. By handing over the money she would allow that world a chance to continue. Her action was a blow against her former life. A blow against the streets of Derby. But she could scarcely admit these underlying reasons for her actions, even to herself. For where would it take her?

The next day, Kitty asked Cluny to meet her in the library for tea. She sat in the chair used by Ann, and Cluny Macpherson could not help but compare the two women. Ann was driven by a primitive determination to survive. Kitty had a great well of compassion and love, but also an awareness of her own frailty and the frailty of others around her. She knew the cost of loyalty and the pain of betrayal. And the greatest pain of being the one who betrayed.

She talked to Cluny of her son. She felt he was too young as yet to know the truth of his parentage; but she had made sure that, after her death, when she could no longer be touched by painful recriminations, there would be someone else, who, holding this knowledge, could tell the boy when deemed suitable. Any promise made by Cluny in his first shock at seeing the boy was not to be seen as a commitment. She smiled at him. They had both, she suspected, expended enough passion on hopeless commitments.

'Not all hopeless, not altogether, madam,' had been Cluny's

gentle response.

'Mr Macpherson, I shall tell you the name of the only other person alive who knows the true fathering of Charles. This is a person who has all the skills needed and the heart too for the task I have given her. It is Ann, my daughter-in-law.'

Kitty looked to him for approval and Cluny had just enough presence of mind to disguise his shock. He kept his face still but he felt despair grip his heart. Now they were undone. Ann Walker would use this to her own ends, of that he was sure. She would be ruthless when it came to betraying this house for her own survival. He had begun to suspect that she may have killed Echan Dhu. There had been some darkness in her eyes when she spoke of him... but he must not let his consternation show. Ann must think she has succeeded in deceiving all of them.

'Very good, madam. I could not have made a better choice.'

Kitty smiled, well pleased with his reply. She asked if Cluny had made any progress with the matter which had brought him to Ashbourne. He replied that he thought most things were now clear. He did not want to lie to Kitty but he did not want to alert Ann. Cluny understood perfectly the workings of a small group such as this. Ann would soon be absolutely sure of her success.

He was proved right. Ann showed herself to be very friendly in the next few days. She walked with Cluny around the garden and down by the Henmore Brook, over the bridge by the Church and along by the water meadows there. She talked of nothing serious but Cluny sensed that she was consolidating what she thought to be her character in his eyes. She was his friend. A simple woman who had found happiness and safety and who was aware of her good fortune. Cluny quickly became bored by this play acting. Two days after their meeting in the library, she invited Cluny to ride out with her onto Calton Moor on the Leek road. She thought it might be similar to his homeland and please his eye. Cluny had ridden through there on his way to Ashbourne. He had thought it a bleak and lonely place to ride out and one uncommonly suited to ambush. What if Mrs Walker were a Government agent and had arranged for his abduction or his death? Cluny weighed it up. It was not so very likely and he was aware that in this drawing room game of cat and mouse he was playing he could hardly refuse her suggestion with any show of politeness and without raising her suspicions.

So they rode out together the next morning.

o o O o o

September the 22nd 1757

On the same day, far away in an overcast Chantilly, Prince Charles Stuart was meeting Choiseul, the French minister for foreign affairs. The matter to be discussed was the imminent French attack on the English garrison at Minorca. As Charles walked up the broad stone steps of the Palace De Chantilly rain made dark spots on his yellow silk coat.

At that moment in Derbyshire the air was bright and clear with that first satisfying edge of coolness that predicts the English autumn. Ann wore a bright red riding coat and a black hat with a fluttering veil. Very easy to be picked out by an ambushing party, thought Cluny Macpherson and wondered again about the sense of his going at all. But Ann turned on her horse and shouted at him to get a move on with all the appearance of such genuine excitement at the idea of their journey that he put all thoughts of ambush aside.

They rode their way along Church Street, past the bulging walls of the Elizabethan Grammar School. Ann pointed at it with her whip.

'Look at that, Mr Macpherson. They did not allow for the

weight of stone and added on two more floors. Now the people of Ashbourne fear for the building's collapse!'

Their horses, sensing an outing, were frisky because of it. Ann's mount kept sidestepping and making exaggeratedly fearful jumps, shying away from anything else on the road. Cluny could see that she was a good horsewoman, only restrained by having to ride sidesaddle. He drew alongside of her.

'You ride well, madam.'

Ann laughed. She had only learnt how to do this a few months ago. Lessons every day from a ladies' riding instructor: how to sit, how to hold the reins, how to dismount in voluminous skirts. The instructor had been shocked when she had wanted to gallop on the third lesson. But she had been fearless. Galloping across the fields around Ashbourne had been exhilarating. The only horses she had ridden up until then had been the stolid, slow moving packhorses as they came into Derby market, where children could get some beer for helping the jaggers out as they manoeuvered the busy streets of the town.

Cluny spoke again, 'You wouldn't need to ride in that confounded way because you're a woman if you were in my country. Highland women do as they wish.'

'I'm sure they do, Mr Macpherson,' said Ann, and with one adroit movement of her leg, she sat astride of her horse. It wasn't easy since the saddle was designed otherwise, but it was possible. By the speed at which she rode off, it was obvious that Ann had done this before.

They reached Calton Moor and then were dipping down into the village of Calton itself. High and bare and barren, its inhabitants eked out a living from the unproductive land by quarrying and lead mining. The houses of Calton village itself were grey and low. Built to withstand bad weather, not to let in light or promote comfort.

Ann turned to him as they entered the village. 'I think this must be like your wild homeland, Mr Macpherson. You will like this place better than Ashbourne.' She laughed and spurred her horse on to ride ahead.

Cluny looked around him. This place was not like the Highlands of Scotland. There the light rushed and shifted over the mountainsides. Water hurtled over stone and cloud came sweeping down to meet the land, creating a mysterious world, half spirit, half earthly, wherein legends were made. Ann and Cluny reined their horses in by the church.They stood on a narrow track, watching as the grey quarrymen of Calton trudged past on their way home from a morning's work. There were no legends in their souls, of that Cluny was certain.

They rode on through Calton village and down the steep track to the Manifold valley. Ann pulled her horse up by a wooded fold in the landscape called Beeston Tor. She moved off the track and signalled to Cluny to follow her. This was it, he thought, ambush; yet his instincts, fine-tuned by his experience of guerilla warfare, told him otherwise. He looked around. The countryside about them had that still, undisturbed feel to it which told him that they were the only people to come that way recently. The trees were still; no birds flocking. The sheep were grazing in a formation which he recognised from his homeland as being their early morning pattern – if left undisturbed. Knowledge of this kind was what had kept Cluny alive and free in the months after Culloden. So Cluny took a step which may have seemed foolish to an onlooker who knew some of the circumstances. He directed his horse off the road and entered the cool green shade of the wood.

He could see Ann's red coat ahead of him in the darkness. As his eyes grew accustomed to the dim light he saw that she had dismounted by a small stone building. It was the remnants of a miner's bothy. There were many such buildings to be found all over this countryside, abandoned after fruitless efforts to find lead. He dismounted and led his horse up to her.

Ann turned to him. In the half light her pale face gleamed, drawn tight into hard edges by her fear. 'Cluny Macpherson, there is a purpose to this morning's ride.'

He nodded. He had thought as much.

'In five days time I want you to leave Ashbourne.'

Ann stopped, expecting him to protest, but Cluny said nothing. He stood, very calm and still, watching her closely. There had been a slight tremble in her voice. Her eyes flickered over his shoulders, to the right and left of him. Was she watching for her accomplices? He tensed and brought his right hand nearer his hidden Skean Dhu. She noticed his actions.

'You are safe, Mr Macpherson, at least from me. Now listen. There shall be a box inside this place, in the earth under the stone in that corner. She indicated the place through the entrance. 'In it you will find two thousand Louis D'or. This is the money I took from your countryman two years ago.' She was silent for a moment, then decided on the truth. 'Less one thousand Louis D'or which I intend to keep. Look around carefully, do not mistake this place when you return and do not come down this track at night. Movement in the dark of night arouses suspicion.'

'Madam...' Cluny opened his mouth to speak but was not sure what to say. He was only certain that he believed what she said. The matter of fact admission of the substantial payment to herself of one thousand Louis D'or convinced him of that.

'Mr Macpherson, do not say anything.' She paused. 'A day ago I found out that Charles Walker is the child of your Bonnie Prince. I have thought of little else since. I know very little of your cause but I do know that this means that the danger to my family from this money has increased many times. If you are to be found carrying this money I do not want it to happen near Hulland House. There must be no connection. I have made a promise to Kitty that I shall tell Charles of his parentage after her death. I assume that you will make sure that this information is also given to trustworthy people in your homeland?'

Cluny nodded.

'Mr Macpherson, I have nothing more to say to you, except to wish you well on your journey.' She turned and remounted her horse. He noticed how her hands shook as she adjusted the bridle.

He watched as Ann kept her head low as her horse picked its way through the trees and then saw her lean forward and urge the animal into a wild gallop down the rest of the slope to the riverside. At that rate, she won't live to tell the boy anything, thought Cluny Macpherson. He continued to watch as Ann slowed to a brisk trot along the riverside path and disappeared around a corner into a copse. There must be another way back to Ashbourne. She will use that to bring the money here, he thought. He spent some time familiarising himself with the wood and its surroundings. When he was satisfied that he could find the place again, he rode back up through Calton and onto the Ashbourne road, to be back at Hulland House in time for the evening meal.

Ann Walker continued to treat him in the same friendly manner that she had shown to him in the few days after their meeting in the library. Kitty did not indicate by any action her new relationship with Ann, and James and Edward treated him with the same affable disinterest as before. Cluny was interested only in getting home to share this momentous fortune and all that it implied with the men who had fought alongside him for so long. He slept badly. He left Ashbourne at dawn on the morning of the twenty seventh of September. By eight of the morning he had retrieved the box, and retraced his steps back through Calton to the northern road. To his knowledge he had been seen making this double journey by two farm boys and one old quarryman, who had stood outside his cottage in Calton and followed Cluny's journey through the village one way and then back the other with mild interest.

If Cluny had happened to glance over his shoulder as he returned up the track by Beeston Tor he would have caught a brilliant flash of light from the wood on the other side of the river. If he had seen that flash, he would have immediately known that it came from early morning sunlight reflecting from the lens of a spy glass.

Chapter 7

Parties

Lapiz lazuli. That was the colour. Amanda Walker leaned forward to look more closely in the mirror. Jewel blue. The colour of her dress and the colour of her eyes. She turned to view the sweep of her gown in its full glory. Yes. The marvellous London corset, with its fine steel struts gave her waist a delicate vee shape, accentuated by the fine lines of stitching which spread out from the centre of the bodice to separate over her padded bustier. The front of the bodice was low and encircled with creamy lace. Amanda could see that this dress was designed to make her bosom the centre of any man's attention. It was London fashion, brought over from France, with whom we are at war, thought Amanda. But that makes it all the more desirable. The bad French, with their wicked clothes. She placed her hands on the panniers, which, by the use of more steel, this time in hoops, covered with some padding, sprang out from either side of her tiny waist in a marvellously exaggerated parody of the curves of the female form. Amanda was not sure how to place her hands on these panniers. She practised for a few moments and eventually found that demurely clasping them in front of her was the best option. She was highly satisfied with this dress. Bodice of blue silk with a raised pattern of ribbons winding across a darker background. Petticoats of paler blue and the panniers on either side in frilled loops of another complementary shade of the same colour. More lace and then tiny blue velvet ribbons at her elbows. Yes, Ann had been right. Keep to blue, with only some rich lace for contrast. She picked up her hair brush and tiara from the dressing table and rang for Mary.

In the summer of 1757 Amanda was twenty years old and

had been in Lichfield for most of the season, staying with the Boothbys at their house there. When she visited Ashbourne it was with ill-concealed impatience and she spent much of her visits planning her next escape.

She had tired of the society of Ashbourne by the age of nineteen, and although content to stay for a while after her brother's marriage to Ann, and to return for the birth of baby Adam, eventually her own needs had become paramount in her plans and she had arranged a constant round of visits to friends whose common denominator was that they lived elsewhere.

Amanda had still been in Lichfield when Ann and James had made their visit to Matlock Bath and she had only returned from a summer visit to Cheltenham the day before Cluny Macpherson left Ashbourne. More than other members of the family, even more than James, Amanda had reached some understanding of Ann's character. She was curious now to see that Ann looked and acted with more freedom and high spirits than she had ever shown before. Perhaps taking the waters really did work.

For her part, Ann was free for the first time of dread. She had begun to expect that her life might simply carry on as it was. She had begun to lose her fear of the future. Cluny Macpherson had gone and they had heard no more of him. She was determined to make this life in Ashbourne real. More real than her past, so real that the threats which still eddied and swirled around Hulland House would be reduced by its domestic power. Amanda had returned from Lichfield and Ann set about planning parties and outings for her sister-in-law, teasing her with the prospect of meeting anew all the eligible young men of Ashbourne. Amanda was happy to stay for part of the winter season of 1757, if only to show off her new, unassailable Lichfield sophistication to her erstwhile tormentors in Ashbourne.

The first event which Ann arranged for Amanda's

entertainment was a small affair, a supper with dancing which included the Dales from The Ivies and four other Ashbourne families. Card tables were set up in the library for those who preferred whist or quadrille while two fiddlers were engaged to play music for the dancers. Amanda enjoyed her new status as a woman of fashion. She watched the Misses Dale shrink before her eyes as she talked of the balls and parties she had attended that year in Lichfield and in Cheltenham. She startled a pleasant but inexperienced young farmer's son by flirting with him until he blushed and left the room in some confusion. His excuse being that he had to see to his horse which had begun to go lame on his journey over from Tissington.   Amanda considered following him to the stables to tease him further but decided that it was not worth getting her gown dirty.

She had contented herself with trying to entertain the extremely eligible Mr John Hodgson, the nephew of Mr Brian Hodgson who lived across the street in The Grey House. Mr Brian Hodgson had kept the Old Hall Hotel in Buxton and had retired to Ashbourne only ten months before. He still had a comfortable air about him that suggested he was taking care of everyone he met as his guest. John Hodgson had none of his uncle's easy manner. He was a serious young man who was to inherit his father's trading company in London. He was already apprenticed to the business and his purpose in being at this party was to make himself known to the Walkers. His father had said they could be useful. He had no idea how to flirt with Amanda but was determined to let no opportunity of creating a relationship with this family slip through his fingers. This was why, at the end of the third set of dancing, he had found himself kissing, or being kissed by a hot, breathless Amanda on the steps leading down from the open dining room doors to the gardens of Hulland House. He found this, his first experience of kissing a woman, very difficult. It certainly wasn't arousing. He was completely engaged with trying to work out which of the bits of the ensemble pushing itself up so closely to him was human and which were decorative appendages. The panniers which appeared so light and soft when Miss Walker danced turned out to be made of a hard frame, covered with some sort of padding. They made it impossible to approach Amanda from any other direction but head on. This made his attempts to kiss her seem uncomfortably like assaults, but he tried not to let this dissuade him. When he encircled her waist with his hands he found that she seemed to be encased in some sort of metal tube. The fine blue silk was stretched over some rigid base. How could she move in all this? But move she did. Amanda slipped out of his arms and skipped down into the garden. Mr John Hodgson watched her with respect. He could never move in so supple a manner while armoured as she was. He followed, determined to do his part. Perhaps another kiss? He saw ships lying in docks and bales of lapis lazuli silk glistening in warehouses.

Amanda was very pleased with John Hodgson. She had never come across so determined and direct a man. He seemed to be completely self assured. Must have had many women, she speculated, as he grasped her firmly about the waist again and took hold of the back of her head to kiss her full on the mouth. He brought his head back for air and looked down at her breasts, two full and preposterously round moons, moving up and down just above and to the front of his hands. He considered touching them. They seemed real. He could see a small blemish on the rise of the right one. He looked for some way of making contact but, short of putting his hand down the front of Miss Walker's dress, rather as one might put one's hand into a sweetie jar, he could not see a means of entry. The bodice was like a shield. He decided against it but then worried that Miss Walker might think him remiss. She might think he was not attracted to her sufficiently. He had a solution. He bent down and began to kiss and lick all parts of Amanda's breasts which could be reached, making noises of appreciation as he did so. She was amazed. This was not impoliteness, she was sure, but passion. His tongue pushed in underneath the creamy lace of her bodice and just managed to encircle a stiff little nipple. Mr Hodgson was surprised. His first reaction was to recoil, thinking he had come across some buttoning device. Then he realised what it was that he had found and tried to consolidate his position by burrowing even more determinedly down into Amanda's décolletage. Just as Mr Hodgson closed his teeth over the nipple of Amanda's left breast, the doors of the dining room began to open and Amanda leapt away. Luckily Mr Hodgson had the presence of mind to release his grip on her nipple as she jumped. With his saliva still glistening on her skin they returned to the crowded dining room to take their places in the fifth set. Fiddles played out a jig and, as they crossed and recrossed the floor, Amanda fell in love. Mr Hodgson let his eyes travel around the room. He looked at all the breasts so carefully presented for his interest. He marvelled that he had never noticed them before.

Later that night, having danced seven sets with Amanda and three with the Misses Fletcher, an exhausted Mr Hodgson sat by the fire in the drawing room of his uncle's house. He found himself unable to think of anything but the moment his teeth had closed over Amanda's nipple. A serving maid came in to heap up the coals on the grate. More breasts. He looked down the dip in her bodice as she leaned over the fire bucket. She sensed his interest and turned to look at him. She was from a hamlet near Upper Padley and had lain with many farm boys, but never with one of the gentry. She came over to him. Young Mr Hodgson found himself succumbing to something insistent in her eyes. He pulled her down on top of him and slipped his hands inside her bodice. Her body was hot and smooth. Plump with good feeding at the ex-inn keeper's house. She had large, heavy breasts and short sturdy limbs. She stood with her legs slightly apart. His hands searched everywhere. So this was a woman's body. Hard nipples, wet between the legs. Round and firm. Palpable and, in this case, calmly compliant. He pushed her back onto the floor and she guided him in. She could tell he didn't know what he was doing.

Kitty sat at the quadrille table and tried to concentrate on her game. She detested quadrille. So slow, especially when played with Mr Longden, who questioned every move. She could see across the hall to the dancers in the dining room. Amanda flashed into view regularly, her appearances dictated by the form of the dance. She looked graceful and happy. She could see Ann, sitting by the wall with James. Her hand lay lightly on his knee and they were laughing in a teasing public way at something out of Kitty's sight.

Kitty had chosen Ann to be the bearer of her secret after some consideration. She could not imagine turning to her sons. Her relationship with them was quite formal although affectionate. As she and her husband had risen in society they had treated their children as they saw other parents of rich families do. When James, the eldest, was seven, the boys were given a tutor and then, as they got older, they attended a boarding school in Staffordshire. Like many women of her position, their mother hardly ever saw them alone. They would either be with a nursemaid, their nanny or, as they got older, brought by their tutor to display their prowess at reading or logarithms. Sometimes she thought about her own mother, sitting with her children on her knee in front of the kitchen range. But that was not how the rich behaved.

James and Edward had become successful men. They saw trade as an opportunity for them to use their intellects to outwit the opposition. Although they were glad to be out of the tannery they had no intention of turning their backs on their father's work as some children of the new rich had done. They intended to build on what he had done.

In 1757 the two Walker brothers were expanding their father's business into something he would not have recognised. Where he sold his excellent tanned hides on the Derby market, his sons bought and sold a whole range of luxurious goods through the port of London. This constant flow of goods fed the appetite of the growing prosperity of England under Hanoverian rule. Most of the needs of the ordinary people of an area like Ashbourne, so typical of much of England, were serviced by local craftsmen. Chairs, beds, cotton and woollen fabric and china were produced nearby. But trade was expanding and, like other merchants, the Walker family were beginning to bring fine goods from Europe onto a rich home market. James and Edward travelled to the international port of Amsterdam to locate new sources of supply and visited the fashionable dealers of London to establish the next product to source. They were considering the purchase of a London house, much to Amanda's delight. This would provide them with a base from which to do business in town.

In the third week of October, a few days after Ann's house party, Amanda persuaded her eldest brother, Edward, to be back from London in time to act as a steward with Mr Brian Hodgson for Ashbourne's first formal winter assembly. The previous winter, Amanda had enjoyed the formality of the Lichfield season, where regular balls and gatherings were held between October and Spring. These assemblies or balls were the most convenient way imaginable for the young gentry of a town to meet and display both their availability and their wealth. The meetings had to take notice of the social order and had therefore to be set up by reliable members of the local society who would lead off the dances and arrange entry to supper in order of rank. Edward Walker was easily persuaded by his sister. He knew that most of Ashbourne saw him as a most eligible bachelor and that he enjoyed the near adulation of the slightly older Ashbourne spinsters. To organise such an event was to arrange an evening of his own amusement.

The assembly was held in the Walkers' own warehouse, by the Market Cross. It was the empty shell of a Quaker meeting hall which had closed some years before. It was a substantial, square building with tall windows, a sprung oak floor and large fireplaces. Amanda supervised the lighting of fires and the cleaning of the floors in the days before the ball. She had garlands of ribbons and paper flowers looped around the walls to give the rooms a more festive air and she ordered a marvellous cold supper of duck, beef, pies, trifles and cheese to be delivered, at 10 o'clock on the evening of the ball, from The Blackmoor's Head on the other side of the street. At midnight there would be a further refreshment of mulled wine and biscuits. Throughout the evening a small ensemble of musicians would play and, of course, for those so inclined, card tables would be set up all around the room. It would be perfect, or as near to perfection, as the imagination and purse of the Walker family could reach. In Amanda's case, in the matter of seeking pleasure, that was very far indeed. It would be the setting Amanda wanted for dancing and flirting with a particular young man whom she had met only days before. John Hodgson.

John Hodgson had found himself unable to resist repeating and intensifying his exploration of sexual pleasure in the form of the serving maid from Upper Padley. She was prepared to try anything, which was quite as well, since, like Amanda, John Hodgson's imaginative capacity for seeking pleasure in any new situation was extensive. He had not known anything about sex when he first kissed Amanda Walker, but ten days later, when he led her out onto the floor of her uncle's warehouse to dance Major Buckstone's reel he knew more than most people in the room. Of course, the serving maid and her five sisters knew more than any of them, but they rarely were called upon to be inventive. John

Hodgson had been a rare treat for the maid from Padley.

Amanda knew nothing of this rapid initiation. She had been convinced of the pleasing sexuality of John Hodgson's nature when he had so determinedly kissed her back in the garden. Without considering the meagre basis for her decision, but trusting in nature and instinct as her narrow education had taught her to do, she was sure she had found her perfect partner. It only remained to go through the formalities of marriage before she would possess him and he would possess her. Amanda had mistaken a mixture of boredom and lust for romantic love but no one would explain that to her. Certainly not her mother, who had made the same mistake twelve years before. Certainly not her sister in law, who danced away the evening with James and their friends, glad that her secret lessons with Mr Corbyn, Ashbourne's only dance master, had been so successful, and unaware of how to classify love at all.

As they talked between dances, John Hodgson began to admire Amanda greatly. She was a lively, direct girl. Her glossy dark hair, bright blue eyes and sinuous body spoke of energy and health. She moved quickly and was decisive. She threw her head back in abandonment when she laughed and then answered his comments on stock-holding with perception and no forbearance. If he made a generalised, unsubstantiated statement for effect, Amanda brought him back to the specific. Although Amanda's social manner was an enchanting mixture of sexual teasing and genuine humour she abandoned all artifice when discussing business. Soon she was deep in discussion with Mr Hodgson about the cost of a complete refurbishment of these rooms and the prospective financial returns on them as a centre for Ashbourne's winter gatherings. All the time they spoke, Amanda kept imagining Mr Hodgson's teeth upon her flesh that night at Hulland House. Although her mind still retained the ability to make rapid arithmetical calculations, Amanda was aware that she was beginning to feel somewhat faint.

She would be a marvellous business partner thought Mr Hodgson. He could see them walking down the docks of Shoreditch together. King and queen of an empire which would straddle the world. He found himself longing to attack the fortress of her clothing once more and, still socially innocent, he intended to do so as soon as possible. He did not stop to consider the implications of his intended actions, only the strategies necessary to conquer each section of Amanda's clothing.

Suddenly, Amanda fell forward into Mr Hodgson's arms. At first, he thought that she could resist touching him no longer, for he had been aware of the way she had been looking at his mouth and he also remembered his teeth closing around her nipple. But then he realised that she had fainted. He was a fairly slight fellow and Amanda a substantial young woman, dressed in full evening attire but he manfully grasped what he thought were her legs and tipped her over into his arms. He straightened up with some difficulty and, amid a throng of concerned well wishers, and, accompanied by her mother, he carried her out to a waiting carriage. Amanda came round before the carriage door closed and begged her mother that Mr Hodgson be allowed to accompany them home. Kitty agreed, aware that she had left her sons and Ann to supervise the assembly and that she might need help negotiating Amanda up the steps. It would not be suitable for male servants to be called to assist her daughter. Mr Hodgson was only too happy to oblige and he sprang into the carriage beside Amanda.

With Mr Hodgson's assistance, she was able to walk into Hulland House. But she declared herself too agitated to go immediately up to her bed and in need of a soothing posset of brandy and milk.

'Mr Hodgson, you have been so kind, will you take some milk with us?' asked Kitty, still a little nervous about being left alone with Amanda.

The milk and brandy was soothing, and, in the quiet half light of the drawing room, Kitty soon fell peacefully asleep. Amanda and John Hodgson were wide awake.

'Mr Hodgson, my mother will sleep soundly for several hours. I often used to make her a posset if I wished to escape the house of an evening,' whispered Amanda.

Mr Hodgson nodded. He didn't know quite what to do next. 'Come with me.' Amanda got up and held out her hand to John Hodgson. They crept up the wide staircase, more afraid of being seen by the servants than of awakening Kitty, who had looked completely at peace when they had left the room. At her bedroom door, Amanda stopped and turned to face her partner.

'Mr Hodgson, will you marry me?'

'Yes,' replied John Hodgson, and as a trader, his word was his bond.

Amanda's room was dark. John Hodgson had the impression of heavy perfume and thick fabrics. The small grate held a good fire, as did the grate of each bedroom, ready for the return of the family from the assembly. They lay down together beside the fire and commenced to teach each other. Amanda taught John about the multifarious fastenings of a lady's dress and then John Hodgson taught Amanda some of the things the maid from Padley had taught him about sex.

Ashbourne Christmas 1757

John Hodgson and Amanda declared their intention to marry in December, and on Christmas Eve, the Hodgson and Walker families were to hold a celebratory party in the long room at the Blackmoor's head. The Hodgsons had been arriving from London all of the week before the event and Ann had lost count of them. There were aunts and uncles, cousins, nephews and close friends of the family. All to be introduced, entertained to tea in the drawing room and found a bed. Happily, most of them stayed with Mr Hodgson at the Grey House. He was enjoying playing landlord to his relations. Two days before the party, Kitty, frantically trying to finish the arrangements, had asked Ann to take tea with the latest visitors.

Ann rather enjoyed this ritual. She would enjoy being the sole representative of the Walker family this morning. She dressed in a fine green velvet gown, a delicate fichu of tissue silk around her neck and a small lacy cap on her powdered hair. She considered a patch but knew it would be too racy. Before she went downstairs at ten o clock, Ann visited Amanda in her bedroom.

'Suitable?' she held her arms out and turned slowly around. The figure curled up in the bed muttered agreement.

'Amanda, you haven't looked,' cried Ann.

Amanda rolled over and opened her eyes. 'Perfect,' she murmured, 'everything is perfect.' If she could, she would stay in her bed until the wedding ceremony and then invite Mr Hodgson back to it immediately. Amanda was living in a kind of sensual dream, where every action was supercharged with sexual potential, and she could hardly bear to drag herself out of this state to deal with the reality of dresses, relations, food and wedding vows. All she wanted was Mr Hodgson, in her bed. Perfect.

Ann left her sister-in-law and went down to the drawing room. Some visiting cards lay on the card table. A Miss Jemima Gilbert, a pale blue scalloped card; a Mrs Jedidiah Brook, a white card with heavy black ink and a Mr Francis Etherington, another white card but without the heavy ink, would all be pleased to call upon the Walker family at ten of the morning to pay their respects. Ann knew Mrs Jedediah Brook, a non-conformist of the highest principles. A dreadful woman. She did not know the other two at all.

Snow began to fall. At first light and then more heavily. Ann went to the window and watched the flakes drift downwards. The street became white and, as Ann turned back into the room, she saw that the increased reflection of light seemed to intensify the patterns and colours of the drawing room. She half closed her eyes and stared into the fire, a game she had played in each reception room of the molly house. The glow spread into an orange conflagration which wildly engulfed everything else in the room. She opened her eyes wide again and the fire shrank back into its grate. The room returned to its placid normality.

In the hallway, the doorbell rang and she heard the serving man ushering in a visitor. Ann picked up a book and sat down to receive her guests.

Only one guest entered the room. It was Mr Francis Etherington.

'Good morning, madam.'

He was pleased to see her.

Ann likewise.

'Thank you. I came on horseback. The others will most probably be in a carriage.' He looked towards the window. 'They may have some difficulty traversing the streets.' There was an awkward silence. 'Or, they could have intended to walk, in which case they may arrive soon...' his voice tailed off and his hands strayed to the edge of his shirt.

Ann rang for tea. She invited Mr Etherington to sit down by the fire and warm himself. He did so, sitting awkwardly on the edge of the seat. She looked at him as she asked him the usual questions. Mr Etherington was a tall, dark haired man, dressed in a new-fashioned tail coat of the softest uncut brown velvet, with a perfectly white linen shirt and neck tie. Impeccable. Even his boots were dry and shone with polish. He must have wiped them before he left the stables. He was of a slender build with long fine fingers which he kept deliberately still on his lap. Ann had the impression that if freed from this control, Mr Etherington's fingers would pull incessantly and nervously at the nearest loose thread.

She estimated that he was in his early twenties.

'I am glad to meet you, Mr Etherington. You are a friend of my future nephew -in-law?'

'Yes, we worked together on some investments made by the Hodgson family.' He smiled deprecatingly, lest this made him sound too important. 'Not a banker in the league of Toplis or the other great London financiers but...' he shrugged his shoulders.

Ann smiled. She liked Mr Etherington, with his nervous fingers and his self deprecating smile. He took tea with the most serious attention, as if afraid that he might make the terrible social gaffe of spilling some. He refused some cake; Ann was sure because he lacked the confidence to negotiate two items on his lap. After a few minutes, Mary came in to tell Ann that Miss Jemima Gilbert and Mrs Jedediah Brook sent their apologies but they would not venture out today. They requested the pleasure of visiting the Walkers on the next morning. As Ann became involved in sending suitable replies Mr Etherington took the opportunity to take his leave.

The Christmas Eve party 1757

The Christmas Eve party was well attended. The Walkers had hired the long room at the Green Man and it was filled to the brim with Ashburnians straining to look at each other and Hodgsons straining to see the prospective couple. The room was hot, for, determined to make their guests comfortable, and mindful of the snow outside, Kitty had had fires roaring up the chimneys all day. It was only the recently introduced fashion for dresses of the lightest organza which allowed the ladies to be at all comfortable. The men, in their frock coats and cravats, just had to bear the inconvenience as best they could. Ann, aware of her role as an established wife, had kept her shoulders respectably covered with layers of expensive and heavy brocade and was consequently in real danger of over-heating. She left the main room and went to sit by an open window in the furthest part of the upper hallway. She could see down into the inn courtyard below and, after her eyes had become accustomed to the gloom, she was amused to make out the figure of Mr Etherington, leaning against one of the stable doors with his cravat thrown off and his jacket wide open. His manner was relaxed, almost abandoned. His head was resting on the doorjamb and he was obviously enjoying the cold air and the snow which brushed across his upturned face. He probably found this sort of event somewhat of an ordeal, thought Ann. Crowds of people and dances to perform. She would seek him out to put him at his ease. There were many young ladies of this district who would be rendered speechless by his gentility and good manners. And they would be at least as shy as him so they would not notice whether he could dance or not.

Half an hour later, in the crush of the main room, Ann was able to speak with Mr Etherington.

'Did you enjoy your brief escape,' she teased.

He looked startled. 'My escape! What do you mean?'

'I saw you outside a moment ago. You looked considerably cooler than you look now.'

'Did I?' replied Mr Etherington, brushing down his hair with one rapid movement, 'and how did you see me?'

He looked so embarrassed at the idea of being spied on that Ann took pity on him. 'I only happened to glance out of the hall window as I was passing... I wasn't even certain that it was you until you confirmed just now.'

Mr Etherington smiled apologetically. 'I would not like you to think, madam, that I do not appreciate the honour of the invitation I have to this event.'

Ann put up her hand to stop him. She could not resist teasing him. 'Mr Etherington, please, no more. You can make recompense for your abandonment of the proceedings by dancing at least two sets with Miss Arabella Fletcher.'

Mr Etherington looked genuinely horrified. Just as Ann had surmised, he did not like to dance. His increasing confidence evaporated, 'Only if I could dance one set with you first?' It was a desperate plea not a polite request. 'To bring me back into the way of it. I rarely dance, you see.'

That self deprecating smile again. Ann agreed. It meant rejigging her card but she was willing to do so. This young man was only expressing the fears which could still assail her when faced with the combined presence of the dancers and talkers of this society. And she was quite pleased that he trusted her enough to express his fears.

As the music started they took their places and Ann prepared to assist Mr Etherington through The Dashing White Sargeant and The Bluebell Woods. Her dancing classes meant that Ann was able to guide Mr Etherington firmly through the steps. His hand was damp and as they stepped close in the turns she heard the rapid intake of his breath and caught the acrid smell of his sweat, made more pungent by nervousness and exertion. She found herself a little shocked by her reaction to the smell of him. She was briefly amused by her fastidiousness. This is new, she thought wryly. Images of her past, the casual intimacy of the molly house, redolent with the smell of human bodies, came to mind. She turned her head to glance round the room. How different this was.

The people in this room were symbols made up of flesh and embroidered bodices and stitched into their velvet jackets; each body attached to a name and a property. And just as the new red brick facades beginning to line Church street followed a strict pattern, so the code of behaviour of this society meant that only in the momentary closeness of a dance in a crowded ballroom could two people not legally contracted to each other have their mouths so near as to breath the same air.

Ann, as the dance proceeded, was aware of Mr Etherington

only as the body that she met and touched in a rhythm dictated by the dance. To reach his outstretched hand at precisely the right moment was her aim at one moment and to turn away from him and to curtsey to the man to her left was her aim at another. And all of these movements repeated over and over again. Every couple down the long rows of the dance concentrating on their experience of the same brief, but heady, moments of intimacy.

'Mr Etherington,' said Ann, as they left the floor, 'you gave me the impression that you could not dance. Why, that isn't true, sir!' Mr Etherington only smiled.

The truth was that Mr Etherington was the worst dancer with whom Ann had ever stood up. Hot and clumsy with his eyes fixed upon Ann's face throughout each set, he had stumbled his way through, reliant upon her signals. The floor was remarkably crowded, however, and he should manage to pass muster with Miss Fletcher.

○ ○ ○ ○ ○

On the morning of December 27th Ann came downstairs to the library to find her husband and Mr Etherington deep in conversation.
James looked excited. They had been discussing a plan to circumvent the power of Amsterdam by bringing coffee directly from the Dutch plantations to a warehouse in London. Mr Etherington could arrange finance for this proposal. Ann sat down and listened to their discussion. She noted that Mr Etherington seemed much more confident in this situation than at the Christmas ball or when making his first social visit. It was often the way, she

thought. Young men were trained to make decisions which could affect many lives but were unable to be at ease outside of the workplace. She thought of her own young son, perhaps she could teach him differently. He was over one year in age now and had at last become for Ann a simple pleasure; she loved to feel the heavy weight of him when she picked him up. She watched James as he talked with such animation to Mr Etherington. James would like another child. Perhaps she should give him another son or a daughter.

James invited Mr Etherington to dine with them that evening and before the meal he called his mother, brother and Ann to the library.

'I wish your approval for a scheme which I have drawn up with Francis Etherington.' James turned to his brother. 'Edward, you already know about this, of course. It will tie up a lot of the capital available from the business but only for a short time until the ships begin to bring in the coffee.' He looked around the room at them all. 'Then the returns could be substantial, perhaps a fortune. Francis Etherington can guarantee finance for the purchase of the warehouse and an assistant to Mr William Pitt, a senior man in the government, has indicated to him that the government would be willing to support any attempt to outwit Amsterdam's cartel of dealers.' This was James' trump card. Ann could tell by his voice that he was impressed by the thought of the government helping them.

'Mr William Pitt, the government man,' said Kitty slowly. 'So Mr Etherington knows the likes of these. Amanda's husband-to-be has interesting friends.'

'This is just the sort of opportunity which will come to us as we take our business from the confines of Derby to the capital.' James was obviously eager for their approval. Edward was quiet. He had not taken to expansion in the same way as James; he preferred to work with their original product, fine leather, and, although they were no longer tanners, he had continued to first develop and then expand the production of kid gloves and other luxury items. Edward, like his father, was a craftsman, more interested in how to make something than in how to sell it. He was, however, prepared to agree to James' plan. James was in charge of that side of things.

And Kitty also agreed to the plan. It seemed too good an opportunity to be passed by. Ann watched James. He wanted to do this so much and she could see absolutely no objections to his scheme. Tonight, when they were alone, she would tell him that she might like another baby, perhaps in a year or two. Without ever discussing it, he was aware that she controlled this aspect of their lives. Ann knew that he had no idea that all women who could afford it were attended by an enormous sub-world of practitioners who would assist the end of a pregnancy or preferably prevent one happening. They gathered particularly where ever the gentry went to take the waters. Towns like Buxton and Bath had many small rooms and offices in their side streets where women could visit, unseen, or at least, uncommented upon. Those who had no money to spare, helped each other, and Ann had learnt for herself who to see and what to take to ensure that, just as no disease should take its hold, neither should an unwanted pregnancy occur. She had been more successful than most in her efforts because she was very careful in the application of her information.

Watching James now, Ann determined to talk to Francis Etherington that evening over dinner. She wanted to show a welcome to this new business partner of her husband's. She was sure this was the beginning of a long and fruitful relationship.

'But, Mrs Walker, you cannot be serious.' Francis raised his head up like a startled horse and clutched at his wine glass for comfort.

'Why not, Mr Etherington?' Ann was annoyed. Sometimes

these comfortable people just could not see. 'The poor cannot afford to pay for medicines for their children so they should be given them freely and this service paid for by the rich. It would save money in the long run because there would be less, less poverty. These children would...'

'Would clutter up the streets in adulthood meaning more mouths to feed and more crime. That would be the result of intervention.' Francis slapped his hand down upon the table, convinced that his argument was invincible.

'How do you know?' asked Ann. 'How do you know? If these things are never tried then we will not make any progress. Have you seen the conditions under which people in our cities live?' She leaned forward to be sure of keeping Mr Etherington's attention.

He leaned back over the table and looked at her with the same directness. 'Have you?' he asked, keeping his eyes on her face.

Ann wanted so much to say, 'Yes I have, because I lived like that, like an animal on streets which you only ride through.' Francis carried on staring at her, and Ann thought for a moment that she might actually say those words, to win the argument. Then she drew back and realised the foolishness of that course of action. To destroy this life around her for the sake of the momentary thrill of winning a point against an inexperienced young man.

At the other end of the table, Alice Beresford, hearing the raised voices and sensing a debate about political reform, took the opportunity to bring in her favourite topic. Alice was a prison visitor. She was part of a group of young gentlewomen who had formed The Christian Women's Prison Visitors. That her husband hoped to stand for parliament was only part of her purpose in pursuing this cause. Any visitor to an English prison in the mid-eighteenth century would have had difficulty justifying the horrifying conditions under which the prisoners had lived.

Alice Beresford, listening to Ann's infrequent but passionate comments about the state of the poor, had been attempting to persuade Ann to join them for some time. Ann always refused. She was only pleased that Mrs Beresford's interest in prisons had not taken hold until well after her own escape from Derby Gaol. That she had not been amongst those Christian Women who had read the name of Ann Dance on a list and decided to have her released. She sometimes toyed with the thought of revisiting the prison as a reformer but the danger far outweighed the possible pleasure. Mr Greatorex might recognise her, even though she were dressed finely and part of a group of intense young gentlewomen whose visits he tried assiduously to avoid.

'The poor are indeed a problem, but shouldn't we first address the problems in our prisons?' called out Mrs Beresford. She was addressing Ann but Francis Etherington intervened.

'My dear Mrs Beresford, prison is for wrong-doers, why would you want to improve their lot?' He leaned back in his chair to turn more conveniently towards her. Ann was surprised. His tone was patronising and dismissive: he sounded like another of the narrow-minded smug men of commerce who often sat at her table. But Mrs Beresford was used to this. 'Mr Etherington, if any of your business ventures were to fail – Heaven forbid – you would be placed beside murderers and pickpockets to take your chances. Can that be right?'

There was an almost imperceptible pause in the flow of conversation as all the members of the Walker family thought of their planned venture with Mr Etherington... and then thought of Mr Etherington's fine figure sitting amongst the most depraved of people in a dim prison cell. It could hardly be contemplated. It should not be contemplated.

'No, madam, it cannot be right, I will grant you that.' Francis Etherington, seemingly in a quandary, picked up a knife from the table and then laid it carefully back in its place. 'But, as I am never likely to experience it, may I be so bold as to say it does not concern me.' There was the sound of relieved laughter from around the table.

Ann picked up her spoon and carried on eating her pudding. The reply of a man who is about to do business. Nothing more. She was disappointed by Mr Etherington. The conversation turned to other things and Ann had no reason to speak to Francis Etherington again that evening.

The next day as Ann sat in the library embroidering a neckerchief for Adam, Francis Etherington appeared in the doorway. He hesitated and Ann looked up. She was surprised to see that he appeared to be in a state of some agitation. He stood by the doorway staring at her. Then he entered the room, coming to stand by her chair.

'Mrs Walker,' he began, 'you think less of me, I fear?'

Ann knew instantly that he referred to the dinner conversation of the previous evening. 'Pray sir, I don't know what you mean,' she said, with a look of concern. This felt like a confrontation, one which she wished to avoid.

Francis Etherington sat down in the chair beside her. He carried on talking in a rush, his face turned slightly away from her. Ann watched him as she listened. She could see the dark edge of his hair under the line of his short tail wig and the remains of powder around his neck where his servants had attended him. Suddenly Ann saw him in his room, in the morning. Talking, giving instructions to his manservants. He would not have carefully considered his words to them as he did now to her.

And what had he been like when the servants had left, when there was no on watching him? When he was unguarded, what were his actions? Quick? Or slow, hesitant, considered? Did he sit for a long time thinking of what to say? Had he planned last night to see her alone

215

today to explain all of this?

Francis Etherington was speaking. She must pay attention to his words.

'Like you, I find the way in which our country is divided abhorrent. I see the misery on the streets of our towns.' He took a deep breath. 'But I am caught up in the world of finance. Where men put up money on a whim or... or... not a whim.' He sought for words, 'but on the substantiation of a belief. Faith that the man they are dealing with can be trusted to take care of their money above all else.' He turned to look at her. 'Do you understand?' he questioned. 'Do you see my trap? I must appear as a money man, I cannot act any other way. However I might feel. Sympathy for the weak is not what the men who put their trust in me expect.' He paused, and looked down at his hands. 'Or do you decide on me as a charlatan?'

He looked up at her again and she carefully put down her embroidery to give her time to think. There was something so directly appealing in this man's form of address that she wished to tell him the truth. That she knew of the necessity of acting out a part and that she also knew all there was to know about the lives of the poor. But it was not possible.

'Perhaps you are a charlatan, perhaps not,' she finally said, getting up and turning lightly away from him. Her tone was deliberately teasing.

'Is that all you have to say on this subject?' He was surprised by her reply. And she knew he was angry.

Ann clasped her hands together in front of her and addressed him directly. Her voice was low and serious. 'Mr Etherington, I cannot tell what you believe, and it does not matter, because it is what you do which is important. You and I can discuss the poor or imagine the horror of prison conditions but it is Mrs Beresford who takes action. I admire that.' She got up and went to the fireplace to ring the servants' bell. 'Now, would you take tea?'

Francis ignored her question. He stood up. 'You obviously do think me a charlatan, madam. One not worth engaging with in a real conversation.' He took his leave with so little ceremony that it would have been described as rude by anybody watching.

Ann stood alone in the library. So Francis Etherington meant what he said. His reaction to her disbelief was proof of that. He did not want to have her think of him as an unfeeling man of trade. Well, she did not. She had been aware of his difficulty in changing the mood of the party from disquiet to relaxed assurance. She had sensed the effort it took to choose the right words as he hesitated mid sentence, but, nevertheless, she had also seen that he was prepared to find the right words to further his dealings. Not, therefore, a man of principle, however he might protest; but a man with, at the very least, a conscience, as the last few minutes had proved.

Mary wondered why Mrs Walker was smiling when she brought in the tea things.

Chapter 8

The wind was becoming stronger and the party of tourists beat a retreat to the confines of the hay barn. This visit to the ancient stone circle of Arbor Low was a foolhardy enterprise in the early days of spring, but the weather had seemed fine when the party, consisting of James, Ann, and Kitty in one carriage and Amanda, her fiancé, Mr Hodgson, and his friend Mr Etherington in the other, had set out. Now the sky was dark grey and swirling and rain came at an angle into the barn. The party retreated further in to the shelter of the barn to escape the storm.

Mr Johnston and Mr Etherington were visiting Derbyshire to finalise the arrangements for the wedding in May. Francis Etherington was to be best man and took his responsibilities very seriously. He had made John practise his speech in front of the Walker family until Kitty had said that young Charles could say most of it off by heart and even Adam could lisp. 'My dear family...'

This outing was arranged by Amanda as a pleasant escape for everyone from speech-making and dreadful decisions about the flounces on her chip bonnet. She went to the door and squinted into the rain. 'I do believe I can see some blue sky,' she called cheerfully to the huddled travellers. They stared back disbelievingly at her. But there was some blue sky and Amanda was determined to lead the party up the cinder path to the ancient site.

They had spent some time the night before crowded round the fire in the Devonshire Arms reading aloud in turn from a pamphlet which she had brought with her about the Druid connections of Arbor Low.

'This could be the very heart of Mercia, the great kingdom

of England's past,' she had told them.

When Amanda had finished, Ann picked up the pamphlet. A lecture in St Oswald's hall to be given by the Reverend Samuel Pegge of Whittington, Who has Researched the Histories of Ancient Derbyshire.

'Don't you find it exciting, Ann?' Amanda swept her skirts aside and sat down, pulling her chair near to Ann. 'You know, I went expecting to be bored but I was most certainly not.'

There had been a pile of freshly printed pamphlets by the door, and she had picked one up and used it to fan her face in the stuffy lecture hall. As she listened to Mr Pegge, she had been first amused and then intrigued by his account. The wild country of the Peak district with its spirits and ghostly battles lay just beyond the regular gardens of Ashbourne. Amanda felt enticed by the proximity of this other dangerous world. Of course, its danger was contained by its existence in the past and it could be safely viewed from this modern age by a young lady with access to a good carriage. She had decided a visit to the site would be a fitting contrast to the sophistication of London coffee houses for her guests. And so here they were.

James went to the partition between the barn and the stable and called to their coachman. 'Michael, go to the farmhouse and ask Mr Cooper to have his wife prepare us something hot. Hurry.' He walked back to the company. 'We should be warm indoors in a moment,' he said. 'Let us wait for the rain to stop this infernal sideways pelting and we can cross the yard.'

Michael returned to say that there was only a ten-year-old boy in the house. His parents were out on the farm and he was only left behind because he had a sickness.

'We will have to go back to the Devonshire.' James had tired of this jaunt and would rather be on his way back to Ashbourne, to a good fire and his own idea of supper, but he felt that the Duke of Devonshire, a coaching inn on the Buxton road, was a fair compromise.

'But James, the sky is getting a little blue and we have waited this long,' Amanda was not pleased to give up so easily.

John Hodgson intervened, 'James, could Amanda, myself and Francis not stay some time longer? You take the other coach back to the Devonshire and wait for us there?' John was given a grateful look from Amanda. He beamed back at her. His beloved.

This seemed a reasonable solution to James. He, his wife and his mother went to the Devonshire and were soon enjoying the very best of service and foodstuffs that the delighted landlord could produce.

In the kitchen, the landlord leaned on the dresser and talked to his wife. 'Gentry once always means gentry again, if you treat them right.'

His usual customers were poor payers from the Manchester coach or even worse, his barns were filled with pack horse men on the old tracks and carters using the new turnpikes to cross the Peak district from Manchester to Derby. None of them had any money and many tried to skip off of a morning without paying. Give him gentry any day, even if you had to fawn all over them.

He stole a glance at his wife's face. She still looked sullen. He kept his wife in the kitchens, he knew that she wouldn't fawn on any body. She had no idea how to treat customers but he liked to say that she was the baker of the best bread in Derbyshire. A craftswoman. Proud of her trade. His loud, public praise for his wife's bread was his only control over her. She was wild. She made him nervous. She might bolt, and then where would he be? You couldn't find bakers out here on the moors. Just farmers' wives who sloped off for lambing or harvest.

He went back into the dining room. Ann bit into a piece of the bread and reassured the hovering landlord that he was not mistaken. Definitely the best bread she had ever eaten.

She would have preferred to stay at Arbor Low. She was drawn to its bleak aspect and its mysterious history. The wind and the rain only enhanced its appeal. She left Kitty and James eating more of the famous bread and walked over to the window. Amanda had been right. The sky was clearing and the day taking on that fresh aspect of early spring, when a fuzz of green could be seen on the trees and the wind could change from threatening gusts to a gentle breath. But at that moment the wind seemed to be increasing in strength and she saw the stables lads banging-to the shutters in the inn yard. Beyond the yard, clouds swept across the high moorland, finding no obstacle in their path.

She caught sight of a horseman riding slowly down the Manchester turnpike. He was riding straight into the rising wind. His head was down, his face and body mostly covered by a voluminous cloak, which every now and then would break free and flow behind him. He would brandish first one arm and then the other in an attempt to gain control of the cloak, in a parody of a romantic hero riding into battle. He was having a hard time keeping his horse on the forward route. It kept veering off to the fields on either side of the road and the rider had to constantly pull hard on the reins to bring it back. As the two got nearer, Ann saw that the horse was nothing more than a poor farm pony, not the steed of a hero, and probably unused to being ridden on hard roads. It would not be shod and the road underfoot would be painful. No wonder it was veering off, thought Ann, and why would any rider force a horse without shoes on to a turnpike? Unless he were uncommonly stupid.

The horse turned into the inn yard and the rider gingerly pulled back the hood of his shabby, mud splattered cloak. Ann saw that it was Francis Etherington.

He would probably never have ridden an unshod horse

before and must have wondered at his difficulties. Ann wondered why in heaven's name he had returned to the inn in such an uncomfortable way... surely nothing had happened to Amanda? She rushed out into the inn entrance, holding her shawl around her, unable to wait if there was to be any bad news.

'Mr Etherington,' she cried, as he came across the yard. Her voice could not be heard above the wind and Francis looked at her in puzzlement. He took her arm and ushered her into the doorway of the inn. Hardly any wind entered past the protection of the thick bulwarks of the old inn porch, built to withstand worse weather than this, and Ann could speak freely. But she suddenly found that she was very afraid. She did not want to ask Francis Etherington what disaster had taken place. She looked at him, willing him to speak first.

'Mrs Walker, what is the matter?' He could see her distress but was at a loss to understand its reason. 'Why have you come running out like this?' He took her arm. 'Here, come into the hall.'

Francis brought her across the threshold into the hall of the inn. It was surprisingly dark after the yard, and Ann could only just make out Mr Etherington's face in half shadow. She could not see his expression for an indication of any disaster.

'Has anything befallen Amanda or Mr Hodgson?' Her voice seemed thin and airless. She took a deep breath. 'Tell me, please.'

For a moment, Francis was quite silent. 'Amanda? John? Why no. No. I rode back because I thought you might like to join us at the Low.' He looked out of the open door, as the wind lifted the last leaves of winter off the ground. 'The weather was appreciably better a half an hour ago.'

He turned back to her. In the dark of the hall, she sensed, rather than saw, him smile. 'The others are well. Or they were when I left them. To be truthful it is not so enjoyable to be with two lovers the week before their wedding. Their conversation was uncommonly silly.'

Ann laughed, partly with relief. She could well imagine Amanda and her beau. It would be a little embarrassing and very boring to be alone with them, and they, if they noticed, would be glad that Francis had left them to it.

'I was given some farm pony and an old cloak by the boy at the farmhouse. I had difficulty controlling both of them.' Again he smiled. 'I had thought we could take horses from the inn and ride back, but,' he gestured to the open doorway, 'it is much worse out there than I had expected.'

Ann looked beyond him to the inn yard. She wanted to tell him that she had been used to walking miles in weather like this. It did not frighten her, but she knew that James and Kitty would be horrified at the thought of it. She felt a sharp pang of disappointment as she realised that she could not go. Then the clouds parted and a flash of bright blue sky appeared. She watched as the clouds continued to roll back and the blue sky spread into a great swathe of colour. A stray shaft of sunlight lit up the hall. Spring weather, thought Ann, unpredictable.

Francis Etherington was also looking at the blue sky and Ann knew that he was thinking the same as her. If it stayed for a few minutes then they could, without seeming too foolhardy, choose to go riding.

He spoke, hardly looking at her for confirmation. 'The weather seems to be changing. I'll go and have two horses saddled. We may be able to ride back after all.'

She turned and ran up the stairs. At the half landing, she stopped and looked back at him. There was something comical about the way he stood there, holding his cloak clutched to his chest, looking up at her. She laughed. 'Mr Etherington. Go! Before the weather changes back again! Make sure that you get two good horses. I will be down shortly.'

Their ride up the turnpike was relatively easy. The wind

was behind them, ballooning out their capes and pushing them on. The inn horses were lively, excited by the wildness of the day, and so both Ann and Francis had to concentrate on directing them. At last, they saw the sign for Monyash lane and were relieved to turn off the turnpike. Immediately they were out of the wind and plunged by contrast into an almost eerie silence. The lane was a deeply worn track. It had been trodden down by a constant stream of travellers over the centuries and now had steep sides lined at the top by tightly bunched trees. Over the years these trees had arched across the pathway, creating a great tunnel of leaves and branches. The horses were calmed by the silence and picked their way quietly along the path. Ann could feel the heavy thud of her horse's hooves on the springy peat of the track and could hear the comforting, rhythmic chink as the bridles were shaken from side to side by their motion. In this silence she could even make out the sound of Francis Etherington's breathing. The track broadened slightly and Francis drew back alongside of her.

'Mrs Walker.'

She tilted her head slightly and prepared to listen, but he said nothing more. She glanced at him. He appeared to have gone into some kind of reverie.

They carried on riding for a few moments and then Ann could wait no longer. 'Mr Etherington, what is it you want to say?'

He looked at her briefly and then leaned over and took hold of her horse's bridle.

'Could we walk a while? I wish to speak with you.'

Ann nodded agreement. They both dismounted and walked on down the track, holding their horses by the reins.

'Madam, do you think of me as a...' he paused, 'a charlatan? You did not answer me that day we spoke. You remember it, do you not?'

Ann nodded. That word again. He spat it out with something close to disgust.

He continued, 'I have often thought of our conversation at dinner. I cannot believe that you took it as lightly as you implied. You do think less of me because of it. Do you not?' Ann hesitated for a moment. Mr Etherington demanded the truth of her, and she wanted to give it. He was right, she had thought less of him after that night.

'Mr Etherington. You,' she corrected herself, 'we, cannot purport to have a social conscience while living the life that we do. We are cocooned by our wealth and can so easily mouth sympathy for those less fortunate than ourselves while all the time continuing to enjoy our good dinners and soft beds.'

He started to speak but she held up her hand, 'I tire, Mr Etherington, of hearing fine Christian principles spouted over laden tables or in glittering ballrooms. I tire of hearing myself speaking in this way. But at least, I hope I am honest enough not to pretend hurt feelings if someone should find me out. We are all charlatans.' Ann walked on a little faster. There was more she would like to say.

'So we are all charlatans. You would count yourself firmly in this number?'

Ann nodded in reply.

He frowned. 'But, Mrs Walker, in order to live, you must compromise. Nothing is as simple as you suggest. It is not possible for me to change my whole life in order to assist those less fortunate than I but I can recognise their difficulties. I can sympathise as a fellow human being.'

Ann could hold it back no longer. 'Poppycock, Mr Etherington. Poppycock. Just so many words. Easily said. You are a pampered young man, whose only worry is whether or not you can increase your standing in the eyes of others of your class. You see the poor as animals, whose conditions you might improve just as you might give a horse fresh bedding or a dog a decent meal.'

'Madam,' he said, and his anger matched her own, 'I hardly think you can speak of yourself differently. When you visit the almshouses in Ashbourne, you are the same as I.'

'No,' replied Ann. 'No! Mr Etherington, for I came from the poor. I have known what it is like to sleep on the same straw as the horse you might ride and I have seen the eyes of rich young men like you look me over as if I were horsemeat.'

She had pulled her horse to a standstill and, in her anger was standing very close to him. To her, at that moment, he represented all that she abhorred and feared in his class. She had met his like in the dark streets of Derby, diffident, shy, so polite; being persuaded by his friends to take a prostitute. But his kindness, his diffident good manners all reserved for his own kind. He, and his friends jeering in the background, would see her as simply a useful commodity. For a moment, the years which intervened between her life then and her life now disappeared. She felt filled by fear and anger. She was standing in Saddlergate outside the Greyhound surrounded by his like. Ann raised her hand and hit him hard across the face.

Francis Etherington did not react to the blow at all at first, his eyes stayed fixed on her face and then he raised his hand briefly to his cheek as if in surprise. Then he shook his head as if to clear it. 'Mrs Walker, I begin to think we are the same. I know we are the same. From what you say... I suspected... I was not born to this life either. I was a child in the poorhouse at Gray's Inn.'

He looked at her as if he expected her to have some knowledge of this place.

Ann shook her head. 'I don't know it.'

She did not want to hear this story. He was eager to tell her, but she was not ready to listen. To allow that he might understand, have experienced a life similar to the one she had so fiercely described.

Her hand still smarted. She looked at his face and could discern a red mark across his cheek. 'Your face...' She raised her hand, but Francis Etherington was not to be diverted. 'It is of no matter.' He dismissed her concern with a shake of his head. 'I speak of The Foundling Hospital.'

Now Ann remembered, yes, of course, she had heard Mrs Beresford talk of it. Mrs Beresford would like to follow its pattern in Derby. Ann had seen the plans.

'I was given a token of my mother. A carved figure. Like a wooden doll. I have it still. I keep it about me.' He drew a small crudely carved figure from his jacket. No bigger than his hand. He handed it to Ann. She examined it. It was a common enough story. A child with only some small scrap of evidence of parentage. The figure did give truth to what he had said. 'Most of us had something like this. A knitted blanket, a necklace or a charm on a leather string. A token.' But Ann remained suspicious. Surely he could find his birth mother if he so wished?

'Where is your mother now?' She asked. She knew the Foundling Hospital had excellent records. She remembered Mrs Beresford telling her carefully, with great emphasis, that they had only ever lost the identities of four babies.

Francis shrugged his shoulders. 'I have no idea. I asked about her. There are records. She was given a receipt for me. But my name was given to me by the hospital. I do not know my mother's name. If she wishes to find me she can. But I cannot find her.'

Perhaps that was true, she thought.

He hesitated, then spoke more quickly. 'Do you have a token, Mrs Walker? Were you in such a place.' He sounded sure of her reply.

Ann opened her mouth to explain, then stopped. 'No,' she said, and handed the doll back to him.

Ann felt her horse strain at its bridle, trying to get to the grass on the bank beside them. She let the bridle slide out of her hand and Francis Etherington did the same. The horses jostled for position and then steadily began to rip up and chew as much of the sweet grass as this break in their journey would allow them. Francis and Ann stood and watched them. He put the doll back in his pocket.

'I do not understand…' he began.

She turned to face him. 'I said no. I do not have a token. I was not abandoned in a foundling hospital.'

'Ah. I have been mistaken.'

She sensed him draw slowly, carefully back from her.

'I apologise,' he said. 'I may have offended you. It was not meant in such a way.' He smiled anxiously.

'I am not offended.' To reassure him she returned his smile. 'You do have something, a part at any rate, of my background. My life was not always like this. Before I married James I was the wife of a poor packman. He died, and I made my own way as a seamstress… then I met James.' She smiled again. 'Now tell me. How did you make your way out of the poorhouse?'

'When I was four years old I was chosen by the benefactors. They were part of 'The Guild of London Merchants'. I remember the name so well because it was here,' he touched his chest, 'blazoned on my jacket for years. Note,' he smiled wryly at her, 'not one came that day, one alone would not have felt safe coming down to Gray's Inn. No, we were visited by a gaggle of them. I was showing some promise in arithmetic and calculations. The hospital provided us with some education, better than many such places.'

Ann nodded, Mrs Beresford had said.

'However, there were many boys who had shown promise and these benefactors had to choose between us. And…' He suddenly leapt up onto the bank and pirouetted in front of Ann. 'I was the prettiest so, they chose me.' The horses jumped back. Their concentration on feeding broken for a moment.

Ann laughed aloud, both startled and delighted. Francis watched her laugh, and knew he had won some way into her confidence.

A boy chosen to be a surrogate son by rich London entrepreneurs to make up for all the people they had harmed in their rise through society. Standing in line that day realising that this might be his only chance of survival and the pity of the moment when he knew he had been chosen and all the others like him had not. The sheer chance of it, the arbitrary nature of the action made a weakness in him. A fear. In the end, perhaps it bred a cruelty, too. He had sensed all of this was in Ann too, however little she was prepared to say.

Protected by the canopy of trees and oblivious of the wind which raged stronger and stronger across the land around them, Ann and Francis talked on. Ann did not tell him of her life in Derby. She let him talk to her of his life.

'I left a few friends behind me in the poorhouse that day,' said Francis, 'and I left many people to whom I was indifferent. I remember how the moment before the choice was made stretched out. It felt like hours. I can still feel the silence as twenty boys held their breath. But I would not have given one of them my chance. I would not have turned round to offer my good fortune to some one else.' He looked around.

'Shall we sit here for a while?' He went over to the opposite bank, bending down to touch the grass. 'It is quite dry.'

Ann joined him. They sat down together and he continued to talk in a low voice. 'That is the truth of poverty. You have no honour. You fight desperately to save yourself and, eventually, you tire of yourself.' He put his head back and briefly closed his eyes. 'You begin to know that you are not worth the saving.'

His voice had died down to a whisper and now he was quiet for a long time. They both thought back over the years behind them. Eventually he began to speak again. In hearing his story Ann moved a little towards understanding her own story better. Each of them carried black secrets; things they had done to ensure their own safety.

She chose not to talk of the packhorseman and of Mr Meynell but, as Francis Etherington talked, she watched him with a kind of envy. He seemed unaware of her scrutiny, or perhaps, it occurred to her, he accepted of it, trusting her completely. She envied him that ability to trust. He was engrossed in explaining, describing what it had been like to be a child in London. Sometimes he became silent, lost in thought, and then he plunged on. Talking of his joy at first at being chosen by his benefactors and then the continual, knawing fear that he would not be good enough and would be sent back to the workhouse. And then finally his realisation of the trap which had been set for him. How the crimes they asked him to commit became greater and how eventually he understood that the trail of blame led to him and him alone.

'It was convenient ... I was convenient. I was perfectly what they wanted.' He shrugged his shoulders. 'When I understood why they had picked me – for my gullibility, for my desperation to impress – I was ashamed.' He looked down. 'Ashamed of my own stupidity.'

He picked up some stones from the verge in front of him and threw one violently across the path. They both listened as it clattered against something hard on the opposite bank and the horses raised their heads in alarm. 'I should have been angry, but I was ashamed. Shame. That's what it breeds in you – the workhouse.' He let the rest of the stones drop between his fingers.

'Why are you telling me this?' Her voice was harsh. She wanted to shut him out.

There was a silence and then she heard him say her name. 'Ann...'

To hear him say her name with such quiet longing was a shock. Suddenly she was ashamed of her own cruelty.

'You and I – we are the same,' she said. She would offer him this, a recognition at least, although she could, she would, give him nothing else. 'We, we are both the victims of our birth.'

'Tell me how. How are we the same?' He leaned towards her.

'Tell me about yourself. ' His voice was urgent.

She shook her head, desperate to get him away from this track. 'No. I cannot. I do not wish to.'

He would allow her that. 'Very well. But there will be a reckoning. I will expect the truth from you one day.'

His eyes were teasing, seeking hers out, but Ann found she could not meet his open gaze. She was glad when he began to talk of his past again.

As he talked, she knew with hopeless certainty, that neither of them had the luxury of morality, or of romance. Kitty and her medallions seemed ridiculous now. The hope she had felt for Cluny and his cause seemed misguided. The rush of desire to enter that world which had filled her as she wished Cluny Godspeed in the wood at Beeston Tor seemed a silly delusion. Her life had been a stark choice at every juncture between her survival or the survival of another. By his talk, Francis had had the same experience. He had lived in Holland, in Denmark and in France, and had done whatever his employers had asked him to do.

'The actions I took were never to be discussed. I was sworn to secrecy but I knew that what I did for them was essential to their success.'

'All of Europe seemed to be at war, Ann. Men's lives were the price commonly paid for the success of one faction over another, and I have found myself willing to exact that price. It is as simple as that.'

Then, keeping her eyes on her hands as they lay still in her lap, she asked him the question she knew she should not ask, but could not resist asking.

'Do you mean to say that you have killed men, Mr Etherington?

'Yes.'

Ann felt as if some taught line within her had snapped. She wanted to tell him then about the packman, about Meynell. She took a breath to speak. But almost immediately fear

231

rushed back into her mind and the momentary release was over. She closed her mouth and turned her head away. Why had he told her this much? Was there a purpose behind these confessions after all? She looked back at him, searching his face for an answer.

His mouth compressed into a thin, anxious line. 'I should not have told you this.'

Now he was afraid of her. She had to reply.

'Mr Etherington, many men kill. Have to kill. We are at war. Soldiers must fight.' She sought for an excuse for him. He refused it.

'Yes. We are at war, but the lines did not feel that clear. I did not wear a uniform.'

'Did you mean to kill?' It was too stark. 'Or, I mean, was it in fighting? To defend yourself?'

There was an almost imperceptible pause. 'Do you think it would be more excusable if I killed because there was no other way to – to survive myself?'

Eventually she nodded her head. 'Yes,' she whispered.

'Then... It was.'

He moved his hand until it rested directly above hers. She knew he was about to touch her and she did not move away.

Suddenly there was a roar. Her eyes were filled with stinging dust as a huge gust of wind swept down through the branches above them and swirled over the track. Ann sprang up and as she brought her hands up to her face to wipe away the blinding dust, she felt cold rain spilling from the leaves and splattering over her head and shoulders. She stumbled and then she felt Francis Etherington's hand under her arm, helping her to stand.

She pulled away from him.

'Thank you. I am all right, Mr Etherington. Thank you.'

'I must get after them,' he shouted. He was already running towards the horses who had begun to move off down the lane, their eyes rolling in fear. She felt a fine, gritty mud on her cheeks and between her fingers as the rain and dust mixed together. She looked up and down the track.

It was impossible to see for more than a few hundred yards either way. The trees had thickened to become two rows of hunched black figures, the sky between them livid with the setting sun. The wind roared again through the outer branches. The inn. The family would be waiting for them. They must get back. Francis was leading the horses back to where she stood.

She tried to raise her voice above the wind. 'Mr Etherington, we must go back to the inn.'

'Why?' he shouted back.

'What do you mean? We have to go back.'

And then as quickly as it had come, the wind passed on and they were both awkward in the sudden silence around them. Ann dropped her voice.

'The whole family will be waiting, Mr Etherington.' She looked at him steadily, 'Anxious.' She picked up her riding crop.

Francis watched her. 'Very well. We must go back. But Ann,' he took a step towards her, ' I will not lose you.'

Ann stilled and looked up at him. She noted his use of her first name again. Both of his hands were slightly raised towards her, as if he intended to put them around her. Keeping his eyes caught in her gaze, she moved back.

'You cannot lose me, Mr Etherington, for you have me as a good friend, and you will find that friendship can never be lost.'

He opened his mouth to protest but she leaned forward and laid her hand over his lips.

'You must know how precious my life here is to me; there is nothing which is worth endangering it for.'

Francis Etherington made no reply. He watched her. She was intent on mounting her horse. Already thinking of their return to the inn. He had misjudged her at the end there.

Ann drew her riding glove over the fingers which she had laid on Francis Etherington's lips. I should not have touched him, she said in silent rebuke to herself.

The ride back to the inn was uncomfortable but not dangerous. They arrived at the inn just after the carriage containing Amanda and John Hodgson. No one had begun to miss them from either party because no one had been sure of their whereabouts. Ann had left only a garbled message at the inn before setting off with Francis and it had not been clear where they were going or when they were to be expected. The party was staying overnight at the Devonshire Arms and so nothing more serious than a slight delay to dinner was caused.

February 1758 The Monkey Room Chantilly France

The heavy yellow velvet curtains lifted slightly as the wind repeatedly pushed against the windows of the Chateau D' Chantilly. The Duc de Choiseul sat by the monstrous marble fireplace in the Monkey Room, called so after the strange creatures which decorated its walls and panels. Choiseul luxuriated in the heat from the blazing fire in front of him. It was a cold night. Colder than it had been three years ago, when he had written his letter to Cluny, giving a promise of seven thousand Louis D'or to add to the three thousand sent across England in the box. He had been alone with his pen and his paper that night and he was pleased to be alone now. He thought again of that night. Calculating what was enough to bring the Jacobites on, that had been nicely done. But then to have it all lost. Lost. For three years. Last night, at dinner, he had had to listen to Louis Joseph, the Great Prince of Condé describe the exact proportions of the new tennis courts he proposed to build. The measurements for the base, the correct height for the nets. It had been interminably boring. To his horror, Prince Louis had then suggested that they take a walk around the site this morning. Choiseul had felt unable to refuse, and this morning he had stood shivering as the wind swept across the lake and blew icy particles of snow in between the folds of his great coat to lodge against his silk-clad legs. The Prince of Condé had excitedly talked on of his plans for Chantilly. Interminably. Seemingly unaware of the bitter cold. Choiseul's right hand fluttered across his chest. He hoped he had not contracted some rheum of the lungs. His mission was important, but he did not wish to die for it.

Although he continued to stare steadfastly into the fire, Choiseul was aware, at the periphery of his vision, of the disturbingly violent scenes which were being enacted around him. The walls of the large reception room were covered with images of war and hunting. Foreign, sandy landscapes with strange sprouting vegetation and Chinese men dressed in wide sleeved gowns. Spears, swords and animals and men running for their lives; the images were in such close proximity that they seemed jumbled, as if there was nothing to distinguish man from beast. All could be hunted and killed for sport. The worst of all were the apes. The grotesque man-like figures that were everywhere and seemed to leer out at him from behind the tapestries. They had small human, watchful eyes but huge animal teeth and mouths. Their hands, long fingered and incongruously elegant, reminded Choiseul of those of a Jesuit priest he had once known. Those fingers which had broken communion bread, turned the pages of a prayer book to precisely the right page now everywhere gripped desperately to the branches of weird trees and clung to snaking vines. And always the faces of the creatures stared out, some watching him impassively, some screaming at him in terror or in warning. They were the stuff of childhood nightmares.

Choiseul jerked upright in his seat as the door opened. A manservant entered to announce that Prince Charles had arrived and was waiting in the antechamber.

Charles Stuart, the Young Pretender, the Prince of Wales, Bonnie Prince Charlie... just so many meaningless titles... thought Choiseul, as he rose to his feet.

A tall, heavyset man had entered the room. His shoulders were thrown stiffly back, his eyes were overly bright and, as he walked into the room, a barely perceptible, almost delicate, smell of sour spirits preceded him. Choiseul knew that this man's slow, swaggering walk, a parody of nobility, was only achieved through ignoring the pain he felt. Choiseul also knew that the pain the Prince suffered was caused by gout. His medical bills were sent to the French, after the Italians had looked at them.

'Your Royal Highness, I am honoured by your agreement to talk with me today.' Choiseul's smile held all the tremulous humility and fear of a man in the presence of greatness. He bowed low to the prince. 'I trust your journey from Italy this past week was not too difficult?'

'Choiseul, I am come to make arrangements.' Charles stopped talking abruptly. 'Who is this man?' He pointed to the manservant standing quietly by the door.

'Only a servant,' replied Choiseul. 'If we speak in English he will not understand us.'

Charles' voice became querulous. 'I do not want anyone here but you, Choiseul. I am hounded by agents, day and night. You cannot trust anyone.'

'My Prince, in a place such as this,' with a vague sweep of his hand, Choiseul suggested the intrigue of the whole French court, with its great houses and vast spy network, 'you are better to let a servant stay in a meeting room. If we send him out it will only bring attention to the secrecy of our proceedings.'

Charles thought. 'Very well,' he said and sat down on the sofa beside the fire, indicating that Choiseul should take a place on the chair opposite him. Choiseul was startled to see the body of the Prince immediately slump into the shape of that of an old man. For a moment, the Prince was silent, staring into the fire. The brilliant, flickering light of the fire threw into relief the deeply lined face of a disappointed old man. Choiseul noted that the mouth of the Prince looked incongruously young, like the mouth of a petulant boy. His royal hand, rings of Princedom embedded in the flesh, trembled on the scrolled top of his walking stick. Is this how he sits, thought Choiseul, night after night, dreaming of what might have been...?

Then the Prince roused himself, rapped the floor with his walking stick and turned to the waiting minister of the French government. And Choiseul saw something of what this man must have been. The bright blue eyes were still startling, compelling. When this man turned to look at you, you might indeed feel chosen.

'Now, Choiseul, I have it from Cluny Macpherson that the Louis D'or which you sent us has been at last recovered.' Charles became excited. This was something he had thought long on. This was a possibility. This success of Macpherson's meant that the French would see how well the network of Jacobites in Britain still operated. As he had written to Cluny, it would be of the utmost importance to the furtherance of his cause.

'Yes, your Highness, I believe so,' said Choiseul. The surprising recovery of the box of money sent in 1755 did indeed mean that the French government would consider supporting another uprising. The recovery was of more than money. Charles would know that three thousand Louis D'or was only a token of French support. More importantly, extensive information about Jacobite sympathisers had been sent with the Louis D'or. There had to be a strong network of Jacobites in England to respond to another uprising and this recovery meant that that network must still be intact and operable. That much was now certain. But would Scotland still follow Charles Stuart? Choiseul examined the

Prince. In talking of the money and its implications for the future, Choiseul had indeed detected a change in the man. He was more animated and his body had become more upright. Maybe, thought Choiseul, maybe this try for the English throne could be more than a diversion. It was a great prize. Great enough to risk some further investment. And, of course, if it failed, it would serve to spread thin the English war machine and save some French lives. Bullets and cannon which were directed at Scottish and English rebels at home could not hit French soldiers in Europe.

The two men talked on. The wind died down and the folds of the curtains made motionless parallel lines down to the floor. The footman silently lit up all the great candelabra on the glossy malachite tables; as the meeting continued the light from these candles fell on newly drafted plans for a third invasion of England by Charles Stuart.

Charles left the meeting with Choiseul as a man of far greater strategic importance than he had entered it. His carriage was accompanied by Palace guardsmen who had orders to stay by him at all times. The future king of England had to be protected by his French cousins. And had to be seen to be.

After Charles had left, Choiseul gestured to the footman to come to him. The footman walked across the room and took the seat left by Charles. Choiseul looked at him 'Well, De Vere. What do you think? Do we stand a chance?'

The footman pursed his lips and shrugged his shoulders. 'It is not for me to say. I only do your bidding, Choiseul. But, ca va, even if it fails we will gain time. Our troops in Portugal are in great need of a respite'

'It is more than a ploy to relieve our troops in Portugal, although, I must admit, De Vere, that had crossed my mind. I think that we can give this pretender one last chance. We would gain so much by his success. The King has it close to his heart to see England a Catholic country once more. We have, of course, the blessing of the Vatican Council and all that that will mean for our foreign trade in the future.'

'But,' interrupted De Vere, 'has not the Prince given up the Catholic faith. I thought in London, on his visit in 1750...?'

'Only temporarily. He thought it might help bring English supporters to the cause but it was never a sound plan. '

Choiseul went back to the main line of his story. 'De Vere, the destruction of the Protestant stranglehold on trade is vital if France is to take her proper place in the world. We lag behind, De Vere, the Dutch take our markets and the English steal Italian plans for machinery to make knitted stockings. Old women still knit by hand in this country. That is our industry,' Choiseul made a gesture of disdain. 'We must back this uprising. Send warships and men to create another theatre of war in the north; and then we must be seen to be pushing south from the Scottish Highlands. Do you not agree?'

But De Vere was made uneasy by what he had just heard. De Vere worked on the ground, with these men that Choiseul sent to battle and death so glibly. He could see the struggling bodies, feel the cold, fearful nights, the pain. Hear the emptiness, the silence, of loss.

'Seen to be. Seen to be...' De Vere turned and walked down the room, too agitated by the enormous betrayal he saw Choiseul to be perpetrating to stand still. 'Choiseul!' he turned and shouted back at the figure by the fireplace. His voice was high and thin with emotion; its sharp echo sounded off the walls of the great room. ' What do you plan? To leave our Scottish allies without support? To encourage an uprising and then leave the people to be slaughtered?'

He strode back to the fireplace and slammed his hand down on the table placed there. The noise was a shock between them. De Vere hesitated as the sound died away, then he turned to face Choiseul. Choiseul could not see his expression, the man stood above him, a dark silhouette with the flames behind him. De Vere's voice dropped to a whisper as he leaned towards the seated man. 'For that is what it would be, Choiseul. A slaughter.'

Choiseul shifted a little in his chair. 'I do not plan a slaughter, De Vere, but we must be realistic. We may not succeed. Or, at least, the uprising may not succeed. However, whatever the outcome, the cause of France will be furthered. And the cause of France is what first engages us – eh, De Vere. Is that not true?' Choiseul looked up at De Vere, his head tilted slightly to one side and his eyes wide open, questioning. He was throwing down a challenge to the other man.

De Vere felt a sickness rise in his gullet. His argument sounded foolish in the light of the other man's appeal. It could also be construed as treasonous.... Was there a warning behind the steady gaze of his old friend? De Vere did not owe his first loyalty to the Scots. He capitulated. He knew the politics as well as Choiseul. And Choiseul was right. The cause of France and the cause of Catholicism would be furthered by a third uprising of the Scots. Successful or not.

'Send the warships packed with our men. They should be seen off the English coast, and the Scottish clansmen must believe in our support.' De Vere paused. Now there was a note of warning in his voice. 'But, Choiseul, do not be mistaken. This plan will only succeed if we have the support of the Scottish clans. The plan will not succeed unless we use the real love of these men for their beleaguered country. They must fight believing in their cause. They must fight believing that they can win. They must fight knowing, believing that we are on their side. I know them Choiseul.'

Choiseul nodded. He spoke soothingly. 'We are. We are on their side. We will do what we can.' He was well aware that De Vere had valuable knowledge of their Scottish allies. His closeness to them was his strength, but it also made him difficult to handle at times.

There was one more piece of information he had to discuss with De Vere. Choiseul hesitated. He knew this man well, and he knew that what he was about to say would anger him and hurt him. But there was no other way.

'De Vere. The Louis D'or. Do you remember how it was carried?'

'How it was carried – by a packman. What do you mean?'

'No, I mean the container.'

'The container? No, I assume saddle bags... a strong box. It would be heavy. I do not know. Does it matter?'

'Do you remember Villiers ... from De Bagatelles?'

'Villiers? The calligrapher? The one who wrote those messages on the back of the miniatures of the Dutch royal family. So tiny you had to use a magnifying glass to decipher them?' De Vere laughed at the memory of so many messages being sent by the French secret service in the innocent hands of visiting Dutch courtiers, pleased to be given such elegant images of their king and his family. 'Yes, I do remember him. Why?'

'Villiers was the master of an ingenious plan to get information to the Scottish Jacobites. The names of all our agents and the names of the greatest of the English sympathetic to our cause were inscribed by Villiers in code on the inside of the box which contained the Louis D'or.'

'What kind of box?' asked De Vere. He was curious. Here was something he had not known.

'Just a simple money box. And under veneer pasted to the inner base of the box were inscribed the names. But they were burnt on, De Vere – that was the cleverness. Not possible to erase them and not possible to make a copy of them good enough to fool us – not quickly. We could trust that if the box got through intact, then our secrets were safe. It is too long since we have been able to do that De Vere.'

Choiseul remembered the small, stout figure of Villiers moving with surprising agility around his workshop. Totally engrossed in finding a solution to the problem of inscribing thousands of letters on an absorbent wooden surface. In the end, he came to the conclusion that only burning in each letter with a fine white hot needle would work. No ink or paint invented, and Villiers knew them all, could make fine enough lines on the wood, and no ink or paint could survive the removal of the thin layer of veneer which he had to fit to the inner base of the box to keep the letters hidden from unwelcome eyes.

Villiers had worked in London. It would have been too dangerous to bring the information to him in Paris. He stayed at the house of Lady Primrose in Essex Street, just off the Strand. She had told any one who seemed curious about the quiet Frenchman who temporarily lived in the basement, that he was a French cabinet maker, repairing household treasures. No one questioned it. Even if the country was at war with France, only a French cabinet maker could be trusted with fine veneer.

Villiers had gone now. He was to have appeared to have drowned, and been given a new identity, as was the way of these things. He had wanted to be free of it all, and had bartered his expertise with the box for his freedom. There was some problem, though. Information had not made it clear where Villiers had really gone. He seemed to have escaped them. It was not good. Might he turn? Could he have already turned?

As he thought back to the events surrounding the creation of the box, Choiseul was aware that De Vere was watching him closely. De Vere was no fool. The fact that this plan had been devised and executed without his knowledge would indicate only one thing to him. He had lost his position at court. He was no longer seen as an important player. His involvement with the failed uprising had tarnished his reputation as a man who knew how to pick winners and he had been sidelined.

Choiseul sought to comfort his friend. 'De Vere. No one felt you could be told. You are known to the Hanoverians. If you had been captured this knowledge would have been dragged out of you. You know that it is true.'

De Vere crossed the room and leaned down to the fire as if he was cold. He looked down into the flames. Dragged out of him... for his own protection... a weak excuse to cover his loss of position. How many other great secrets had he in his head, secrets he had helped create in the past? Who had usurped him in his friend's favour? Who? But best not to show his bitter disappointment. He turned round and made an exaggerated moue at Choiseul. 'Fear not, my friend. I am not about to sulk. I know what you say is true. The Hanoverians have me in their sights. You have to protect information. I am not about to stamp my feet and change sides.'

For a moment the two men looked at each other in silence. The words hung in the air between them.

Then De Vere stood up. 'And now I must take off this disgusting livery,' he brushed at the jacket of his servant's outfit, 'I do not wish to be at your beck and call a moment longer.' He laughed. 'You may ask me to fill a bath tub for you and scrub your back or some other such service.'

Choiseul smiled provocatively up at De Vere, glad that he seemed to have accepted the situation. 'My dear man,' he said, unbuttoning his waistcoat as he spoke. 'You do look uncommonly attractive in the livery of the king. I think I shall indeed require some further services from you.'

De Vere stood for a moment, smiling at him, and then he leaned down and kissed the Foreign Minister in a long and leisurely fashion, full on the lips.

Arisaig April 21st 1758

Cluny Macpherson stood by the jetty and watched the longboat of the cutter Calais as it slowly crossed the sound. Behind it on the calm water the mother ship waited patiently at anchor. As the boat drew nearer he saw that it carried De Vere. He was glad. With him he had the Louis

D'or which he had retrieved from Ann Walker. Through the long months of his journey back to the Highlands he had sustained himself by imagining his next meeting with the Frenchman and the look on his face as Cluny spilled the gold on the table. And now he would get his chance to act it out.

De Vere stepped off the longboat and embraced Cluny warmly. 'Mon frére, we have much business to do. Let us get on.' The two men walked up the beach together and entered the same bothy in which they had sat so many months before.

De Vere withdrew parchments from a large leather case. He laid them out carefully on the rough-hewn table and began to systematically work through the plans with Cluny Macpherson. There was much to explain. Many questions for Cluny to answer. Both men were experienced campaigners; they knew that the availability of water for horses and food for men were equally as important as guns and swords. In 1745, the Scottish army had failed to attract enough support from English Jacobites. The groundwork had to be laid more carefully this time. Commitments had to be made in writing, and the key players had to be ready to lead an uprising in London. This was where the information attached to the original Louis D'or would be vital. Before he moved on to discuss this, De Vere recapped the outline of the invasion plan.

'So, Mr Macpherson, on 20th July of this year your Prince will land at Moidart. He will bring with him four French frigates, fully armed and fifty small cannon. These boats will travel round the Sound of Mull and down to Leith by Edinburgh. There they will be met by six more French warships and 10000 men. Together, the French and Scottish army will proceed to York and on to London. Your task is to rally the clans and to destroy the garrisons at Fort William and at Fort Augustus.' He smiled at the serious clansman. 'Simple. Ah?'

Cluny did not smile back. In his mind, he was already out amongst his clansmen, talking, persuading, investing each man with the desire to win.

As the redcoats marched throughout the Highlands and General Cope sat in Fort William putting his signature on schedules for his officers' leave in Edinburgh, De Vere outlined the invasion plans Choiseul and Charles Stuart had devised in the Monkey Room at the Chateau De Chantilly.

After Cluny had assimilated all that had been said and his questions had been answered, De Vere spoke again. 'Now, Mr Macpherson, to another important matter. I cannot believe that you have found this money from three years past. It shows a great daring. We had thought it lost, gone by some chance who knows where. Where is it, my dear Macpherson? Do you keep it safe up here in your wild country?'

Perhaps he feels as I do, thought Cluny, he has to see the money here, on this table, to complete the agreement. Cluny swung the leather saddle bags on to the table and began to empty the gold on to its surface. The Frenchman looked at the gold and then said, speaking very precisely and with some urgency, 'Mr Macpherson, where is the box which contained the money?'

Cluny was briefly at a loss for words. 'The... the box?' he questioned. 'What do you want with the box, sir!' He gestured at the table, 'Here is the gold.'

De Vere indicated for Cluny to sit down and then he spoke very carefully in English. 'The box, sir, has burnt into its inner surfaces underneath a layer of veneer the names of all the Jacobite sympathisers of any import in England.' He paused. 'And the names of all French agents in England.' He leaned forward. 'The box, therefore, is the key to the success of your rebellion. If it has got into the clutches of Hanoverians then we are doomed. Now sir. I had falsely assumed from your message to us in France telling us that you had found the box full of money that you had brought both to your homeland.' His voice rose. 'But I see not. Now sir, where is the box? The lives of many brave people depend on your answer.'

Cluny looked back at De Vere. Why hadn't he been told of this?

'Why was I not told of this?' he asked.

De Vere passed his hand wearily over his face. 'Because when you said you would look for it, I did not think you would ever find it. And, at that time, I had not been told of the significance of the box itself. When the box was lost those in the French court who knew of this scheme waited to see if our agents had been uncovered but for years nothing happened. It was assumed that the information had been safely lost.'

'But then... who knew about this information? Who in the Highlands did you tell of the importance of the information being carried by Echan MacLean?'

'No one in the Highlands. No one in England, except the agent who inscribed the names, and Echan MacLean himself,' replied De Vere. 'This was French intelligence information, gathered by us to help us in our infiltration of government and society in this country. It would have been invaluable information in the months leading up to another invasion and we, of course, intended to share it with you. But we had to minimise the risk of discovery and hence the names were fired into the very wood of the box which carried the money. A letter was sent in the box, to further misdirect any enemy agents but a list on paper or parchment carrying this information would have been impossible, even in code. It was too risky. But hidden under the veneer on the base of a box. Voila! That was a good idea.' De Vere slapped his right fist onto his left hand. Even though he had been distracted by his concern with his political position, he had been full of admiration when Choiseul told him. It was almost foolproof. Almost. He turned to look at Cluny Macpherson. 'So, Mr Macpherson, where is the box?'

Chapter 9

'And so, may I take this moment to reflect on the value of family...' Mr Brian Hodgson smiled at his audience. He had been speaking for nearly twenty minutes and he was just beginning to enjoy it. Ann slipped out of the room and headed down the back stairs of the Blackmoor's Head. She would go to the kitchen and supervise the provision of supper. A perfectly legitimate excuse for leaving the room.

As she passed a room at the bottom of the first flight of stairs, through its open door she caught a glimpse of men sitting round a card table. These were the serious gamblers. The room was gloomy except for the table where a large oil lamp illuminated the faces of the men. Ann was surprised to see Francis in the ring of faces encircling the table. She was about to enter the room and tease him. In his position as best man, he should not dare leave the wedding party. Then she realised the meaning of his presence in that room. She had not thought of him as a serious gambler, but, as she lingered on the stairs to watch, she recognised signs that she had seen many times at a gaming table. His hands on the cards were sure and confident, well practised; his face, like that of any good gambler, was expressionless, but his eyes were unnaturally wide and his body was eager and alert, with none of the nervous diffidence Ann had witnessed on their first meeting. He looked up and caught sight of her. For a fraction of a second, Ann was aware of a calculating mind, assessing the significance of her presence, before he smiled and waved. Without responding, she turned and carried on down the steps. She reached the kitchens and stood by the entrance to the yard.

So Francis Etherington was a gambler. He had not told her

that. More than a gambler. A man who could not be persuaded to stop. She had needed only one sight of him at the cards to see that in him. She knew what an addiction of that sort meant. She had taken advantage of it often enough. Why had he not told her? But then – why did she think that he should? And like many of his kind, he probably would not recognise himself as a man with anything more than a great love of playing the cards out. He would not see how he was compelled. She thought again of his eyes. Wide and unseeing. And then the change.

That look. She told herself that it was the look of the gambler, lost to everything happening around him. But she was aware that her explanation left her uneasy. Had it been just that? She thought again of the change in him when he saw her watching. Something about his manner. He had not just come out of a gambling stupor to recognise her standing there; it had been rather that he had quickly replaced a mask which, believing himself to be out of her view and being distracted by the cards, he had let slip.

A mask for her. To persuade her he was something he was not.

No, surely not. She thought of that day at Arbor Low. His open face as he had talked and talked. He had shared his worst secrets with her, and put himself in danger by doing it. Trusting that she would not use it against him. Francis Etherington would be annoyed, distressed that she had seen him like this. Ashamed. He had left the wedding to play cards. He could not resist their draw. This was a weakness. Something private. Something shameful. Like all addicts, he had weighed up the possibility of discovery and had gone ahead. He would be annoyed to have been found out. Indeed, he certainly would be. But that was all this was. There was nothing else to be uneasy about.

Ann entered the kitchen and stood staring unseeing at the kitchen girls as they speedily decorated the rows of cream puddings with sprigs of mint.

When had he begun this, she wondered? What had led to it? What life had he led? What actions had he taken? She moved restlessly around the kitchen. Where had he been living when it had grown? When night after night he found he had to play. London? Amsterdam? Where did they send him to do their work for them?

She nodded as one of the girls brought over a decorated pudding for her approval.

How much had he lost? Perhaps he could control it. A banker could afford to lose some money.

Another girl asked her if she would like a glass of water. She shook her head.

She knew so little about him.

She picked up a spoon and put it down again.

How little had she told him of herself, yet.

Yet? What did she mean by that? How much more did she think she might tell of herself to Francis Etherington?

A delivery boy stood in the doorway for a moment, looked at Ann, exchanged a longing glance with one of the girls and then retreated.

To tell him everything. That was what she wanted. To share her horrors with him as he had done with her.

She sat down on the cook's chair by the range.

The girls watched her warily.

Ann stared into the fire.

To unburden herself.

She sat back and closed her eyes.

To unburden herself to him. She longed for it.

The puddings were ready.

As the girls started to convey the dishes upstairs, and she was left alone by the grate, Ann finally admitted to herself that she longed, simply, for him.

And behind the admission came the doubt. But what did she know of him?

Since that afternoon on the track by Arbor Low, business

with James brought Francis to their house again and again and she had found she was drawn to his company. The intimacy of that day at Arbor Low had been important to her. It had opened up the possibility of confession. She had watched and listened as someone else discarded caution. Though she had not spoken, the words she had not said aloud hung in the air about them. Each time she had met Francis Etherington, she moved closer to the edge of speech, like someone sliding down a bank towards a cliff edge. And she had begun to relish the danger of this position she was putting herself in. The exhilaration of the fall. She had imagined him to be a safe landing.

Until now. To see him at the gambling table. So certain of his moves. And again she saw his face, unmasked and calculating, staring back at her through the doorway.

She could hear Mr Hodgson's voice continuing in the room above. She should go back.

As she left the kitchen and turned to go back up the stairs she felt a hand on her shoulder. She turned to find Francis standing there. How long had he been standing there?

'Oh,' she cried and stepped back.

'I have been looking for you. Ann, can we talk? Come with me.' Her first name. Something he had not done since Arbor Low. They stepped out to the yard.

'Ann, you know what you have seen. I will not lie. But I must know. How do you think of me now. How badly?'

Ann said nothing, the silence extended. From the windows above she heard the sound of clapping. Mr Hodgson must have come at last to the end of his speech.

He took hold of both of her shoulders and shook her, 'Tell me.'

She looked at him.

'Francis, I know now that I cannot trust what you say. That what you do is driven by the need to play at cards. I know that you are unlikely to ever be released from that need.

That is what I think of you.'
'You know this much of it?'
'I do.'
'Then you know it is an affliction.'
'Yes. But it is after all, self-imposed. Some struggle and overcome it.'
Few succeed, she thought.
'Ann, help me to overcome it.'
Ah, the plea of the gambler.
He had moved closer to her and now his mouth was only inches from her face. She half tipped her chin up as if to meet him in a kiss and then, with a huge effort, she stopped herself. She drew her head back and looked down. She must not.
Again there was silence between them and during it somehow his plea, his appearance of supplication began to turn to a parody in her mind. It was as if he was holding a pose, and the longer he waited for her reply, the less he could manage it. He did not need her help. There was something else. The word charlatan came to her mind. She pushed it away. Francis waited.
'No,' Ann said.
She moved past him, back up the stairs.
Alone, Francis Etherington leaned against the doorpost. He went over the yard, cupped water up from the horse trough and cooled his face. This was disappointing, but there was progress. He went back upstairs to his game.

The wedding celebrations continued for two days after the couple had left. There were tea parties and evenings of cards and a dancing party was got up. Ann enjoyed none of it. She thought only of gambling, of the foundling hospital, of what she had not said, of what she could say. Images formed and reformed in her head. London, lost children, Francis' hand on the splayed cards. His look as he caught sight of her. The sound of her steps as she had mounted the stairs and left him in the yard. His lips parting as she had leaned towards him. The kiss she did not give him.

At each event, Francis Etherington was a figure standing against a wall or leaning over someone's chair, watching her intently. Then, always when her attention was momentarily somewhere else, he would disappear. She never saw him leave. She would turn back to look for him, search the room, and he would not be there. And every time this happened the loss of him felt greater and the need to see him, to talk to him, grew. When he left, the room felt empty. At first, when she realised he had gone there was a slight sense of relief, she was no longer being scrutinised, but then there was disappointment. When he was not watching her, her actions seemed unimportant. Time at these events stretched out into great yawning gaps as she served tea or listened to talk of the weather. The market. Fashion.

At the Beresford's dancing party, Ann stood in a corner. Francis Etherington was not there. She had checked all the rooms. Beside her, clutching her unmarked card, stood Miss Beresford speaking earnestly of her plans for a foundling hospital in Derby. Ann closed her eyes and thought of Francis. Of the moment when he was chosen.

'Ann. Are you well? You seem distracted." Miss Beresford was concerned. She put her hand on Ann's sleeve.

'Yes,' said Ann, 'I am well.' She smiled reassuringly at Miss Beresford.

How was she to deal with this? There was nothing else in the world but Francis Etherington. And it did not give her happiness, or peace, or pleasure.

Ann ran down the final few stairs into the hall of Hulland House. She smiled. She had regained some authority over herself. Francis had been in the house all morning, talking

252

to James, and she had not contrived to meet him once. She could hear his voice, could locate what room he was in but had not put herself in the way of meeting him. And now he had gone. She had done well.

As she crossed the hall she saw a pair of leather gloves lying on the oak table by the door. His gloves. She picked one of them up and examined it, seeing how the leather had stretched and shaped to his hand. She looked around to check that no one was watching her and then crossed the hall to the morning room, carrying the gloves as if they were some secret prize. She shut the door carefully behind her and moved quickly over to the window where she would be half hidden by the curtains. She slipped one of the gloves on, picked up a book and began to turn the pages. She realised that she was holding her breath and let it out slowly, like a sigh. The pages of the book fluttered and then lay still. She turned another page. It was as if it was his hand holding this book. She hesitated, then she put the book down and slowly brought her hand, still in the glove, up to her cheek. This could be his hand here, she thought. Why not. Why can't it be? She dropped the glove on the floor and turned away.

I must stop this. I cannot stop this. The two thoughts came together.

'What will become of me?' she whispered to the empty room.

One restless afternoon, she chose to walk with Adam and his nurse along the Henmore Brook. Ahead of them were a young couple. Servants on their day off. Wearing their best clothes. The boy's jacket stretched over his large shoulders, the girl's woollen dress frayed around the hem. They walked sedately down the path, stating their intentions by being seen together in public. But from time to time they could not resist a sudden, stolen closeness. Body to body, tightly, briefly, with arms around each others' waists. Then the girl would giggle and push the boy away, glancing over her shoulder to see who might be following and tell her mistress. Adam was pulling at his nurse's skirt. He was tired. Ann picked him up and lodged him on her hip. She buried her face in his neck. For comfort. Over the top of his head she kept her eyes fixed on the couple in front of them.

They had reached a large puddle and the boy lifted his girl up by the waist to carry her over. As the girl rose shrieking above him her eyes caught Ann's and held them for a moment. Ann felt the force of the girl's excitement hit her like a physical blow. Such happiness. She lost her footing and lunged sideways, Adam clutching at her neck in alarm. The nurse put her hands out. 'Will I take the boy? He is heavy, madam'.

'Yes, Jess. You go on a little way. I am tired.'

Ann turned and walked back down the river path. This was something which had never entered her reckoning before. Love.

This is what James felt for her. This is why he was prepared to marry her, even though she did not love him. This is what drives you to take a bad deal, because a bad deal is better than no deal at all. Now she understood, that what ever it sprang from, this was not some light thing. It ran deep and dark in her. It wanted to be fed. It twisted her judgment and coloured her actions. She would have to be very careful. Careful of herself, for she was no longer to be trusted.

And it was possible there was nothing to be trusted in Francis Etherington.

o o O o o

Ashbourne May 20th 1758

Moidart
Borrodale
24th April 1758

My dear Mrs Walker.
I thought never to contact you again and what I am about to ask may mean that you will wish you had never become involved with my cause. This letter will come to you by a man we can all trust. I ask you to direct him to where you hid the French money.
There, if no one has taken it, still concealed in the same place he will find the box which contained the money. I took the money but thought to leave the box for convenience. This box is of the utmost importance to my cause and must be brought to Scotland forthwith. To tell you more, madam, would endanger you more than I am willing to do.
Yours in faith
Cluny Macpherson.

Francis Etherington put down the letter and frowned. 'So she does know where it is,' he said. 'And yet, all this time busy falling in love and she hasn't told me. Well, I'll be damned.'

He walked over to the window of the headmaster's study. He looked down on Church Street. Across the road he could see Hemsforth House, the first home in Ashbourne of Ann Challinor. He noted it in passing as he looked down onto the street. He knew about its association with Ann Walker. He had spent some months checking every association with Mrs Walker in Ashbourne. He turned back to the man seated behind the large desk.

'You have done well.' He lodged himself on the edge of the desk and idly picked up the silver sand shaker from its stand and examined it. 'Yes, you see, I knew we didn't have far to look in Ashbourne for someone who would know it was in his interests to help us.'

Mr Harrison nervously moved from one buttock to the other on the slippery leather seat of his chair. He was uncomfortable about this. Mr Etherington had called him back after a game of cards one night and put it to him that his past was about to catch up with him in a particularly nasty way.

The past which involved the death of a girl in most unfortunate circumstances at a cat house – a tidy little earner down a back street in Nottingham – owned by Mr Harrison. He had not known his house of ill repute was a favourite with those who earned their money by providing the Government with information. But, apparently it was so, and, after having a graphic explanation of what might happen to him if he should involve the constabulary in an investigation of this girl's death at the hands of one of these men, he had been willing to forget all about the incident in return for his liberty and the chance to start afresh.

In the weeks after Ann's confession in St Oswald's church, Mr Harrison had been visited by a London man who had asked for an appointment to see round his school. Thinking he was a prospective parent, Mr Harrison had put an afternoon aside to impress his potential client. By the end of the afternoon he had been made aware that his movements were being watched and that his past was a weapon which could be used against him. On being faced with his visitor he realised that there was never any clear escape from the tentacles of this agency. He had felt there was no alternative but to assist the Government with their enquiries. The man assured him that they would be in touch. They expected to have business in Ashbourne.

Now, two years later, when Mr Harrison had begun to think that perhaps the visit from the Hanoverian agent had been a product of his imagination, this Mr Etherington had appeared and was asking questions.

Did he know anything about Mrs Ann Walker? He did. Did he know anything about a packhorseman named Rudge? He did. In the last three years the Hanoverians had established that Ann Challinor was the only possible link in Ashbourne to the disappearance of a packhorseman in February 1755. Now Mr Harrison told the agent everything that he knew about Ann Challinor. She was Ann Dance, escaped from Gaol. A street thief, a gambler and... from her own confession... a murderer. Mr Rudge had been helped to his death. She had as good as told Mr Harrison so. Mr Harrison regretted telling all of this to Francis Etherington, but he was being forced to play his best card. It was the only expedient route to take. The forces ranged against him were too great. All he could do was attempt to save himself; therefore he had made himself as useful as possible to this man, but he was not sure that that had been enough. Etherington had explained that he may be called upon to stand as a witness against Ann Dance. It would be the gallows for her, he thought, and a cold hopelessness entered his heart. There seemed to be death all around him.

In the back of his stables lay a body with blood congealing in its veins. It was the Highland messenger who had entered Ashbourne at four o clock that morning, exhausted and glad to be at the end of his long journey. He had been tracked from Leek by Government agents; they had broken his neck and taken Cluny's letter from him as he passed St Oswald's Church.

As Mr Harrison squirmed and waited for his instructions, Francis considered his next move. He had to decide what to do. He fanned the letter against his face. What would Ann do if she received this letter? Would she help the bearer of it? How would she react? How could he ensure that the box came to him? This would take some thought. A false move now when they were so close would be heartbreaking.

Heartbreaking. Ann Walker was in love with him; he was certain it was the first time in her life she had been in love with anyone. He had performed well. He had become the only kind of man with whom Ann Dance would fall in love. A soul like her own, a soul which had been dulled and sullied by experience and which longed for recognition in the eyes of another. So as not to be alone. He knew this all before he had met Ann that morning in the Walker library. He smiled in satisfaction at the memory of that first meeting. She had been so amused by his clumsy attempts to drink her tea. The freshly polished boots had been a master stroke. And the first meeting of minds on the lane. Not too much then, the restraint of passion. To be assuaged later. Still, she had not been fully taken with him then. He remembered her finger on his lips and then the clear message that she would give no more. But he had changed this; now, where ever she was, he was the centre of her thoughts. He had her.

But now, what to do? Send in another agent to deliver the letter? They had none near enough with a northern accent and how much did she know of the Jacobites. If Macpherson would trust her with this information then she may be party to their recognition signals. Secret codes which could separate friend from foe in a seemingly innocent conversation. They did not know them. In which case their man would be exposed during his first conversation with her. What to do?

St James Palace London May 24th 1758

The box. Sir Christopher Lovell sipped at his morning bowl of tea. They had had such a stroke of luck when they picked up the agent who had helped inscribe it. He was inexperienced and had dallied in London to spend his money while his master, the great Villiers, had stowed himself safely and quickly on a Dutch ship out of Portsmouth. A young Frenchman with money in his pocket

258

in an East Dock tavern is bound to be of interest to the Hanoverians.

They were torturing him as a matter of course, hoping for some minor codes or one or two contact names at a low level, but as his mind and body broke down he told them of this scheme. As they burnt his flesh with hot irons he began to babble about writing with fire. Of secrets. Of a box of money. Of the packhorseman riding through England at that very moment and of the names somehow secreted in the very wood of the box. At first they had ignored him but he began to scream at them, reciting lists of names. They were on his lips as he died. The torturers were experienced men. They were certain this was a genuine confession. Unfortunately they had gone too far and he had died before they could fully understand what it was he had to say, but they were certain that information of importance was somehow attached to this box of money.

The box. Sir Christopher carried on sipping his tea. Even with their extensive network of agents, watching movements through all the market towns of England on the Northern routes, sensitive to any occurrence out of the ordinary, it had been hard to trace it. They had entered Ashbourne twenty four hours too late; knowing there had been an important meeting because Cluny Macpherson had left Scotland to be there. Their only consolation was that it appeared that Cluny Macpherson had been also unable to find Mr Rudge. And now, three years later, the whole series of events began to be clear. Careful observation and information gathering by men in the field had gradually pieced together the outline of the story.

An escaped prisoner, on the run from Derby gaol, had inadvertently become a player in their game of espionage. She did not pose a threat, she was working alone and had little knowledge of the implications of what she had found. She may still have the box but would have to be handled carefully. Not being controlled by any political group made her actions unpredictable. They had hoped to get Francis into position before Cluny Macpherson had appeared on the scene but they were too late, Cluny had come and gone and their quarry in Ashbourne was now more knowledgeable and therefore more difficult to handle.

Francis had been given the brief to work to gain as much leverage on the Walker family as possible. He had been successful. The eldest son, James, had allowed him what could be turned into a stranglehold on the family business and Ann, the escaped-prisoner-turned-lady had allowed him into her heart and, it would seem, was about to allow him into her bed. Even more useful, the latest report from Francis Etherington held the news that the woman could be held to account for murder. Francis had a man who would be prepared to testify in court that she had made confession to him. She was an escaped prisoner and had killed a poor man – Mr Rudge, he would warrant – who had tried to help her, and taken his money. They had her.

Francis Etherington was holding good cards but, as he had said in his report, he was not sure how best to play them.

Sir Christopher Lovell put down his cup of tea and looked at the letter from Cluny Macpherson again. A third uprising. Surely the French could not be serious? Charles was mostly in his cups and the Highlands were laid waste by Cope. The Mediterranean was of far more strategic importance. Yet no one had predicted the success of the rebellion of '45. They would have won London if only they had kept going. How many supporters were there in London? A lot if the French were confident enough to assist a third Jacobite rebellion.

He picked up his cup and stirred in some more sugar. He had a sweet tooth. He leaned over and selected a Bath biscuit from the plate by the teapot. He settled back in his chair.

The help from the French source had been invaluable. Obviously someone very near the top. Some one ready to negotiate, showing them the quality of what he had to offer.

Well, they would have to wait and see. This informant could have even more valuable things to tell them but they would have to let him come to them. Not endanger him by clumsy attempts to contact him. He would be in great danger now, whoever he was. An important man, mused Sir Christopher. Able to direct them to the letter from Cluny Macpherson to Ann Walker. Able to get information to London which told Sir Christopher that the box itself carried on it names of significant importance and that the third uprising was planned for July. It was May now. Two months. They had very little time.

He had to find that box. The information on it was everything to the success of the next two months. Without it his government would not know how to react to events. To know what was a real threat and what was a feint; who was a real friend and who was an enemy.

He went to his desk and sat down to write instructions to Francis Etherington. For this young man had better be as good as his mentor, Jamieson, had said he was. They would have to rely upon him now but he did need some direction. Sir Christopher placed his cup on the silver tray, moved over to his desk and picked up his pen.

Mayfield May 27th 1758

'Mrs Walker.' Francis called across the garden.

She pretended reluctance and half opened her eyes. 'Mr Etherington, I'm dreaming. Leave me alone.' She smiled in his direction, still without completely opening her eyes, and put out her hand to ward him off lazily as he approached. Feigning indifference.

She was sitting in the early spring sunshine, in the garden of Mrs Oakhampton of Mayfield. Mrs Oakhampton had let her Derbyshire house to Mr Etherington for the spring and summer months. Francis was increasingly in Ashbourne, and, as he had said to James, he preferred to rent his own property. He liked peace and a solitary existence. James and Ann were visiting. For an hour, the two men had been talking business and then James had had to return to Ashbourne to meet with his lawyer. Ann had agreed to return by carriage later; and now she sat in this garden, aware that she was alone with Francis for the first time since Arbor Low. She held the idea close to her like a prize as he walked slowly towards her.

She knew that she should have warned James of Francis Etherington's need to gamble. But she could not. If she did then she may never see Francis again.

That was the first betrayal, she thought.

But Francis was a competent businessman, she was sure of it – at the moment. She would keep watch on him carefully. As she would watch herself. There was no good to come of how she felt. It was a hot disease. A restlessness. A want. It made her open to mistakes. She reminded herself that it meant that she could no longer trust her judgement. She felt as desperate as she had done when she had escaped from prison. Running along Derby road, her breath harsh in her chest, her heart pounding. Hunted. But this was worse; for in escaping from prison all her actions had been ones of preserving her self. Keeping alive and free. It was what she had always done. It seemed natural and right. She had never questioned it. It was what she was feeling now which seemed unnatural to her. These feelings were about the losing of self. Of combining with another.

We think as one person, Mrs Walker, Francis had said last night as they played at cards. She had been afraid to look up. The opening of one self to another. Fearful. Yet she longed for it.

Francis watched her as she lay with her eyes closed and her face up to the sun. Something no lady of fashion would do.

Something she would not do in most company. He smiled. She trusted him more than she knew.

Sitting in on that card game at the wedding had been foolish but he had turned it to his advantage. She knew what a gambler was. An obsessive. She had made use of their obsession many times. He could see that she had struggled not to tell him so.

 Then he had been clever. He was pleased with that. He kept away from her but had been there on the edges of every event, watching her. And now he would confide in her, when she was already seeing what she wanted to see. She had lost that sharpness, that wariness that had made her a difficult task. She was a ripe fruit, ready to drop into his hand.

'Mrs Walker, Ann, I must speak with you.' She opened her eyes. He was at the side of her chair. The seriousness of his tone roused her. She sat up and pulled her shawl about her shoulders.

'What is it?'

'You know I am a gambler.'

Something in his manner warned Ann that what she was about to hear would be disastrous for all of them.

'I have long fought to over...'

'Mr Etherington.' Fear made her impatient. She needed to know this bad news. 'Tell me what has happened.'

'I play in London... for high stakes.'

'That is your business,' she said quickly. But as she said it, she knew she was wrong. This would be the business of all of them. I should have warned James, I should have told him.

I wanted Francis for myself. And his secret was to be shared with me alone. Now we will all suffer.

She stood up. 'Tell me. Mr Etherington. For pity's sake.' Her voice quick and hard.

Francis hesitated. 'Not here. Come with me.' He held out his hand. She looked at it but did not take it.

'Come with you? Where?'

'Walk with me.' He pointed. 'By the river.'

She considered him. His face looked drawn, there were shadows under his eyes.

'Please. I cannot stay. I cannot settle. I cannot talk to you here.'

He seemed so agitated, perhaps he would talk more freely if they walked. 'Very well.'

Ann wrapped her shawl closer around her shoulders and walked beside him to the tow path. Although the evening was warm, there had been heavy rains two days before and now the mountain water had reached Mayfield. The river was high and the water swirled a few yards to the side of them, brown and frothy.

'I tell you, Mrs Walker.' Francis had to raise his voice above the sound of the rushing water. 'Every night these past few days I have walked by this water and wanted to throw myself into it.'

'Mr Etherington. That is foolish.' She sounded sharp. 'Foolish to even think of it. Now you must tell me what has happened.'

This was not what he had expected. Perhaps his next move would change her mood. He shook his head. 'Ann. I cannot. I am too ashamed.'

Ahead of them a small landing stage stuck out a short way into the foaming water, its planks awash as the river flowed wildly around it.

Before she could say anything else Francis began to run. He reached the walkway and ran out along its length. It shook from side to side as it took his weight. He heard Ann shouting at him to come back.

He got to the end of the jetty and, holding on to the rail, turned to watch her. She was still shouting at him, the sound of her voice just a thin, frightened sound above the roar of the water. Her shawl lay forgotten on the grass as she ran to the river's edge.

This was what he wanted. She was afraid for him. He glanced down at the planks. They were safe enough. The summer floods looked bad but they were never that strong. He had tested the jetty last night. It would hold him. He looked back at Ann. Now she was in the shallows, clutching at the bushes which straggled there to steady herself. If she was not careful then she would be in and he would have to save her, which was not what he had planned.

Ann held on to the bushes with one hand, freeing the other to point up river. Her feet sank into the soft mud and she lurched forward, almost falling over as the water began to suck at her skirts. 'Francis! Francis!' She was still shouting desperately, stabbing the air with her free hand.

And at last he understood. He turned to look upstream and saw the jagged edge of a huge branch which was rolling on top of the water towards him. Even before he started to run he knew that it was too late.

With a great shuddering jolt, the tree trunk hit the landing stage square on and tore the last few feet of it clear away. Francis was thrown to his knees and then he slid sideways as the remaining planks tilted upwards. For a moment they seemed to stand upright, shielding his body as he clung to them but then, with a crack loud enough to be heard above the water, the wood shattered around him and he fell backwards. The rail was momentarily caught between two of the posts and Francis found himself slammed up against it by the weight of the water. He could feel it straining beneath him and knew he did not have much time. He stretched out his arms and managed to get a grip on one of the posts. Just as he did, the rail broke and he felt the power of the water lift and pull at him. He tried to wrap his legs around the post but it was slippy and the water was against him. He was on the wrong side. He tried to manoeuvre himself around to the upstream side of the post but it was hopeless. All he could do was cling on and fight the water pressing on him from all sides. He looked back to the shore and saw Ann edging out towards him. There was nothing she could do. She could be of no use to him. The shore was no more than twelve feet away but he could not reach it. If he let go of this post he would be drowned in seconds.

The water kept filling his mouth, making it difficult to breath. It tasted of the hills. Bracken and mud and heather. He coughed. He was choking. He tried to gulp air but the cold water filled his mouth and his throat. For a moment he went under. He closed his eyes to keep the water out and tried to bring his head up. And then he felt a heavy blow on his back. He felt himself being dragged off the post and he opened his mouth to scream.

She reached out and stroked his face. It was wet. As wet as the grass beneath his head. And almost as cold. She thought, this is the first time I have touched his face. The contours under her fingers were new, unknown. It was not like touching James, or Adam. Odd that she should think of them now.

They were alone, pulled and half dragged up high on the bank by the river. The two men had gone to get help. Blankets. A litter to carry Mr Etherington, if he were to need one. Ann knew they had been lucky. If the gardeners had not seen them, if they had not known where the boathook lay in the long grass, then Francis would be dead.

Francis opened his eyes. For a moment, he was blinded by the sunlight.

He moved his head to the side and then he made out Ann, crouching beside him. He was sure that she had just touched his face.

The river. A mistake that. More than he had bargained for. He moved his legs gingerly. Good, nothing seemed to be broken. But there was an infernal pain in his back. He tried to locate it. To the side, quite low down. He twisted his head to look, probing with his fingers. His jacket and his shirt were ripped and there was a great welt on his side where the boathook had bruised him. Thank God it had held firm in the cloth of his jacket.

His fingers found the source of his pain. He must have cracked a rib. Perhaps two, but there was nothing else. Ribs would soon mend. He had had worse.

He turned his head to look at Ann. She was staring down at him, her eyes wide and dark. She tried to smile, but she could not. She had thought he was dead. And the fear of losing him was still in her. He could see it. This could turn out well after all. Although he had thought that he was going to die back there in the water. He shuddered. Enough. He must concentrate. He pushed himself up on to his elbows, biting his lip at the sudden pain in his side as he moved.

'Ann. I must tell you.'

'No, Francis.' She could not bear it. Not now. 'Ssh. Wait. They are coming with help. Lie quietly.'

'No. I must talk to you.' Francis lay back down. 'Ann, please let me explain this.'

And then he began to tell her the story that Sir Christopher Lovell had crafted for him in London. Made all the more poignant by his sorry state as he lay stretched out on the grass beside her.

'You know I am a gambler.'

She nodded. There would be no surprises in what he had to say to her. The only thing she did not know that mattered was the amount he owed.

'The men I gambled with in the London clubs have turned out to be unscrupulous, taking advantage of my weakness.'

She shook her head. What else did he expect?

'I was led on to make higher and higher stakes, invited to play with people far beyond my station.' He stared out across the river. 'I was flattered. I was pleased that these people wanted to play with me.' He paused for a moment. There was still a trace of wonder in his voice.

Ah, Francis, I had not thought you would be such a fool.

'Then they called in the debt. Four days ago. I have notice of twenty days to pay them off.' He shifted his body weight to one elbow and rubbed his eyes with his free hand.

'Only twenty days, Ann. But that does not matter. If I had twenty years I could still not pay them. I cannot pay, Ann. I cannot.' He covered his face. 'I will be taken to Highgate.'

Of course, the debtors' prison. Her heart felt like a heavy weight in her chest. Highgate. People died there. By some quick disease if they were lucky or, if they were unlucky, after a long time, when they finally lost hope.

'Ann... There is more. I cannot honour my dealings with James. And we have no surety.' He was whispering now. 'Do you know what that means?'

She shook her head. Of course she knew. But she wanted to deny it. To delay the moment when she had to accept it.

'It means that the Walker capital will be called in to support my debt.'

There was no escape. 'How much,' she said dully. 'How much will be called in.'

'All of it, Ann.' He spoke slowly and clearly. He wanted her to be in no doubt, and as of yet he could not fathom her reaction. 'All the Walker capital and more would be needed. I wanted you to know before the collapse comes. I wanted to explain it to you.'

He sat up slowly and turned to face her, putting one hand to his side. The pain was getting stronger. 'I have not been able to crawl out of the workhouse.' He took one of her hands in his. 'Ann. I thought I could.'

His voice faltered. The line between truth and lies had become blurred.

The workhouse. It was true. He couldn't crawl out of it. He would never crawl out of it. They wouldn't let him.

Francis had stopped talking. It was costing him dear to say

this to her, Ann could see that. She looked down at the hand holding hers. The skin was scraped raw from each knuckle. Blood was beginning to ooze. She thought of his gloves - of slipping her hand into his glove in the library at Hulland House. He could be dead. He could be dead at this minute. The thought filled her mind completely. She closed her eyes and she felt his grip on her hand tighten.

Francis shook his head to clear it. 'Ann. My greatest regret is that I have pulled you back in with me. And your family.' Had it registered? He still could not tell. She seemed to be in some kind of dream.

Ann heard voices behind her. The two gardeners had brought the cook and a housemaid. Ann and Francis were wrapped in blankets and helped back to the house. Francis was taken to his bed to await the doctor. Ann got herself pinned into one of the cook's skirts and insisted on being driven home.
She sat in the carriage, staring out unseeing as the houses of Mayfield passed in front of her. Francis was a gambler, of course she knew that. She had known it could be serious. The expression on his face the night of the wedding party had told her that. Now he had had told her how bad it really was. How bad it was for all of them.
And then the other thought. He was not dead. He might have died today. And she would have lost him.

For two days Ann stayed in Hulland House. She did not go out, even into the garden, but moved restlessly from room to room as she tried to find the best solution to the problem which threatened them all. And underlying all her thoughts was the feel of his face under her hand.
The third morning after the accident she returned to Mayfield.
Francis Etherington was sitting by a fire in Mrs

Oakhampton's drawing room. He had a blanket over his legs and a bowl of weak tea at his side.

She was immediately alarmed. 'Francis, are you ill?'

He waved away her concern. 'No, no. I have had worse falling off a horse. But the cook has made me sit here.'

Ann smiled in relief, then she came to stand in front of him. The window was behind her and, as she spoke, the sun illuminated her outline. He did not realise it but he was seeing what James had seen when he had first noticed Ann. The halo of escaping curls, the downward sweep of the head and the awkward stance. To Francis it signalled his success.

'Francis, I have not been entirely honest with you,' began Ann.

Now we have it, he thought. Sir Christopher was right. She kept some of the gold for herself. But will she tell me where it came from?

'I have some money. A considerable sum of money.' She hesitated and cleared her throat. 'The packhorse man, my husband, had come across a vast sum of money. I have no idea how. I found it when I was looking for information amongst his things.' Information to make my story more convincing, she thought, but she did not say it. ' I have some of it still.'

Still lying, thought Francis. Do not ask her where the rest of it is, he thought, she is going to say. These are her last secrets. She wants to make a gift of it all to me. She has discovered, no, perhaps admitted to herself, that she loves me. He sat very still as she continued.

'The money was French. Louis D'or, bound for the Scottish Jacobites. I found this out much later. It has mostly gone to them now but I have some still.' She looked up. 'One thousand Louis D'or. Surely enough to pay your debts?' She continued to look at him, eager for confirmation.

Francis Etherington put his head in his hands.

It was done. He had done it. He pressed his fists into his face, afraid to look at her for fear that she would see the triumph in his eyes. Now she would do what he wanted. He imagined the satisfaction spreading across Sir Christopher's face as he told him of his success.

He brought his head up. 'Ann. I can hardly understand this. I do not know what to say to you. Except to thank you.' He stood up and crossed the room and put both hands on her shoulders. 'Yes – one thousand Louis D'or. It is enough. It is more than enough!' She did not move away. 'Ann Walker, I thank you,' he said.

He put his arms around her and felt the way she curved into his body. He felt the warmth of her breath on his neck and he noted that there was a tremulous quality to it. He pressed her against him and he felt her heartbeat, rapid and strong. He laid his chin upon her head, looked out of the window and smiled.

They walked out together across the lawns. There were still questions he had to ask, answers he needed to take to Sir Christopher. 'How did you come by the money?' He turned to her. 'You said it belonged to your husband, who was a packhorse man. Where did he get it?'

'No. No… it didn't belong to the packhorse man.'

Ah, she was going to tell him the whole story now. She had the illusion that she was safe. She was helping him. He was no danger to her. Soon she knows she will open her mouth and the words 'I love you' will come out into the air. And these other confessions will make it so much easier.

'Francis, the packhorse man was not my husband. What that means – what that was – does not matter now. But you should know that he was an agent of the Jacobites. I know this will all seem far fetched but I assure you it is true.'

She is careful, not many men would have won this far with her.

Eventually she came to the part he wished to hear. The visit of Cluny Macpherson, and his departure with the money. Now Francis Etherington knew where the box must be. Still where Cluny had left it. In a bothy in the wood at a place called Beeston Tor. He would find it, if it was still there. By the grace of God it would be. Francis filled his lungs with the fresh air of spring. He turned his face away from her to hide his elation. He had managed his part well so far. Lovell would be pleased with him.

There was one last part of the story which he had still to understand and, although it was not essential to the success of his next move, he wished to know. What made this street thief give away a fortune? 'Ann, why did you decide to give the money to Cluny Macpherson? From what you have said to me, he did not connect you firmly enough with the trail. You could have left things as they were and he would have gone away empty handed.'

Ann was quiet. This was the most difficult part to explain and yet the most important part of her story. Why had she chosen to relinquish the money? She began to speak. The truth. It felt as though she was forming it in her mind for the first time.

Ann remembered the day before she gave the money to Cluny Macpherson, Kitty sitting by the window of her bedroom, saying that her fourth child, Charles, was the son of a Scottish Prince. Telling Ann in order that after her death there would be someone to pass on that information to Charles. Saying that Cluny Macpherson was the only other person who knew this secret. Now Ann was linked to them both by this shared knowledge. And it had begun to change her.

She took his arm, anxious to have his full attention. 'Francis.' She walked a little ahead of him. She opened her arms wide. 'Cluny Macpherson has the greatest faith in his people. He will continue to fight for them and they will continue to fight for him long after the possibility of success on the battlefield has gone.' She came to a halt and stood in front of Francis and gripped him by the shoulders. 'Because the real failure would be to turn away from that faith. Do you see, the real success is to hold fast to the truth that you hold most dear.'

She stopped walking and stood in front of him, barring his way. Ann wanted him to understand everything. Her voice changed, became more intimate and unsure.

'Francis, until I met you…'

He held his hand up to stop her.

'No, I must say it. Until I loved you, I did not know what it was to share an idea, or a faith, or a, a love,' her breath caught on the word, 'so fundamental to your life that without it you would die. You would rather die.' She looked at him directly. It sounded like a soldier's swearing of allegiance. A pledge.

He found he could not meet those fearless eyes and he looked over her head, across the river to the fields of Mayfield. The sun was still rising in the morning sky and the larks were rising with it. He could see their tiny bodies spiralling upward as they sang. How could those scraps of bone make such a song, so loud, so beautiful? A song that carried in it the hope of summer.

The box, he thought mechanically. I should get her to take me to it. It would save so much time. 'Ann,' he said gently, reaching for her hand. 'Ann, take me to where the money was left. Take me to Beeston Tor.'

Ann looked at him 'Why?' she asked.

How to convince her. 'Because I want to feel what you felt that day. I want to know this about you. I cannot imagine that you managed this venture so well.' He smiled.

It sounded false to him, but she smiled back and nodded, willing to share everything. As he looked at her he had the curious impression that she was very far away from him; and then, for a moment, everything seemed to be very far away and he existed, briefly, on the edge of things. He lost his balance and stumbled with the strangeness of it and Ann, full of concern, tried to help him. But he pushed her away, explaining that he was better walking alone.

Whatever it was, it would pass of its own accord.

They rode out to Beeston Tor that afternoon, taking the old track by the river. The wood was quiet, the miner's coe stood by the heap of mine spoilage, as it had always done. They entered the broken stone portal and Ann showed Francis the place where the box had been buried. Cleverly concealed by rocks and part of the coe wall and now concealed by grass and nettles. A thick stem of ivy snaked across the stones. It was well established. The box had not been moved.

'How did you get it in there?' asked Francis. His heart was hammering against his chest. He longed to race forward and tear away the earth and stones to see if the box was indeed still there, as it had to be. But he could not. He must not raise Ann's suspicions. If she in any way guessed that he knew the box was there then his whole story would be worthless. Ann went over to the place she had indicated. 'Here, I'll show you. There was a gap between the stones of the wall and... it is hard to see it. I suppose over the years –' A noise outside made her stop mid sentence... Francis was moving towards her to prevent her from digging for the box, when they both heard the sound of talking in the wood. 'What was that?' she said.

Francis went to the entrance of the coe. Two men were walking through the wood. They wore leather caps with a flap down the back and had pick axes on their shoulders. They glanced briefly at Francis. What toffs got up to in the woods was nothing to do with them.

'Two men with pickaxes. They're almost out of the wood, but they seem to be turning round...' he called back to Ann. This would be useful. He did not want Ann to find that the box was still there. She must not bring the box out of its hiding place. Now that he knew where it was, he would come back and take it himself. If it was there. But he was sure it would be. The French source had had it from MacPherson himself.

Ann stood up. 'They will be from the Ecton copper mine. Taking a short cut home to Calton. Francis, I think we should return to Ashbourne. I will be missed. We should take the low road along the river.'

As Francis and Ann left the coe and Francis took one look back to make certain he could find the place where he was convinced the box lay hidden, back on the track leading to Calton the two miners were in conversation with a man on horseback. He leaned down to hear them as they pointed toward the wood.

Mr Harrison

Mr Harrison had been given few instructions by Francis Etherington. He was to dispose of the body of the Highlander and simply await events. Francis might need him again, he might not. As he watched the agent speak, Mr Harrison knew that he had played his part already and was therefore expendable. The agents had brought the dead body to his house as a known safe place and had waited for Francis Etherington to arrive. They had put the letter on Mr Harrison's desk and had waited, taking turns to sit in the dark in his study. They had not let him touch it. It was still sealed with the unbroken seal of Cluny Macpherson when Francis Etherington came to read it.

But Mr Harrison had learnt long ago how to unseal and reseal a letter and how to give a man just enough of a sleeping draft that he hardly knows he has nodded off. He now knew more than Mr Etherington thought he did and his knowledge dismayed him. This was an international operation. He would be more of a danger alive than an asset. He had nothing with which to bargain. But Mr Harrison was not about to give up like a rabbit in a trap. He had been in difficult situations before; nothing with quite the bad feel of this but still difficult, and he had survived. There was a box which both the Hanoverians and the Jacobites wanted very much. Whoever had that box would have an excellent bargaining point. Bargain. He set about following Ann to see what he could glean.

He watched Ann ride out to the house at Mayfield and he had watched her walk in the gardens with Francis Etherington. He had followed them that afternoon and he had seen them enter the wood. From his conversation with the miners he knew where they had stopped in the wood. After he saw them leave he had waited for quarter of an hour as silence settled back over the valley and then he had emerged from the trees on the other side of the river to investigate.

After an hour of patient looking, he found the wooden box. He opened it and scratched at the varnish which covered the inside. Some of it came off but he could read nothing underneath. He turned it upside down and examined the base. He could see nothing. What was it they were so desperate to find? He took the box home and locked himself in the windowless anteroom behind his library. This room was little more than a cupboard but it served well for private viewing when Mr Harrison and his friends wished to enjoy an evening with his extensive collection of what he called erotic art. He opened the box and put in some fine ink drawings of Japanese courtesans. He paused to examine the topmost drawing; such attention to detail. He then laid the box on a shelf by the door. Mr Harrison finished his evening with a brandy in the library and went to bed to sleep better than he had for many nights.

As Mr Harrison slept peacefully, another man threw back his head to the heavens and bellowed vengeance on whoever had been before him.

Every thing living in the small valley around Beeston Tor

started at the sound of such anger echoing in the night. Francis Etherington stared at the ivy strewn in the moonlight across the floor of the coe and the empty, gaping hole where the box should have been. He put his head back and screamed into the night again.

Hulland House Ashbourne

Ann inserted the carving knife she had taken from the kitchen between the floorboards and prised them up, one by one. When she had lifted the fourth one she put her hand down into the cavity and pulled up a linen bag. It was heavy with gold coins, the Louis D'or she had withheld from Cluny Macpherson. The house was quiet. It was market day in Ashbourne and the servants were out at the stalls, only the tutor and Charles were in the schoolroom upstairs. She had no difficulty in returning the knife to the kitchen and putting the linen bag in a picnic hamper which stood on the table. She had requested a picnic hamper from the cook the previous evening. She took the hamper into the stables and waited while her horse was saddled up. She was impatient to see Francis. She could not rest until he had this money in his hands. She was afraid that he had found her story too preposterous. Perhaps he had thought she was only seeking to give him false comfort, and was, at this very moment, sitting alone, trying desperately to think of a solution to his problems. She had that solution. She could hardly believe it herself. How could he believe it? Standing in the wood at Beeston Tor, it had all seemed unreal to her. How must it seem to him? She mounted her horse with haste. There was not a moment to lose. She could not bear to wait to see Francis hold the coins in his hands and know that he held his salvation. She drove her horse to a canter as she rode down Church Street, nodding her head in greeting to Mr Harrison who was walking up the road as she passed. Mr

Harrison watched her ride out of sight. She had on no bonnet and looked remarkably excited. She was riding down the Mayfield Road. Going to meet her lover, thought Mr Harrison, grimly. He feared for that eager figure on horseback. For a moment he allowed himself to feel sympathy; she was riding into the darkest night of her soul.

Mrs Oakhampton's house Mayfield

Francis sat in the library of Mrs Oakhampton's house. He had sent the two servants out for the day and so was alone. He could hear every sound that the house made. The creaking of the beams as the sun warmed the walls into expansion, the swallows squabbling in the eaves and the steady tick of the clock standing in the hall.

He must admit, he was surprised by this turn of events. He had felt a real guilt as Ann had spoken to him in the garden. For a moment, he had failed to maintain his hold on the world he inhabited and had faltered. The force of her emotion was so strong, so pure. She offered him love. Unadulterated by any bartering, any holding back.

He listened to the clock ticking the minutes away. He moved impatiently in the chair. The sun was in his eyes.

But had she had been tricking him, even as he had thought he had been tricking her? He thought of the letter proclaiming his success which he had sent to London. He had very little time. Sir Christopher would be sending other agents out to assist him; important people would be told. What could he salvage from this mess? Very little. He tried to piece together a reasonable interpretation of the events leading up to this moment.

Firstly, Ann had no knowledge of the fact that Cluny had left the box in the hiding place in the coe, otherwise the letter would never have been sent. Neither did she know of the names written on the box. So why would she take it? But who else could have taken it? Had a second messenger from the Jacobites arrived in Ashbourne carrying the information about the box and had he seen Ann that very evening? Or had he taken it without her knowledge? Someone had been to Beeston Tor after them, and disturbed the hiding place which Ann had pointed out to him. So the box was taken before last night. Or something was.

The clock ticked on and, outside, Francis heard the hay carts going down the track beside the house to the meadows. Boys shouting and playing the master with the patient horses.

He thought she might come to him. But how? Would she come to him today, as a different woman? One who admits to being knowledgeable and hardened. No more pretence. Ready to play him at his own game. Could he pre-empt this? How? He heard the sound of a horse approaching the house at a rapid trot. He heard Ann's voice as she shouted instructions to the stable boy, who had been exchanging insults with the hay makers. He heard her quick footsteps as she crossed the hall.

And then she was in the room, standing by the door, breathless and covered with a fine dust from the roads she had ridden so hard. He waited for her to speak. Ann crossed the room and placed the linen bag of money in his hands. 'There it is. The Louis D'or. Did you doubt me? I wouldn't have blamed you. My tale must have seemed a strange one.' Her voice was light. Teasing and expectant. She tried to brush some of the dust from her skirts and laughed as a cloud of white powder rose up into the room.

Francis looked down at the linen bag. He opened it. The unmistakable glint of gold. He looked up at Ann. She was smiling at him expectantly. She had found a solution for him and she was happy. She didn't know.

Francis sat down. Who had the box? Who had it? He rubbed his eyes with the back of his right hand. Ann came to him and knelt on the floor. 'Francis. Francis. Do you not see? It's over. You have the money to pay.' She shook his arm, perturbed by his seeming lack of comprehension. Francis sat up and pushed her away. She was the only link. She had to be.

'Ann,' he began. It would be easier to show her the letter. He drew the letter from his inner pocket and handed it to her. 'Read this,' he said, 'as you can see, it is addressed to you.'

Ann read Cluny's letter. The urgency of Cluny's plea was immediately apparent to her. She looked up at Francis. 'We must get the box to him. To this messenger. Where is he? How do you come by this?'

'He is dead. My men intercepted him two nights ago as he entered Ashbourne.'

'Your men. What do you mean, your men?' Ann stared at Francis. No, this could not be.

'Ann. I, or the people who employ me, have for a long time had an interest in this box. We need the information it contains. We must protect the state.'

Ann continued to stare at him. 'The people who employ you,' she said slowly.

'Francis...' It was the beginning of a question, the edge of understanding, but she stopped. She found she could not go on. She did not want to know any of this. But the thoughts came unbidden to her mind anyway. She could not prevent them.

Francis watched. He could almost visibly see the moment when she understood she had been betrayed. The slight softening of the body as if she had taken a physical blow, then the almost imperceptible reduction of the space she took up as she closed in on herself for protection. But there could be no protection from this. As she sat there, Ann's perception of the world, so newly formed in its marvellous entirety, collapsed in on itself. She had nothing to say. The details of her betrayal did not matter. The mechanics of this man's clever manipulation of her were irrelevant. The change in her view of him as she raised her head to look at him with this new knowledge was complete.

So he was a Hanoverian agent, come to get information. That was all.

She would deal with that later. But now she would deal with this. 'You want the box. Then why have you not taken it? You know where it is.'

'It has gone.' Francis watched her closely. Did she know more? He doubted it, but he had to make sure. 'I went last night to the coe and it was gone. Ann, I must have it.' She moved back in surprise. His voice was conspiratorial, as if they still shared some common purpose, some common feeling. 'You must help me.' He turned to a drawer in the desk behind him and withdrew something from it. 'Read this, Ann.'

He handed her a yellowed piece of paper, a list of some sort. She unfolded it and tried to decipher the faded letters. It was a list, and half way down, she came to words which caused her to move back from him in horror.

A good Reward offered for the capture of Ann Dance, pickpocket and thief, who escaped from Derby gaol on this day February 25th 1755. A handsome faced woman of young age, being five foot five inches high, pale complexion, fair hair and blue eyes, looks very sharp, commonly known as The Sparrow and belongs to a notorious gang of Gamblers. Her father is well known as a pickpocket and lately is imprisoned in Leicester Gaol to take his tryal at the next assizes for the stealing of Great Coats from Melton Fair. Whoever will apprehend and secure the said Ann Dance, in any of his Majesty's gaols in England, and give notice to John Greatorex, Gaoler at Derby, shall receive 10 guineas Reward.

Three years disappeared and Ann found herself again on the run. Alone, with no protection but her own wits. The smell of the damp earth and bands of light filtering through the trees. The man tending his horses who was to have such a far reaching effect on her life. The dark chamber... the dirty pillow... She fought down the rising panic and faced Francis Etherington.

'You would have to find some connection between me and this woman. I fear you would find it hard.' She suddenly thought. 'How did you come by it? How did you finally make this connection?' Where had this information come from?

'Mr Harrison. He told us of your real identity and then it was no difficult matter to obtain the relevant list of escaped prisoners and the words Mr Greatorex used to advertise their escape in the Derby Mercury. Mr Greatorex is a very organised man and so willing to help our agency...' Francis watched her steadily. Ann read the notice of her escape again.

'I have only seen this once before,' she said, 'on the town hall noticeboard in Ashbourne.' Just a flimsy piece of paper, her courage returned. 'It is so long ago. To what purpose can you put this now?' She held the sheet out to Francis as if to dismiss it from any connection with her. Francis did not take it. He continued to look steadily at Ann.

'Mr Harrison is prepared to be witness to your true identity.'

Ann's heart began to beat impossibly fast. Her chest felt restricted. She could not breath. What else could Mr Harrison bear witness to? St Oswald's church. What had she told him that night in St Oswald's church.

What had she told him?

'Ann,' Francis hesitated. 'I have to say to you... it is difficult for me... we have been close...' Ann was surprised by his manner. Now he appeared to absolve himself of blame. To seek her forgiveness. Did he really have so little a grasp of morality or was he still acting his part?

'This money, Ann,' he shook the linen bag of gold, 'I thank

282

you for it. I thank you for the feelings which made you bring it to me.'

What else do you know? she thought. Say it. Say it. Francis seemed to gather himself.

'Mr Harrison will also testify that you murdered the pack horse man that night in The Plough Inn by placing a pillow over his face until he suffocated.'

He moved over beside her and placed his hand on her shoulder. He bent his head until his face almost brushed her ear. 'You will be hanged, Ann,' he said in a whisper.

He took his hand from her shoulder and moved away, and, as he did so, his manner became more public, that of a polite stranger. 'I have no wish for that fate to befall you, madam. If you find yourself able to co-operate with the Government agency which I represent, then I am sure you need fear nothing.' He smiled. 'To another matter. Your husband is relying upon my bank,' he smiled again, 'to stand surety for the coffee venture.' Francis picked up a plum from the salver on the side table and tossed it in the air. Even in her extreme fear, she thought how ridiculous his studied actions and his pompous speech made him seem. 'I'm afraid that venture will fail, if you do not comply with our wishes. So, no heroics, Ann, or your son will become a pauper after your death. And, just think – no mother to turn to...' He laid the plum carefully back on the salver.

For the moment she could say nothing aloud. She was attempting to assimilate all of the information with which Francis Etherington had bombarded her. These are clever tricks, she thought. He has destroyed my safety, the safety of my family, my love and threatened me with the gallows, all in one meeting. What he wants must be very important. He is leaving nothing to chance.

He was her enemy. She had not known. She looked at his face now turned away from her. He could not even look at her, now. He hates being known, she thought. He preferred his pretence, his persona as the ardent lover. She felt the numbness which seemed to have invaded her being from the moment he had begun to talk to her, leave, and instead hate rose in her for him. All the passion of her commitment to him seemed to immediately turn to its opposite without losing force, only changing direction. She was shocked by the power of this change. She wanted to kill him. To act in a physical way. To see him bleeding and broken.

He must think me at my weakest now, she thought. But I am not. I have a strength, a huge anger. She was amazed by it. She had made no effort to create it. It flowed into her body as if from an outside source, sustaining and energising her at this most desperate time. She took a deep, shuddering breath. And, almost to cloak the strength she felt rising in her, she bowed her head down and put her cupped hands over her face.

Francis wanted her to go. He was uncomfortable. He did not want to have her in his sight, have her sitting there in front of him. He had hoped at the beginning of this enterprise never to have had this confrontation. It was distasteful to him. To play his part so well, he had to partly become the character he played. This skill was what made him so successful an agent. Empathy, Sir Christopher called it. He could double guess the next actions of his quarry because he could become his quarry. Their feelings, fears and hopes became his own. In doing this with Ann, he had had to go further than he had ever gone before. So much of what he had said to her about himself was true. For a while it had threatened to enmesh him. He had almost been unable to bear tearing this creation to pieces, but then there was always that other weakness in him. That had to be fed. A longing in him to be praised, to be accepted, by Sir Christopher. To be part of his agency. To do his work. The brotherhood. That had driven him on. 'You must give back the box, Ann,' he continued. Determined to convince her of what she must do.

'I do not have the box.' Ann brought her head up and spoke with some force. 'Why do you imagine that I do? Do you think that I am the centre of some Jacobite ring?' She stood up. 'Francis, you are not being reasonable. Think back over the last few months. How could I be the centre of this? You must have watched me...' her voice tailed away as she thought of his duplicity. Yes, of course he had watched her. Her argument was reasonable, but Francis Etherington knew that if the Jacobites had been watching them, if they had taken the box, then Ann was the only one with the connections to take it back for him. If there had been some other unforseeable mishap then he did not wish to contemplate the consequences for himself. Francis was a man with only one chance of survival; impressing upon Ann the necessity of what she had to do was his only hope. Ann was the key.

A few minutes later Ann walked out of the Mayfield house. She had been given the task of finding the box. If she did not succeed she would be taken to court and tried for murder. Mr Harrison, a respectable headmaster, would bear witness against her. No court would acquit her. She would wait, like Mary Dilkes, with a bible in her hand, no doubt given to her by the sobbing Ashbourne branch of the Christian Women Prison Visitors. And, then, one morning, she would be led out into the daylight and hanged. James would find that his venture gradually turned from a promising enterprise to a dragging failure and her son would be left in a similar position to the one in which his mother started. She could not let this be.

But Francis must imagine that she had more influence than she had. Finding the box was an almost hopeless task. It could have been taken by anyone. She stood for a moment in the entrance of the stables. The stable boy was elsewhere but he had left his work on the tack table. She walked over to the table and picked up a broken stirrup that lay there. It felt heavy in her hand. She lifted it higher and imagined bringing it down on the back of Francis Etherington's skull. She could return to the house, overpower him and take back the money. At least then the family would be saved from destitution. Francis had been clever to use her love to bring him to the box and to make her willingly give to him the only protection her family had. So clever.

She looked back through the stable doors to the house. It would be impossible to go back and overcome him. A wild idea. He would be on his guard, and she had no strength at this moment. Her limbs ached and her heart beat heavily in her chest. She wanted to lie down and weep but she would not. She had to act. The only place to begin her search was at the place where she had last seen the box. She put the broken stirrup down and shouted for the stable boy to saddle her horse.

She returned home and went to her room. She put on the riding jacket she had worn on the day she had visited the coe with Francis and, at the same time of day as her visit with Francis, on the same horse, she went out on the Leek road. She rode through Calton and down to the track which passed Beeston Tor woods. She waited for over an hour by the side of the track but no one was to be seen.

Ann did this for three days. Each day expecting Francis to come to Hulland House and tell her there was no more time.

Beeston Tor May 31st 1758

On the third day as Ann sat on the verge by her horse, two miners came through the wood. The same two men who had passed the coe before. Ann sprang up to speak to them.

'Gentlemen. Do you remember seeing me here?' she asked. The men looked at her with suspicion. Would it be better to say no or yes? They hesitated. They both clearly remembered Ann but self-preservation was their greatest motivation, not truth. She seemed extremely distressed. Ann drew some money out of her pocket. She showed it to them. They immediately relaxed. Money changing hands always was a safe proposition. You knew where you were with bribery.

'That day, did you see anyone else here. Or any other day,' she asked.

They had. A man had stopped and enquired after her and her companion.

What had he been like?

'On horseback so hard to tell,' said the first man.

'Tall, dark, thin. Town clothes. A gentleman, although he didn't offer us any money,' added the second.

'Was he from round here?' asked Ann.

'I couldn't rightly say,' said the first man again. 'His horse wasn't tired, so he couldn't have ridden far.'

'Somebody local, but who?' thought Ann. 'Have you seen anyone else here?' asked Ann. 'At any time?'

'No, Ma'am, but if you want to find out what happens in these woods, visit Jeremiah over there on the other side of the river. He lives on that slope. Sees everything. Been there for years. Got a spy glass.' The second man pointed in the direction of the river. 'Shouldn't be there by rights. Not fit to work now. But he used to be a forester and Mr Okeover never turned him off. He's harmless. The winter'll get him one year.'

'Will he speak to me?' Asked Ann.

'Oh yes. Jeremiah likes to talk. You'll have trouble stopping him, Ma'am,' said the first man, and they continued their journey up the track. Well satisfied with their money and the information they had given for it. Fair exchange.

Ann urged her horse over the river and stood on the edge of the wood. Sure enough, after a few minutes, she could make out a bent but agile figure making its way towards her.

The man stopped in front of her and looked up.

'I know you.' He spoke in staccato bursts. 'You've been here. With men. Different one each time. What's your game then?'

Ann got down from her horse. 'Are you Jeremiah ?' she asked.

'I am.'

'Can you... Will you help me?'

The old man looked at her for a while. 'Got any more money, or did you give it all to those miners?' he asked, nodding in the direction of the two men plodding up the hill. 'Yes, I have more money,' said Ann. He was going to help, good, but what did he know?

Jeremiah knew a lot. Two years ago he had watched Ann come down the track with Cluny Macpherson and then, on the very next day, he had watched her hide the box. He had gone over to check what she had hidden and had been wise enough to put the gold back where he had found it. He would be the first one to be blamed if something went missing around here. And he loved his wood. He wouldn't want to live anywhere else. He had seen Cluny ride up the track early one morning and he had again checked. This time to find the box empty. He worried then, for a long time. But no one ever came to blame him. Months later he had seen Ann reappear with another man and he had seen that man return at night and go to where the box had been hidden. He had heard Francis Etherington bellow in disbelief in the darkness of the night.

But after that last visit by Francis Etherington he had seen another man question the miners and then return to take this box away hidden under his cloak. Now, that was the smart one, in Jeremiah's opinion.

Jeremiah had been in these woods when the Jacobites had ridden through on their way to Derby. He had seen them trail back defeated, spread out in disorder over the countryside, and had witnessed four boys from Wetton beat a rebel to death by the turn of the river. They had been

288

heroes to the village, saying they had fought off a horde of soldiers but Jeremiah had seen them cracking the skull of this one man with great stones as he lay, defenceless, half in the water.

He had no time for any one. Not even this pretty woman standing in front of him, with such beseeching eyes. But he had time for her money.

'Did you see anyone take something from the coe in the woods over there,' Ann pointed to Beeston Tor. 'I have more money. How much do you want?'

She wasn't a very good negotiator, thought Jeremiah. He considered what would be a fair price. 'I could give you a description of the man who took the box,' he said.

Ann nodded her head, 'Tell me your price.'

'Well, for a description I want twenty pounds.' Jeremiah kept his expression neutral. It was a small fortune. More than a top miner could earn in a year.

Ann sighed in relief. Twenty pounds was nothing. Less than she spent on candles in a month. 'Of course, you can have that.'

'But.'

Oh no. What else does he want, thought Ann.

'But,' went on Jeremiah, 'for fifty pounds you can have his name.' He squinted at Ann in the dappled light of the forest. She was very quiet. Had he gone too far? He was out of his league with this one.

'His name,' repeated Ann. 'Yes, I'll pay fifty pounds for his name.' She held her breath. Jeremiah took the opportunity to fill the silence.

'You see, I go into Ashbourne for market and such like. And I like a gamble. There's one man I always see at the cockfighting down Compton. He's a strange one. Dressed in black. Takes himself very serious. I've asked after him. I take note of people. And I've found out his name. Mr Harrison, The headmaster. He's your one.'

'Mr Harrison came here?'

Jeremiah nodded.

'He took the box.'

Again, Jeremiah nodded.

Ann had money with her. She brought one hundred pounds out of her pocket, and, as she counted out fifty notes for Jeremiah he realised he had been too cheap. Still, fifty pounds was a lot of money. Jeremiah began to feel that particular warmth which the thought of spending a windfall always brings.

Arisaig May 31st 1758

De Vere walked along the stony beach. He was impatient. It was all very well for Choiseul to have these marvellous ideas but he was not the one risking his neck in a country bristling with redcoats. And he could hardly sleep for these infernal insects which attacked his flesh day and night. Only the thickest smoke from a green fire would drive them away and that was too dangerous a course to take. De Vere thought he would almost prefer to face the redcoats than put up with being bitten continously. He laughed. He could see Choiseul's face. Quizzical and sardonic. Driven out of hiding by insects, my dear De Vere, you are getting soft.

He thought of the letter sent to Ann Walker. He had ensured that Cluny had included information about the box and the imminent uprising. Then he had ensured that the Hanoverians had captured the letter. He hoped he had ensured that he would live, protected by the English state. He had no wish to return to the French court and wait for his wine to be poisoned or an irresistibly sweet little boy assassin to run a stiletto through his neck. The English were his only hope. London. He longed for the comfort of a city. Not this huge bog of a land so beloved of every Highlander. Never to go back to Paris. Tears came to his eyes. Betrayed. Betrayed by Choiseul. Why had he not fought for him? How could he have let the council close De Vere out of their innermost proceedings? Overcome by his loneliness and isolation he sank down on a sodden, moss covered rock and wept.

Eventually, De Vere stood up and wiped his face. He started to climb back up the rocks to the bothy. He must stay alert. Falling into despair was indulgent and would leave him vulnerable to attack. There was no guarantee that his plan would work. Cluny Macpherson had left the Highlands a few days before to find out what was happening in Ashbourne. Cluny could prevent De Vere's plan from working. He was clever. Careful but opportunistic. He knew when to take a chance. He may snatch the box from under the noses of the opposition.

De Vere stepped around a sheep, sitting resolutely on the path. In a way, he half hoped Cluny would snatch the box. His loyalty to the Jacobites had been part of his persona in the Highlands for so long that it had begun to take root. And he was still a French man. If the box was captured by Hanoverian hands then many French agents in England would die. Their throats cut in the dark or their bodies found on river banks. De Vere looked back across the grey sound. He thought bitterly of the men who had forced him to become an informer. Choiseul. He could have given De Vere warning that his position in the council was compromised. Why had he not? Because he had to survive himself. De Vere knew that there had been jealousy in the court over his relationship with Choiseul. They had been lovers for some time. Perhaps they had both known that at some time there would be a price to pay, but for Choiseul to allow him to pay it alone. He drew his cloak about him. The clouds lowering on the far hills foretold another wet, miserable night.

Chapter 10

May 31st 1758, Ashbourne

Ann left Jeremiah counting his money and rode back to Ashbourne along the low route. The horse made its own way. Its rider was deep in thought. She knew who had the box but how to get it off him? Threats? Violence? She had no need to become involved in that. She would pass the information on to Francis Etherington and her part of the bargain would be complete. But she would at least ask for her gold back before she told him. She must protect the interests of the family as much as possible, even though that was very little.

How far would the Hanoverians take it? They would have their information. They would be secure. The rebellion would be smashed. Surely the Walker family would be left alone. She thought of the men waiting in the Highlands for the landing of their Prince. They were doomed to fail, however great their hope and however hard they struggled. And she would have played a part in that failure. Cluny's letter, asking her for help, had given information to his enemies which would finally destroy him. And she was about to play her part in that destruction. If she gave the information to Francis Etherington there would be no hope for the rebels. In the next few hours what she did would affect thousands of people throughout the country. How could she save one family with that as its price? Ann struggled with these arguments all the way back into Ashbourne. She went upstairs and sat by her window to think further. How important was Francis Etherington? If he disappeared now, how much would it matter to his employers? She suspected not much. His function was important but his survival was not. If she could remove him from the situation and substitute some useless box with meaningless code scribbled on it and send it to London... but how? She opened the window and leaned out. The air was soft and the distant sounds of the town were comforting. Church Street was almost empty, only a drover's cart going towards the market place. Silent and respectable. Safe and secure. If she could kill Francis Etherington... and take the box... and substitute it... She had to try. She drew her head back into the room.

She had to try, or she would be like him. Like Francis. A piece of thin tissue. A substanceless creature. No truth to hold on to. She would be lost. She would be bound to his kind in shame. She realised that she had no compunction about planning his murder. How to do it. He was not dying, like the packman. She forced herself to think of it. He was not naïve like Mr Meynell. Francis Etherington would be watchful. He knew her history. He knew what she could do. She decided on her course of action. First, Kitty must be told and warned to take Charles and Adam away to somewhere safer than Ashbourne had now become for them. Then she must make a replica box and somehow convince Francis that it was the real one. She must also visit Mr Harrison and persuade him to part with the real box. Her courage failed her for a moment and she sat down on the bed. All of it was impossible. Her plan was the plan of a halfwit. Kitty and the children could not travel fast enough to escape detection. Francis Etherington had examined the real box, he would not be fooled and Mr Harrison held the trump card. He was not going to let it go easily. Ann lay back on the bed and stared at the ceiling. It was impossible. She curled over on the bed and closed her eyes. She could not do it. She could not save them all. Strangely, she slept. And when she woke with the afternoon sun on her face her thinking was calmer.

There were the Jacobites and her family. It might only be possible to save one by sacrificing the other. And she had to try to save her family. It was all that any morality would ask of a woman. Would Mr Parker not agree? Ann raised her hands into the pyramid of prayer. She remembered Mr Parker teaching her the strange words. Like a spell. *Pater noster, qui est in caelis. Adveniat regnum tuum....* Mr Parker told her that if she spoke these words she would always be given help. Ann did not know what that was, only that it was a hidden, powerful thing and saying these words was a great source of pleasure. God would find her, said Mr Parker. He could see everything and was good. Ann could never quite see how this fitted with the church's insistence on the need to struggle against evil. Fight to be good and choose the right road. Why did you have to fight? She had asked. If God is so powerful, why doesn't he help you straight away? If he loves you, why does he not ease your pain? The questions of a child, said Mr Parker.

Now, as she lay on this bed, in this house, in this town of Ashbourne, she wished that prayer could bring her an answer. She unclasped her hands and let them fall to the bed on either side of her. That would not happen. She thought of Adam, and then she thought of men dying in battle. The pictures came unbidden to her mind and stayed there as long as she lay on the bed.

Beeston Tor June 1st 1758

The second time someone came asking Jeremiah for information about the goings on over on the Tor, Jeremiah had asked for one hundred pounds. He had decided that his information was worth more that he had thought. His questioner had handed over a bundle of money without remonstrance, and had waited patiently while Jeremiah counted it and put it into a small leather pouch. Now the pouch was gripped tightly in Jeremiah's hand. Blood from his slit throat dripped steadily over the pouch darkening the leather to black. The pouch was empty.

Cluny Macpherson had arrived at Beeston Tor early that morning. He had concealed himself in the undergrowth by the track and had watched for some hours. Nothing moved on this side of the river but over on the other bank, someone was going about his business. Cluny saw birds rise and settle. He watched a thin wisp of smoke rise above the trees. After a while, he saw sun catch on a spy glass and he made his move. He clambered back for half a mile to the copse were he had left his horse grazing. He mounted up and rode down the track in full view of the opposite bank. He entered the wood and made his way to the miner's coe where he had left the box. He examined the disturbed earth without touching it, all the time waiting for a sound at his back. But no sound came. No one entered the wood after him. His being here was not a threat. Cluny trailed a stick in the earth. The last person to look here had not cared to conceal his actions. Why not? Was concealment no longer necessary? Or no longer possible?

Cluny mounted his horse and left the shelter of the wood. He crossed the river, dismounted and settled down to wait just in the perimeter of the trees. He fully expected to be ambushed. It was a desperate measure, to bait an enemy attack, but he had little time and no other options. He was surprised when, instead of an attack, an old woodsman had come through the trees to speak to him. The man had told Cluny what he had seen in the last few days. He did not tell Cluny that he recognised him. He did not think it prudent. When he had finished speaking, Cluny had taken his Skean Dhu from its scabbard on his leg and had slit the old man's throat with one efficient move.

He had to leave no chance of detection. An old man who would tell anything for one hundred pounds was not to be left alive. But now he had the information he needed. The box was in the possession of one Mr Harrison, whose school was on Church Street in Ashbourne. But what of Ann

Walker? She had come down to the coe with a man. Who? Not a Jacobite. Cluny had made enquiries along his route. There had been no reply to send to Scotland. He knew there was a Government agent in Ashbourne and that the Jacobite messenger had been assassinated. His body lay in the lee of the Henmore Brook bridge at this very minute. Best not to claim it. Let the Hanoverians think they were further ahead than they were. This agent fitted the description of the man who came down the Tor with Ann Walker. Had she turned? She was often seen with him, even at times when she should not be. He could no longer rely on Ann Walker to support his cause. Kitty. Kitty and the young Charles would be in great danger. If Hanoverians had captured his letter, which seemed likely then Charles, as a son of a Jacobite Prince, had better be taken to Scotland for there was no safety here. What of the invasion? The English would know from his letter that it was imminent. What a fool he had been to put that information in a letter. His head ached with it all. To Cluny the box represented the lives of loyal supporters. If he could bring it safely back to Scotland, if the government agents had not yet got the information in it, then the network could stay in place and there would be hope for the third uprising.

Mr Harrison was teaching in his largest classroom when he was informed that a man wanted to see him. He asked for the man to be sent to his study and left the classroom. Was this it? he asked himself as he walked along the corridor. Had they come to negotiate? He must plan what to say. He stopped by a window and looked out on his garden. All he wanted was a chance to carry on his life. He liked it here in Ashbourne. The society of the town was easy and the common people respectful of his position. He wanted nothing to do with espionage and murder.

He had formulated his opening sentence and had taken breath to utter it when he entered his study and immediately was thrust against the wall behind the door by an unseen assailant. He twisted his head round and inadvertently added to the momentum of a sharp knife as it sliced through his right ear. The knife, he could now see, was in the hands of a wild looking Northener. Mr Harrison started to tremble with shock as blood saturated his collar. Cluny put his arms under Mr Harrison's armpits and lifted him onto a dining chair. He dealt him a heavy blow to the side of his head and held his left hand over Mr Harrison's mouth and nose. Mr Harrison struggled and then went limp. Cluny pushed the limp body onto the floor and broke two fingers on its left hand. Mr Harrison came to, groaning in pain. He tried to cradle his left hand in his right but Cluny rolled him over on to the floor and held his right arm high behind his back. 'What have you done to me,' wailed Mr Harrison. 'My hand. For God's sake, can't we talk?'

'No,' said Cluny into what was left of Mr Harrison's right ear. He snapped the ring finger of Mr Harrison's left hand against the butt of his knife. The bone broke with a tiny sound. 'Oh, my god,' moaned Mr Harrison. He wanted to faint to escape this agony but all of his faculties were bent on survival. He remained fully awake and horribly responsive. His heart pounded blood along his veins, some escaping through his ripped ear. His nerve endings sent miniscule but powerful messages back from each site of damage and pain raged in the parietal lobes of Mr Harrison's brain. His senses were heightened. His eyes could see the detailed carving on the handle of the knife Cluny Macpherson was holding between his legs. 'Oh no,' thought Mr Harrison, 'Oh no.' He felt the searing pain as the knife cut into his scrotum and he gave up all hope of negotiating with this man.

'You want the box,' he said. 'I'll give it to you.' He waved his arms in the air, trying to find purchase. 'Let me get up. I'll get it for you.'

He led Cluny into the windowless room behind his study and took the box from the shelf. He tipped the Japanese sketches out of the box, and handed the box to his tormentor. Cluny examined it inside and out and then pulled Mr Harrison towards him in what Mr Harrison thought for one wild moment was a gesture of affection. But as Mr Harrison's head came to rest lightly against Cluny's shoulder he felt something like a pin prick and then a great pain which spread across his chest as the knife entered his struggling heart. Mr Harrison sank to the floor dying as Cluny left by the front entrance of the school, carrying the box under his arm.

The upper housemaid found Mr Harrison's body soon after Cluny had left. She entered the room and, being a pragmatic girl, did not scream but stood still and used her eyes to examine the body, with its blood at the crotch and at the heart. The man who had just left must have done this. Mr Harrison was dead. She then saw the door to the private antechamber was open. Breathing heavily with fear of discovery and the proximity of a fresh corpse, but too curious to resist this opportunity, she walked over and saw the Japanese prints scattered all over the floor. She bent down to examine them more closely. She picked them up and chose two of the more explicit ones to hide in her apron pocket.

She, and all the other servants at Mr Harrison's school, had long suspected that he would come to a bad end. They had heard that the most depraved things went on in the antechamber. Many of the younger servants, male and female, lived in fear of being invited in to that dark place, although none of them ever had. Mr Harrison had obviously been murdered by a jealous lover. A lover crazed by unnatural acts. The maid went to tell cook.

The next day, as Ann awoke tired and without hope in her bed, the town of Ashbourne was abuzz with the murder of Mr Harrison. The town guard had eventually been called to the school by the hysterical butler, who thought that his wife in Derby would think he was somehow implicated in all this perversion. The two assistant teachers had taken to their beds, to show how shocked they were. They were considerably worried about their wages and had already begun to slip out of their rooms on forays to accumulate small pieces of silver to supplement their probably much reduced income. The cook was the only person in the house who remained calm and carried on doing her job. This was because although she had always valued her job it was only now, in the midst of this disaster, that cook happily found her importance increased in other people's eyes by the recent events. The kitchen had become a centre of discussion and comfort. The three maids felt it best to weep continuously in the corner, although they had all taken the opportunity to visit the cold pantry with the upper housemaid to look at the Japanese prints.

Ann heard the news at the breakfast table. Kitty had been told a most lurid version by her personal maid and she was cheerfully retelling the story to Ann when the under parlour maid entered the room. 'Beg pardon, Ma'am, but there's a letter come for you.' She handed Kitty a silver salver with a folded and sealed letter upon it.

Ann barely noticed the letter or the interruption of Kitty's story as she read it. She was trying to fit this latest information into her scheme of things. Mr Harrison dead. Not by a lover, thought Ann, but by the hand of Francis Etherington. He had made the same discovery as she had. Now there was no hope for the family, for Charles or for Ann herself.

Kitty stood up abruptly, still holding the letter in her hand. She handed it to Ann without speaking, but her eyes were large with fear.

Madam, your child Charles is in the greatest danger from Hanoverian forces. You must make sure he travels North

immediately and you with him. There is a stone with this letter which should ensure that you get help from true Jacobite men and women on your journey. God speed you. I hope to see you in my homeland before long.
Cluny Macpherson.

Kitty held out the stone for Ann's inspection. It was a curiously worked disc, with a complicated pattern of interwoven snakes and circles inscribed upon it. They were copies of ancient Celtic symbols which could be found carved on rocks and tombs across the Highlands of Scotland. Neither Kitty nor Ann knew this, but the very alien nature of the symbols seemed to lend the disc the power of a talisman.

'Ann, what shall I do?' queried Kitty. The letter had said tell no one but Kitty could not imagine that that instruction included Ann. Ann stared back at Kitty without speaking. Ann knew that she would have to take this information to Francis Etherington. It had not been Francis who had visited Mr Harrison during the last day, but somehow Cluny Macpherson. He had returned to Ashbourne, and, by the sound of this letter, had left again. He would be travelling north now. He must have tracked down the box to Mr Harrison and had recovered it.

Mr Harrison was dead. The words repeated over and over in Ann's mind. He was dead. He could not testify against her. Ever.   It would be difficult, no, impossible, for the Hanoverians to have her accused as a murderess without a reliable witness. And her identity. Who would believe that she was that poor unfortunate street thief? No-one. With Mr Meynell dead there was no-one who had cared to examine her closely enough to be able to recognise her after all this time. The trap had been sprung. Cluny Macpherson had inadvertently freed her from Hanoverian control as surely as he had freed Mr Harrison from the burden of life. Ann jumped up and clapped her hands.

'Ann, how can you be like this? What is there of joy in this news?' Kitty was not sure if the letter or Ann's apparent reaction to the news it contained was the more disturbing.

Ann took Kitty by the arm. 'Kitty. Do not fret. There will be a solution. For the mean time, do not make arrangements to take Charles away. Wait. Do nothing yet, Kitty.' She dropped Kitty's arm and strode out of the room. She must visit Francis Etherington and tell him of these developments. How must this change the situation? With Mr Harrison gone there was only the finances of the family in Etherington's control.

It was doubtful if Francis Etherington would survive this failure long enough to put the ruin of the Walker family into operation. And what purpose would it serve the government? The box had gone.

Ann rode out to Mayfield and into the yard of Mrs Oakhampton's house. It seemed quiet. She tied up her horse and pounded her fist upon the door.

There was no body there. She waited for some time until a gardener appeared and she could question him.

'Where is Mr Etherington?' asked Ann.

'He's gone to London, Ma'am and should be back today. Likeways, the kitchen staff are coming in today to light the range and cook some supper, so's he must be coming back.' Ann nodded acknowledgement.

Back today – but why go to London? Had he gone to tell his masters that Ann Walker was unable to do anything but help them? That the box would soon be theirs? Were his masters already uneasy about Francis Etherington? After all, he had let the box slip through his fingers once. Now it had gone out of his reach forever.

Ann got down from her horse and tried the door of the house. Of course it was locked and she looked around for some of the kitchen staff to arrive and let her in. There was no-one. She wanted to get in. What might she find in there which she could use? She walked around to the back of the house and searched for the tiniest sliver of an opening in a shutter or a window. She was rewarded for her trouble. Just above the cellars, on the steps leading down to the kitchen, she spied a small window which had been left loose. It was probably the window of a pantry. Ann pushed the sash gently up, unbuttoned her riding skirt and laid it across the window sill. She lifted herself up onto the sill. She bent over and entered the house head first, gripping the sill and bringing her legs up after her in a compact ball.

She landed with both feet on the floor and stood up in one fluid movement. And then she stood completely still and listened, as she had learnt to do as a child. She almost expected to hear her father's low, urgent voice outside the window, telling her to get a move on. She pushed the thoughts of her father away and looked around the room.

It was a pantry. Dark and musty. She pulled her skirt off the sill and rebuttoned it around her hips. When she pushed at the door it opened easily. Not locked, thank God. She walked across the flagged floor of the kitchen and climbed the stairs to the main house. This is the house that I came to in the hope of making love. The house where I told Francis all I knew, where I offered him the gold which could have protected my family. Ann stopped. She could hear a steady tapping sound, coming from one of the rooms upstairs. She listened. The tapping continued.

Ann rose up the staircase as quietly as she could. The sound came from the master bedroom. The door was ajar and from where Ann stood at the head of the staircase, the room looked empty. But the steady, intermittent tapping continued; like the sound of someone drumming his or her fingers on a table. Ann walked slowly across the hall and pushed the door of the bedroom wide open. As the heavy door slowly swung open she could examine each part of the room as it came into view.

There was nobody there. The sound came from a window blind which was being pushed in and out by the breeze through an open window. Ann crossed the room and closed the window.

She turned round and looked at the bed. She put her hand on the pillow. This is the bed where I could have lain with him, she thought. And enjoyed it, believing him to love me. Was it possible to derive real happiness from an unreal thing? A question to be answered by the Reverend Parker's books.

How could he have professed love in his actions, his speech and in the very movements of his eyes upon her body? How clever must he be. How without scruples. And why had she been tricked by him? She had seen enough good tricksters in action; had been one herself. So why..? How...? How was he able to so completely persuade her of the reality of his love? Love.

Already the word sounded ridiculous. Too fancy, too overused. She considered that most of the street women she had known would have told her that this state of affairs was all too easily possible. Most men acted this way, and most women were taken in. Ann smiled. This was the kind of advice she would receive outside the homes of the gentry, on the streets.

But that was not enough. There was more to it. The women on the streets of Derby might not have it, but then it was not in their interests to see themselves as anything other than victims. Hardy, surviving victims. Worthy of sympathy, Your Honour.

In matters of love both men and women could be easily fooled. But why? Why could even the most astute, the most suspicious of people become drunk on another person and lose all reason? How had she done this? How could anyone?

She sat down on the bed. Maybe in this matter each person was locked into their own interpretation of events. Even as you thought you were becoming close to one other human being, in reality you were only coming closer to what you thought they were. You made them up. You 'found' your love. The words implied that this love existed separately, waiting for you, but it did not, thought Ann. It had no existence. It was merely an extension of your existence. You put flesh upon its bones when you were ready for it. Was this how things worked? She thought of Amanda and John Hodgson. John did not seem to be at all the man Amanda spoke about, and Amanda certainly was not, Ann knew, the woman who John thought he had married. Did knowing the truth of another person not need to be there for love to exist? She thought of James. Did he love her? Yes, he did. She felt ashamed.

She thought of Francis Etherington. Now, at last, a great grief rolled and crashed in on her. Like an inexorable wave of pain and loss. So great that she did not cry out but sat on the bed where they had never lain together and waited for it to pass. He felt separate yet the same. Not created by her but created for her. And she had been created for him. Ann could not deny it. That was how she had felt it. And she had been wrong.

She heard the sound of voices. The kitchen staff were arriving. Ann had been sitting in the bedroom for some time. The shadows on the floor showed that it was well after noon. Would Francis Etherington be back soon? Should she wait to tell him her news or go? The door from the kitchens to the hall was opened. Ann was amused to hear that the cook thought that thieves had broken into the house. She was sending one of the girls out to find the gardener to see if he had noticed anything. Ann came out of the bedroom and walked down the stairs. 'Cook,' she called out. 'You should fasten your pantry windows better. It was no trouble at all for me to enter.'

The cook could think of no suitable reply. She was glad that there had not been a break in but, on the other hand, here was this, this trollop coming out of the bedroom (Mr Shoesmith from The Green Man had said she was a trollop and he was a man you could believe). She would probably complain to Mr Etherington.

'I'm truly sorry, Ma'am' she said, bobbing a curtsey to Ann. 'You are so right. We could have been broke in.' She turned and made her way down to the kitchen to shout abuse at the kitchen maid.

Ann went to the study where Francis had told her of his gambling debts and sat at the desk. She opened the drawer to her right and saw a large brass key. Ann stared at the key. She picked it up and rolled it between her fingers. It was the key to a strongbox. A strongbox, she suddenly knew with a rush of certainty, which contained her money and which was secreted in this house. She turned around in the chair. But where?

Now could she put her knowledge of Francis Etherington to use, just as he had used his knowledge of her? Could she enter his mind and follow his intentions? If she could, then she was on the brink of completing a circle of safety around all of those people who were most close to her. She could hear her own breathing as she stood up. Think. Think. Where would he hide the money? Hurry. He might be back soon. Ann moved to the centre of the room. She shook her shoulders impatiently, to release tension. Be calm. Become him. Become Francis Etherington.

He would not be afraid of any action from her, with her passionate interest in the money. He thought he was safe from her. So he would not have hidden it from that kind of danger. He would just be protecting it from the servants, or the casual burglar, trying to earn a living. Where would she look if she had been sent into this house by her father? If he was waiting outside at this very moment, ready to give her a good cuffing if she came out empty handed? If she were ten years old.

Her hands were damp. She wiped them on her skirt. Where? She moved into the hall, listening all the time to the distant sounds from the kitchen. There were three bedrooms on this floor but only the biggest bedroom was in use. The other rooms would be shrouded in cloth and possibly locked. Too obvious, thought Ann. She looked up to the stairs which led to the servants' quarters above. Too inaccessible. She began to walk down the stairs. She realised that she was walking as she had when a child on a job like this. Hardly making a sound, walking on the outside rim of each foot, slowly putting the weight on each step. From underneath her came a loud crack. Ann jumped and gripped the banister. The noise had been like the sound of gunfire. Must be a board out of place on the stair tread. Badly out of place. Moved recently and put back in a hurry.

Ann quickly crouched down on her knees. She slipped the brass stair rod out of its brackets and pushed the carpet aside. The inner plank of the tread lay at a slight angle. There was a gash of unvarnished wood visible where the board had been hastily put back askew. Ann ran down the stairs, picked up a paper knife from the study and returned to prise up the plank. There was something there. She could see it. White. Made of cloth. She pulled out the bag of Louis D'or which she had given Francis two days before. She had been wrong on that detail. No strongbox. She went up the stairs and put the key back in the drawer. Then she went to the morning room and sat down to wait.

Francis rode into the courtyard of his house and shouted for the stable boy. He was still preoccupied with his meeting in London and did not take note of Ann's horse tethered at the other end of the stables. He had been summoned to London by Sir Christopher, who had expected him to appear with the box. Francis had explained the disappearance and had speculated that it had fallen into Jacobite hands. They had listened to him in almost complete silence. Then they had given him their reply. He had been given the freedom to do as he liked. All the power of the agency would be put at his disposal. He would be expected to succeed.

The atmosphere in the room at St James Palace had been difficult to read. Jamieson, who had taught Francis everything he knew, seemed friendly but Sir Christopher was enigmatic. The box was of the utmost strategic importance. Although both men seemed to accept Francis' explanation of the arbitrary and unresolved disappearance of the box, he sensed that they were displeased with him. To have been so close to taking it and to have put it back into hiding. For the niceties of preserving his cover in Ashbourne society? It seemed far fetched even to Jamieson. 'Francis,' Jamieson raised his eyebrow. 'Francis, have you fallen in love with this woman?'

Francis considered before he answered. It was a valid question. He had to examine his reactions to see if his answer should be in the affirmative. It was certainly not an idle question. If he had become involved in that way, then someone else should be sent to finish the task of the recovery of the box. 'No,' he answered, 'I have not. To live as I have for so many months. It is difficult sometimes to separate your real self from the character you play. Perhaps that did happen but, on reflection, I acted to preserve my cover, because I did not know whether it would be needed or not.' He gave a slight nod of his head, 'I stand by what I did. My cover had to be maintained for as long as I was able to do it.'

Sir Christopher looked at him for a moment and then relaxed. 'Very well, Etherington. But it is as well that you be wary of this possibility, so be vigilant. If you suddenly find that the life of, say, one woman, seems more important than your country then I am afraid that we would have no more use for you. Now, to other matters.'

There had been a further development. A Frenchman had turned informer. Some one of importance. Francis was glad to regain some credibility by being able to advise Sir Christopher as to who that was. The evidence pointed to De Vere.

De Vere. Francis knew that De Vere had not attended two high level meetings recently. He could well be out of favour. His affair with Choiseul made him a target for jealousy. He had also been closely associated with the failed second uprising. Perhaps those who wished him harm had gained the upper hand in the French agency. De Vere could give the whereabouts of a Jacobite letter from the Jacobite stronghold. He was thought to be in Scotland at this very time. His role would be to carry the invasion plans to the Scots. His next move may be to barter the invasion plans for asylum in England.

If he survived. It was an extremely dangerous game he was playing. Living closely with his allies and yet planning to change sides would leave him open to detection. Hard to act out a part continuously. Day by day. Francis knew of De Vere, knew the way he worked. The two men were not unalike. They each worked well in the field because of their peculiar ability to become the man they impersonated. The loyal friend. The reliable confidante. The soul of discretion. The innocent party. The true love. How was De Vere faring now, thought Francis, cold and alone, amongst enemies who thought of him as a friend?

'We must simply wait. We have no other option. De Vere will come to us when he can. We cannot risk contacting him ourselves.' Sir Christopher was adamant. If De Vere died without handing over the invasion plans then they would have lost a great opportunity. The utmost sensitivity was required in this matter. For that reason they would not inform General Cope of the prize in his midst. He would probably raze the country to the ground in a fruitless search. De Vere would have to survive on his wits for the time being.

As Francis listened to Ann give him an account of the brief but deadly appearance of Cluny Macpherson, he realised with horror that the very thing which he had wished to avoid most had happened. Cluny Macpherson had the box. If he had stayed in Ashbourne... if he had set watch on Harrison... Francis felt a rising panic. He imagined his return to the room of Sir Christopher and his attempt at an explanation. But he probably would not get that far. He would be dead in the next few weeks. Expendable and expended. He would have to follow Cluny Macpherson and attempt to take the box from him. He realised that every moment he waited meant that Cluny would be deeper into Jacobite territory. As Cluny moved North, to take the box and succeed in returning with it safely would become increasingly harder for Francis. He looked at Ann. She seemed very self contained. She sat on the window seat, her hands clasped in front of her and her eyes down, very still. Why should she be so calm? He may have lost his chief witness in her murder trial but he could still ruin her family. But she sat there composed and quiet... although, if he looked at her closely, he could see that her chest was rising and falling quickly as if she had been exerting herself.

Francis sprung off his seat and grasped Ann by the arm. He dragged her into the hall and halfway up the stairs. He pulled back the stair carpet, forced the planks of the stair tread apart with the heel of his boot and discovered the empty space underneath. He pushed Ann against the banisters. His hands were round her neck. 'Where is it?' , he asked, his voice trembling with a dangerous mixture of fear and anger. Ann slowly brought her head up until her eyes looked directly into his.

He saw in those eyes such fury and such a challenge that he relaxed his grip in shock and moved away from her to the other side of the stair, pushing himself up against the wall, his eyes still on her face. He knew then that he would not find out anything from her. She would die before she told him. He had become something evil to her and she wished him destroyed.

'The money has gone, Francis. Your informer is dead. You

have no more cards to play.' She spat the words at him. Her anger propelled her forwards and she almost lost her footing. She lunged clumsily across the stair, gripping the lapels of his jacket in her hands and pushing him down until he sat crouched on the stair tread. He seemed too startled to defend himself. She stood over him. 'Get after Cluny Macpherson,' she shouted, 'it's all you can do.' Then she leaned down to him to whisper in his ear as he had once done to her. He felt her fast breath on his face and recognised the faint scent of roses on her skin as she leaned over him. The same scent had been on her two days ago when he had taken her in his arms. When she had trusted him. Loved him. Her mouth was close to his cheek.

'You won't win, Francis. He will kill you,' she whispered. Her certainty terrified him.

He stood up, pushing her down one step and shouted back at her, 'Cluny Macpherson is a fool. He will give the box to his French ally.' He mimicked the oily voice of false friendship. 'And his French ally, the great De Vere, will take it to General Cope.'

'I don't believe you. I know nothing of De Vere.' She leaned away from him. 'You are a liar. What do you know of the loyalty which drives such men as Cluny Macpherson? You.' She paused... there were no words for him, for his kind. 'You are nothing. Just an honourless lackey, running for your masters here and there.' Her voice was full of derision. 'That is all you are, Francis. Nothing. Nothing. You are beaten. You know it. And now your masters will get rid of you, because you are no longer any use to them.'

She pushed him aside and ran down the stairs.

The truth of her last words caused Francis to lose all reason. His only satisfaction was to convince her that her world was false, as false as his. 'De Vere is the French liaison with the Scottish Jacobites. Only he is much more than that. He is an informer. How do you think I knew you were the one who knew where the box was?" He started to come down the stairs, pointing his finger at her. 'How, Ann, how?' He shouted. 'Because De Vere told us to look out for a messenger carrying a letter to you.' Again he pointed at her. 'So you see, your Cluny Macpherson is riding back to be betrayed... just like you, Ann. My love.' His voice dropped to a sneer on the last words. He wiped his sweating face with the back of his hand. 'You can do nothing. No message of yours will get through quickly enough to save him. The rebellion will be no more than a rout of the Highlands. And there will be no safe place to hide in England for any Jacobite.'

Ann began to run along the hall. She stopped when she reached the door and looked back at him. His face was beginning to change. He was going to beg her to help him. He was a man facing the certainty of his own death and he wanted someone to share the dread which was wrapped around him at this moment.

There was nothing more for her to say here. As she left the house, she heard Francis screaming after her. 'So you see, Ann. You are finished too. Cluny Macpherson is finished. No one wins in this game. No one.'

Ann rode home to Ashbourne. If Francis was telling the truth, and Ann was sure that he had been, then Cluny was about to suffer the most deadly betrayal. She must write to him and find a messenger to take the information. She had to use the talisman. But there was very little time. She knew nothing of this Frenchman De Vere, but obviously he was an important link between the French and the Scottish Jacobites. His betrayal would be disastrous for the Jacobite cause. When she rode into the courtyard the first thing she did was to go into the tack room. There was one young lad there, cleaning a saddle.

'Did Master Cockayne from Mayfield bring some thing for me?' she asked.

'Aye, ma'am,' replied the stable hand, getting up and going over to the corner of his room. He extracted a linen bag from a saddle bag and handed it to her. It contained money. A lot of money. He and the stable hand from Mrs Oakhampton's house had discussed it. Mrs Walker had come running out of the house and told the lad to get over to Hulland House as quick as possible by the back way, through Snelston. He did as he was told. The gentry were for ever asking strange things. The two young men had opened the bag and handled the money, but had wistfully put all of it back. However much they would like to, they knew that taking any of it would lead to too much trouble. Didn't recognise the coins anyhow, might be pretty worthless, on case of point, as the stable hand from Mayfield had pointed out. Probably no landlord in Ashbourne would touch them without asking questions. That's when the trouble would start. Now here was Mrs Walker come asking for it. Looking very lively and determined. Probably enjoyed her visit to Mayfield. They could do what they liked, these rich women. He handed her the saddle bag and carried on smearing the saddle with sheep fat.

During the afternoon, Ann spoke with Kitty. That evening Ann asked James to speak to her in the library. When he entered she handed him the bag of Louis D'or. 'James, before you say anything, let me speak. This money is ours. Rest assured that I have not stolen it. I want you to put it safely in a bank.' She unfolded a piece of paper which she had been carrying. 'The Toplis Bank on Fleet Street, London. It must be this bank, James. I know we do not use this bank but that is why I want the money to be put there. I have come to the knowledge that Francis Etherington may not be the most reliable of financiers. We must prepare for the worst.'

James watched her. He had suspected this. He wasn't blind. His wife, with her closed, secretive ways, had never been this free in the presence of another man. Well, so be it. She had thought herself in love with Francis Etherington. Not a likely candidate. More of a clerk than a lover, he would have thought. It probably had never come to anything. Whatever it had been, it was obviously over. He drew deeply from his glass of wine and drummed his fingers lightly on the arm of his chair. He traced the pattern of leaves in the silk brocade of the armrest with his finger. Perhaps she had finished it and feared that Etherington would wreak revenge by destroying their business partnership. James doubted that he would. The venture was a great success. Everything they tried seemed to be blessed and their plans were coming smoothly to fruition. But Ann must fear that her banker would respond to her rejection by cutting off his nose to spite his face. And James would go along with this. If this was his wife back to him then he would ask her no more questions and put the money into Toplis' bank. Rates were good there anyhow. But how had she come by this money?

'Ann, you must tell me,' he held up his hand, 'I will do as you ask, but, how did you come by this money?'

Then Ann explained to James that his younger brother was the son of a great Jacobite Prince and that this money was part of the protection which would always surround this boy. The protection of those who loved 'the king over the water'. She told James to go and talk to his mother. Kitty sat in her room, waiting to speak to her second son, holding the two medallions and wondering at the great love which had made the Jacobites send this money with Cluny Macpherson for her, and wondering at the marvellous secrecy of Ann, who had never told her of this.

That night, Ann professed a headache and retired to bed early. She slept in the second bedroom as she sometimes would if she felt ill and did not wish to be disturbed. James and his mother dined alone and talked of their father, of the Jacobites and of love. They grew to an understanding of each other as the evening went on which they had never thought to have had. 'Ann,' said Kitty, 'has carried a great burden for us, James. For me,' she paused. 'But you. Do you feel she has betrayed you?'

'How?' His reply was too quick.

'By keeping things from you, James. By not letting you in.' She stretched across the table and laid her hand on his, 'By closing you out. As I have done.'

His faced twisted momentarily and she watched as he looked away from her to hide his grief. Then he looked back at her. 'Tonight I am content with my mother and my wife. I am glad of them both.' He attempted a smile.

At eleven of the clock Ann slipped out by the servants' door and took her horse from the stables. The lad woke up as she was saddling it, but Ann put her hand to her lips and shook her head fiercely at him when he appeared in the stall. He retired back to his comfortable pallet. The mistress knew best. Her business if she wants to go gallivanting about in the night. She's playing it close to the wind, though.

Ann rode out on the turnpike to Leek. She rode for about forty minutes until she came to an inn, high on the moor. The Dragon's Nest. This was the place. She had heard Cluny talk about it. He had stopped to water his horse there, was all he had said. But Ann knew that he would not stop at any place where he did not feel safe. She walked into the noisy taproom. There was a momentary hush. It was not usual to see a lady of quality riding out alone on a dark night. Also, there was something about Ann's manner which commanded attention. She went to the landlord where he stood by the bar. Out of her pocket she took the talisman. 'I would have some ale, good sir,' she said. 'and, I found this outside, would it belong to any one here?'

The landlord looked at her. He held out his hand. 'Give the stone to me, ma'am,' he said, 'I'll ask around.'

A young girl brought a mug of ale to the seat by the fire which Ann had taken. She sat quietly, slowly sipping from the mug. Around her the usual level of talk in the inn resumed. After about half an hour, when she had finished her drink, Ann stood up, placed the mug on the bar, nodded to the landlord and walked out. She was about to mount her horse when a hand descended on her shoulder. A man with a hood around his face stood beside her. 'Come with me, ma'am,' he said. He led Ann to the back of the inn, where there stood a small row of miners' cottages. He led Ann in to the first cottage. By the light of the fire, Ann could make out a young thin-faced woman, dressed in breeches and riding boots. She had the cool air of the night about her and had clearly only just arrived at the cottage. She was holding the talisman in one hand. 'Who are you?' she asked Ann.

'I am someone who knows Cluny Macpherson well. I need you to get this letter to him as fast as is possible.' Ann stood up. 'I must return to Ashbourne before I am missed. Get this letter to Cluny Macpherson, that is all I ask you to do.' Ann looked at the young woman. She moved a little closer, the better to be seen in the firelight. 'Get it to him,' she repeated. The woman nodded her head. 'We will,' she replied, convinced now she could see this rich woman's face that she was not an enemy.

Arisaig Scotland   June 12th 1758

'Get out! Get out ! Or you will be burned alive!'   The old man's face was contorted with fear. It flashed before De Vere in the confusion of smoke and flames. De Vere crawled out from his hiding place under the stacked lobster pots and made for the door of the bothy. He could only crawl painfully slowly because in one hand he dragged a saddle bag. The saddle bag contained the box and a rolled sheaf of papers which were the plans for the third invasion of Scotland. He reached the door and was roughly flung into a huddle of prisoners by two red coated men. The army of General Cope was continuing its systematic rout of the Highlands with no idea that amongst their prisoners were some of the most important of their enemies. De Vere had no intention of staying as an enemy of the British state, but he was not going to explain that to anyone in this rabble.

Not unless it became absolutely necessary.

It became absolutely necessary about one hour later when De Vere realised that the main function of the temporary garrison at Locherichthead was to execute as many prisoners as possible. The gallows stood in a sinister row. Five of them, to facilitate a quick dispatch of each incoming load. The prisoners were housed in makeshift pens set along the bleak shores of Loch Ericht. Stronger structures were not needed as they did not stay there very long. Any men who tried to escape provided a diversion for the bored troops as they chased the Highlanders across the barren landscape and cut them down.

De Vere sought the attention of the only officer among the troops. No one responded. The air was thick with the murmur of Gaelic prayers and all eyes were drawn in horrified fascination to the twitching bodies which festooned the five gallows. It was only as he was being dragged out of his pen towards these gallows bellowing French insults to his captors that he was noticed. The officer came over to him. He inspected the cut of De Vere's coat and boots. De Vere said nothing, letting the man make up his own mind.

'Where are you from?' questioned the captain.

De Vere decided to speak in English. His voice was calm and clear. 'I am from the French court and I wish to see your General Cope. He knows that I am in this area and is waiting for me to make contact. I have things of importance for him.' He patted the saddle bag which was gripped in his left hand.

Captain Porter considered the man in front of him. He was certainly foreign. Probably French, as he said. What would a Frenchman be doing up here if not that he had some connection with the Scottish rebels?

'Very well. We will take you to Fort William. But first, give me the bag.' Captain Porter put out his hand.

De Vere stepped forward and faced the captain squarely.

'This is for the eyes of General Cope. He will not want you to take it from me.' There was such confident menace in De Vere's voice that the captain let him keep the saddle bag beside him. He still had it when he was marched into the garrison at Fort William and placed in a cell to await an audience with General Cope.

The general was intrigued by the news that a Frenchman had been captured; and still more intrigued by the fact that this Frenchman said that he was expected to make contact. First he knew about it. But then communication from London or even Edinburgh could be haphazard. He had been told to increase his patrolling of the Western coast and substantial reinforcements were on their way by boat from Liverpool. London thought there was the possibility of a third invasion but it seemed unlikely to Cope. No rebel commander of any experience could expect to have any success in the Highlands. The Jacobite rebels were depleted; their equipment destroyed or captured. Only massive help from the French could give them any chance of overwhelming the forces ranged against them. The French. Perhaps he should see this Frenchman. Find out what he has to say.

De Vere entered the office of General Cope with profound feelings of relief. He sat down where indicated, directly opposite the general.

'Tell me what you have to say,' asked Cope.

De Vere was confident that his indication of the transference of his loyalties would have been conveyed to the man sitting opposite him. The English spy lords would have prepared their army chiefs for his defection. Cope had been waiting for him and would know what he had to offer.

'My dear sir. I have to say to you that I am happy to meet with you. It was not easy... getting this far on my own. However I have succeeded in bringing you the box.' He had decided to deal with the box first and then use the invasion plans, some of which were still safely in his head, as a final

317

negotiating stance. With a flourish, he pulled the box out of the saddle bag and placed it upon the table.

Cluny had handed the box to him only twenty four hours ago. He had then slept briefly and left. Eager to get out amongst his supporters. Eager to organise his army. De Vere realised that Cluny was in that state of tension which is induced by the imminence of battle. The fine tuning of the senses, the sharpening of the wits. It was what made battle so intoxicating for some men. So Cluny had slept lightly and had gone in the grey mist of early dawn. Too early to see the redcoats approaching from the East. No matter, in the last twenty four hours, De Vere had feared for his life. But now he had reached safety. He could feel the ache of relaxation beginning its spread through his weary body.

General Cope stared at the box. It looked like a very ordinary money box. Quite substantial but unremarkable. Perhaps it held money? Often he had found the most obvious answer was the correct one. He pulled the box towards him and opened the lid. There was nothing inside. He looked up at De Vere sitting with a complacent smile on his face.

'Sir. This box is empty. Why do you bring it to me?'

De Vere felt uncomfortable. This was not what he had expected. How could Cope not know? 'The box, sir. Surely you have been told. It has the names of all the French agents in England and the names of all important Jacobite sympathisers.'

General Cope examined the box again. He lifted it up and examined its underside, and then he opened it and looked again around every corner of the interior. Apart from a very professional coat of varnish on its inside surfaces, this box was unremarkable.

'Sir, I ask you again. Why do you bring me this box? There is nothing in it or on it that I can see.'

De Vere became exasperated. He leaned forward and gesticulated wildly with his elegant hands. General Cope moved back from this whirlwind of fingers in consternation.

'Sir. The names were burnt on to the very wood of the interior of this box and then they have been covered with this veneer to protect them from unwanted eyes. Look. Look. See.' De Vere leaned across the table and tapped the interior of the box. 'How fine the wood is on the interior. Too fine. No moneybox requires such work. Prise it up. Prise it up. If you remove the veneer, then, voila, you will have the information.'

General Cope saw the sincerity in De Vere's eyes. He arranged for the Frenchman to be given a private room with a jug of water to wash himself and some of the general's own tea to refresh him. The box was sent to the tack room to be examined further by Cope's chief intelligence officer and a woodworker who knew about solvents.

De Vere washed himself and drank the fine tea provided for him. He suspected that this garrison would eat well and he looked forward to a fine meal as he drifted off in to a light sleep. Four hours after he had entered the barracks De Vere was ushered back in to the presence of General Cope. He took with him the bag containing the invasion plans. The General sat behind the table as before and beside him sat another man. They both watched De Vere solemnly as he entered the room and sat down.

When De Vere was settled, the General spoke. 'This is my chief intelligence officer, Mr Chambers.' He indicated the man on his right. 'He has examined your box thoroughly.'

De Vere nodded. Good. Good. Now they could move on to the important negotiations. He always enjoyed this sort of bargaining. Everything had a pattern, a flow to it.

'Mr ...eh... De Vere,' the General searched for his name. Again De Vere nodded. He approved of formality. 'Mr De Vere, there is nothing on your box.'

De Vere sat upright in his seat. 'Nothing on the box. My dear sir, have you been careful and thorough in your examination? I hope that you have not destroyed something of such importance.' He stood up. 'Where is the box? I must see it. You have failed to use the correct solvent, or you have not used enough.'

'The box is here.' The chief intelligence officer spoke for the first time. He put some pieces of wood on to the table. It was the box. Reduced now to its component sides, lid and base. It was meticulously clean. Every bit of glue had been scraped from its inner surfaces. A thin rectangular strip of veneer, released from the tension of being attached to the inner base of the box, lay curling on the table. De Vere leaned forward. He picked up the pieces, one by one. They were free of any lettering. No burn marks were visible. Only on the base was inscribed, almost certainly by a hand holding a hot needle, the words:

Flower house
The den
Look Love Follow
The box

'First the flower house,' murmured De Vere. Where were the names? What had happened? For one wild moment, De Vere thought that the men opposite him had planed away the surfaces to erase the names. He carefully put the sides of the box together and peered at his construction for evidence of tampering. Every thing fitted perfectly. The dovetail joints were smooth and sound. General Cope and Mr Chambers watched him. De Vere continued to try to understand what had happened.

Villiers had made a decoy, and this was it. He had made a decoy and sent it through England with Mr Rudge. When the veneer was removed only these few words would be found. But they would be a clue to a Jacobite supporter important enough and old enough to know that "flower house" was the original code name for the home of Lady

Primrose. Her house on Essex Street was the one used by the Prince when he had visited England secretly in 1750. So the real box was with Lady Primrose. Flower house. The first box was still in the house where Villiers had done his work. The words on the box were a guide, an indication. It was very possible that even Choiseul did not know of this insurance ploy by Villiers.

De Vere looked up. 'Gentlemen, this is a decoy,' he began, but he was interrupted by the General raising his hand. 'Mr De Vere. The box does not have any names on it and now you tell us that it is a replica. Why are you carrying a 'decoy' through Scotland?'

The grim faces opposite him drew him back to the present. For the first time, De Vere considered that the lack of names on the box would condemn him in the eyes of these men. He had been so intent on understanding how he had come to be guarding a replica box that he had not yet thought of their reaction. Ça va. The next few moments might be difficult but he could have found another bargaining chip for the future. Now, to consolidate his present position.

He reached into the saddle bag and drew out the papers. He held them in front of the two men. 'The box. It is difficult to explain, although all will be made clear. It will just take a little time. But these, gentlemen are the invasion plans of the French government. Or at least some of them. I offer them to you in exchange for asylum.' He brought the papers out of the saddlebag and smoothed the thick folded sheets out on the table. When he was satisfied that the papers were as flat as possible and that other two men could see each sheet clearly he began to explain the meaning of the French symbols and words which littered them. The general and the chief intelligence officer looked carefully at De Vere's map. They took their time. Eventually Mr Chambers drew back and general Cope followed suit. De Vere continued to talk, unaware that his audience was losing interest.

'This is certainly a map of Scotland,' said Chambers, 'but as for these being realistic plans for the invasion of this country by the French,' he shook his head and pursed his lips, 'I do not think so, sir.'

General Cope had watched Mr Chambers' reaction very closely. Now he turned to De Vere. 'You have not convinced us that your information is of any use to us,' he said.

De Vere was astounded. He could not believe the stupidity of these two men. 'These are the invasion plans for the third rebellion,' he shouted. 'The third rebellion!'

Mr Chambers stood up and turned to the general. 'Shall we have him shot?'

General Cope shook his head. 'He is obviously a madman. A box with names on... the invasion plans of the French army... I'm superstitious, Chambers. They say you should always spare the mad. They mean no harm. Have him thrown out.'

He waved a dismissive arm at De Vere. 'Mr De Vere, take your plans and leave. We wish you no harm. In fact, you have amused us for a while. It can grow tedious in this northern territory. We can tell people about you over dinner, can't we, Chambers?' Chambers nodded silently.

De Vere was thrown out of the Fort William garrison. He stood for a few moments, looking at the bleak landscape in front of him. The relentless rain had already soaked through his greatcoat and his feet were sinking in the muddy cart tracks which made up the road to the fortress. But De Vere hardly paid any attention to any of this, except to wipe away the rain from his eyes with a quick, impatient movement. He could still hardly believe what had happened. That the chief of the English army in the Highlands could be so foolish as to pass up the chance of taking into his hands the evidence of a great plot against the crown...

De Vere thought back over the meetings. Chambers. Who was he? It had been his condemnation of De Vere's map which had swayed General Cope. Chambers had paid too little attention to the papers...it was as if he knew what was there already…

De Vere's mouth opened in astonishment. He turned back to look up at the garrison. As if his eyes might meet those of Chambers in a flash of recognition. Chambers was a spy. A Jacobite spy.

De Vere turned and started to walk down the road, away from the fort. In the intensity of his desire to understand what had happened to him and to formulate a plan for his survival, he forgot the first rule of any operative in a foreign land. To protect himself from immediate danger by concealment. He was still clutching his saddle bag when he was attacked by two men who had noticed his fancy clothing. A fine Englishman on his own. An unhoped for opportunity. The men had followed De Vere for half a mile, until his path had taken him into a dip in the road, surrounded on either side by birch and elder trees. From here De Vere could no longer be seen from the fort, as his followers knew.

He caught sight of his attackers an instant before they took hold of him and dragged him off the pathway. He tried to scream but as he opened his mouth, his jaw was cracked with a heavy stone. The men were efficient. One of them pulled De Vere's head back. The hot flood of pain as his broken lower jaw was pulled out of place by the movement forced out of De Vere a strange, roaring noise from deep within his chest. The second man took a piece of twine and pulled it tight around De Vere's throat. The roaring stopped. The men opened the saddle bag and shook it upside down but there were only some papers in it. Nothing of any value. Disappointed in their haul from such a rich looking man, they each gave the body a ritual last kick before they set off over the hill pass to Killiecrankie. They were uneasy now. Their task was to watch the fort and report back. There might be trouble for this. They shouted to each other as they ran. Best say nothing. Plan the same story if any trouble is caused.

The men disappeared into the bracken, their voices growing fainter until in the copse there was only the sound of the rain spattering heavily on the leaves of the birch trees. Soon the body of De Vere was a sodden heap and the plans for the third rebellion lay, an unreadable mass of inky paper, beside him.

As the rain gathered force and the day darkened, General Cope took the wood from the box made by Villiers and threw it on the fire in his office. Impregnated as it was by solvent, it made a fine blaze.

Chambers cradled the bowl of whisky and hot milk in his two hands. His plaid cloak and his sheepskin boots lay steaming by the glowing peat fire. He looked across at Cluny Macpherson.

'No, I could not save the plans, Cluny. They are lost in the mud of the road to Killiecrankie. But I did prevent Cope from taking them seriously.' He sipped again at the bowl. 'The man's a fool.'

'He does not have to be very clever, not with the arms and the men he has,' said Cluny Macpherson.

He picked up some of the peat stacked by the door and placed it around the edges of the fire. 'How did he get his troops to the very shores of Arisaig without us seeing, Alastair? How? Where were our lookouts, our sentries? I had been away but a few hours.'

Alastair Chambers looked at Cluny. The man was near exhaustion, he thought. Not the exhaustion which can be righted by one night's deep sleep but the exhaustion of the soul, which goes on a long time. Sometimes to death.

'Cluny. Where does this put us now? We have been betrayed by the man who was the strongest link to our allies. When they hear of this, they will surely not back an invasion? None of us can be sure what information has been compromised. None of us can safely trust the next French representative, whatever credentials he brings.' Alastair leaned forward. 'And Cluny, if De Vere, whom we have known so long, can betray us then what is happening at the French court? The tide has shifted away from us, I fear.'

Cluny said nothing for a while; the only sound was the hiss of the burning peat. When he did speak, his voice was tired and low, 'Alastair, I have taken this betrayal hard. There is no purpose in denying it. De Vere was a man I trusted. He came with the Prince in 1715 and again in 1745, and each time I sensed a brave and loyal man in him. I was wrong. I will pay for that mistake.' Alastair tried to protest. Cluny shook his head. 'No, Alastair, I know what you are going to say, but it is true. I was the one closest to this man. I should have seen the trickery lying in him.'

'But what of the future? What of our men preparing for battle?' Alastair thought of his own younger brother, too young to fight in 1745, now ready and willing to die for his Prince. This new generation of young men could not go out to be massacred as before. 'Cluny,' he said gently, 'Cluny, it has to stop. It will be no better this time. For god's sake, it will be worse, much worse.' Alastair picked up a birch log and threw it on the fire.

Cluny Macpherson said nothing but bowed his head down as the flames jumped and danced in front of him. Eventually he sat up straight and spoke. 'Alastair, you must go back. However stupid you say General Cope is, you will be missed. And to the other thing. Yes, it has to stop, and, here in the Highlands I must be the one to stop it. There will be no rallying to the banner. I will send word of this to his Highness, Prince Charles, and I will inform Choiseul that he sent us a traitor.'

'What of this box? The one which De Vere says does exist. Is it merely a figment of the French imagination?' Alastair smiled at the memory of De Vere trying to convince General Cope that his fantastical tale was true. Cope believed himself a practical man, not easily fooled. The more subtle aspects of warfare often passed him by. But any one would have had difficulty giving credibility to De Vere's story. 'Is it true?' asked Alastair. 'Is there another box?'

'Tell me again what there was on the box,' said Cluny.

'Nothing,' replied Alastair. 'No names. No list. Just the words 'first the flower house'.'

'You are right, Alastair, it means nothing,' said Cluny. 'Now go.'

'Cluny, I believe you are protecting me,' replied Alastair Chambers, as he pulled on his damp boots. Cluny only smiled.

He wanted Alastair to leave. A letter from Ashbourne had been handed to him just as Alastair arrived and he had not been able to read it. The less Alastair knew about the network, the better. If Alastair was caught, right in the centre of the Hanoverian Empire, he would be shown no mercy. All his secrets would be torn from him.

Hulland House Ashbourne

Ann pulled back the curtains in the bedroom overlooking the garden and looked down to the work going on below. Kitty was having a fountain installed and the arrival of three workmen had caused the under housemaids to find a lot of slop buckets to be emptied on the back garden. Ann sat down on the chair by the window. It was a low chair and so she could watch at her leisure as Mary walked up and down the path, flirting with the workmen. There would be no chance of Ann being seen. After an interval she grew tired of watching Mary and her mind turned to its usual track. What had happened to her letter to Cluny Macpherson? Had it got through? Did he now know that De Vere, the French agent was a traitor?

Francis had disappeared from Ashbourne. He had told James he had banking business in London and then had gone. For over three weeks they had heard nothing from him. Ann assumed his usefulness to the Government was at an end so he would be left to fend for himself. She thought it was quite likely that they would never hear from him again. James had been at home constantly since she had told him of her doubts about Francis Etherington. She realised that James knew her very well. He knew that something had happened between her and Francis but he preferred not to confront her with his knowledge – yet. He watched her for long periods during the day, as if he were attempting to gather evidence. Ann rather enjoyed this scrutiny. It was not that he was gathering evidence of a threatening kind, rather knowledge about something dear to him. Ann left the bedroom. As she reached the head of the stairs she realised that there was the flurry of some one arriving in the hall. She leaned over the banister and saw Amanda handing her bonnet to one of the maids. Amanda looked up and caught sight of Ann. Ann could see that her face was serious. What could have happened? She ran down the stairs to be met at the foot by Amanda. 'Ann, the most dreadful thing has happened. Francis Etherington has been found dead. Hanged in his apartment in London. John is staying to make arrangements, apparently Francis has no family... What do you think of it? Isn't it the most dreadful news?'

'Hanged. How did he hang?' asked Ann. She could only think of Francis Etherington breathing into her ear and saying, 'you will hang, Ann...'

Amanda put her hand on Ann's arm. 'He took his own life. Apparently there was a note. It said very little.'

'What did it say?' asked Ann sharply. 'What was this very little?'

Amanda led Ann into the library. 'Ann, sit down,' she said. 'He was afraid that he had made some rash decisions and that he faced ruin.' She cleared her throat. 'Ann, you know how involved we all were financially with Francis, well, I'm afraid we may all suffer very badly indeed through this.'

'Very badly. How badly?'

'John fears that we may be ruined,' said Amanda.

Ann wanted to say. No, we will not be, because I once murdered a man and I still have a substantial sum of money because of it. She remembered Amanda questioning her so closely during her first months in Ashbourne.

'Amanda, you need have no fear. There is money enough for us all. Kitty will explain to you how. It is Kitty's story. But do not ask her yet. Wait until she has understood all of this. And now I must find James.'

James was standing by the window in the drawing room. He turned as Ann entered and she knew he had overheard Amanda's news. He contemplated the picture his wife made standing by the door. The door he had first seen her at, as it so happened. He felt that rush of love which her appearance always engendered in him. 'You heard Amanda, James. Did you not?' she asked.

'Yes, I heard the news. And you are right, Ann, thanks to our Jacobite benefactor we have enough money to ride out this storm.' He turned away to look out of the window.

Ann felt compelled to tell James more. 'He did not die because of me, James,' she said softly.

James turned back to look at her. He smiled. 'I know,' he said, 'you are not a murderer.'

He turned away to look out of the window again. Ann stood in the doorway for what seemed like a very long time. Although her mind raged with the possibility of what to say next, she did not speak.

James and Edward went down to London to attend the funeral of Francis Etherington and to settle matters at the bank. Thanks to the Jacobite money as they now all called it, the family was able to survive the losses incurred by the collapse of Etherington's dealings. He had been gambling heavily for years, it appeared, and his debts were extensive. The day after the funeral, Mary came to Ann in the drawing room and said that a young woman was there to see her. 'Show her in to the library,' Ann directed, and she made her way there to meet her guest.

Ann half expected a visit from the Government agency. She was certain that Francis had not committed suicide but had been murdered by his former colleagues. Would the agency loosen its hold on her now? Or would they attempt to secure her silence in some way? She did not know, but each day she waited for the call of an unknown person at her door.

When she entered the library she saw at once that it was the thin faced young woman from the inn on the Leek road. The young woman stood up when Ann entered but Ann waved her to her seat. She sat down and prepared to listen. 'Mrs Walker, I have come with important news from Cluny Macpherson.' Ann nodded. The young woman continued. 'He thanks you for your letter. It came too late to save the plans for the invasion but your information helped to confirm what he had discovered. Now, he has a request to make of you.' Ann's heart plummeted. What could he want? 'The box which he took was just a copy, a replica.' The woman spoke as if she had learned this off by heart. 'The real box, with the information on it, is still in the house where these boxes were made. The house of Lady Primrose in Essex Street. Mr Macpherson asks you to go to London to the house of Lady Primrose and bring the real box back to Ashbourne with you. The rebellion will not take place in the near future but people will die if the names on that box get into the wrong hands. If you get the box you are to bring it to the Dragon's Nest and show this.' She leaned forward and gave Ann back the stone talisman and with it a piece of strong cloth on which were printed the words:

Flower house
The den
Look Love Follow
The box

'Mr Macpherson knows that he asks much of you. But he asks it, nevertheless.' She stood up and went to the door. She put her hand over the handle and stood there. 'Because there is no one else to ask.'

Ann went forward as if to detain her. 'Is that all?' she asked. 'There are no more instructions?'

For the first time the woman smiled. 'When asked that question by others, Cluny Macpherson said that you would not follow instructions any more than you would ride side saddle.'

Then the woman was gone and Ann was alone in the library with the talisman in her hand.

Chapter 11

June 23rd 1758 Whitehall, London

The man hunched over the fire in the wing-backed leather chair leaned across and took another Bath biscuit from the tray at his side. It was his sixth biscuit and Sir Christopher Lovell was no more comforted by it than by the previous five. This was a very bad do. A very bad do indeed.

56 Grafton Street London June 23rd 1758

The house on Grafton Street was tall and narrow. Ann had an impression of white stone pillars and polished marble underfoot and then she was inside. Away from the noise and dust of the street in the coolness and order of a long hallway. Amanda was coming towards her down the hallway, made breathless by the effort of moving so fast that her legs were pushing against her voluminous skirt like a wader against the tide. Delighted to have her sister-in-law in London. 'Ann! James!' she cried breathlessly. 'Come in! How marvellous to have you here. How was your journey? Are you exhausted? I will ring for some tea. Or do you want to go up to your rooms first?' She paused for a moment to catch her breath and then led them into a square elegant drawing room. The furnishings were rich and the seating was comfortable. As Amanda chattered Ann sank into a deep sofa covered with cool brocade. She closed her eyes. The next few days were going to be difficult.
Tonight, when she wanted only to rest and think, she must attend an assembly in honour of Mrs Caroline Curzon. A birthday celebration, a masked ball, which was to be held in the Curzon's London house on Audley Street.

Nathaniel Curzon was ambitious, he had recently inherited the land and house at Kedleston in Derbyshire and he coveted a seat in the House of Lords. When he had been contacted by Sir Christopher Lovell he had been excited. He sensed an opportunity. And when he had sat in an austere office in Whitehall hearing Lovell's request, he had understood immediately that it was a matter of great importance that he should issue an invitation to his wife's birthday party to an obscure Ashbourne family of merchants. The Hodgsons and the Walkers – Who were they? But they seemed to offer him the chance to do something for the government, and to bring, as Sir Christopher had murmured, his peerage possibly a little closer.

Amanda was greatly satisfied to have received an invitation. A little strange, for she had never met Caroline Curzon at any function. But she supposed that there was something of a Derbyshire connection here. And that this was evidence of how well the family were doing. They were moving into entirely another level of London society.

Even though the final part of their journey to London had been tiring, Ann and James felt they must attend.

Audley Street London June 23rd 1758

Three hundred members of London society attended the masked ball to celebrate Caroline Curzon's birthday. By six thirty, Audley Street was blocked by a series of opulent carriages. The street was filled with the noise of horses stamping and neighing in panic as their coachmen attempted to pull back or dive forward whenever they saw an opening. All attempting to roll up promptly at seven o clock to disgorge their glittering, bejewelled occupants so eager not to miss the first entertainment of the evening.

As the carriage which held Ann and her family approached

Audley Street, Ann saw figures packed on either side of the road. Some were cheering the sight of this wealth, but others stood silently. On the corner of Audley Street Ann could clearly see two pickpockets, a man and a woman, working a mark at the front of the crowd. These two were unaware of, or uninterested in, the fact that they could be seen so easily from the carriages. They knew that the people in the carriages would have no real interest in the crowd. The woman's face, as she turned to the chosen victim, was a picture of helpless, ladylike suffering. She clutched her shawl to her breast with one hand and reached out the other for assistance. Now she will faint, thought Ann. As the woman sank to the ground and the mark leaned over to help her, Ann saw her partner move in and remove the man's pocket book from his britches. Ann became aware that Amanda was gently shaking her arm. 'Ann. Ann, listen to me. Time to put on our masks.'

Ann looked down. The masks were pretty things made of silks and feathers. Ann's lay on her lap. She had chosen the simplest one sent from the costumiers, white velvet with diamanté encrusted around its edges. Amanda was carefully clasping the fasteners of a bright blue silk affair, and James was struggling with a black and white harlequin mask made of papier mâché. John Hodgson had already put his mask on. It had a beaked nose with pale feathers sprouting from each side and he looked very much like a large barn owl. Some of the tension inside Ann suddenly released. She laughed aloud with the relief of it and prepared to enjoy this evening. Wedged securely against the door of the carriage as it bucked and rolled across the cobbles, with her velvet mask covering most of her upper face, Ann felt confident that there could be no danger to her in the hours ahead.

As she stepped up the wide steps and into the great entrance hall, Ann realised that the first entertainment had already begun. It was a troupe of Russian acrobats who had been entertaining London society all season. Their presence indicated the importance of the house, and therefore the importance of the party, for only a large house could have a hall big enough for their performance. Above the bobbing heads of the guests thronging the great hall Ann saw their curled bodies, first one by one, then together, then separate again, rising high up into the heights, making arcs of red, purple and blue against the stark white of the stuccoed walls. The Curzons had had three thousand candles lit throughout the reception rooms. The silks and the diamanté of the costumes shone and shimmered as their wearers moved constantly about. The effect was of one vast moving, restless light. And above it the arcs of blue, then red, then purple rising almost, it seemed, too slowly to maintain their trajectory. Ann stood as close to a wall as she could and watched it all.

The acrobats landed together on the floor, bowed and ran out. As soon as they had gone, three men, wearing white loin cloths with their oiled upper bodies shining in the flickering candlelight, marched out from a side door in one of the walls and took up their places on a dais in the centre of the inner reception room. Behind them came a young woman, her slender body wound in yards of white silk. She carried a brazier. On her back, held in a kind of sling, were what appeared to be long sticks of wood. At a signal from one of the men, she placed the brazier on the floor, took one of the sticks from the sling and dipped it in the brazier. There was a murmur of delighted fear from the watching guests as the stick burned brightly. With a flourish, she handed the burning stick to the man nearest to her. He took it, held it aloft briefly and then swung the stick down until he had placed at least a quarter of it in his mouth. The crowd gasped. Even louder when he withdrew the stick from his mouth, still burning. One by one the men were handed sticks and repeated the actions of the first. As the last man was holding his burning stick above his head in triumph, Ann noticed that the young woman had begun to unwind herself from her covering of silken cloth. She had chosen to hand a corner of it to an important-looking man in the crowd and was slowly moving away from him. He watched, smiling. She knows her business, thought Ann. As the dancer turned across the floor, the wide strip of material unwound behind her until it all lay discarded. Now she was dressed only in jewelled circlets around her breasts and a tiny skirt of heavy silver fringing, which hung from below her waist. She raised her arms above her head, clapped twice and waited until all eyes were upon her and all murmuring had ceased. Then she began to dance.

Ann had never seen a body move in this way. Every part seemed to undulate and flow. The roundness of her breasts seemed to merge in to the dip of her waist and then spring upward again. The woman moved around in a full circle with small tapping steps and Ann saw that the lift and dip of her buttocks mirrored the movement of her breasts. She moved faster and faster, her hands clapping furiously, her body turning more and more quickly and then she suddenly sank down until her forehead touched the marble floor of the entrance hall. She leapt back up after a moment of complete silence and stillness in the room. To a great thunder of applause, she then bowed low, picked up the brazier, and ran from the room, followed by the fire eaters, still carrying aloft their flaming sticks in a kind of ceremonial procession.

People turned to their neighbours to exclaim over what they had seen, an almost naked woman. How daring of the Curzons. To have such an entertainment! But now musicians could be heard in the ballroom. The gentle, measured notes of the minuet. The ball had begun. People crowded towards the the ballroom to take up their positions in the dance. For a moment, Ann found herself pressed up against the man in front of her.

Before she had thought of it, her hand had slipped down and found the wallet lodged in the shallow pocket of his breeches. Once her fingers closed on the familiar feel of leather she knew there was no going back. She had to complete the lift. And quickly. She pulled the wallet out, flipped it up until it lay flush against her wrist and, holding it tight into the folds of her skirt, she moved backwards into the crowd. At least twenty steps away. That was how you did it. Her heart was hammering but she had to dip her head to cover a smile. It was so easy.

Then she was horrified by what she had done. Why had she done it?

Fool! Fool! Fool!

So much depended on her and now she had jeopardised it all for the thrill of picking a rich man's pocket. She moved against the crowd until she was against the furthest wall from the ballroom. She would let them all leave, too dangerous to drop it from her hand now, even in this crowd. She looked around. Perhaps an antechamber or an alcove. Out of sight.

Soon Ann was left almost entirely alone, still standing close to the wall. Don't rush. Don't rush. She put her hands behind her back, still holding the wallet, and laid her head back against the marble pillar behind her, feeling its coolness even through her thickly wound and pinned hair. The mask felt hot and uncomfortable, but she would not take it off. Flimsy as it was, if she had to run at least her identity might be protected for a while. Her fear subsided. No one would expect a pickpocket in this great marble hall. The pickpockets were all outside. And those huge footmen with their great white wigs would prevent any of them getting in. She started to laugh then put her hand to her mouth as a servant crossed the hall and looked at her curiously. She must not draw attention to herself.

It had been the pickpockets on the street. Seeing them. She had wanted to be on the pavements with them. So simple. Taking enough to get by. Never being greedy. Never hesitating once you'd both agreed your target. She closed her eyes for a moment and began to go over in her mind what she had to do tomorrow. Was it possible? Could she do it? She sighed. As she opened her eyes she realised with a shock that she was not the only person in the entrance hall. A man was watching her from across the other side of the hall. She took as much in of him as she could. He was stout and his shoulders were hunched as if he spent his days poring over books. Not a guard then. He certainly couldn't give chase. But perhaps there were others. She looked around quickly but could see no one else. She looked back across the room. The man's legs were slightly parted to enable him to rock back and forward. He held a glass of wine in one hand and had tucked the other into his satin waistcoat. He seemed relaxed. In no hurry. But he was staring at her. As far as she could make it out. It was hard to guess at what was happening under his mask, which was black and covered his eyes and the sides of his head.

And then he began to cross the empty expanse of stone floor. Ann gently dropped the wallet to the floor and stepped back so that it would be covered by her skirts. Her mouth was dry. She swallowed hard and tried to breath evenly.

He reached her and put out his hand. 'Sir Christopher Lovell, ma'am.' She brought her right hand from behind her back and touched his briefly, trying to see his eyes behind the mask.

His handshake surprised her. It was usual to kiss the hand of a lady… or to grip the arm of a thief. She gave a wry smile. The handshake was brisk and business-like, but instead of drawing away at its finish, he continued to hold her hand in his and stare at her. Ann felt for the wallet with her foot. It was still there, safely under her skirt. Then she felt him grip her hand more tightly and he pulled her closer to him with a sharp tug. There was something brutal in him. This was nothing to do with the wallet. What did he want?

'I'm sorry sir. I do not think we have met.' She was aware that her voice shook.

'No. No, we have not. You are Mrs Ann Walker, I believe.'
He indicated the mask, 'I saw your carriage arrive.'
Watching for her then. Alarm spread through Ann and the
wallet lay forgotten. Be innocent. Be innocent of everything.
'I am, sir. And you?'
'Sir Christopher Lovell,' he said his name again, bowed and
dropped her hand.
'Indeed, I do not think we have met, sir. In fact I am sure of
it.'
Sir Christopher looked at Ann for a moment.
'No, as I said, we have not met. But I know a little of your
family.'
'Really?' Ann smiled gracefully. 'Then sir, tell me more. Do
you know my husband James Walker?'
But Sir Christopher Lovell did not answer. He leaned
forward as if to get a last look at her and then simply turned
and walked away. She realised that she had been measured
and then dismissed.
Sudden anger flashed inside her. She lifted her skirts and
kicked the wallet violently across the floor. It slithered
noisily to the centre of the room. He must have heard it but
he did not turn around.

The family left the ball at four o clock in the morning. As
they stood at the top of the steps waiting for their carriage
to draw up, Ann looked over her shoulder. There was Sir
Christopher Lovell standing in the shadows at the edge of
the entrance hall, watching her.
In the carriage driving home Ann was glad that everyone
was too weary to talk.
Sir Christopher Lovell. He had announced himself to her as
if she would recognise the name. But she could not.
Impossible to explain. But it could not be good. As she had
looked back into the house she had realised that his mask
reminded her of something. The black helmet worn by
executioners. Her spirits sank.

Essex Street London June 24th

'I am going to take a walk this morning.'
Ann looked around the breakfast table.
'To reconnoitre the area,' laughed James.
Amanda waved the butter knife in the air, 'James! You are too unkind. You make it sound as if Ann is setting up a military operation. Whereas she is only going out to spy where the best shops might be.' She smiled at Ann.
'Oh no, I insist that my term is accurate,' he had replied, still laughing. He had held Ann's eyes for a fraction too long but she had no time to worry about that now.
She approached Essex Street from The Strand. Very few people were about. All trade deliveries to the London houses lined here had finished long before and the gentry were not yet ready to sally forth and engage in their daily establishment of hierarchy through meetings and card leaving.
At the door of Number 15 Ann handed her card to a manservant, who raised his eyebrows in surprise at this unfashionably early visit. She had not wanted to draw any attention to herself but she had little time. He returned to the door quickly and ushered her in to a quiet room just off the hall. The curtains were still drawn but Ann could make out that the room was lined with books and furnished with a large desk. It smelt like a place where men would meet late at night, a place redolent of brandy and cigars.
The door opened and in came a small woman dressed neatly in morning muslin and a mobcap. She walked across the room and opened the heavy curtains. The early morning light revealed a face softened and lined with age and a gown which Ann could now see was sprigged with bright yellow primroses.
Ann smiled, 'Lady Primrose?' The woman nodded.
Ann went on. 'I have come looking for something.' The woman nodded again.

Ann reached into the small pocket of her jacket and brought out the amulet. She handed it to Lady Primrose, who held it up to the light, scrutinising the inscription upon it.

'Look, love and follow,' she said slowly, turning back to Ann. 'The motto of the Jacobites.' She turned away from Ann and gazed out of the window. 'Tell me what you want.' It was an uncompromising command.

Ann was uncomfortably aware that there had been no rush of fellow feeling between them. If anything Lady Primrose seemed uninterested. Nevertheless, this was the house to which Cluny had sent her and Ann had to trust his judgment if she was to proceed at all.

She told Lady Primrose of the need to find the real box, the second box. She did not say why. Lady Primrose did not turn around until Ann had finished speaking.

Her face was in darkness and Ann could not read her expression.

'And you have been told that this box is here?'

Ann bent her head slightly in affirmation.

'And the man who made this box is called.... Villiers?'

Ann bent her head in agreement again but her confidence in the situation began to deteriorate. A nervous thrill of fear darted across her body. She instinctively looked at the door for a means of escape.

'There is no escape, my dear,' said Lady Primrose softly. 'You do realise that, don't you? Or did they recruit you without telling you?' She sounded almost playful. 'Don't worry. You are safe here. Or as safe as I can make you.' Lady Primrose walked across the room to a cabinet. She took out a bottle of French brandy and three glasses. She calmly poured three drinks and handed one to Ann.

'I have been asked to show you to someone. Wait here.'

Ann waited alone in the dark study. Eventually the door opened and Lady Primrose re-entered. Behind her came the figure of a man, wrapped in a thick travelling cloak. The man stepped forward, threw back his cloak and held out his hand to Ann. Ann felt obliged to stand up. She felt some other gesture was expected of her but did not know what it was. She looked down at the extended hand and proffered her own in return. As their hands met, Ann noticed that on the third finger of the hand extended to her was a ring. The motif on the ring was the same as the one on the talisman.

'This is your Prince,' said Lady Primrose. The playfulness of her previous tone had been replaced by one of respectful anticipation. Ann felt that the two other people in the room had a role for her to play. The hand in hers felt clammy and soft. The eyes in the face in front of hers were a bright, startling blue. But they expressed an expectation of adoration which Ann felt unable to fulfil. The words the Prince spoke to her were of encouragement and thanks but Ann was left with the impression that she was of little interest to this man. He longed for a return to the centre stage. She might be a means to help him get there and so was worth some time and some attention. Two other men wrapped in cloaks entered the room and the Prince left with them. Ann had an overwhelming sense of anti-climax. The Young Pretender. Bonnie Prince Charlie. How many of the Highlanders who so loved him had met him? Looked into those calculating, greedy eyes as he talked of winning his throne? That people would die for him, he saw as his right. The right of kings. Ann was doubtful. Somehow he did not impress her as a man of honour. But would men like Cluny McPherson follow him unless his cause was an honourable one?

As the Prince left the room with his bodyguards, Lady Primrose sat down behind the desk. She lifted a pretty lacquered box off its surface and opened it. She offered it to Ann. 'Would you like a cigar?' she asked. Ann shook her head. Lady Primrose took her time to cut and light a long cheroot, and when the room was filled with its pungent scent, she spoke. Her tone surprised Ann with its vehemence.

'You are a fool,' she said. 'Do you see who you endanger? The Prince can and does visit his loyal followers in London but he is never safe. Care must always be taken.' She spoke with much more precision and emotion now, 'I have no idea why you are involved in this... this,' she waved her hand in the air, 'this melee... but you shouldn't be.'

She slapped her hand on the desk with such force that Ann jumped. Lady Primrose leaned towards Ann and spoke harshly and rapidly. 'What do you mean by coming to my door so early in the morning? I assume you have only just arrived in London?'

Ann nodded.

'So now it is clear to anyone watching this house... to any servant who has other reasons than my payment to want to be in my employ, that you have something to pass on... or something to pick up. You fool. You jeopardise everything and everybody with your stupidity.'

Ann opened her mouth to explain and defend her behaviour. Lady Primrose intercepted her before she could form the first word.

'Don't bother,' she said. 'Don't bother with your tales of romance and loyalty. With your new-found sense of purpose. Your loyalty to the cause, or – ' At this point she gave a dismissive snort. 'Or even more banal, your great love for some Jacobite rebel, who has stolen your heart, and who you will follow to the ends of the earth.'

Her eyes travelled over Ann's impeccably fashionable gown. 'My dear, you are simply bored and would like to be a heroine in your own adventure.' She stood up, and leaned across the desk. Her eyes stared full into Ann's own. 'The reality if you, or I, are caught, is a filthy cell, with dung around your ankles and your body eventually, slowly, painfully becoming used and broken until you either die or are thrown out on some back alley. What do you know of that?' Lady Primrose picked up Ann's card, 'Mrs... Mrs James Walker.' Her voice finished on a note of derision and the card fluttered back on to the table.

After a moment of complete silence in the room, when the only sound was of a cart passing in the street outside, Ann heard her own voice in reply, slow and firm and clear. 'I know very well what it is like to be in the circumstances you describe, and I know how to escape from them...' she glanced around the room, 'more than you might from this house, this street, this city... Lady Primrose.' There was equal derision in Ann's use of the name of her hostess. 'Now,' she continued, noting briefly that the other woman's expression had changed from contempt to a mixture of surprise and curiosity, 'the box.'

After half an hour, she had learnt nothing from Lady Primrose.

Villiers had used the basement of the house and it would not have been prudent for the lady of the house to know more than she had to about his actions. She had visited the basement after he had gone and there had been traces of his work, wood shavings, varnish, some cloths but nothing incriminating, nothing informative.

After this fruitless discussion, Julia Primrose left the room to dress for the day. She would return, and they would continue their meeting in a proper manner, like any other ladies of fashion becoming acquainted with each other.

Ann got up and went to the window. She watched the street with its small trickle of passers by. Would it contain a spy, following her, watching her? Watching this house? She realised that Lady Primrose was right. She was not equipped for the task Cluny had set her. But Cluny would know this and would have chosen someone else if he could. She must complete it. For there was no one else.

Ann turned back into the room and sat down on a sofa against the wall backing onto the hall. On the wall opposite her was an imposingly dark and grand oil painting showing a woman, sitting on a large ornate oak chair and holding on her knee a plate or shield of some sort. Around the edge of the plate some sort of motto was written. Ann got up to see what it was. The lion and the fox lie down together, she read. And as she sat down again, Ann noticed that around the edge of the cloth thrown across the back of the chair some initials were picked out in gold thread. L,L,F. Three intricate letters, entwined with each other. The name, Lady Lucy Falconer was painted in thin lettering along the bottom edge of the painting. Obviously this was her portrait. Perhaps some part of the family of Lady Primrose or the previous owners, thought Ann.

Julia Primrose re-entered the room. 'Well, what do you want to do?' she queried. 'Look all over the house? I can't think of a better plan. Can you? If he had a box to hide and your clue is Flower House then it must still be here.' She looked around her. 'This is the most unlikely spot; no one comes in here. It is my 'den' so to speak.'

'What did you say?' said Ann, thinking of the piece of cloth Cluny had sent her:

Flower house
The den
Look Love Follow
The box

The inscription on the inside of the decoy box which De Vere had offered to General Cope. Flower House was this place but no one as yet had any ideas as to what the other clues could mean. But this room was the den.

'The box must be here.' Ann got up and began looking around .

'Why?' Julia was startled by Ann's sudden activity.

'Because of the clues: the next one is 'The Den', ' said Ann. 'Then, Look Love Follow and then The Box. Let me write them down for you. Perhaps you can add to their meaning. Perhaps you carry the information of the whereabouts of the box without knowing it.'

Ann went to the desk and wrote down the clues, handing Julia the sheet of paper.

'Julia looked at the sheet of paper, mouthing the words under her breath and shaking her head. 'No,' she said slowly. 'I cannot think. Look Love Follow is the Jacobite motto of course, more usually written as three entwined letters... but...'

'Entwined letters!' Ann was pointing at the painting as she leapt up. 'Look,' she gripped Lady Julia's arm in her excitement. 'Lady Lucy Falconer – see the initials here!' She jabbed her finger at the painting.

LLF, in gold thread, on the cloth draped over the chair on which sat Lady Lucy Falconer.

Ann cast her eyes over the painting again 'and the den – where fox and lion lie down together. We must be on the right track.'

Both women sat down on the sofa opposite the painting and continued to stare at it.

'What else..? What else...?' Ann's eyes strayed down to the piece of furniture directly below the painting. It was a large side table with an upper part combining two side pillars with a small rectangular cabinet between. Something about the size and shape of the cabinet was familiar. Ann struggled to understand why. Where could she have seen it before? Then, with a sudden shock, she recognised it. It was the box. Or at least it was something very like it.

She rushed forward and ran her fingers over the front of the cabinet. Yes, she was certain. It shared the contours and dimensions of the box which she had carried and concealed for so long. As she looked closer she realised that this central cabinet had an emblem in brass screwed to the front of it. It carried a simple but memorable design which was exactly the same as the design on the lock on the money box that Ann had looked at so often in the past few years.

They hurried to prise the cabinet out of its setting. Taking the cabinet out was not difficult. Whoever had concealed it there had anticipated this day. It came away from its side struts with surprising ease. Eventually it sat, more or less intact, on the desk in front of them.

Lady Primrose looked at Ann. 'What are we looking for?' she asked.

'I ...I don't know. Something hidden on the wood itself... like the other box.' Ann shrugged. 'I'm so afraid of destroying anything of use. What if we scrape away the varnish and scrape off the names?'

'Then obviously we stop scraping. We will only lose one, at the most,' said Lady Primrose.

She traced the inscription on the brass. She saw that it was made up of the letter L repeated and then a curved F. Anyone looking at it would have thought it the motif for Lady Lucy Falconer, gazing serenely out from the painting above. Never suspecting the letters to indicate the motto of the Jacobites The most secret information, here in Essex Street, in 'the den', for three years, in front of everyone who passed through this room.

'This isn't a box, it can't contain anything. It can't conceal anything . Look,' she held it up for Ann's scrutiny, 'it has no bottom. It only has five sides of equal weight and width.' She turned the false cabinet over and the rough wood of its inner sides was exposed. For the first time, a name and address was revealed to them.

'What is that?' said Ann. Her heart jumped under her ribs.

'I don't know. The name and address of the furniture maker, I suppose. This isn't an especially good piece, it will have come from a little workshop somewhere.'

'When did it come here?' asked Ann.

'I don't really know,' Julia shook her head. 'My father bought it somewhere... I think...'

'After Villiers' visit?' asked Ann.

'Yes, yes, definitely. It was a gift from my father for my birthday. That's why it ended up here in my room.'

Julia picked up the cabinet and read out the address.

'The Patisseria Valeria, No.15, The South Gloucester Road, Kensington Village'.

'That is strange,' Lady Primrose traced the address with her fingertip.

'Why?' Said Ann quickly.

'This isn't a furniture manufacturer. Patisseria. This must be the name of some Italian bakehouse. I have never heard of it. It means nothing to me.' The two women looked at each other.

Then Lady Primrose spoke. 'You must tell me more.'

It was a statement rather than a request.

So Ann explained to the woman who sat quietly opposite her how events had brought her to this room. After she had finished Lady Primrose sat silent for a while. When she replied it was in a series of rapid instructions.

'Leave here now. Leave this box,' she gestured at the table, '...cabinet, with me. Tomorrow you will receive an invitation to visit me here in the morning of the following day. Accept this invitation in writing and come to visit at the time agreed. I will have more news for you then. Do not indicate to anyone what we may have found.'

Ann spent the next day unable to rest. She hoped she appeared calm and tried to maintain an interest in all around her, but eventually, in the afternoon, she retired to her room, saying that she felt tired. At least, when she was alone, she could pace and think without interruption.

At last, she sat in front of Lady Primrose. 'Well,' she said.

'Ann, there is nothing in or on these pieces of wood.' Lady Primrose indicated the neat stack on the desk between them. Ann was suddenly filled with hopeless disappointment. She looked down at her gloved hands, lying useless in her lap. What would Cluny do now?

Lady Primrose was speaking again. 'The information on the

cabinet is only the name and address of the patisseria. No code. There must be some kind of contact to be made there.'

'I'll go to it,' said Ann, standing up and moving towards the door.

'Yes, you must go.' Lady Primrose took her arm. 'But be cautious,' she said. 'Many years have passed, this could have turned into a trap. Do not leave my house and go straight to this address. Wait for at least one day. Wait until tomorrow.'

Waiting again. Ann was about to disagree, she had no time to wait but she realised that what the other woman said made sense. If they were being watched then the more time between her visit to Essex Street and to Kensington Village, the better that would be.

'One more thing. Go as a lady with a party to plan, or a wedding cake to buy. Have a clear, legitimate purpose for being in that shop.'

'Yes,' said Ann.

26th June Glen Alder

Cluny continued to stare into the eyes of the elder MacDonald.

'No,' he repeated. 'Calum, it is certain death.'

The elder MacDonald stared back. 'Cluny,' he smiled, 'it is always certain death. Haven't you read your scriptures? Death and resurrection are the only certainties.'

Cluny was not to be deflected by the other man's easy charm.

'Without French aid, we are doomed.'

'Doomed? That's a strong word. A word for the superstitious. Where's your courage, Cluny? Or have you lost the appetite for this fight?'

'Calum,' Cluny shook his head. 'We have been struggling a long time. The French have not aided us each time we have asked. There will be no difference this time, unless we can get English support it is murder to take our men south.'

From the doorway of the bothy, the younger MacDonald spoke. 'He is right, father. We cannot win without the French. And without that list we will not have French support, let alone know who our allies are in the south.'

The older man stood up. 'Ach, John. Have you no stomach for this fight either? Am I among friends of the Stuart cause or not?' His voice showed his derision and frustration.

The younger MacDonald watched his father for a moment. 'You are among true leaders of the clans, father. We will not have our men killed for nothing. Lives wasted because we followed a headstrong old man who did not think beyond what came out of his foolish mouth.'

There was an electric silence as the elder MacDonald chose his course. 'Very well, John,' he eventually replied. 'But have a care of your own tongue. It has little respect.' He bowed formally to Cluny, ducked out of the entrance and strode off to his waiting horse.

Cluny felt his body relax for the first time in the last three days. It was over. He had hardly hoped for this outcome as the talks had wound on and on. But with the MacDonalds in agreement, the other clan chiefs would fall into line. They would wait for news of the French fleet. They would wait until Cluny had agreed tactics with the Bourbon government.

He knew what they did not, that *there* was where the power lay, not with Charles.

26th June 1758 Patisseria Valeria

Patisseria Valeria was part of a small group of shops on the high street of Kensington Village.

Ann passed down the street twice in her carriage, each time taking in as much of the frontage of the shop as she could, before asking the driver to stop and wait a hundred yards further up the road by a watering trough. The shop seemed perfectly normal. Perfectly bona fide. A dark green door and a big window under a striped awning. The name Patisseria Valeria written in elegant gold curlicue lettering along the ledge above the window.

Ann strolled down the high street. It was busy with morning activity. Each man and woman who passed Ann looked inquisitively at her. She suspected each one of being a government agent until she realised they were only interested in her dress. She hoped Amanda's sense of London fashion was accurate enough for her to blend in with these crowds.

As she approached the shop she could see that each sparkling pane of the broad window revealed a different sweet delight. Towers of delicate chocolate leaves in white and brown. Flat, squat bright red strawberry tarts, creamy white chiffon pies and heap after heap of golden ratafia biscuits, overflowing from little china bowls set along the inside of the window sill.

She pushed open the door. A bell jangled and two customers turned to look at her briefly. Ann saw that a young dark haired girl was the only person behind the counter. The shop was a calm comfortable place. Smelling of sweet, warm food. Ann realised that she was disappointed. She felt a little foolish. She had somehow expected an air of conspiracy. But this was just a cake shop.

There may have been a connection. But it had been too long. Whatever trail there had been was lost.

'Can I help you madam?'

It was her turn to be served.

'Do you know of a gentleman named Villiers?' asked Ann abruptly, ignoring the advice she had been given.

The girl slowly shook her head. 'Villiers... No, I'm sorry, Madam.' Ann turned to go before the girl asked any questions. Hearing the girl speak the name out loud made Ann realise how dangerous her direct tactics were.

'Madam, wait.'

Ann looked impatiently back from the door. She hoped to politely discourage any further conversation. The more time she was there, the more that was said, the more danger grew. 'I will ask Master Valeria. He may know this gentleman. Did you say Villiers?' At the top of the two steps which led to the back shop, the girl paused. ' Is that a French name, Madam?' Her voice was raised.

A man examining the chocolate towers turned sharply to stare at Ann.

In a shop near London asking for a Frenchman, I must be mad indeed, thought Ann.

'I suppose it could be,' she replied, trying by a deprecating smile to disassociate herself from the very Frenchness of the name.

The girl disappeared up a step into the back shop. After a few moments during which, to Ann's relief, the man left, the girl reappeared. 'No, I'm sorry, Madam. He does not.'

Ann had the presence of mind to purchase four strawberry tarts, which the girl placed in a cardboard box. Now at least I look as if I had a legitimate reason for being here, thought Ann, as she stepped back out onto the street. Although four strawberry tarts will not convince anyone who recognises that name. And still I am no nearer finding the names. Or Villiers. Or anything.

 She was lost in thought as she sat back in the carriage until she realised that the driver had stopped in a park of trees and neat shrubs. Ann put her head part way out of the window. 'Where are we?' she called to the driver above. 'Why have we stopped?'

People milled down the road, people cantered past on a parallel cinder bridle way and Ann could see an impression of a white stone palace through the great elms which encircled the flat expanse of grass.

She heard a sharp click and felt the carriage rock slightly. Ann turned to see the girl from the counter at the patisseria get in. She held up her hand as Ann tried to speak. 'Come every day to drive here,' she said, and then she had opened the carriage door and dropped back down onto the driveway before Ann could detain her.

No 18 Lazard Street 26th June 1758

'Why does she ask for Villiers?'
The speaker stood at the window. Although the body was short and stout it was corseted and stitched into a fine example of London fashion. Sweeping satin panniers came to a hairsbreadth of touching the polished floorboards, but as they did not, the body seemed to float unattached to the ground as the speaker turned to face the man sitting on the other side of the room. Then, as the figure moved, the panniers tipped upwards, the whole skirt held in one belled shape by the unseen metal cage which underpinned it. With this movement, the illusion of floating was broken. Exquisitely worked slippers came into view. Satin of the palest cream edged with tiny pearls around the front and toe. A glimpse of plump, creamy silk-encased ankles above. The figure moved forwards across the room, one hand extended to display a tiny lace handkerchief only just held by the most extreme finger tips of the left hand. The hand swirled in an elaborate figure of eight and the figure curtsied.
It was impossible to talk to Villiers when he was like this, thought Alberto Valeria as he sat patiently on one of the uncomfortable chairs in Villiers' boudoir.
For twenty minutes Villiers had been strutting up and down in his finery, delighted to have a new audience. The visitor suspected that Villiers found his life at Lazard Street somewhat boring. But there were things which had to be discussed. This woman may spell danger or she may bring the answer they were seeking. Only Villiers had the

knowledge to unravel the truth from the possible lies in this situation.

'Henri, we must decide on what action to take.'

Villiers changed his demeanour. He strode across the room and sat down by his visitor. His face under the thick paste was mottled with excitement. 'I know this. I of all people, know this.' To emphasise this point, he struck his right hand with the balled fist of his left. The lace handkerchief fluttered, forgotten, to the floor.

Villiers' painted face suddenly, incongruously, took on the aspect of a sad clown. The carefully drawn arches of his brows rose up into his forehead and his thin mouth was pulled down on either side in an exaggerated moue as he thought out the possible solutions to their problems

'I know this,' he repeated. 'You must send her to me. The news from the north indicates that she can be used. She must be used.' He shook his head, and the tiny curls of his wig flopped to and fro. 'But it is not likely that she will succeed. She will die, this Ann Walker. She will simply be another death.' And the visitor watched as the eyes in the grotesque face opposite him darkened with sadness.

Admiralty House, London

Lord Newcastle tapped nervously on the desk in front of him.

'But Christopher, we publicly disbanded the Committee of Secrecy at least 30 years ago. It has remained out of the public domain ever since. How can I suddenly tell the House that this committee has been pursuing Jacobite traitors since then? And... and ... that many of them, the very members of the House, have been investigated by agents of that very committee.'

'This is a situation of the utmost gravity, my lord. As first minister, you have to address it. There appears to be a real possibility of a Jacobite rebellion, fuelled by the French. The House must be alerted. There are traitors, Lord Newcastle, and we need all to be vigilant.'

Newcastle stood up and started to walk up and down the room. Sir Christopher Lovell was pleased, he had him. Whenever Newcastle paced, then he was truly agitated.

'Christopher... this woman... you say she is a thief, escaped from gaol?'

'Yes.'

'She is the only lead to this list of Jacobite sympathisers?'

'Yes.' Sir Christopher watched the first minister of His Majesty's government enter his trap.

'She is masquerading as the wife of a merchant?'

Sir Christopher nodded.

'Is he implicated?'

Sir Christopher hesitated. There was something unclear about the relationship of the Walker family to the Jacobite cause but he could not fathom it. There was proof of nothing. And Newcastle would only go so far. Finally, he shook his head firmly. 'No, my lord.'

'She is a spy, then. For the French and for the Jacobites. Is she not?' Newcastle looked to Sir Christopher for confirmation.

'Yes, my lord.'

'Then we must have her killed.'

Newcastle took up his hat and moved quickly to the door. He felt slightly sick. He did not like to think about death. As he reached the door another unpleasant thought re-entered his mind. He turned. 'And, Christopher. No more talk of making the Committee of Secrets a public entity. It would not help my position in the Commons. Not at all.' He smiled thinly. 'It served Walpole well out of sight. And it will serve me.'

'Of course,' answered Sir Christopher. 'If we can prevent the network of sympathisers from consolidating then the rout of Forty-Five can be repeated, without the addition of public pressure.' He smiled reassuringly at Newcastle.

A few moments after the first minister had departed, Sir Christopher left the building by a side entrance and made his way to Lincoln's Inn. There, on St Mary Street, he entered a narrow town house of unpretentious appearance and made the arrangements for the quick dispatch of Ann Walker. He returned to his chambers well satisfied with his afternoon's work. He had thought it would be more difficult to get Newcastle's agreement to the murder. Newcastle was squeamish, unlike Fox. Sir Christopher had liked working with Henry Fox. Pity he had left office after so short a stay in power. But, no matter. Newcastle, faced with the spectre of Commons uproar at the disclosure of the continuance of the existence of the Committee of Secrets, had seen the authorisation of the murder of a spy as definitely the lesser of the two evils.

Sir Christopher rang for tea and Bath biscuits.

Chapter 12

28th June 1758 London

On each morning after her instructions Ann rode through the park in her carriage. Sometimes, unable to bear the airless heat of it, she would get out and walk under the trees for a while, but this could prevent anyone approaching her so she would soon climb back into the carriage and take her seat.

Every time she climbed into the confined space of the carriage her sense of foreboding increased. She felt like a rat in a trap. Her last conversation with Lady Primrose kept returning to her mind. Be careful Ann. Always be aware that you could be killed for this. If not on the street then on the gallows as a traitor.

Killed. She had hardly considered it. Killed for what? Lady Primrose had talked of the cause. Ann did not have one. Or not enough of one to die for. Was she a Jacobite? If she was caught she would be treated as one. Did that amount to the same thing? Would she become one as she was tortured or as she was walked out to the scaffold?

She slumped back against the uncomfortable seat. She could not escape the consequences of each action that had led her here. Caught, she would be treated as a rebel. As a traitor. But she was one without conviction. Without the powerful embrace of belief. She would die coldly. Not as a martyr, or with any God to sustain her. She would have no last glorious words to shout because she had no cause. She shuddered, remembering how the law could so casually put Mary Dilkes to death.

And then, on the third day, Ann was startled by a beggar leaping up to her carriage window. He stood on the side step and spoke quickly and urgently to her in the few moments he clung on to the door.

'....in a day or two, go to Bertonelli's house on 18, Lazard Street and name yourself as Mrs Walker.'

As the carriage swept out of the park, heading back to Grafton Street, all thoughts of capture, of failure, left Ann's mind.

Bertonelli's house 18 Lazard Street

Ann had no idea that she was being followed. When she left the house in the morning of the day after she had spoken to the beggar at the window of her carriage, she did not see the two men who accompanied her throughout her visits around town. Who glided in turn after her figure as it entered the carriage or paused on a step or walked slowly along The Strand. Who watched her talk in a lively manner to Amanda's friends or who took in her glance as she read the news on the front of the London Gazette. "French overrun Hanover."

The men were there the next morning when Ann left the London house alone. She walked quickly down Grafton Street and turned in the direction of the West End. Her first tail was happy to keep his distance. In her pale yellow gown she was easy to pick out from the crowd. He only needed a quieter spot. A place briefly unviewed. Enough time to attack and leave clear evidence of a street crime. He and his partner would have to act quickly. They had been told this was an urgent matter. When his companion signalled that things were comfortable, they would move in for the kill.

Suddenly his quarry stopped in the middle of the street and turned abruptly. She began to retrace her steps. She was walking quickly and brushed past her would-be assassin before he had time to melt into the crowd. The material of her gown swept over his feet. He could have reached out and detained her. He caught sight of her face as she passed by. She looked preoccupied, unaware of her surroundings. Her mouth was slightly parted and her cheeks were flushed. She looked excited. Not afraid. Eyes not darting from left to right. Not like most of his victims, who knew that someone was tailing them, an assassin was closing. Who were experienced enough to know that their actions had led to this reality. Whose breath trembled in their throats. This woman did not look like the prey; she looked like the hunter. But what was she doing?

A few feet further on and Ann had passed her second follower. A few moments later and she had gone back up the steps of the house in Grafton Street and disappeared from their view.

Half an hour later she reappeared from a side door. The two men had taken up positions to cover both doors. They suspected that Ann, for all her apparent innocence, had sensed their presence. As the figure in the yellow gown moved quickly down the side street, again she was followed by the two agents. This time her journey appeared to be in the direction of Cheapside, and took her over Westminster Bridge. She kept to the inside of the pavement and seemed at great pains to avoid being conspicuous. The two men sensed that their target was wary and more careful than before. They had to act quickly. Another day and their intended victim would be super sensitive to their presence. Their chance would have gone.

Westminster Bridge was wide and there were few walkers on it. Carriages were more common. At the centre of the bridge the assassins saw their chance. With practised ease they closed on the figure in front of them. One man slid a narrow blade up and under the elaborate costume, piercing the skin, grazing the ribcage, puncturing the right lung and entering a few millimetres into the heart, and the other man adroitly heaved the slumping body over the parapet. As they heard the splash, the two men were already fifty yards away from the scene of their attack, and one hundred yards away from each other, moving in opposite directions across the bridge. A sleepy cart driver, crossing the bridge from the Dover end, stared at the spot where he thought he had seen a murder but, unbelieving, he shook his head and looked back along the heaving sides of his cart horses. This load was too heavy for them. He would have to have words with the haulier.

The body hit the stone supports on its way down. By the time it entered the water, the neck was broken, the right eye socket smashed and the cheek torn from almost all of one side of the face. The yellow gown billowed out, trapping air and keeping the body partly afloat. It came to rest hidden from view under one of the arches of the bridge, snagged on a rusting metal stanchion which protruded into the water there.

The body rose and fell on the water of the tides for hours until the dress was impregnated with granules of dark mud and the wounded face took on a softened, bloated look. As the sun was going down, two boatmen found it as they skulled down river on their way home.

'Did she do herself in?' asked the younger man, as he heaved the sodden body into the boat.

'Probably. Love problems usually. This'll not be the last one you'll see.' The older man unhooked a purse from the waistband of the dress. He rubbed some of the slimy mud off and tiny golden sequins glittered from his hand. 'This was a pretty little thing,' he murmured. He opened it. 'Look. Can't be robbery.' Inside were some coins and two calling cards, their letters still clear:

Mrs Ann Walker,
Grafton Street.

He stared at the cards, baffled. He couldn't read but he wasn't about to admit that to the young lad. He looked up towards the shore. 'We'll have to find someone to sort this out. She looks like gentry, by her clothes.'

'Will there be a reward?' asked the younger man.

Mr Bertonelli's house

Ann continued her journey towards Mr Bertonelli's house. She pulled the print scarf over her head. Not because she feared detection but because she relished its anonymity. No one in the busy streets would recognise this serving girl with her straggling hair and bent body as Mrs Ann Walker. She smiled as she recalled the astonished and greedy look on Susan's face when Ann had offered her the yellow gown in return for her Sunday best. Susan had been most delighted of all by Ann's leather shoes with their turned heels. At this moment, Ann could distinguish the clipped sound of Susan's wooden pattens on her feet from the other street sounds around her. She hoped that Susan would not get into trouble. Ann had told her that she was going away, but Susan knew that she was only to say this to Mr Walker. Susan was to tell Mr Walker that his wife was going to stay in the country with some friends and that he was not to worry, she would contact him soon. It was a prank, she had told Susan. Susan had nodded. Anything was possible from the gentry. Ann told Susan to go upstairs to the maids' bedroom and stay there for the rest of the day, out of the way of the other servants. Ann would tell cook that Susan was ill.

Twenty minutes later, holding Ann's shoes in one hand and picking up the skirts of Ann's fine yellow gown in the other, Susan climbed down the back stairs and slipped out of the side door, on her way to Cheapside to show her family how well she was doing. She was afraid of meeting cook crossing the Westminster bridge after market and so kept her gaze averted from any one she saw approaching. She kept near the bridge wall for fear of stumbling on the fancy high heels. She thought the two men who accosted her were arresting her for theft of the dress, and was attempting to tell her story as the breath failed in her body.

Ann turned into Lazard Street. Ahead lay Mr Bertonelli's house. Number 18. Ann slipped down the steps to the basement. It was so easy to enter a house posing as a servant. Ann was pleased by the success of her disguise. The idea had come to her as she had set out for the first time, walking towards this house. As Mrs Ann Walker, Ann could not walk around London without being noticed. But, dressed in Susan's clothes she was free, unnoticed and invisible. She tried the door to the scullery. It was unlocked. Ann pushed it slowly until she could see that the narrow passageway room beyond was empty. A further door to the kitchen was partly ajar and Ann could see the newly stoked fire in the range burning brightly. She stepped in and made for the narrow back stairs to the upper house. On her way she picked up a bucket by the coal hole and half filled it from the coal bunker. Carrying this she would be unquestioned.
Ann appeared at the head of the servants' stairs to the exotic sights of Mr Bertonelli's molly house. Unable to concentrate fully on anything but her purpose in being there, at first Ann was only able to gather an impression of colour and activity. As she stood at the head of the servants' stairs she began to make out more detail. She could see that Indian fabrics, sparkling with tiny mirrors, hung at the windows and incense sticks burned in copper containers standing on the tiled hall floor. Two men in turbans and flowing white dhurbas passed Ann and after them ran a man dressed in the full costume of a Bengali dancing girl. His movements were light and fluid. He made a convincing dancing girl. Apart from his long, dark and curling moustache. A tall,

fair-haired man appeared at the door of what appeared to be a small sitting room. He wore a long white gown and carried a circle of roses in one hand. He smiled at Ann as she passed. Ann fleetingly thought of Mr Davidson. Behind him, in the room, she glimpsed an altar with candles and, above it, what looked to her to be a blue and white image of the Virgin Mary.

Although there were people sitting around the large hall, some separate, some in couples, no one else gave any notice to Ann. She crossed the hall and entered what appeared to be the main receiving room. Sitting at the other side of this room, on a red brocade sofa, wearing the impeccably cut morning dress of a town gentleman, was a large muscular man of middle years. He had an aura of physical energy and impatience, as if he had either just come indoors from some busy activity or was about to leave to take part in the same. He had papers scattered around him and was questioning what appeared to be the cook, who stood defiantly before him.

'Cook, a rack of lamb does not cost this much. Your book keeping is inaccurate. Do you take me for a fool?' He stood up and leaned forward. 'Does all this give you licence to cheat me?' He gestured to the glittering room, and the dancing girl, who was running back across the hall, weeping. His eyes were fixed on the cook's face and his stance uncompromising. The cook eyed him up and decided on retreat.

'No, sir,' she mumbled, conceding defeat.

The man seemed satisfied. He waved his hand. 'Then rewrite your books,' he said.

The cook turned to leave. As she passed Ann she gave her a sharp and curious look.

Fear of discovery ran through Ann. There was little time. Ann had to speak to Mr Bertonelli, for this surely was him in front of her, now.

'I am Ann Walker, I was told to come here. You have

something for me?' Ann placed the coal bucket directly in front of Mr Bertonelli so that he would have difficulty in escaping to raise the alarm. She need not have feared. Mr Bertonelli was obviously used to dealing with the unexpected. He took a moment to examine her outfit and her face.

'Ah, yes, Mrs Walker. Come with me'

He took her to a small study off the hall, closed the door quietly behind them and then retrieved a package from a deep cupboard in the corner of the room.

'This is what you want,' he spoke quickly, as he handed Ann the package. 'Put down the coal bucket. We will go upstairs to the topmost floor and find you something else to wear before you leave. Cook will know that you do not belong to the servants of the household - and she has no particular reason to help the French cause.' He shook his head. 'If you have been followed...'

Ann opened her mouth to protest. He raised his hand and spoke a little louder.

'If you have been followed and someone is questioning her right now, Cook will say that she saw a servant in this house who had no rights to be here. We must get rid of that servant.'

Mr Bertonelli led Ann up to an attic bedroom. He ushered her in.

'I will send someone to assist you. Please sit quietly here and wait.'

Mr Bertonelli left the room and Ann sat down on the bed.

Now she had time to think out her plan. To escape from London in the clothes of a working woman had seemed a better way of getting the information she would carry back to Ashbourne and the Dragon's Nest than any other she could think of. She had only thought of it as she had walked out that morning. She would prefer to leave without informing anyone of her departure but she could not leave

James without any knowledge of her whereabouts. However, she knew she had seriously compromised his safety by giving him the message that she had left town.

Susan was also a concern. The fact that she knew what clothes and what character Ann had chosen as her disguise was a serious flaw in the plan. Ann had indeed better find another identity as quickly as possible. It was not only Mr Bertonelli's cook who could offer information about her. Ann suddenly remembered Lady Primrose's words.

Mr Bertonelli's matter of fact acceptance of the great danger she was in made the idea of her own death more tangible. She fought to prevent her fear of her own death from taking over her thoughts. If she did not ignore it, she would not be able to act. It was almost impossible. Images of her own death seemed to constantly run behind everything else in her brain. She had the greatest desire to run away. Her breath came fast and her heart raced. She did not want to die for a cause. Someone else's cause. From which she was excluded. But again, she realised that she was set upon a certain path, some of the factors in this situation were out of her control. She could not simply stop and leave this game. She would be pursued until death whatever she did now. Tears of self-pity rose in Ann's eyes.

A soft knock on the door caused her to jump off the bed and crouch behind it, her body tensed and alert. The door opened and a man entered.

He came round behind the bed and stared down at Ann. He was carrying a bundle of clothes. Ann slowly stood up, feeling foolish.

'You are going to be a young man of about my age and size,' he said. 'Hold your feet up.' Ann slipped off the pattens and held up one foot.

'Hmm... I'll see ...' With that, he left the room.

Ann proceeded to put on the clothes. First she opened the package given to her by Mr Bertonelli. Inside, as she had been promised by the beggar, were the leather strip of tiny inked names and the silken belt, with a slit on the underside, near the small brass buckle. Using a pin from her hair, Ann methodically fed the leather strip into the slit and along the length of the belt - without first reading any of the names. She did not want to dwell on why it might be a good idea at some point in the future that she did not know these names. She knew that at least no one could drag them out of her if she were captured.

The belt complete as a hiding place, she stood up and fastened it around her waist. After that came a woollen vest and a then a fine cotton undershirt. On top of that she put a coarse linen shirt and then a woollen waistcoat, with many buttons. On top of that, a leather jerkin and then a heavy, lined and pocketed, worsted jacket. She pulled on fine woollen leggings and leather breeches, cotton stockings and long woollen socks. She was dressed for a journey in foul weather, for, although it was early summer, the nights were still cold and there had been freak storms on the midland routes. Soon, all that lay on the bed was a cloak, leather riding gloves and a satchel, such as might be slung over your shoulder when riding.

Ann sat down again. They obviously intended her to ride out of London. She hoped someone would point her in the right direction. How far was it to Ashbourne? How long had it taken their coach to reach London? How long before the list reached Cluny, waiting in the far north. Ann rubbed her hand over her eyes. Would James return to Ashbourne? Would he get there before she did? How much could she tell him about her actions? Finally she thought of her son, safely enclosed in the house on Church Street. Surely no one would harm him?

The list lay curled around her waist. If she gave it now to Government agents, would she make Adam safe? As she sat on the bed, staring unseeing out of the window, it came to Ann with shocking force that Adam would only be truly, finally safe if she were dead. As long as she lived and knew, or was thought to know the information in the belt she could feel pressing on her stomach, then Adam was the best possible hostage. He was a lever to prise her open. Thinking it mattered whether she read or did not read the names on that list was a fanciful piece of naivety on her part. No opposition could take the chance of allowing her to survive. She went to the window and stared up and down the street. She could feel her breath shuddering in her throat. She could imagine a knife cutting through her neck. She wanted to run. Now.

The door opened and, for the second time, Ann's heart leapt in her chest.

An old man, dark haired and neat of body, quietly entered the room. He brought the scent of lavender with him. Ann became aware of her own hot smell of fear. She moved back, nearer the window.

 He sat down on the bed and indicated that she should sit beside him. She took her place beside him. She could think of no other action to take. If he had come to arrest her then he would have other men in the house. She could not escape. She sat down. There was nothing else to do.

'Why did you come asking for Villiers?' he said, turning at right angles to stare intently into her face.

Perhaps he was from the Jacobites. How to show what side she was from without endangering herself further?

'Lady Lucy Falconer advised me that he cannot be surpassed in the matter of the repairing of fine veneer, and it is so difficult to find someone of that high standard in London at the moment.' She looked back at him, mindlessly.

A slight smile played around the man's lips. He held out his hand.

'Monsieur Henri Villiers, Madame. I have been waiting a long time for this day and curious to see who it would bring me.' His eyes searched her face, as if to check what he thought he had seen there. Then he rose from the bed and made as if to leave, satisfied with what he saw.

Ann gripped his sleeve to prevent his leaving. 'Monsieur,' she spoke quickly, her words coming out in a rush, 'tell me why did you not send the letters on the box?' She had lain awake on many nights since being given this task to complete and that question had been burning in her brain.

Villiers hesitated. ' I should not have come to see you. But I could not ...'

He seemed to make a decision and sat back on the bed beside Ann. Villiers began to tell her his story.

In 1754, he had been sent to London to create a foolproof method of getting the vital information of the names of all the major Jacobite sympathisers in England to the waiting Scots. A third rebellion could not go ahead without that chance of cooperation and support for the army as it proceeded south. Ignorance and gullibility had ruined the second uprising and it could not be allowed to happen again. Friend had to be distinguished from foe. The ingenious idea of the names being placed under a thin layer of veneer had been Villiers' own conception . He had experimented in the basement of the London house until he was satisfied that the concealment of the names was undetectable. Inside and out, the box would simply look like a plain but solid piece of carpentry. Under the fine sliver of wood with its glossy coat of varnish he had painstakingly burnt the names of over a hundred key supporters of the Jacobite cause. Many from the great Catholic aristocratic families who had suffered such a reduction in status under William's reign. The Tory backbone of the Jacobite cause in England.

This was to be Villiers' last job. He had agreed to it only on one condition. That afterwards he would be allowed to all but disappear, in his own way and in his own time. The French spymasters had agreed.

Villiers was under the strictest instructions to work alone. If he were to disappear afterwards, the French wanted as little possibility of the exposure of this information as possible. But he had not followed his instructions.

Villiers looked at Ann and sighed. 'You see, madame, there was a young man I loved.' He hesitated before the word 'loved'. 'But this is a confusing story. For I did not meet this man until after I had made my deal with my masters. To them, I was to drown at sea. But I had already chosen my life. To live here.' He raised his arm to encompass Mr Bertonelli's strange house. 'And then I met Gino and I had even more reason to fight for my secret life here. I had hoped to live that life with him… with Gino Fratelli…' His voice died for a moment.

He had chosen to see out his days in a molly house in London. He looked at Ann quizzically. Did she know what a molly house was? He raised his eyes and tipped his head toward the door. Ann nodded her head in reply. Of course. Ann did indeed know what a molly house was.

'A particularly English phenomenon,' sighed Villiers. 'The English are so much more tolerant than the French. So much more prepared to accept that the ordinary man may have many different ways of living.' He smiled. 'I think it is because you change religion so often in this country. It is only political power which sends you to war, never fanaticism, never the desire to rework the secret lives of your people.'

Villiers gave a small laugh, and shrugged his shoulders at the impossible narrowmindedness of the French.

The molly house, the world into which Villiers wished to disappear, was owned by an Italian named Bertonelli. He was prepared to take Villiers on as a partner, the two men had found an immediate rapport when Villiers had first sought the house out, but there was a problem. A

Frenchman would attract unwelcome attention. And so, Mr Bertonelli insisted that Villiers became, to any who were inquisitive about his new business partner, an Italian like himself. Maybe a cousin, a shared boyhood from his own village. The English could rarely distinguish between the sound of their language being spoken with an Italian or a French accent. It would do.

But Villiers was a perfectionist, meticulous in every detail. It was what had made him so successful. And so to help him learn some of the Italian language he had taken on an assistant. Gino Fratelli, a wood worker from Lucca, who had been employed in London for over a year. A fine craftsman.

But Ann understood that that was not the whole of the story. For Villiers' voice lowered and softened when he said the name of this young man. Before he uttered the name there was a gap, as with the word 'love', a tiny fraction of a silence, and after it a gap, and into those gaps poured all the desire, the anticipation and the pain that saying out loud the name of his lover still caused this man.

Villiers had fallen in love. And had jeopardised the whole of his mission because of it. He had fallen in love. With a young man who eventually showed the depth of the love which he returned by resisting to death the work of the government torturers.

Villiers had compromised his security to take a chance to get what he wanted, to take his freedom at last. And he had lost. But the price of his failure had been paid by the young Italian. Ann could see the pain this confession was causing the man sitting beside her. He paused for a moment. In the silence, he turned his head slightly away from her in an attempt to keep his feelings private.

He saw the lean, smooth face of Gino Fratelli. His upper lip. A perfectly crafted curve, made of flesh. He felt again the companionable warmth of his presence in the dark basement as they worked on the wood together. The excitement of sensing his closeness when he came near to watch Villiers as he worked on the intricate dovetails that would bind each edge of the box in a perfect right angle. The admiration in his voice as he carefully examined each finished piece of work. Bellisimo, bellisimo. His kindness when Villiers was sick with river fever and could not work for the shivering. Take this, drink a little, here, let me hold your head, you foolish man... you are sick.

Ann heard Villiers catch his breath. Drawing air in as if he had been under water. He cleared his throat and carried on. It was Gino Fratelli who had been picked up by the government agents and Gino who had attempted to resist telling his name to his torturers. It was their incompetence in killing him which meant that they never learnt his identity. For he could surely have held out no longer against the pain. It was only the fact that Villiers knew certainly that Gino knew none of the names which were to go on the box which meant that Villiers finally decided to go ahead with the partly altered plan. That and the thought of his freedom, so near. Worth one last gamble to reach it. Don't tell the spymasters, carry on. Find a way out. The box had not gone when he heard word of Gino's capture. He had time to change things. He burnt the box, the hours of work reduced to ash, and set about creating the decoy.

Villiers knew that, although Gino had not been party to the names of the English sympathisers, he could talk of a box and of concealment. Easy enough for a competent English player to see the rest of this game. That route to the Scots Jacobites could never be taken. So Villiers devised a compromise. He would send the box, but he would not put the names on it. If it fell into friendly hands the information that was there would lead those friends to him and to the names; if not, then the information was safe.

Flower house
The den
Look Love Follow
The box

These words had successfully led the Jacobites to him in the shape of this intense young woman, who watched him carefully as he finished his story.

She had not been prepared to believe the story that Villiers told her. Ann had pursued this in her mind constantly. Only a man of great loyalty and experience would have been chosen for the job of getting the names across England and such a man would hardly take so many chances in a matter of such importance. She had come to the conclusion that it was not possible. Unless he had turned. Unless he was attempting to betray the Jacobite cause.
But here was another reason; one which convinced her.
 Now she could see how Villiers would be prepared to compromise the security of his masters. To weigh up the costs and benefits of his actions and to take chances. And finally to risk living in a country at constant war with his homeland, a place fraught with danger, in order to pursue this quiet obsession. For the truth was that for Villiers the world outside the molly house was where danger and foreignness had lain all of his life.

 He stopped and waited for Ann's response.
'I was not prepared to believe anything you said.'
'I know. I would have come to the same conclusion as you. How could a man who has been so careful to follow instructions all of his life, make such wild decisions? Stretch the resources of the networks so impossibly. Two boxes...Veneer... Coded messages sent over years on flimsy wood. Preposterous! True. I should not have done it. But I was trying to take something for myself.'

He rubbed his hands across his face. 'Something from all this. And in doing so I confused the issues. Three years ago a young man died, not for the cause but because of my selfish purpose and since then I have lived with the possibility that many may die because of what I have done. I have tried to reset the balance as best as I could.'

He touched her arm lightly. 'And now you are here and I have told you everything. This is very dangerous for me. But you would have accepted nothing less. Now you must trust us.'

Ann nodded.

Villiers left the room with a feeling of distaste in his mouth. She was calm and prepared to do her best now. He had prepared her. But she would die. He sighed. He thought he had done with all this.

Ann was only alone for a moment in her room. This time when the door opened she did not jump off the bed. She was no longer afraid, but she was eager to get on the road.

Her dresser was standing in front of her with a pair of riding boots.

'Quickly give them to me. I must go.' Ann pulled them on. They were too large but wearable. The man handed her a small brown bottle.

'Put this on your skin. It will darken it. Put it more heavily around your cheeks and under your chin. It will give somewhat the impression of a beard.'

Ann rubbed the tincture over her face. She was then handed a wad of money in a sturdy leather money belt and she was ready to leave. She followed the man down stairs. The hall, which had been so busy, was now deserted. Her guide took Ann out to the stables in the mews at the back of the house. Ann asked him what road she should take, and, on receiving the information, she left, without any polite thanks or a backwards glance. Her mind was set on the days ahead. The young man watched her leave the yard and turned back into the house. He resolved to put all thought of her and all conjecture about her task out of his mind. It was best. Unusual circumstances like this and people acting out of their usual context, as this woman was doing, always signalled danger for those who became part of the plan, however briefly. Rarely did any of these actions lead to a successful conclusion. He allowed himself the indulgence of one thought on the matter. She had asked for the road to Ashbourne.

A woman in disguise, on horseback, to ride over a hundred miles alone carrying something very secret.

Her death was certain.

He stood for a moment, squinting up at the sunlight just visible through the roof tops, then he crossed the yard and shut the heavy wooden gates after her.

Ann picked her way through the crowded streets at a steady pace. It was only when she was clear of the crowds and was on the muddy Northern road with its constant flow of cows, pigs and geese, all being herded the other way into the city that she took stock of her situation. She had been given a good horse and a substantial amount of money. She could ride in daylight and stay overnight in inns along the way. Her sex was unlikely to be discovered since no one took their clothes off on a long journey, even to sleep. Or she could sleep by day in hidden places and ride by night. It might be quicker and she could escape detection more easily. For the moment she would simply ride as far as she could on this first day. Whatever she did, it would take her at least four days to reach Ashbourne. She had to concentrate, stay alert. Avoid detection by government agents. They would be bound to be looking for her. The man watching her so closely at the Curzon's ball had been aware of her circumstances, she was sure of it.

Sir Christopher Lovell. Was he the spy master? Was this the man who had ordered the death of Francis Etherington?

With difficulty Ann tried to move her mind away from thoughts of Francis Etherington. Now she could see how you could be caught in something beyond your control. To the extent that you no longer see your personal reactions and desires as being of any importance. Her despair as she had understood Francis Etherington's betrayal was not important. Those feelings were not important. To get to Ashbourne with her information was what mattered.

Hour after hour Ann rolled astride the broad back of her horse. Back and forth. Back and forth. The land ahead bobbed and ducked in time to the rhythm of the horse's movement. She began to feel detached from time and from her surroundings. The urgency with which she had left London that morning had left her. The constant motion of her horse as it cantered steadily forward, lulled her into an almost hypnotic state. The measured chink of the bridle brought another day clearly back to her mind. She remembered riding up to Arbor Low with Frances Etherington on that stormy wedding outing. Then walking their horses in the protection of the trees along the Monyash bridle track.

Ann jolted forward as the horse stumbled slightly and then recovered. He was tiring. She shook herself back to the present. A fine drizzle had set in over the last hour, wetting her face and causing her to screw up her eyes, blurring her vision of the road ahead. Ann felt weary and confused. It was time to find somewhere to stay for the night.

She alternated between day and night time travelling to throw off any pursuers. There were many large inns where one man and his horse could go practically unnoticed, as long as he paid up. Outside Nottingham, she sheltered during the third day in a barn and travelled over night on the old pack horse route into Derby and beyond to Kedleston. Her journey had taken longer than she had anticipated because of her obsession with throwing off her pursuers. She was careful not to be too easy a target for the agents she was sure would be following her. Sometimes she would stand off the road for an hour at a time, concealed in a copse or an outhouse, watching down the road she had just covered, waiting for her would-be assassins.

As her journey progressed, she became obsessed with the thought of the agents sent to kill her. What would they look like? Would she sense their presence? The image of Sir Christopher Lovell's watchful eyes haunted her. She became convinced that she was right. He was the spymaster and her days were numbered. On the fifth evening of her journey she found herself nearing Ashbourne on the route she had originally taken four years before. Would agents have got ahead of her and be lying in wait? She decided to spend the night in Bradley woods, about one mile outside the small town. She knew it well and the Hulland end, away from the possible packhorse encampments on the Ashbourne meadow side, should afford her some protection. To arrive in Ashbourne with a horse, obviously exhausted from a long journey would cause some comment. Her disguise could be uncovered. One night of rest and she could be any traveller from Derby, on business in the country. As she led her horse into Bradley Woods, the beginning of this all came back to her. It had been here where she had slept, exhausted, on her first night out of prison. She remembered the packhorse man, swaying in front of her as they had entered Ashbourne. Then she put him out of her mind. She had no time to mourn him now.

On the morning of the 5th of July, Ann walked her horse gently down the road into the southern end of Ashbourne. The weather had improved and she was hot in her heavy clothing, but, apart from the cloak, she felt she could take nothing off for fear her disguise would be made worthless. She made her way to The Green Man coaching house, her own superstition meant that she could not use the nearer

Plough Inn. She passed it on the crossroads as she turned to her right into Compton. The place where this whole string of events had been put into motion by her actions. She realised bleakly that her past actions meant that she could not take any higher moral ground than the men whom she was convinced were tracking her now. As Francis Etherington had said 'You are a murderer, Ann... and murderers die for their deeds.' Assassin, murderer, spy, soldier. What did it mean?

The Green Man was busy. Fine carriages stood in the courtyard and the stables looked full to Ann, as she dismounted from her horse. As she waited to speak to the yard man, Ann watched one carriage driver carefully decorate his carriage with black ribbon. When the doors were beribboned, he went into the stables and reappeared with a stable boy, leading two fine black hacks. Each with a black silk rosette on their bridles.

Ann went over to speak to the stable boy.

'I wish to put my horse here for the night,' she began. The boy shook his head even before she had finished speaking.

'Sir. We have no space. You can put your horse to graze by the river in Turner's farm meadow. He pointed in the direction of Church Street. We have a lad there, watching the horses. But that's the best we can do until after the funeral.'

'What funeral?' asked Ann. She was curious. This was Ashbourne. It would be someone she knew. 'It must be someone important if you are so busy with such fine decoration.' She nodded her head towards the beribboned carriage.

The boy's face took on a suitably serious look. 'The Walker household have suffered a terrible loss,' he intoned. He seemed to be repeating the unfamiliar, formal words parrot-fashion. Gentry funerals were good business for The Green Man. Ann was too stunned to reply for a moment.

Then, 'Walker of Church Street?' she asked. She realised

that her voice was her own but she was too shocked to attempt to disguise it. The boy did not seem to notice.

Was it James? Had he paid the price of Jacobite involvement with his life? Even though his father, his mother and now his wife were far more guilty traitors than he. Ann felt her knees give way. She wrapped the bridle hard around her fingers and leaned on her horse for steadiness. Oh, James. You did not deserve this, her throat constricted painfully. She swallowed and shook her head. She could not even mourn him in public.

'When did Mr Walker die?' she asked.

The boy looked at her, taken aback. 'Not Mr James Walker, but his wife. She died in London. A terrible accident on the river, so they say.'

Ann looked back at the boy, not understanding at all.

'Mrs Ann Walker,' she whispered.

'Yes, Mrs Ann Walker...' his voice faded from Ann's ears as he proceeded to repeat his information about Turners' field. Ann gradually registered that she must leave the yard of The Green Man and she slowly did so. Leading her horse out along Church Street to Turner's farm. To reach it she had to pass her own home, Hulland House. As she walked slowly in the road, she tried to make sense of this news. How could she be thought dead? How could there be a body? Her body. In a coffin. Due to be buried in the soil of St Oswald's Church. As she approached Hulland House she could see the black ribbons on the door arch and the black drapes at the windows. This had to be a hoax. Somehow James had arranged a mock drowning to save her from the Government agents. He must always have known more than she had realised or he had said. She hurried forward. She would enter the stables, quarter her horse and ask to see him urgently. Keeping her disguise, of course. He had to know immediately that his ruse had worked. For here she was, alive!

As she reached the crowd in front of the house, a gleaming

hearse made the clumsy turn out of the narrow courtyard. She had an impression of glossy darkness and plumed feathers as the horses pulled left, towards the church, but it was those who followed who caught and held her full attention. For here came James, flanked on either side by his brothers. He held Adam in his arms, clutched close to his chest. And in one brief moment, as she looked on his stricken face, Ann knew that this was, for James, no hoax. The woman he loved was being carried in a coffin a few feet in front of him, dead and cold. Here was a man who had contained his love for her in her lifetime but who could not contain the dreadful pain of losing her to death. Ann dropped the reins and took a step forward, oblivious of the people around her. She had to go to him. To touch him, to see his face change as he turned to look at her and slowly realised through the fog of his pain that his wife was here, alive, in front of him. But she could not. She knew that she must not. She looked from side to side; people around her were all craning to see as much of the funeral procession as they could. No one seemed interested in her, but there could be agents in the crowd, waiting for her to appear. If she took those few steps to his side now, she would be condemning James to death.

 She watched in horror as the cortege turned in the direction of St Oswald's Church. Behind her came the impatient stamp of horses' hooves as carriages lined up to carry their important owners the few hundred yards from The Green Man to the graveyard. A man touched her shoulder. She gave a small cry and lept away from him.

'Your horse, sir, ' he said simply, holding out the reins. He was looking at her curiously and she realised that her disguise as a man was wearing thin.

She took the reins and led the horse back down the street. She had no idea what to do or where to go, but she knew that to stay in the crowd would mean that she would be discovered. She could not sustain her deception much longer. She had to get somewhere quiet and calm herself. In an unbearable state of dread and agitation, she mounted the horse and rode a short way out on the Wirksworth road. She came to Atlow Green, a small triangle of grass where cattle and sheep could graze as they waited to enter Ashbourne for market. She dismounted and sat down by the side of the road.

How could she be dead? Dead. But about this she had been right, there were agents out to kill her. What had happened? Who was in that coffin? A boy was collecting hay in a field opposite to where she sat. She got up and called him. Would he look after her horse for a fee, while she walked back into Ashbourne to attend the funeral of Mrs Ann Walker? Yes, he'd be very willing.

'Do you know what happened to the poor lady?' she asked him.

He eyed her. 'Well, I've heard some.'

'And what's that?'

'You family – or close friend, maybe?'

Ann shook her head. 'No, just thought I'd pay respects. Our company does business with the Walkers.'

Satisfied that he was not going to be blamed for impudent gossiping the lad told Ann all he had heard.

'Well, you know that it has been rumoured that Mrs Walker had a sweetheart, a fancy man ?'

Ann shook her head. No, she did not know that this was common knowledge.

'Well, he was from London but had himself a house over that way.' The boy gestured with his right hand in the direction of the river and Mayfield. 'But she broke it off, see. And he went back to London. He killed himself and she followed. They say she flung herself off Westminster Bridge this week.' He sat back on his cart and stared expectantly at Ann for a response.

'Why, that is so sad,' she said, after a pause.

But her story teller thought differently 'Sad. Sad it is not.

Stupid more like.' He jumped off his cart and took the reins of Ann's horse. 'I''ll mind him until you get back. I'll be here the rest of the day. I've all top field to do.'

Ann walked into town. Westminster Bridge. She had been nowhere near Westminster Bridge.

Had never walked there. None of this made sense. On reaching the town she made her way back to The Green Man. By buying some ale and sitting quietly in a corner, in half an hour, she had pieced together the whole tragic event of her death.

Susan must have put on the fine yellow dress and had gone out visiting.

Although what Ann heard in the inn, as she sat quietly in the corner was that Ann Walker had gone for one last time to an old trysting point of the lovers' and, dressed in her lover's favourite colour, had thrown herself from the bridge. Her face had been horribly mutilated by the fall, and then the fishes had eaten at it, although she still wore the beatific smile of one who is certain she is going to see her love.

The perpetrator of this tale, a footman in Ann's own household, whom she had always found painfully shy, relished every moment of the telling, as did his audience.

Poor Susan. No one would probably even wonder why she had disappeared at the same time as her mistress. Servants were ten a penny. No one would imagine that she had been killed in error. A case of mistaken identity. Her face damaged by the fall, no one, not even James realised that the dead woman in the yellow silk dress was Susan, and not his wife.

Ann wondered if he had heard this lurid version of her death. Perhaps that is what he would find most believable, anyway. What else could he believe? The reality was even more preposterous. Susan had been murdered in her place by men intent on preventing a Jacobite conspiracy from bearing fruit.

Ann took her attention away from the tale teller, who,

flushed and happy, was now downing his third pint of ale to a chorus of curious questions from his supporters.

Ann Walker was dead. Dead to the government. Dead to the agency. Dead to Sir Christopher Lovell. James and Adam were safe. As long as Ann stayed dead. Could she stay away from them? For the forseeable future she had to. But Adam was only two years old. It would be likely that he would not remember his mother in a few years. How could she leave him? But if she did not then he could die. She must stay away.

Yet, having made this decision, Ann was drawn irresistibly to the Ashbourne house. She left The Green Man and walked along Church Street, which was now almost empty. Earlier she had passed the carriages of the mourners, gathered for some ghastly funeral tea at the small assembly room opposite The Green Man. Ann had no desire to enter that room. She realised, however, that most of the Walker household would be there, including Kitty and Adam. She could enter Hulland House undetected, for the last time. She would do it.

Ann stood in the shade of the large branches of an elm tree, in the back garden of Hulland House, and looked up at the familiar windows. Not that she had ever looked at them like this before. As a thief. About to enter. What did she intend to steal? Mementoes of her life there. Of her husband, of her son.

And the money which still lay secreted under the floor of the nursery. Some of the money she had taken from the packman. Money she had even kept from Francis Etherington, from James. A small amount by the standards of a conspiracy of traitors. But enough to now provide her with a new life. With that in place she could wait until it was safe to return.

The house lay silent in the afternoon sunshine. No movement at any windows. Ann threw a stone at the scullery door. It rattled with startling noise against the wooden surround. Ann waited patiently for fully three minutes. Nothing happened. Nobody came. She moved silently forward, quickly across the grass and onto the window sill of the back kitchen. The sash was loose and unlocked. As always. She slid it up and jack-knifed in. Her feet made the slightest thump as they hit the floor. She kept them perfectly still where they had landed and relaxed her body. The interior of the house was cool and dark after the sunlight outside. She waited for her eyes to adjust.

Then up the stairs, into the nursery on the right. Adam's bed lay neatly quilted. Ann stopped as painful longing for the touch of his body swept over her. She picked up a shoe from the floor and slid her hand inside. The contours were as familiar as his face. She had put this shoe on his foot many times. She bent her head and drew in the child scent of him from the interior of the shoe. Then she laid it carefully back beside its partner.

She crouched down on her knees and reached under the high cot side. Inserting her fingers in a small groove made for this purpose, she slid up the plank which ran directly under the length of the cot. Reaching to the furthermost corner of the hiding place, her hand closed over the cloth bag which held the gold. Here were the Louis D'or. All that was left of them. Most had gone with Cluny Macpherson. Some had gone to Francis Etherington and then to James but always this bag had lain under the floor beneath Adam's cot as a safety net against any eventuality.

She would leave something in its place. Something which would prove to her son who she was if that were ever needed. Ann opened her leather jerkin and pulled up the linen shirt she was wearing. She unbuckled the silken belt and drew out the talisman, the stone circle with the words Look, Love and Follow inscribed. She was about to place it in the floor cavity when she remembered with a small shock that also around her waist she carried the list of names. Cluny. Waiting. Relying on her. She had to get to the

Dragon's Nest. She needed the talisman to prove who she was.

But Adam. She had to leave something of this day, of her last entrance into this house for the forseeable future.

She could leave half of it here. She stayed crouched on the floor, unable to find a solution to this problem and unable to leave without completing this gesture. Leaving some symbol of her constancy. She was thinking incoherently. The need to leave something for her son was driving logic out of her mind. Ann looked around desperately for some way of breaking the stone in half. With the right tool it would be easy. A careful blow with a hammer or a small wood axe would probably do it. They would be in the house, but downstairs. Did she have time? Time before her own funeral party returned. She had to chance it. She had to leave a future message for Adam.

Ann stood up. As she did so she heard a sound. A sound which was out of place in an empty house. It was the sound of someone coming slowly up the stairs. Silently, Ann turned back and put the plank gently back in place. She picked up the bag. There was a slight clink as the coins knocked against each other. The steps on the stairs stopped. Ann reviewed her options. They were few. But there was a small possibility of escape.

She shook the bag gently and the coins clinked again. The steps on the stairs restarted, with more confidence. Ann took two large steps to the window and opened the catch. As the steps came down the hall she pushed the window open, threw out the urn which stood on the windowsill and in the same movement twisted round to dive under the sofa which sat by the fire. The urn landed on the terrace below with a loud crash. Ann pulled the rug which draped the sofa in front of her and thanked the Lord that she had played hide and seek so often in this room that she knew all the tiniest places where you could still find space to squeeze away. Someone entered the room and ran to the window. Ann could just see the worn down shoes and thin ankles of Jess, the nursemaid. Jess began to shout for help through the open window and then thought better of it. She ran out of the room and back down the stairs. Ann began to wriggle out from her hiding place.

And then she heard why Jess had run downstairs. The family were returning from the funeral. Suddenly the hall was loud with noise. There was little time. Ann leapt from the room and climbed the stairs to the attic floor. She twisted through the half sized door at the end of the attic passage and found herself in the roof space, with the length of the building in front of her. She crouched down behind the travelling trunks by the outer brick wall. She could hear voices downstairs. People moving about. Occasionally she could hear the muffled voice of her son and the voice of James as he reassured Jess. Ann had guessed correctly. The family would accept that a would be thief had been disturbed and had got away with nothing.

Ann crouched in the attic until it was dark and the house had fallen silent. She explored the feeling of being close to them but without their awareness. It was like a bolster against the years ahead. She tried to be aware of every moment she sat there in the dark, at the topmost point of this house. With people who loved her lying below. It was almost the only way she could fully realise that she had existed in this life. For these people. Having a reality as a wife, mother, friend. She was afraid she would not remember. And then she would lose it all, for she might not have the courage to come back. To claim her place. As the dark hours ticked by she came to know that this is what she would struggle with in the years to come.

St Oswald's Church clock rang out two o clock and she stepped silently out of the attic and crept downstairs. She crouched on the first floor, listening intently into the darkness. Nothing. She began to move forward, and then she froze.

From the front of the house came a muffled choking. The sound of a man crying. Light from an oil lamp flickered and then steadied into a thin band under the door of the bedroom at the end of the hall. Their bedroom. It was James, awake and thinking of her. Ann darted back to the shelter of the stair turn as the door opened. She watched as James slowly crossed the hall and entered the nursery. For a moment he was outlined in the soft glow of the nursery light. His head was bent and his shoulders slumped. She bent her own head down and fought the need to get up and follow him into that room, to see her son lying there, to have James put his arms around her. To have him listen to her whispered explanations. She felt as if the very essence of her being was flowing out of her into that room; she wrapped her arms around her body and closed her eyes. She must resist it. The feeling was so strong she felt that at any moment James would sense her presence and find her. She had to get out of the house. Fate had dealt her an opportunity to safeguard her family and she must take it.

She crept past the nursery door and half slid her body down the wide stairs, across the entrance hall, down into the back kitchen and then she was out. It was always easier to get out of a house than get in. She had learnt that many years ago. The streets were silent. Windows and doors tight shut against the night. She moved without sound from the shadow of one door to the next. As she did so, a small part of the exhilaration of being out alone at night, that power over those who sleep owned by those who do not, returned to her from the past. She allowed it to give her some comfort. Soon she found herself on the Wirksworth road, softly whistling for her horse. The lad had unsaddled the horse and laid the tackle down by the hedge. Ann blessed his honesty. She left some money under a stone nearby where he had put the folded saddle blanket.

As the church clock struck the half hour, Ann was riding back past Hulland House. All was quiet. She looked up at the soft glow of the night light in the nursery as she passed. Safe.

And as long as she remained dead to them then they would continue to be safe. A coldness crept over her. She could feel the bleakness of the years ahead. The longing that would come to have sight of her child again. To touch him, to know his thoughts. She felt weak with fear for him. There was so much time ahead of him and she would not know of him, of how he was. She would not be there.

And there was James.

She had learned something both sweet and painful, something she could hardly bring herself to name. It was at once the most immense and the most ordinary of things. She reined in her horse and looked back at the town, its buildings only just distinguishable in the moonlight. Men and women slept there in each others' arms, as they had always done. She thought of James and the things which had remained unsaid between them. He had understood what she now knew. That it was only possible to live fully in this world if love was at the very core of your life; if you did not then you lived forever in a half light and you were diminished. But there was a price to pay for embracing love. And James had known that too. It left you open to harm, and to great pain. Again, she saw his anguished face as he had followed her coffin. She had seen his face then as if for the first time. She relived that desire to run up to him, see his face alter, slip her hand under his arm, and take her place beside him. But she knew she could not. She was condemned to exist on the edges of other people's lives for long years. Watchful, separate.

Ahead of her loomed the structure of St Oswald's Church. In the graveyard were the remains of Susan. Soon there would be a tombstone with Ann's name on it. Or one of her names. Not Ann Dance, or Ann Challinor but Ann Walker. Ann pulled her horse in to the side of the road and dismounted. She tied the horse to the church gate post. She looked up and down the street and then hurried down the pathway of the graveyard. Soon she came to a freshly dug grave. Ann opened her shirt and tugged the talisman free from the belt. She quickly dug a hole in the fresh earth. Down, down until she judged it safe but all the time afraid that she might touch the coffin, aware that on the other sides of the wooden boards lay the disfigured, swollen body of Susan, taking her place. She pressed the talisman into the soil and filled in the hole. She stood up and stared at the grave. One day she would return and dig out the talisman to give to her son, who would be standing here beside her, who would know who she was, however long it had been. The words sounded in her head, but she did not believe them. For a moment, her resolve left her. She sank down by the grave and covered her face with her hands.

There was a whirring sound as the church clock clanked into action. She looked up. It was four o clock in the morning and around her light was creeping across the cemetery. The mist on the water meadow below the church briefly took on a luminous, unearthly glow which faded even as she watched it. The long meadow grass turned from grey to green and the line of trees alongside the Henmore Brook slowly appeared from the darkness, their easternmost leaves lighting up with gold. There wasn't much time.

There was one last thing she had to do. She undid the buckle of the silken belt around her waist and slipped it out from under her shirt. It felt warm from her body. She drew the leather strip out and laid it in the grave alongside the talisman. She carefully covered them both with soil.

Let Cluny think that she was dead, and with her death was lost all chance of the safe delivery of the list. Without the names there would be no French support. Without the French support the clan chiefs would not dare to go ahead. She sat back on her haunches. She knew now that many men would be saved.

She had seen the inexorable power of the English government when she had been in London. Around families like the Walkers, over some of the dinner tables at which Ann had sat, listening and watching, she had seen that a new way of living was taking shape. James and his brother dealing on the docks in Holland. Men like them did not want a Stuart king. There was an air of terrible doom clinging to the Jacobite cause. It was in the bitter assessments of Lady Primrose, in the watchful eyes of Sir Christopher Lovell. Perhaps the real death of it for her had been in the weak hand of The Young Pretender, when he had greeted her with fine empty words in the house on Essex Street. As the Prince had taken her hand in his own soft clasp, she had begun to understand that men like Cluny could have a terrible wrong-headed courage.

There must be no third rebellion.

She got up and walked back to her horse. On the ground by the cemetery gate she saw something black. She bent and picked it up. A crumpled black ribbon. It must have fallen from one of the horses pulling her funeral cortege. She put it in the pocket of her jerkin, swung up onto her horse and rode out on the Leek road.

Epilogue

Cluny Macpherson walked out on the side of Ben Alder and read again the letter confirming Ann's death and the complete loss of the list.

'And you are certain that the English do not have it?'

Alastair Chambers nodded his head. 'My Lord Cumberland has been told of its loss.' The English government certainly did not have it.

Cluny watched two buzzards circle lazily in the sky above him. This would change everything.

He looked back at Alastair. 'And she is dead?'

Alastair Chambers nodded. 'There is no doubt of it.' A soft wind rustled the bracken at their feet, above them the eerie cry of the buzzards could be heard faintly on the wind.

'It is likely then that Ann Walker has given her life for a cause that was not hers.'

Alastair Chambers nodded again.

A weariness came over Cluny. He thought of Ann Walker telling him lies in her dusty drawing room in Ashbourne. Telling him that Echan was a traitor. Standing her ground even though she knew he was close to tracking her down. A brave woman.

Alastair was watching him anxiously and saw Cluny lift his hand up as if in salute. Then Cluny turned and beckoned to him. They walked back up the path together.

Then to Alastair's astonishment Cluny began to laugh. At first a chuckle then a full throated roar as Cluny threw his head back and let the tension of the past few months fall away from him.

'Alastair,' Cluny took a deep shuddering breath and brought himself under control. 'Alastair I have something to tell you.' He laughed again. This time at Alastair's puzzled face. He imagined how that expression would change in a moment to one of delight and amazement.

For in a moment Cluny would tell him the greatest of news – the news that a child of the Stuart line was safely hidden in the heart of England's Hanoverian state.

o o O o o

Acknowledgements

Although this story is essentially a work of fiction, many of the main characters are taken from history and I am indebted to Fitzroy Maclean for his account of Charles Edward Stuart and of Cluny Macpherson,the keeper of the Arisaig treasure. For the molly houses I have to thank Tim Hitchcock, senior lecturer in history at the University of North London and his 'English Sexualities 1700—1800'. I must also thank Dr Gary Winship of the University of Nottingham for introducing me to the work of the philosopher Louise Andreas Salome and particularly her critique of Freudian theory which relates so closely to the transdressers of the molly houses. Jeremy Black's 'Eighteenth Century Britain 1688 – 1783' gave me the European political backdrop to the story and Lisa Picard's 'Dr Johnson's London' provided endlessly fascinating accounts of eighteenth century city life. My research in Derbyshire relied upon Derbyshire Library Services and particularly, the 'marvellous microfiche' in the Local Studies Library. Weekly articles by the journalist Carol Frost and the work of Ashbourne Local History Group, edited by Adrian Henstock, gave me thorough and reliable sources of information about Ashbourne in the eighteenth century.

As a guide to research, I have to mention 'The Age of Reform' by my great uncle Llewellyn Woodward, which served to remind me that good sources are an essential first tool, and Constance Woodward, my grandmother, who made me read his work at an early age. For the inspiration to write about the hopes and desires of the people of the Scottish Highlands I am indebted to the poetry of another distant family member, Sorley MacLean, whose fierce honesty and clarity of observation have been part of my literary upbringing, and last, but not least, to the work of the Scottish poet James Aitchison, whose words have always fed into my imagination.

Fiona Mairi MacLean MacLeod